Dr Grahame Howard was born in London in 1953 and his family moved to Norwich when he was four years old. His childhood, particularly the eccentric behaviour of his father, is documented in his first book, 'The Tales of Dod', published in 2010. He returned to London to study Medicine at St Thomas' Hospital Medical School, from where he graduated in 1976. Following a series of junior doctor posts in London and Cambridge he was appointed consultant Clinical Oncologist in Edinburgh in 1986. His subsequent career was spent at the Edinburgh Western General Hospital, specialising in prostate and testicular cancer, eventually becoming Clinical Director of the Edinburgh Cancer Centre, an examiner for the Royal College of Radiologists and assistant editor of Clinical Oncology. His second book, 'Spoz and Friends', documents the writer's life as a medical student in the 1970s, and relates with humour the faltering transition of these young men from schoolboys to newly-qualified doctors.

# THE EUTHANASIA PROTOCOL

## GRAHAME C.W. HOWARD

Matador
9 Priory Business Park,
Wistow Road, Kibworth Beauchamp,
Leicestershire. LE8 0RX
Tel: (+44) 116 279 2299
Fax: (+44) 116 279 2277
Email: books@troubador.co.uk
Web: www.troubador.co.uk/matador

ISBN 978 1784620 950

British Library Cataloguing in Publication Data.
A catalogue record for this book is available from the British Library.

Typeset by Troubador Publishing Ltd, Leicester, UK
Printed and bound by CPI Group (UK) Ltd, Croydon, CR0 4YY

**Matador** is an imprint of Troubador Publishing Ltd

*To June*

*With grateful thanks to Dr Gordon Booth for his support and guidance.*

# CONTENTS

# PROLOGUE

Two men sat quietly on the hillside enjoying the warmth of the early summer's evening and gazing at the peaceful loch lying below them. A few feet away from them was a small grass-covered hummock at the head of which was a boulder crudely engraved with the names, Ruth and Hope. The sun was sinking behind the mountains opposite them but its burnished rays still bounced and glistened on the gently rippling surface of the water. The men appeared to be in their fifties and were wearing dun-coloured woollen ponchos drawn in at the waist by a rope belt. Their uncovered arms and legs were muscular and weather-beaten. The slimmer of the two men absentmindedly played with a stone before lazily tossing it away down the slope in front of him. His wiry, straw-coloured hair was short and patched with white, while his tanned face and arms were covered in a profusion of scars. Although disfigured by the wounds of a hundred missiles, his face was still somehow handsome and his blue eyes retained a piercing clarity.

The second man – short, stocky and slightly overweight – was an ex-Enforcer. It was he who broke the silence. 'Giles,' he said quietly, 'What do you think life was like before The Protocol?'

'I only know what the old man told me.' Giles tossed another stone from the little pile in front of him and watched it roll down the hillside. 'In the Great Wars of Religion whole populations were destroyed and vast tracts of land laid waste, left unfit for habitation by the weapons – the poisons, viruses and radioactivity – used in their struggles. The Protocol certainly brought peace and stability to the western world for a time.'

'Where did it all go wrong then?' asked the Enforcer.

Giles sighed as he gazed across the loch. 'I think it was the Euthanasia Protocol that changed the balance.' He paused for a moment to examine the stone he was holding. 'After that had been introduced and accepted, the Protocols evolved from being a useful guide for society, to becoming a force in their own right. As Doreese once said, they became "wise." ' Giles tossed the stone down the slope, then picked up another which he absentmindedly manipulated while staring unseeingly into the middle distance. After a while he continued. 'The old man was undoubtedly well-intentioned when he drafted the Protocols and was horrified after they were misinterpreted and slavishly adhered to without any recourse to commonsense or intelligence.'

The ex-Enforcer thought for a moment. 'Then the Mandys and Doreeses of this world used them to their own ends, to grasp and then hold on to power?'

Giles smiled to himself. 'I think you give them more credit than they deserve. I believe they had completely lost the ability to think for themselves let alone have a cogent strategy. The capacity to analyse information and make decisions had been expunged by the State with its endless systems and committees. Then,' – and here Giles turned to look at his friend – 'the leaders of our so-called intelligent society believed the Protocol to have some sort of supernatural power – a theistic significance – and our fellow human beings found it easier to adhere to the Protocol: verbatim and by rote, than to think for themselves. Inevitably interpretations of the texts differed. Sects were formed and then faction fought faction until the momentum could not be halted.'

'Now that it's destroyed, what will happen?'

Giles looked at his friend, the man who had hunted him down and had then saved his life – not once but three times. 'There will be a new Protocol: a new prophet. A new god will emerge who will be the one and only god – as were all the others before him… ' Giles hesitated for a moment, '… or her.' He chuckled quietly, 'That is, until the next one comes along. Then there will be religious unrest, followed by violence and war and the circle will once again be complete.'

'Can't we learn from our mistakes, Giles?'

'Mankind has many good qualities but learning from the past is certainly not one of them.' Giles smiled to himself and tossed another stone down the hill where it rolled for a time before coming to rest a few yards away.

Giles and the Enforcer chatted quietly as they watched the sun descend slowly behind the mountains. Neither of them heard the approach of a skinny man with long lank hair and a swelling on his left cheek. Like some predatory animal, the man crept forward silently through the forest behind them and, once within range, lay down on his belly, silently loaded his rifle and took aim.

# PART 1

# THE EUTHANASIA PROTOCOL

# ONE

'Ladies and gentlemen of the Cabinet, there can be no doubt that this is *the* most pressing problem for our country at this moment in time.' The Prime Minister had spoken these words in his most earnest tones while his sleek countenance bore an expression of the utmost sincerity. He looked around the table at his seated ministerial colleagues to add emphasis to his statement. There were a few nods and some grunts of acquiescence.

'I need hardly tell you,' he continued, 'that the average age of our citizens is now well over one hundred years and that fewer than five percent of the population are income-earners. The demographics of our society have changed out of all recognition since the end of the last century and the present situation is socially and financially unsustainable.' He paused briefly. 'An unbelievable ninety-eight per cent – yes *ninety-eight* per cent – of all our resources are consumed caring for those over eighty.' the P.M. once again looked along the table to ensure that his colleagues were paying attention before continuing: 'Left unmanaged, this situation can only deteriorate until our society completely disintegrates.' He paused here to score a political point. 'I might add that previous governments have never tackled this issue and have only allowed the crisis to escalate. This administration *must*, and *will*, address this problem once and for all.'

His speech complete, the Prime Minister sat down heavily on his chair at the centre of a long table around which were seated his most senior colleagues. He then turned to the Minister of Health. 'Charles, you kick off, would you. How on earth have we got ourselves into this deplorable situation?'

The Minister sighed and rose rather reluctantly to his feet. He knew that the blame for the age-crisis would land on his doorstep and that his department would be in the firing line, albeit rather unfairly. 'Thank you, Prime Minister,' he responded somewhat unconvincingly while waving a sheaf of papers clutched in his left hand. 'Essentially, ladies and gentlemen of the Cabinet, the problem is that insufficient people are dying. It's as simple as that. There has been an exponential growth in the elderly for nearly a century now and, as our Prime Minister has stated, this is commercially and fiscally unsustainable.'

'Yes, but *why* aren't sufficient people dying?' demanded the Prime Minister.

'It stems, P.M., largely from previous governments' crass mismanagement of the elderly.' The Minister said this hoping to divert some of the blame for the current situation away from himself. He glanced briefly at his papers before continuing. 'The problem is that we seem to have eliminated the more common causes of death. For example, at the beginning of the century, cancer and cardiovascular disease killed enormous numbers of people but these diseases have now largely been eliminated from the population by a combination of genetic manipulation and laboratory-grown spare parts. Coronaries *used* to account for a good fifty per cent of deaths amongst those over sixty. *Now*, at the very first hint of chest pain, people nip down to their local clinic and are given a spanking new heart. The Chief Medical Officer informs me that some folk are on their third or even fourth upgrade.'

'What about a good old-fashioned influenza pandemic?' interrupted the P.M. 'That used to do the trick. In the old days a sturdy new 'flu virus would wipe out a good proportion of the elderly every winter.'

'Genetic manipulation, Prime Minister! We have genetically engineered viruses so that they are no longer dangerous.'

'Well. Can't we un-engineer them so they are lethal once more?'

'That would be too non-specific. We would run the risk of losing a significant proportion of our younger population, something that would be disastrous. In fact, I am informed that there are some data that suggest younger people could be *more* susceptible to such attacks.'

'Mmm.' The Prime Minister stared unseeingly at the papers on the desk before him. Then his eyes widened with enlightenment and he suddenly looked up, 'I know,' he said. 'Accidents! We need more accidents!'

'We've made those illegal, P.M. Recent legislation has virtually eliminated the risk of accidents. In fact, as the Cabinet will be aware, it is a criminal offence for a member of our society to take any significant risk whatsoever. The Risk-Averse Act has made it an felony for anybody to do anything that might conceivably cause harm to themselves or others.'

'Oh, bugger!' was all the P.M. could say.

'I know!' The Minister for Foreign Affairs looked around the table and then at the P.M. before continuing: 'How about a war? Years ago we were able to kill off whole generations with a war or two.' He looked excited as though he might be on to something.

'Wrong age group,' replied the P.M. glumly. 'We can hardly send a battalion of nonagenarians to invade a foreign country.'

'The stupid thing is,' continued Charles, the Health Minister, 'that many of our elderly don't really want to carry on living but we've given them no choice. I've visited a number of our establishments and they just sit there in complete boredom, waiting for something to happen – which it never does.'

The P.M. paused and thought for some time while those around the table also fell silent. At length he declared, 'Somehow we need to ration life. How about… ' he looked at the Minister for Health, '… banning medical interventions in all those over seventy? That might do the trick.'

'The problem there, P.M., is that your proposal would mean most of *us*, around this table, would not receive any care.'

'Mm. Well, we could make it eighty,' said the P.M. who was seventy-two.

'Sadly, that wouldn't help either, as most treatments are now preventative and all the DNA manipulations necessary are performed early on in life – in the first few months – and protection is life-long.'

'Can't remember when I last saw a baby,' muttered the Homes Minister.

'I saw one last week,' said Lady Carter, who was Minister for Babies.

'Did you say that some of these old folk actually *want* to die?' The P.M. looked at the Health Minister.

'Well, yes. That appears to be the case.'

The P.M. was pensive for a moment. 'Do you remember in the latter part of the last century, when we still had some of those ghastly diseases that we've now eliminated, some people actually *wanted* to die?' He looked around the table. There was now a sound of shuffling and an expression of alertness and interest on some of the ministers' faces, as though they might at last be on to something.

Someone muttered, 'Yes, that's true.'

The P.M. continued. 'As I recall there was a huge debate about euthanasia, and all sorts of people got involved.' He paused and then added with a smile, 'Including the Church, of course.' There was a chuckle from around the table.

'Ah, the good old days,' murmured the Minister of Health.

'There are still some about,' said the Homes Minister.

'Some what? Good old days?' asked the P.M., confused.

'No. Some theists.'

'Really? Is that right?'

'Apparently,' the Homes Minister nodded gravely, 'but mainly in rural areas such as Norfolk, and of course in Dalriada.'

'Anyway,' continued the P.M., 'we're digressing. What about reintroducing euthanasia – on a voluntary basis of course.' There was a dubious silence in the room the only noise that of papers being shuffled. Then the Minister for Health broke the silence.

'Personally, P.M., I'm not convinced that the uptake would be very high. They may be bored and tired of life but I suspect they wouldn't be queuing up to be exterminated.'

'Bad word, "exterminate"; better not use that. Overtones – you know.' The P.M. gently rebuked the Minister.

'Of course. Sorry, P.M.'

'What we need is an *incentive*.' There was silence around the table as all eyes turned to the person who had uttered those words. He was Justin, the newest member of the Cabinet, appointed as Junior Finance Minister. This sudden focus of attention embarrassed him and he coughed several times before timidly continuing, 'How about a *financial* incentive scheme – Sir.' The P.M. and the rest of the Cabinet continued to stare at him. The new boy was unnerved and coughed several more times before muttering, 'Sorry – bad idea,' then again, slightly more loudly, 'Sorry.'

The P.M. was the first to respond. 'No. No, not at all, Justin,' he said thoughtfully. 'That might just work. If the capital costs involved with setting up such a structure (or perhaps we should call it a "service") is less that the cost of housing these poor souls, then economically it could be viable. Of course we would need some sort of sliding scale, a kind of health "means test". The nearer someone is to a natural death, the less the award would be.'

The Minister for Health was still not convinced. 'It's not much of an incentive, is it, saying to someone, "Here, take this money and we'll kill you tomorrow?" '

'Kill's *not* a good word, Charles. Better not to use it.'

'Sorry, P.M.'

'No. We would give some of the terminal award, perhaps fifty per cent, up front a few months or a year or so before the "event" – we'd better call it that – and then the balance thereafter.'

Charles was having trouble keeping up with the rapidly developing initiative. 'But how can one pay a dead man?' he asked.

'Better not use the term, "dead," – you know; emotive.'

'Sorry.'

'No. It would go to the next of kin or someone nominated by the newly-deceased, after the – "terminal event." '

'Mmm.' The Minister was still having trouble with the logic. 'Mmmm,' was all he said.

The P.M. continued, 'It would not only prove an incentive for the client (better to use that word rather than "stiff" or "corpse," – too emotive) but also for the family. The old person's life becomes a resource, a family asset, almost like a house in the old days when people owned their own properties; but with this scheme every living person automatically has an asset.' He paused, before adding excitedly, 'It's *brilliant*.'

Justin, the newest minister, had now regained his confidence and was worried that it might be forgotten that this had originally been his idea. 'Prime Minister,' he said, 'this ticks many boxes. Not only will it reduce the number of elderly useless… '

'Better not use the word, "useless," you know… but do carry on.'

'Sorry, I should say, the economically less viable people in our society, but it would actually income-generate. In addition, the administration of such a scheme would require a whole new branch of the civil service and a management structure potentially creating thousands of new jobs which would be funded *by* the scheme. In effect it would be self-funding.'

'Yes,' agreed the P.M. 'I envisage a sort of commission system: maybe ten per cent going to the executioner – bad term; executioner, – perhaps, assisting practitioner for euthanasia, or APE for short, would be better.'

The Minister for Health was beginning to catch up. 'I see! It's a bit like voluntary early retirement, back in the old days when people were employed?'

The P.M. was pensive for a moment and then, with the utmost *gravitas* and wearing his most serious demeanour, he pronounced. 'Gentlemen,' he glanced at Lady Carter, 'sorry, and Lady. I think I might be on to something here. It is of course all highly sensitive and we would have to make this scheme socially acceptable or my idea would be thrown out before it could be up and running.' The newest Minister sighed; he knew he had already lost his battle for recognition.

'We'll need to set up a working party, behind closed doors of course, and its remit will be to flesh out this concept and look at the economics. Marketing will be crucial. I see this operating along the lines of a public duty. Something like, "Tired of life? Realise your final asset." Or, "Elderly useless relative? Trade him in for ready cash." – No, that's not a good slogan, but you get my drift. We could have a help-line, those always seem to go down well with the voters, a *Death-Line*, or something punchy like that. Of course it would need close regulation like education and telecommunications, so we would need an equivalent: a *Deathcom*. The structure and the protocol need to be worked up. Do I have agreement and support for that?'

There were murmurs of assent from around the table.

'Right, Charles. I think it falls to your department to work this up. Although in the longer term the Department of Health may hardly be the correct department for overseeing this project.'

'Happy to do so, P.M.'

'Thank you, Charles.' The Prime Minister sat back in his chair with the satisfied expression of someone who has just solved a knotty problem. Then, after just a brief self-congratulatory moment, he pressed on. 'Right. Next item. Now what's all this about a problem with the climate? – Gerry?' He nodded towards the Minister for Disasters, who slowly rose to his feet.

The Minister for Health knew that he had drawn the short straw and he left the meeting feeling quite disconsolate, bowed down under the weight of the albatross that had been placed around his neck. *His* post had once been one of the most prestigious in the Cabinet but, over the years, as all the major illnesses had been conquered and ill-health had ceased to be a significant political issue, his role had become increasingly marginalised. He was now, in effect, merely the head of an administrative body that ran a preventative medicine service, rather like the head of the police or any of the other civil service departments. It was only for historical reasons that his was a Cabinet post at all and he was sure it would not remain so for much longer. The Homes Minister was now far more important since he and his department had a massive budget with which to manage the ever-increasing social problems associated with longevity, paradoxically caused by the successes of preceding Health Departments.

The problem with an ageing population was not that people were unwell; in fact they were generally quite fit. They might not be Olympic record-breakers but they could manage most physical tasks and were capable of light manual labour – if there had been any to do. Nor was it true that they were intellectually so impaired that they couldn't function independently. Most were reasonably intelligent, as all the common causes of dementia had been eliminated. No – the fundamental problem was that there was nothing for them to do. There were very few jobs available and almost all of those were reserved for the under-fifties, so that everyone at least had a taste of what it was like to work at some time during their life. Everyone else was bored. They had nothing to do. No *raison d'être*. They could attend courses, and most did – lots of them. It was not unusual for someone to have completed half a dozen university degrees by the age of fifty. Of course it had been recognised long ago that such qualifications didn't guarantee work – far from it – as there were simply not enough jobs to go round.

Years ago some idiotic politician had reckoned that if two per cent of the population went to university and subsequently went on to well-paid, full-time employment, then if *all* school leavers went to university everyone should get top jobs. This fundamentally flawed policy had inevitably led to the creation of a vast number of highly-qualified, unemployable unemployed, while at the same time annihilating the pool of those skilled in essential and rather useful trades such as building houses or fixing leaking taps. The dole queue was littered with astrophysicists, ethical botanists and medieval historians but with no one who knew how to mend a fuse. What had crept into society was not a physical or mental illness but a kind of moral decrepitude. The only successful industry and by far the largest employer was the Social Care Service itself.

For most people, life amounted to a period of schooling followed by twenty years or so of courses or post-school training – and for what, one may ask? Perhaps maybe five years or so working in, or managing, a home before becoming a resident until death arrived maybe fifty years or more later. For many, death came as a welcome release and attempts at suicide were common. The risk-averse legislation, however, required that attempted suicide should be severely punished and one politician, in all seriousness, had recommended that the death penalty should be reintroduced for persistent offenders. For some years social unrest had been a problem and the government had felt compelled to introduce a degree of censorship. Certain books and films considered undesirable and likely to lead to social unease were banned. The 'A' list consisted largely of religious texts, the subject of which had been the cause of so much carnage and evil three decades earlier. The 'B' list consisted of books such as Orwell's *Animal Farm* and *1984,* which, it was thought, might incite civil unrest. Then there were books considered to be "undesirable" on the 'C' list, such as those written by Hemingway and Solzhenitsyn amongst others, which were considered to be depressing and liable to weaken the spirit and general moral fibre of society.

The Health Minister himself was in his mid-seventies and beginning to develop the lassitude that was so common at that age. That evening, he thought long and hard about his new remit. He knew the P.M. had given him this project in order that he might fail, thereby providing an excuse to sack him from the Cabinet. The more he thought about his brief, however, the more he viewed it as an opportunity and by the time he finally fell asleep he was as enthusiastic about this commission as he had been about anything for many years. He had been given the task of designing a whole new Service: one which, if successful, would change the demographics of society and save the country from spiraling into terminal infirmity and moral turpitude. It was also a chance to get one up on the Homes Minister.

When Charles awoke the following morning, his enthusiasm for the task was undiminished and for the first time in twenty years he was impatient to get to his office and begin work. He arrived early and immediately summoned his most able junior secretary. 'Giles,' he said, 'we have been given a brief by the P.M., an important one. Would you call a meeting of the *whole* team, no excuses, for ten o'clock, please?'

'Certainly Minister,' replied the young man, slightly surprised by his Minister's zeal.

# TWO

The old man stood motionless, huddled against the cold, peering intently at his reflection in the shop window. 'Why is it,' he thought to himself, 'that as we get older our ears and nose get larger while the rest of us shrinks?' He frowned and looked more closely at the image gazing back at him. 'And how is it that my spectacles have suddenly become so huge?'

The old man was preoccupied, his brow furrowed with puzzlement as he pondered over the reflection in front of him. He was tall and slim but stooped – slightly untidy – as old men often are. Strands of thick white hair straggled down the nape of his neck and curled over the collar of his once fashionable overcoat. He stared into the picture window barely recognising his own reflection. There, staring inquisitively back at him, was a complete stranger: an old man, a geriatric caricature. From among the jowly folds protruded a nose, bony and hooked, and his ears, peeking through the wavy whiteness surrounding his face, appeared inordinately large. An oversize pair of spectacles seemed to consume the rest of his face giving him an owl-like appearance. Below his chin hung a dewlap where tufts of grey whiskers had escaped the efforts of his razor that morning. Between his neck and shirt-collar – from which hung a loosely knotted, woollen necktie – was a gap through which a few sparse grey hairs protruded. There was a faded, red silk handkerchief in the breast pocket of his crumpled, threadbare overcoat and just visible beneath was a charcoal-grey, pin-stripe waistcoat, once part of a stylish three-piece suit. Well-worn, dark-green corduroy trousers hung from his waist, their turn-ups just covering the tops of once elegant black brogues, now cracked and moulded to the contours of his feet. His knuckles were swollen and distorted, gnarled like the roots of an ancient tree and on the little finger of his left hand was a gold signet ring inscribed with the letter 'G'. In his hand he grasped a crumpled, white-plastic, carrier bag with an indecipherable red logo, within which were six sausages and a book.

For the third time that week he peered into the window of the shop, or studio as it was supposed to be called, and looked through his reflection to the advertisements beyond. The deals on offer seemed competitive, the business was registered with the department, and the letters A.C.E. after the proprietor's name proclaimed him, or her, to be an Associate of the College of Euthanasia, therefore fully qualified for the job. Of course, now he had a poor prognosis his situation had changed irrevocably. Just a week before he'd had no life-threatening disease that he was aware of, but then he had decided to pay for a pre-euthanasia assessment. To his surprise – according to the printout now safely stored in his wallet – his lifespan could now only be measured in months and thus any offer would be financially less attractive. The corollary of course was that, if he signed up to the voluntary scheme, the duration of his life that he lost would be commensurately less.

The old man didn't really want to die. It was just that he didn't particularly want to live either. He had spent the majority of his seventy-six years just struggling to exist. For the last forty odd years, since he had been unceremoniously stripped of both his job and his wife, he had done the same thing day after day. He was tired and bored. His numerous qualifications (more than he could remember, as he had long ago lost all the certificates) could not guarantee work. Thus, after his spectacular fall from grace forty years before, he had never worked again. Living in a State-funded home, the recipient of a small allowance, the years had gradually and inevitably transformed the exuberance and enthusiasm of youth into the monotonous, hopelessness of old age.

He had not set foot outside Nowton for thirty years and was tempted by what the practitioners and monitors quaintly called a 'terminal holiday' funded by the pre-mortem payment. He didn't actually need the money as he had a considerable sum saved but he might as well take whatever was on offer. At his age and with a less than favourable prognosis, that would not be a huge amount. 'But even with a modest grant,' he thought, 'I'd have enough money to travel almost anywhere in the world and stay in expensive hotels if I so wished.'

His mind wandered. 'Where on earth would I go?' he asked himself. He had no particular desire to visit far-flung places, no expensive tastes to savour or ambitions to fulfill. 'I could make that decision when I know the size of the payment,' he thought. 'I might even get a special offer since I've no relatives or friends to whom I can leave the post-mortem payment. It'll all be recouped by the State in the end anyway. There's no doubt I would be doing the right thing. It would be for the good of the State.' He rocked to and fro on his heels as he gazed at the colourful images of smiling people in exciting locations enjoying their happy terminal holidays.

'Are you thinking of doing it?'

The old man had been alone with his thoughts and this unexpected question delivered in a boyish, treble voice made him start. His hearing had become dull and he hadn't heard the approach of the thin boy whose reflection was now visible in the window beside his own. The youngster turned his gaze from the interior of the studio to the old man and smiled openly and honestly. 'Are you thinking of doing it, old man?' he repeated.

The old man was startled and annoyed at this unexpected intrusion into his private thoughts and he turned as quickly as his aged frame allowed. 'None of your business, son,' he said, his lower lip quivering with anger.

'Sorry! Didn't mean to upset you. No offence meant.' And the boy turned to walk on. The old man immediately felt ashamed of himself. He was inherently a polite and courteous person but he was scared. Alarmed by the new age, frightened of a world he didn't fully understand, intimidated by a new generation, and scared of people he couldn't trust. The lad had started to drift along the street, his hands thrust deep into the pockets of his tatty jeans.

'Hey, son,' the old man shouted. 'Hey, young man. Come back. I'm sorry. I really didn't mean to be rude.' The youngster stopped, turned and looked back at the old man who, relieved that the boy had halted, continued. 'I'm sorry, I didn't mean to be rude. I'm just not used to people talking to me.'

'That's okay, old man,' replied the boy, 'I'm not used to people talking to me either.'

'You must be freezing. Look at you! You've hardly got anything on.' The old man stared at the boy shivering in the February cold. Apart from his jeans, all he wore was a short-sleeved T-shirt and his slim young frame was shaking uncontrollably. He looked about twelve or thirteen, and had a handsome, open, honest face with blue eyes above which was a thatch of wiry, short, almost blond hair. His shoulders were hunched forward so that he could thrust as much as possible of his bare arms into his trouser pockets and there was a bluish tinge to his lips, though his face was now creased into a warm, engaging grin.

'You must be freezing!' the old man repeated.

'Well, it is a bit chilly,' the boy admitted.

'Where're your clothes? You should go home and get a coat. You'll catch your *death* like that.'

The youngster was pensive for some time and seemed at a loss for words. 'So, are you *really* thinking of doing it?' was all the boy said in reply.

The old man's gaze returned to the shop front. 'Possibly.'

'Why?'

'None of your… ' The old man stopped, anxious not to repeat his earlier rudeness. Surely the boy could have no ulterior motive in his questioning; he just seemed to be friendly and surprisingly inquisitive. 'Well to be honest, son, I'm not sure I want to carry on. I've had the medical – you know – where you go into a cubicle and get a printout, and it looks as though I haven't got that long to go anyway, so I thought I might as well try to get some money by volunteering. Maybe get a few bob for a holiday into the bargain.'

'Sounds reasonable,' the boy replied. 'To be honest I'd consider it myself but I'm not allowed to.'

The old man was outraged. '*You*! You,' the old man repeated, aghast. 'You're far too young, You're just a boy. That's ridiculous. Your whole life's ahead of you.'

'Yeah, you're right. I wouldn't really. I've got things I want to do. It's just that things aren't too good at the moment.'

'How d'you mean, son?'

'Oh – just things.' The boy looked at the ground. 'Anyway I'd better get moving; I'm getting cold standing here. Nice talking to you. Bye, old man.'

For the second time the boy turned to leave and started to shamble along the windy Nowton Street. His bare feet slopped around in worn trainers and his shoulders were hunched against the cold.

'Hey, boy,' the old man called. 'Where d'you live? I'll walk with you.'

The boy continued to walk.

'Hey, boy. I said, where are you going?' There was no reply so the old man started to follow. He could no longer walk quickly but shuffled along as fast as his legs would allow, following in the steps of the youngster who was no longer visible.

'Hey, son! Come back,' he shouted along the now empty street.

The boy turned into an alley which ran between two terraces comprising mainly shops. This narrow corridor channeled the cold wind, which now whistled through the youngster's meagre clothing. He took shelter in a doorway and shivered wildly. 'Yes,' he thought to himself, 'this is *not* good. I can't survive like this for much longer. I must find warmth or the old man's right, I'll freeze to death.' But his pockets were empty. 'No money, no warmth, no future,' he said quietly to himself.

The old man turned the corner and peered down the alley. After a few seconds hesitation he set off in search of the boy. Halfway along he found the doorway in which the lanky youngster was now shivering uncontrollably.

'Look, son, I need to know where you're going, because if you don't get warm soon you'll be frozen to the spot.'

The boy hesitated. Even at the tender age of thirteen, he was fiercely independent and it was anathema to him to be beholden to anyone; that was part of the reason that he was in this position in the first place. However, he also reluctantly realised that the old man was correct and that he was in a perilous situation. He thought for a moment then between shakes managed to say, 'Look, old man, this is my mess and I'll have to get myself out of it. But the problem is I'm homeless. I've got nowhere to go and all I've got is what I'm standing up in.' Having admitted to himself that he was now in real danger and couldn't see a way out, he opened up and continued. 'I really hate to ask and I've never begged before, but if you can help me in any way I would be most grateful. For the first time in my life I just don't know what to do.' The cheeky grin had gone and was replaced by an expression of despair.

The old man was still wary. He had been caught out by scams in the past which had lost him money and he knew worse had happened

16

to others. He was of a mind to interrogate the boy further but there could be no disguising the blueness of his lips and the shaking of his body.

'Here, son. Come with me and we'll get warm and have something to eat.' The boy nodded his gratitude, too tired and cold to argue or to question.

\* \* \*

The café was warm and comforting and after a quarter of an hour, as the food and drinks arrived, the boy had finally stopped shivering. The old man drank his coffee in silence as he watched the youngster devour a large plateful of fried food. It was expensive but he had insisted that the boy had everything on the menu, eggs *and* meat along with piles of potatoes. The boy ate without talking, only stopping occasionally to gulp from his mug of sweet, weak tea.

'He must be hungry,' thought the old man, 'there's no disguising *that*. Okay, if I've been swindled out of the price of a meal, so what? There's no shame in that.' Somehow the old man was tempted to trust and believe in this boy. 'First impressions are rubbish,' he thought. 'I've been caught out that way before, but this young fellow has an honest face, and he *is* as skinny as a bean pole.'

'What are you thinking, old man?' asked the boy as he drank the last of his tea.

'That you must be hungry and cold.'

'I'll not argue with that.' The boy gave a wide smile of pleasure, no – more than that – of deliverance.

'You couldn't fake that relief,' thought the old man and he was won over. There could be no doubting it: this boy was not a devious vagrant, beggar or wide-boy. He was just down on his luck – cold and hungry.

'Aren't *you* eating anything?' the boy enquired.

'No, son. At my age you don't need to eat much and I had something at the hostel, first thing.'

'Is that where you live?'

'Yes, and have done for the last forty years.'

'Gosh!' The boy wiped his mouth with a paper napkin. 'So why are you thinking of the Protocol?' he asked in all seriousness and with a naïvety that was engaging.

'Well, we all have to die sometime and my printout says I've got months rather than years, so I thought I might realise the only asset I have and use the money for a holiday.'

'Sounds reasonable to me, but what do your relatives think? They might not agree.'

The old man smiled: one of those slight smiles that facially is but a hint of the mirth felt inside. 'They normally do,' he said with a chuckle, 'since they are beneficiaries of the post-mortem payment. Anyway, I don't have any relatives, so it's not a problem.'

'What happened to them all?'

'Not sure. I just never had any. That's how it's always been. The State has looked after me from childhood. I guess I owe it something.'

'Same as me,' said the boy as he settled back in his chair with the satisfied expression of someone whose hunger has been satiated, thirst quenched and shivering calmed.

The old man smiled at the boy. 'So why are you on your uppers? You must have some clothes and belongings?'

'Well, I was in the State children's home until a week ago, but then they discovered that I don't exist.' The boy said this in a wholly matter of fact way.

'What d'you mean? *Don't exist?*'

'Well, apparently I'm not on the national database, so therefore I don't exist.' The boy looked into his mug to check that it was empty.

The old man looked puzzled and the boy continued nonchalantly. 'I've been in the home for as long as I can remember. It's quite nice, as boring as hell of course but it's warm and you get fed. The staff are stupid but that seems to be a prerequisite for being in any position of authority.' (How true, the old man thought.) 'Anyway I was caught reading a banned book and the caretaker went to register my offence. He tried to log me on and access my records but only got a default message saying, "You are logged out or invalid hypervent request," or something like that. In fairness he tried several times but essentially there was no record that I existed. Initially I reckoned that was a good thing because I wouldn't be reported – but then I was summoned to the board. They told me that as I was didn't officially exist they couldn't have me as a resident any more, as it was against regulations.'

The boy looked at the old man and smiled at the recollection. 'Also any belongings I had couldn't possibly be mine as someone who doesn't exist can't own anything. So I was thrown out just like this.' The youngster's face showed no self-pity but creased once more into a wide cheeky grin as he looked down at his T-shirt and jeans.

'The idiots! The *unbelievable morons*. I just cannot believe how stupid and unthinking our race has become,' the old man fulminated, his face suffused with anger. After a moment he asked more calmly, 'What are you going to do?'

'Well, I was just considering the options when I saw you and thought I'd say hello. I've slept rough for a week but the last two nights have been really freezing.' He gazed briefly out of the café window – misted and streaming with condensation – to the cold, bitter street beyond before turning his attention back to the old man. 'I'll think of something. I always do,' he added with an optimistic smile.

'No one will touch you if you're not on the database. You're a social leper, an outcast: you have now officially fallen below the radar of the State's social services. You no longer exist.' The old man paused for a moment to allow what he had said to sink in then the crow's feet around his eyes imperceptibly deepened, 'That's quite an achievement for one so young!' He looked at the boy who had been restored, by a simple meal and some warmth, to a naïve, cheery adolescent with a broad, cheeky smile, unreasonably content and at ease with a world that had dealt him a cruel blow. 'What was the book?' asked the old man.

'It's called *Nineteen Eighty-Four*, by a man called Orwell. Heard of it?'

'Oh! Yes that's on the 'B' list all right. I'm not surprised you were busted for that. It's many years since I read it. What'll you do now.'

'Well, old man, thanks to you, I'm fed and watered so I think I'll wander down to the subway and try to find somewhere out of the wind to get some kip before the police come to throw us out at nightfall.'

'Then what?'

'I'm not sure. Possibly just keep on the move till dawn, then bed down again.'

'You'll freeze to death!'

'I'll rob a blanket from a washing line or something like that. Anyway you've been a great help, old man. I was beginning to get a bit depressed with my situation but I feel a lot better now, thanks to you.' The boy sat forward and made a move to stand up.

'Don't go, boy,' said the old man. 'I'm having another coffee. D'you want anything?'

'Are you sure? You've already done more than enough to help me.'

'I'm sure. I'm enjoying your company. I haven't talked to anyone like this for thirty years or more.'

'Okay, thanks. Another tea and one of those cakes would be nice,' the boy indicated some enticing sponge cupcakes covered with a thick layer of chocolate.

And so they talked about their respective lots in life: of books and writing, hostels and homes. After a while the old man delved deep into his plastic carrier bag and brought out his prized possession, a battered, dog-eared copy of *Brave New World*. 'Here, I'll swap this for a read of Orwell,' he said.

'It's gone. Confiscated. Destroyed I expect,' replied the boy.

'Never mind. You take this, but don't let anyone find you reading it. I don't need it any more, I know it virtually by heart.'

'The boy grinned broadly with excitement. 'Well, *thanks*, old man. I really appreciate that.' As the boy glanced excitedly through the grimy pages of his new book, the old man watched him and thought, 'I haven't had such an engaging conversation for decades. This boy is intelligent, optimistic and mature well beyond his years. Even though the State has told him he doesn't exist he's just shrugged that off as a minor inconvenience.'

'What would you like to be when you're older, son?'

'Well, to be honest, my priority at present is survival. But in an ideal world I'd have liked to be a writer or maybe a journalist. You know, one of the old-style ones, the ones who told the truth, not just ghost-wrote what the State invented.'

'Quite an aspiration for someone who doesn't exist.' The old man hesitated for a moment. He knew he was now entering emotional territory which he'd not visited for forty years or more and had promised himself he never would again. 'Look, son,' continued the old man, 'I can't let you disappear into the subway with nothing but a T-shirt, a pair of jeans and a battered copy of Huxley to keep you warm. I'm happy for you to come back with me to my hostel. There's a guest room for relatives and I'll say you're my long-lost nephew – or possibly great-nephew would be more believable. I'd like to help you get back on your feet again.'

'Thanks, old man, but I hate being beholden to anyone. I appreciate your offer, believe me, but I prefer to be independent. You've already done more for me than I deserve.' The boy stood up. 'And, by the way, you do what you want, but you might be better *not* to sign up to the Protocol just yet, as you could do a very good job helping waifs and strays like me!' The boy smiled, pushed his chair back and extended his hand to the old man who took it and accepted the firm handshake. Then, without hesitation, the youngster stepped through the door and back into the cold February afternoon, the worn-out book clasped in his hand.

* * *

The encounter had intrigued the old man. It had reawakened feelings and emotions which he had buried long ago. He had been reminded of the boundless enthusiasm and energy of his own youth and of his aspirations to become a great writer and politician. After returning to his small one-room bedsit he sat for a while and pondered over the events of the day. He then ate two of his sausages and went to bed.

Between periods of fitful sleep the old man thought about the boy and made a decision to try and find him the following day. So, at first light, he rose, dressed quickly, stepped out into the bitter cold of the early morning and headed for the subway. It had been the coldest night of the winter so far. There was a hard frost on the ground and he could feel the rock-hard, frozen soil through the worn soles of his shoes. There was no one in the subway: the night police had seen to that. He began to wonder what might have happened to the boy and the more he reflected the more his imagination took flight. 'How old was he?' he asked himself, 'Surely not yet in his teens.' He had been crazy to let the boy go without warm clothes or somewhere to stay. But that hadn't been *his* decision, it was the boy's. The youngster hadn't wanted to compromise his independence – or to owe anything to anyone. 'The boy's not *my* responsibility, for heaven's sake.' But the more the old man, quite logically, justified his actions of the previous afternoon, the more he became concerned and agitated. He was now genuinely worried as there could be no doubt that without shelter, the boy, like so many homeless people each year, would die of hypothermia. He walked faster, wandering around the streets of Nowton, down alleys and paths which he hadn't traversed for years. Initially he told himself that it didn't much matter if found the boy but after two hours he became increasingly despondent and finally accepted that he was desperate to see him again to confirm that he was still alive.

Mid-afternoon, his search fruitless, he returned to his hostel. He was tired from his walking and his body ached, being unused to such exertions. As his muscles throbbed, so his mind spun in turmoil and it began to dawn on him that he actually cared for this boy. He hadn't truly cared for anyone for several decades and he had forgotten how uncomfortable that emotion could feel. The more he wondered, the more he worried. He certainly couldn't report the boy missing. Even if he knew his name, the lad didn't officially exist and the police would not search for someone who wasn't on their database. No one thought for themselves any more and it wasn't wise to question the *status-quo*, the operators of the system, the puppeteers, the computers and databases; as he had found to his own cost all those years ago.

As dusk fell the old man could sit still no longer so he gathered up his plastic carrier bag and his tired legs, put on his ancient overcoat and stepped out once more into the street. It was even colder now, the dark, brooding clouds were laden with snow – no one could survive the coming night without warmth and shelter, he thought. The homeless, the vagabonds, the tramps and those who were not allowed to exist, would be culled during this cold snap. 'Can you die if you don't officially exist?' wondered the old man.

He wandered aimlessly along the same streets and avenues that he had walked earlier on that day. He lost all sense of time and unknowingly found himself once again outside the Euthanasia Studio. He looked unseeingly into the warm inviting interior and the well-lit window dressings. 'Yes, it's tempting,' he thought, 'a few weeks in the sun before a gentle demise would be an appropriate end to an unsuccessful life.' He decided that the following day he would go in and enquire what deals were available.

'Thinking of doing it, old man?'

The old man turned so violently that, for a moment, he lost his balance and nearly fell over. On seeing the boy, his face lit up with recognition and an immeasurable sense of relief. '*Boy*, you're all right!' he exclaimed. 'I was so worried.' The youngster was smiling broadly but he was blue with cold and his face pale and drawn. 'Boy, you're safe, I was so worried.' The old man looked in wonderment and delight at the lanky, hunched figure. 'You look awful. I was truly worried. I came out to look for you, I thought you might have died from the cold.' The old man's words tumbled out and the boy just stood, hands deep in his pockets, shivering, his book held firmly under his arm.

'Is that offer of shelter still open, old man? Because if it is, I would like to take you up on it.'

The old man just smiled. 'Of course it is. Let's go back to my hostel before you freeze to death.'

'Thanks, old man. Here, I'll carry your bag for you.' The boy took the old man's carrier bag in one hand and they walked the short distance to his hostel, arm in arm.

# THREE

'Charles,' said the P.M., 'the floor is now yours. Please give us your plans for the Euthanasia programme.'

The Minister for Health rose to his feet with as much alacrity as the seventy-six year old could muster. In his eyes, however, was a gleam, a glint of ardour which his colleagues had not seen for many years.

'Thank you, Prime Minister.' He glanced around the table at his Cabinet colleagues. 'Since you charged me to take on and develop this initiative six months ago we, at the Department of Health, have been very busy. Fellow Ministers, I have brought with me today my junior secretary. This young man… ' and he nodded in the direction of Giles, a handsome, intelligent-looking man in his thirties, '… has been instrumental in the process and I must acknowledge his contribution, along with that of the whole Department.' The Minister paused for a moment as those around the table glanced at the young man while mumbling and grunting in a generally appreciative way.

'I should like to share with you the key features of our proposals and then would be happy to take questions.' The Minister took a deep breath and calmed his voice. For the first time in his life he felt that the rest of the Cabinet were actually interested in what he had to say. It was certain that his proposals would impinge on all the other governmental departments as it was so fundamental to the whole administration and structure of society, and his colleagues were well aware of this.

'To begin with, ladies and gentlemen, it seemed inappropriate for the Department of Health to lead on this initiative so I have set up a sub-department called the Department for Intelligent Euthanasia, or D.I.E. for short.' The Minister paused in order to garner approval for his neat and witty little acronym.

There were grunts of approbation from around the room while someone from the far end muttered, 'Very good; that's very good,' and tapped the table.

The Minister then continued: 'I see this Department being independent of, but running in tandem with, the Department of Health. The job of the DoH is to keep everyone healthy until it is time for them to enter the End of Life Pathway, that's when D.I.E. takes over. This Department will report to a Parliamentary sub-committee.' Charles was now in full flow and beginning to enjoy himself. 'The substructure will be run on a regional basis and the actual service will be delivered by Euthanasia Practitioners. These professional euthanasiologists will be extensively trained and will use, as the basis for the procedure, technology developed many years ago for those who had terminal illnesses and wanted to end their lives. The service will be delivered through a network of Studios; one per hundred-thousand of population and each Studio will normally be staffed by one practitioner and an assistant. The service will be overseen by Euthanasia Monitors who will supervise the running of the studios and police the system in general, including tracking Protocol-violators or Non-adherents as they will be known. There will of course be an independent watchdog, "Ofdeath," which will report directly to me.'

The Homes Minister interrupted. 'Surely that's not *entirely* independent, Charles?'

'It's independent enough.' There was a sharp intake of breath around the table at this curt response. Charles continued: 'The Protocol itself is still being refined and is necessarily quite complex. There will be an assessment of prognosis based on age and general health, with the financial awards varying accordingly. We envisage fifty per cent being awarded up-front, and the remainder after the event – but this of course could be negotiated and I can picture entrepreneurial practitioners offering special deals. They will be paid on a commission basis which will ensure active competition and a high quality of service.' The Minister paused and looked at the Prime Minister. 'Perhaps I should just stop there for a moment P.M.' he said.

'Thank you, Charles. An excellent piece of work, I must say. Now: any questions at this stage?' He looked around the table.

The Minister for Homes, still smarting from his put-down, coughed and raised his hand.

'Charles, this is all very well but there will be those who will simply take the money and – to use the vernacular – do a runner. How do you foresee dealing with that potential problem?'

'Yes of course, that's an important point.' Charles adopted a conciliatory tone. 'The business of policing the system will be the responsibility of the Euthanasia Monitors with a team of Enforcers. They will screen and track candidates in the same way as we do for all other Protocol violators such as... ' and he hesitated for a moment, '... say, over-breeders, and if there is any sign of default or non-adherence the Monitors will have the power to detain the client to ensure compliance.'

'What about those who simply change their mind?' asked Lady Carter.

'There will be an appeals process whereby, if a client's situation changes for whatever reason, or even if there is just a genuine change of heart, they can apply to appear before a Euthanasia Tribunal. The decision of the tribunal will be final.'

'I see, Charles. But what will their terms of reference be and how will we ensure fairness and equity?'

'Well, Lady Carter, that will be down to the... ' he hesitated briefly and looked directly at her, '... *The Protocol.*' The Minister said these words with deference and an almost religious fervour. He paused for a moment in order to emphasise the significance of what he was about to say. He then continued, almost in a whisper: 'The Protocol is the nucleus, the fundamental tool, the very nerve centre of the whole project. It is crucial to the success of our whole initiative and is still being developed by my young colleague here and his team.' Once again the Minister looked at his Junior Secretary and then around the whole room to ensure inclusivity. 'As Ministers may know, in the distant past doctors used protocols for all manner of things, mainly to make decisions for them when they didn't know how to manage their patients. They are essentially algorithms which are designed to aid decision-making. Ministers will remember that *Life Protocols* were introduced to aid government over thirty years ago by a previous administration and have proved extremely successful. In fact those Protocols have become the backbone of our society. What I am suggesting is that we just extend this tried and tested administrative system and add an End-of-Life Protocol, a sub-section of which will address euthanasia. We will design a Euthanasia Protocol so tight and so accurate that it cannot possibly go wrong. In it, all potential scenarios will be addressed and appropriate responses and solutions defined. The Euthanasia Protocol will be the nucleus, the engine-room: the living, beating heart of the End of Life Pathway.' The Minister's voice had risen as he had delivered those final words and as he finished it seemed as if he might even thump the table with his fist, something that was generally frowned upon; but he stopped short and merely smiled at the P.M.

The P.M. was as entranced by his Minister's rhetoric as were the rest of the Cabinet. 'Can you give us some more detail of this protocol please, Charles?'

'I'd like to ask my Junior Secretary to do that, if I may, P.M.'

'Yes, of course.'

'Giles, would you be kind enough to talk us through the details, please?'

The young civil servant stood up and, with a friendly and confident expression, smiled briefly at the P.M., and then at those assembled round the table. 'Well, Prime Minister, the Protocol will have several different sections. The first will address phase one of the process whereby the patient, or client, initially signs up to the programme. We have a one-hundred-page document explicitly addressing all the client's rights and what is expected of both parties. The Practitioner or the Assistant will talk the client through this and, once it is signed, the protocol must be adhered to.'

'Is there an opt-out clause?' asked Lady Carter, who was showing clear signs of being a bit of a lefty.

'No. We feel on balance that it wouldn't work, but we do have our appeals system.'

'Carry on.' The P.M. glanced at his watch for he was now beginning to feel more than a trifle peckish.

'The second part of the protocol is the personal contract. The individual details will, of course, vary from client to client, for example the size of the payment, and the post-agreement lifespan or PAL. Here, there would need to be considerable flexibility as to how much is paid up-front – that is the pre-mortem payment, or PREMP for short – and how much after death, the post-mortem payment or POMP. We will also need to have absolute clarity about to whom the POMP is payable. There will be a separate section defining the local process, including which euthanasia systems are in place. These will of course vary across the country taking into account regional culture and personal preference.' The young man took a breath, tugged a red silk handkerchief from his breast pocket and wiped his spectacles with it. 'Then there will be the tribunal protocol, which will essentially be a computerised process to ensure absolute consistency and safety. This is far too complex a process to leave to the whim and capriciousness of human beings. It is already over a thousand pages long and is not yet finished. The tribunal is the sole – and final – court of appeal.'

'What happens if a client changes his mind but has spent his pre-mortem payment?' Lady Carter was not going to let this issue drop. The P.M. audibly groaned.

The Minister for Health looked surprised at such a banal question and took over from his junior. 'Well, he'll just have to *repay* it.'

'But what if he has no money left?'

'That technically would be a protocol violation and punishable by what we call, "project completion." '

'You mean euthanasia?'

'Yes.'

'But that would be against the client's will.'

Cabinet members were becoming exasperated by this continued questioning but Lady Carter would not be silenced. Charles continued: 'In rare situations, yes. But occasionally an individual may have to suffer for the greater good of the Protocol and thereby of our society. The Protocol must prevail. Non-adherence is unthinkable and would result in chaos. We simply cannot have everyone doing their own thing, willy-nilly, whenever they want. That would be *ridiculous*.' The expression on the Minister's face was pugnacious and challenging as he looked directly at the Minister for Babies, but she would not be bullied.

'What have the human rights groups got to say about this?'

The Health Minister was puzzled. His recollection was that all such groups had been replaced by the relevant protocol years ago. 'They will be represented on the tribunal panel,' he said, confident in the knowledge that he had given no thought whatsoever to whom would be on that particular group.

The P.M. stepped in, 'Ultimately, I suppose it's all about selection. If the criteria are tight then these problems shouldn't arise.'

'Absolutely, Prime Minister,' agreed Charles who was pleased to move on from Lady Carter's inquisition.

'And then, of course, there's Ofdeath,' added the Homes Minister who, realising the mood of the cabinet, had decided to come on-side. 'What if the client *can* pay the money back? Let's say he has relatives who want him to stay alive?'

'Lady Carter,' chuckled the Homes Minister, 'that's *hardly* likely to happen, is it?'

'That would be up to the Tribunal to decide,' replied Charles.

Quiet then descended on the Cabinet room until the P.M. broke the silence. 'That's very comprehensive, Charles. You've done a very good job. To be honest, I thought you'd make a complete arse of it but you've come up trumps in my book.'

'Thank you, P.M.' The Minister flushed with pride and smiled at his sidekick.

'Any idea of uptake?' asked the Junior Finance Minister, whose idea this had been in the first place. He had sat glumly through the proceedings so far but now felt that he should engage lest he be seen as a lefty whinger.

The Junior Secretary stood up to respond. 'Well, Minister, that's such a fundamental issue we decided to perform a pilot – on the quiet – of course. We approached the residents of two homes in the north. Nominations were invited from the managers and the relatives of residents. Oh yes; and of course, the residents themselves. The results were interesting. As a result of this initiative we discovered that relatives visited more frequently and communicated with their loved ones more often – clearly a good thing, I'm sure Cabinet will agree. Furthermore, the potential clients themselves felt that they now had something to offer, that they were no longer merely a drain on the family and the State, but a potential financial asset. We had a twenty-per cent application rate in the over-nineties. Compliance was high, at nearly a hundred per cent.'

The Minister then added, 'In fact it would have been a hundred percent but two clients died pre-mortem.'

'How can you die pre-mortem, for heavens sake?' asked Lady Carter.

'Well, you know what I mean. They died before we could euthanase them.'

'And is that a protocol violation?'

'Absolutely. Totally unacceptable behaviour.'

'Oh. I see,' said Lady Carter shaking her head in disbelief.

'Where were these homes exactly?' asked the P.M.

'Nowton and Stownome, Prime Minister,' replied the Junior Secretary.

'Hardly representative. The median age there well exceeds the national average,' observed the Prime Minister.

'That's true, but it was for exactly that reason that we felt these were ideal towns to test our systems and this pilot shows that the process *is* viable.'

'And the cost?' asked the Finance Minister.

The Health Minister once again took over. 'This initiative is economically sound. In fact we estimate that it is cost-saving. We have introduced the concept of a "unit saving per euthanaised life year", or USPELY for short.'

'Doesn't exactly trip off the tongue,' muttered Lady Carter.

'No, we will have to find a better acronym, but the important thing is that we have calculated that we will save about a hundred thousand pounds per USPELY.' The Minister turned his gaze from Lady Carter to the Prime Minister. 'We also conducted a satisfaction survey after the event. The results were very promising, with ninety-five percent of relatives happy with the process. The only criticisms concerned the amount of the award and some haggling about how much should be pre-mortem compared with after the event.'

'How about the clients?' asked the P.M.

'Well, obviously they couldn't respond.'

'I know *that*, but was there much non-compliance?'

'No. None at all.'

'Well done, Charles. We'll put it to the House in the next session, but I think it is fair to expect it will be passed so I would ask your new Department to begin setting up the processes straightaway. The sooner we get started the sooner we'll see results.'

With barely a murmur from the usual lefties, the Bill was passed, just as the P.M. had anticipated. The Minister for Age-Control, as Charles was now known, organised a national network of Euthanasia Studios and initiated an impressive marketing programme, while his junior secretary, Giles, set about completing the various documents that would constitute the End of Life Protocol.

# FOUR

After the briefest of hesitations the old man pushed open the door of the studio and was immediately comforted by the relaxing warmth of the interior. Outside the late February winds were icy, penetrating the meagre fibres of his threadbare overcoat and chilling him to his very soul. Once inside, however, his confidence, built up by weeks of staring into the studio window at regular intervals, vanished as soon as the door had swung closed behind him. He became unsettled and fleetingly considered turning on his heel and walking back out into the cold winter wind.

As he hovered near the entrance and considered what to do next, a lady appeared from nowhere and glided up to him. At first glance she seemed a mere girl, certainly not more than thirty he thought. She was attractive and pretty in a slightly obvious fashion. Her formal dark-blue suit hung slightly uneasily on a figure which somehow gave the impression that it would be more comfortable in jeans and a T-shirt. On her feet she wore elegant, shiny, high-heeled shoes where trainers would have looked more natural. Heavy, blonde shoulder-length hair framed a round, yet pretty face which displayed just the right amount of makeup for her to look mature and professional, but not *too* sexually alluring. Her lips bore a touch of colour and the merest hint of a smile. Somehow she managed to combine the *gravitas* of an undertaker with the cunning of a used-car salesperson. As the old man vacillated, she approached at just the right pace. Like a hunter on an open moor she was too quick to allow him to follow his first instinct which was to run away, but not so fast as to startle him. She halted at precisely the correct distance from him – one and a half arm-lengths away, close enough to be friendly but not so close as to unsettle him. She had been trained well.

'Good morning, sir. I'm Mandy and I'm the Euthanasia Practitioner.' She offered her hand which he tentatively grasped. 'How may I help you today?' She paused for a moment and when there was no response continued, 'Perhaps you're just browsing. Or maybe you'd like to discuss some particular issues that are concerning you?' The old man said nothing. He had been completely wrong-footed by this girl. He hadn't seen, let alone spoken, to a young woman for years and even at seventy-six he found the girl's attractiveness disconcerting. It was rather like going into a barber's shop for a packet of condoms and unexpectedly finding that the sales assistant was a attractive young woman. Sensing his unease, she took a half-step back, clasped her hands in front of her and tilted her head at the perfect angle to demonstrate sincerity, kindness and efficiency, all in equal measure.

'Would you like me to show you around?' she offered, a slight smile dancing on her lips and around her eyes.

'Thank you, yes. That would be m-most helpful,' the old man stuttered. 'Yes, I would like a look around, please, and maybe a talk. I haven't made up my mind yet.' The old man hesitated for a moment before adding, 'But I've had the medical,' in order to demonstrate that he was serious about his intent.

'That's no problem, sir. Please call me Mandy.' Her face lit up briefly with an almost coquettish smile. Mandy was far too professional to look overtly attractive in a sensual fashion but she knew well how elderly men responded to her undoubted curves and mildly flirtatious ways. It was how she used to get her own way with her grandfather when she was a young girl. For female clients she usually sent out her male assistant who had similar skills. She had instantly taken the measure of this old man, an old roué she surmised, and she had been correct.

Having not spoken with a female for some ten years, the old man felt shy and nervous just being in the presence of this pretty girl, 'For God's sake,' he thought, 'I nearly blushed.' 'All right... M-Mandy,' he stammered.

'Good,' she replied in a business-like tone. 'I can look at your printout later – that is – *if* you decide to go ahead. Many of our potential clients find it helpful if I guide them through the whole procedure, step by step, and if you are interested we can then do the paperwork.' Mandy raised her well-groomed eyebrows in a gesture of reassurance.

'That would be most helpful... er... Mandy. Thank you.'

'We'll begin with the waiting room.' She turned and led the way into an adjacent room. It was the size of an old fashioned drawing room and was similarly furnished with two comfortable-looking upholstered settees, a low coffee table on which lay the current edition of *Euthanasia World*, and a desk, presumably to facilitate any last-minute paperwork. The walls and ceiling were tastefully decorated in measured tones of grey and burnished gold, while framed images altered every few seconds as did the background music.

Mandy stood in the centre of the room and looked all around rather proudly. 'This is where you would be received on the day of your Event,' she said. 'You are allowed to bring a maximum of three people with you and,' she drew his attention to the pictures with a sweep of her arm, 'you may of course choose your own decorations and music. We have a library of over a thousand pictures and fifteen hundred sound tracks.' She smiled at the old man before continuing. 'The final paperwork is completed here and details such as the payment confirmed.' Mandy paused for a moment. 'Right, now let's move on.' She walked to a door at the other end of the room, opened it and passed through. 'If you come this way you will see that we are now in the Final Event Chamber.'

The room where they were now standing was of a similar size but here there was little furniture, just a couch and table, while the walls were bland and colourless. 'You will see that this room is undecorated. That is so that we can personalise it for your Event. We have a huge choice of scenarios from which you can choose. Let me show you an example.' Mandy lifted a remote control, pressed some buttons and suddenly the whole room was transformed. The walls became a shimmering deep, rich red and a magnificent sunset appeared in what appeared to be the middle distance. The old man looked down to find that he was now standing on a brilliant-white Pacific beach and an emerald green sea lapped at his feet. So realistic was the illusion that he even stepped back for fear of getting his feet wet. Mandy smiled, seeing the amazement on the old man's face as she continued to manipulate the remote control. Suddenly they were transported to a lush jungle clearing. Tons of water tumbled and foamed over the top of a waterfall to settle into a placid pool seemingly close enough to touch. The sound of crashing water mingled with the raucous cawing of parrots and other exotic, brightly coloured creatures.

'I can see that you're quite fascinated by our range of environments,' said Mandy smiling. 'We have a large selection of atmospheres from which you can choose. These are what we call, "Event Pathways", which are a combination of holographic internal room effects and programmed electrical deep brain stimuli which will offer you virtually any sensation you desire.' She looked at him. 'As long as it's legal of course.' She gave a gentle professional chuckle of just the right volume and length.

The old man looked puzzled. 'I don't understand.'

'Don't worry. Most people don't – to begin with. The whole concept is to transform your Final Event into a deeply satisfying and pleasurable experience. Perhaps it would help if I gave you an example.' Mandy pretended to think for a moment, her face a picture of sincerity. 'Say you wanted to pass away as though you were sitting on a beach in the Caribbean with the sun setting while sipping a pina colada. We would chose the appropriate room ambience,' and with the press of a button she returned them both to the Pacific shoreline. 'That's the ambience,' she said, 'but that's just part of the experience. We can create the actual sensation of being there by deep brain stimulation through small electrodes which we attach to the back of your head. We can give you a complete sensation of the place: the smell, the warmth,' and again she chuckled professionally, 'even the taste of the pina colada.' She resumed in a more matter-of-fact and business-like fashion, 'We have one of the biggest selections of Event Pathways in the whole of the country. They are all in the brochure of course, but others include just lying in bed next to a loved one, or there's dying in battle; that's popular with our younger clients as is scoring a winning goal in the World Cup. We also offer making love, either gay or straight. We call that "The James Bond." ' She smiled at her joke and paused to let the information sink in.

Seeing that no questions were forthcoming she continued. 'Now I know you'll be wondering about the process itself. Well, it's ever so easy.' She went over to the small table and picked up what seemed to be a wristwatch from a box lying there. 'This little device does it all. We just attach it to your wrist. Would you like to try it on?' She smiled as the old man shook his head. 'No! That's not a problem, most clients don't.' She fingered the instrument. 'Then we set the programme and it is subsequently activated by a remote control or a time switch.'

'How long does it take to… ' the old man hesitated, '… well… work?'

'Usually about five minutes.'

'Okay. Thank you… er, Mandy. I need some time to think about this.'

'Of course, it's a big decision. Would you like me to have a quick look at your prognosis printout to give you an idea of what deals might be available and what sums are involved?'

'Yes please. That would be most helpful.'

'Good, let's go back to the office.' They passed through another door and the old man found himself back in the front of the studio where a handsome young man was now talking in subdued deferential tones to an elderly woman.

'That's Paul, my associate,' explained Mandy. 'Right, let's have a look at your printout.'

The old man retrieved the now slightly grubby printout from his wallet and handed it to Mandy who, after a brief glance, fed it into a computer on the table in front of her. 'Now, let's see what the Protocol comes up with,' she said turning the screen so that they both could view it. After a few seconds some text and numbers appeared on the screen. After scanning these for a moment Mandy said, 'Well, as you know you have a relatively short-term prognosis. The USPELY… ' Mandy looked at the old man who had registered confusion, '… Oh! I'm sorry, I should explain, that's the unit saving per euthanased life year,' the old man nodded his understanding, 'is around 150,000. That's not brilliant but it's something. We could of course negotiate the details if you decide to go ahead but we are looking at an event delay of, say, six months – that would be your terminal holiday – together with an award of two hundred thousand pounds, half up-front and half later. Of course there is no POMP if you die before your event day.'

'POMP?' The old man looked at Mandy, puzzled.

'Sorry,' Mandy chuckled, 'That's post-mortem payment.' She then hesitated for a moment while her *gravitas* returned. 'I shouldn't really be telling you this until you've signed up, as strictly it's considered coercion,' here she leant towards the old man in a conspiritorial fashion, 'but we do have a special offer on at present when we're adding an extra ten percent up front but that is for this week only.'

This said Mandy sat back in her chair, looked up and gave the old man a bright and engaging smile. 'Do you have any questions?' she asked.

'No I don't think so,' replied the old man, 'that's been most enlightening.'

'No doubt you'll want to go away and consider things, but don't forget the special offer is for this week only and of course the award decreases according to the Protocol's sliding scale on a day-by-day basis. Here's some literature and my card, so please don't hesitate to get in touch if I can be of any further help.' The practitioner stood up to end the interview. They shook hands and quite suddenly the old man found himself back out on the street and once more facing the icy winter wind.

The old man felt stunned, amazed at how matter-of-fact the whole process had been. One could almost forget that this was his *life*, his very existence that was being discussed. It had been more like negotiating the purchase of a car than dealing with the end of his life. As he wandered slowly back to his hostel, he reflected on how, initially, the concept of voluntary euthanasia had caused disbelief, followed by a sense of outrage. However, since the process had officially been inaugurated, slowly at first when a few suicidal old folk were paid to have their lives ended (which was what they wanted anyway) the idea quickly became widely accepted. 'It's amazing how easily society becomes desensitised: numbed to what was originally considered to be quite unacceptable behaviour,' the old man thought. 'It's a bit like thieving, or even murder: the first time is the hardest. Once you've done one it becomes easier; after a few it becomes acceptable – and then very quickly the norm. That must be how genocide becomes possible.'

In fact within ten years of its introduction a process, which had initially caused public outrage, rapidly became an integral and accepted part of the culture – as natural as death itself. Of course most of those in the targeted group didn't care too much anyway. Past the age of a hundred, most had the lassitude syndrome, were bored with life and the idea of receiving a payment for what would probably happen quite soon anyway had its attractions. Some cash for a terminal holiday and leaving the rest to their loved ones made sense to many elderly men and women. The Euthanasia Protocol soon became a natural extension of the Life Protocols. For many years these had defined, controlled and administered all aspects of life. Everything – from conception to education, employment to imprisonment – from pubescence to senescence was addressed by a Protocol. Now it seemed only natural that there should be one to manage the process of dying. It was a vast industry and the protocol division of the civil service had rapidly become by far the largest. Very soon there were protocols about the Protocol and then protocols about those protocols, and so it went on.

Back at the hostel the youngster was awaiting his return.

'Where have you been, Old Man?' The old man's eyes brightened as he looked at the boy's open and appealing face. He had meant to tell him about his plans but simply said, 'Just out for a walk, son. I'm hungry. Fancy going to the café?'

'I'm up for that,' said the boy with an enthusiastic smile.

* * *

A week later the old man was sitting uncomfortably on the opposite side of a desk to the chief warden. 'I'm afraid I have no choice,' said the warden. 'I've checked the Protocol and he can't stay any longer. We cannot use our guest facilities for someone who is not on the database.' He looked at the old man and removed his spectacles, 'I know you say that he is your great-nephew but officially the boy doesn't exist.'

The old man had no idea how the warden had discovered the boy was unregistered, but that didn't matter; what mattered was that he *had* found out. 'Chief Warden, you know as well as I do that's a piece of nonsense. The fact that there has been some protocol error is hardly the boy's fault.'

'I know that but we have to follow the protocol. Look – the procedure's clearly stated here. D'you want to see?'

'No that's not necessary, I'm sure you're right. But the Protocol's an ass. You know that.'

'I wouldn't let anyone hear you say that if I were you.' The warden looked at the old man, surprised and concerned by his tone. 'You know, I could expel *you,* as well as the boy, for associating with him and getting me into this mess in the first place.' The Chief Warden was genuinely concerned about the situation that he now found himself in. Residents of state homes rarely broke the rules but this was a clear case of deliberate protocol violation which would reflect badly on him and on the home.

The old man was growing more and more annoyed, an emotion he had not felt for a long while. A few decades before he would have reacted angrily to such a piece of crass nonsense: called the warden an intellectual pygmy or worse, might have become physically threatening. However, over the years he had learned that standing up for one's beliefs and challenging the official dogma in that way was always counterproductive. You couldn't argue with those unthinking aments, those human automata; and the frustration of being unable to connect intellectually with such thoughtless State employees had in the past resulted in friction with the authorities. His defence of commonsense against protocol driven idiocy had, long ago, cost him both his job and his woman.

'All right, give me forty-eight hours and I'll guarantee that he will be gone.'

The Warden hesitated. He knew that every minute the boy was in the hostel his own job was on the line and, if it were discovered that he had used State facilities for an unregistered person, he would be summarily dismissed and replaced by one of the several hundred younger men and women waiting for a job such as his. However, he also detected the fury that the old man was barely keeping under control. If the old man chose to, he could leak the story to higher authorities and that would be it – he would be a resident in his own home.

'Okay. But not a minute longer. I want the boy out by midday on Thursday. D'you understand?'

The old man didn't even bother to respond, but rose wearily from his chair, turned his back on the warden and left the room.

Once outside, he breathed a sigh of relief. He knew that if he had so wished the warden could have had him arrested for misleading the State and the boy thrown out on to the street where he had found him.

The old man was now completely focused and knew exactly what he had to do. In a strange way he felt relieved as a decision over which he had vacillated for so long had now, in effect, been made for him. There was no alternative. He went back to his room, donned his overcoat and walked to the studio.

Later that afternoon he took the young man to what had become their regular rendezvous: the café. The boy was wearing his new leather jacket and a warm woollen jumper and socks, along with his usual T-shirt and jeans. Sitting opposite him the old man thought how much better the boy looked than when they had first met. 'Young man,' he said, 'how would you like to go away; go on holiday somewhere?'

'I'm happy here, with you,' the boy replied, without looking up from his plate.

'No. I mean both of us. We could stay in a hotel or rent a house. See somewhere different, somewhere other than Nowton.' The boy briefly looked up from his plate, 'That sounds nice. Where d'you have in mind?'

'I've always had a hankering to see some mountains. We could go to Scotland.'

'Scotland?' the boy looked puzzled, 'where's that?'

'You know, up north.'

The boys face suddenly beamed with understanding. 'Oh! you mean Dalriada?'

'Yes! Yes, Dalriada, They've changed all the names since I was your age. I still think of it as Scotland. I'm old enough to recall people calling Sri Lanka – Ceylon.'

The boy finished his food. 'I'd be up for that,' he said, 'but I've no money. You'll have to go on your own.'

'I'd pay for us both, I wouldn't go on my own.'

'No, I've already taken too much from you, I couldn't do it.'

'Look, I want a holiday, but I'm not going without you. Are going to stop an old man from having a holiday?'

The boy thought for a moment and realised that the old man was deadly earnest. 'Are you sure you can afford it? You've already spent far too much on me.'

'Yes. I've been saving up. For years I've had nothing to spend my money on and now I have quite a lot. I've always fancied a holiday, but couldn't be bothered. Now, with you, it would be fun.'

'Well, I'm not going to turn down the offer of a holiday, I've never had one. Thanks, old man. You know I'll never be able to repay you?'

'I don't want you to. That's the deal.'

'Fine. Shall we go in the summer? I think that's when people usually take their holidays.'

'No, we're going tomorrow.'

The boy looked up with surprise. 'Why so soon?' he asked.

'Well, I'm not getting any younger and I'm not as fit as I used to be, so as I see it, the sooner we go the better.'

'Well, I'm not doing anything else and Dalriada sounds nice. Can we go on the train? I've always fancied a train ride. I used to watch the trains all the time when I was younger: wonder who was on board, where they were going and think what fun it would be to travel on one.'

'Yes, we shall go by train. Apparently it's one of the most exciting journeys in the world.'

'Are you sure people who don't exist can have holidays?' the boy said with a smile.

'Oh yes,' said the old man with feeling, 'they have the best holidays – as they don't have to end.' He smiled fondly at the boy, 'Pack your bag, young man; we're off at first light tomorrow.'

Although street-wise and experienced well beyond his years, the boy still had the naiveté of a child and didn't think to question the old man further, but just gratefully accepted this piece of good fortune.

Thus it was that the following day, at seven o'clock in the morning, the old man and the youngster slipped out of the hostel with all of their combined possessions contained in two plastic carrier bags and, without a word to anyone, they simply disappeared into the urban morning.

# FIVE

Once the Bill had been passed, the Department worked rapidly in order to introduce its euthanasia policy as quickly as possible. Although initially beset by reactionary opinion from thoughtless minority groups, skillful marketing and a gentle, sensitive introduction meant that it quickly became accepted as yet another integral part of the State's management structure.

Each region of the country was required to introduce the policy slowly and delicately, beginning on a small scale. Initially it was advised that perhaps one or two elderly individuals, non-controversial clients such as those with little insight or an active desire to die should be encouraged to volunteer for the programme. By starting with such carefully selected cases, preferably with high-profile, media-friendly relatives, the population quickly became desensitised to the concept of voluntary euthanasia and accepting of the procedure itself. Large financial awards, particularly at the beginning, aided subscription and euthanasia rapidly became something that was perceived to be not only beneficial for society but also entirely justifiable for the greater good of the State. Even the health scientists, that most reactionary of groups, who had initially opposed the Protocol as anathema, were soon won over and commenced work on a euthanasia default to add to the health and monitoring chip inserted into all individuals at birth.

Gentle but persuasive marketing along with carefully monitored, positive media coverage allowed the programme to gradually expand. Within a year of its introduction the Protocol had become the main topic of discussion in pubs, on chat shows and at home. Soon everybody knew someone, or knew someone who knew someone who had undergone the procedure. Even those who didn't actively support the principle, now accepted that the Protocol was an inevitable part of life to be grudgingly accepted, rather like inclement weather. Officially of course it was still voluntary, but there was that invisible force: peer pressure to be proactive with the older members of one's family, to be reckoned with. Comments from a neighbour such as, 'I see your great grandad's still hanging on then,' were usually enough to initiate a family discussion. There was now a tacit acceptance that once over a hundred years of age everyone should buy into the End of Life Programme with its euthanasia option, and many considered it at a much younger age.

The benefits were there for all to see. Within the duration of the government that introduced these measures the median age of the population had reached a plateau and soon after showed a small but tantalising fall. It was a vote-winning policy and ensured the Party an overwhelming election victory, allowing it to enjoy a third successive term.

Recipients of the post-mortem payments spent their awards on all manner of things, saying to themselves and to anyone else who would listen, that this was what, *he* or *she* would have wanted. Charles, Minister and head of D.I.E., proved to be skilled at designing and organising the network, appointing and training an army of practitioners, assistants and tribunal members to run the service.

Giles worked tirelessly on the protocols which numbered over thirty in all. His contribution was recognised by promotion to Senior Under-Secretary and the award of a State wife – a rare honour. He was given the choice of some ten women and eventually chose a pretty brunette with dark, appealing eyes. Having a State wife gave Giles considerable status and the award was reviewed biennially. The concept was that a senior civil servant who was unmarried, like Giles, would have access to a partner for formal occasions as well as for personal support and comfort if so wished. Rather to his surprise, it quickly became clear to Giles that life was far more pleasant with his partner than it had been previously and he was delighted when the State agreed to fund his wife for a further two years. Soon they grew very fond of one another and what had initially been an arrangement of convenience soon developed into a loving relationship.

It was the Dorset Tribunal which proved to be Giles' undoing. As the senior author of the Protocols his opinion was not infrequently sought in difficult cases and he was not surprised when, some three years after their introduction, he was asked to attend a tribunal hearing as an independent external adviser.

On the day of the tribunal he read the background papers while on the train. It appeared that a young woman had signed up to the Euthanasia Protocol on the understanding that she had a rare untreatable disorder that would prove fatal within an estimated five to ten years. Because of her youth, relatively long prognosis and inevitable requirement for expensive state care as her disease progressed; her award had been substantial. Central to her reasoning was the knowledge that her son, who was disabled, would need financial support after her own death.

The problem arose when the woman's diagnosis was reviewed and judged to be incorrect. She was then delighted to be told that her life expectancy could now be considered normal and unsurprisingly wished to withdraw from the agreement on the basis of a change in circumstance. She had applied to the tribunal confident that the euthanasia order would be overturned on her returning the pre-mortem payment. The committee members, however, were undecided and could not agree an appropriate outcome as the protocol did not appear to cover this highly unusual circumstance. Although the woman's change in prognosis was exceptional and the decision to rescind the euthanasia order seemed to be quite straightforward, whenever the chairman (whose job it was) typed the new information into the database and requested an overrule to the euthanasia order, the computer simply read: INADEQUATE INFORMATION – REQUEST DENIED. After an unusually heated meeting when the members of the tribunal were evenly split between complying with the order and overruling it, the chairman decided to seek help from the Department and asked the Minister for advice. Charles immediately passed this on to his Senior Under-Secretary to resolve. As an interim measure, the tribunal upheld the order but deferred completion pending advice from the D.I.E.

'Seems quite straightforward,' thought Giles as he watched the sprawl of urban London rush past. 'A clear case of change of circumstance. The order should be overruled. Don't know why they need me to tell them that.'

Giles was slightly late and when he arrived was surprised to find the tribunal chamber empty. He had expected the meeting to be in full flow by then, with the client sitting before the panel in the prescribed fashion, and a lively debate proceeding as to the legality of upholding the appeal. After Giles had scanned the looking the room for a moment, the silence was broken by the creaking of a door. A man entered the chamber and began to walk over to Giles, his hand extended. He sported a straggly, untamed beard and wore an open-necked shirt, a cardigan along with casual green trousers, while sandals covered his otherwise bare feet.

He shook Giles' hand. 'Ah. Under-Secretary, how good of you to come, although I fear we have brought you out on a wild goose chase.'

Good, thought Giles, it looks as though they have done the sensible thing. Then he said, 'I suspect so. But that's fine.'

'Yes, I'm pleased to say that we have resolved the case.'

'I must say it seemed quite clear to me what the appropriate course of action should be.' Giles smiled at the chairman.

'Yes, on reflection it was, but I only realised after we had requested your attendance. Subsequently it became apparent to me that the Protocol was quite clear on the matter and as chairman I acted accordingly.'

'Good. Could she repay the pre-mortem award?' asked Giles.

'That was never a problem. She hadn't spent it.'

'Okay, so it's all resolved then?'

'Absolutely.'

'Good. Well, as I've come all this way I may as well say, "Hello," to her and wish her well.'

'How do you mean?' The chairman's expression had changed from one of amicability to surprise and puzzlement.

'Well: congratulate her on her change of circumstance.'

The chairman's countenance was now one of complete confusion. 'You can't see her,' was all he said.

'So you've released her already. That's fine. I'll be on my way then.'

'No... ' and he hesitated, '... No. She's been Completed.'

On hearing this the blood drained from Giles' face, his amiable expression vanished and his eyes widened in disbelief. 'What d'you mean by, "she's been Completed?" '

'We upheld the order – as the Protocol demanded.'

'What!' Giles was dumbstruck. '*What*! You haven't euthanased her. Tell me you haven't.'

'Yes.' The chairman had now become calm. He realized that the secretary was furious and that he was now fighting for his career as tribunal chairman. His eyes narrowed. 'Yes, Under-Secretary. Yes. We reviewed the Protocol and there was no reference to a change in diagnosis, so the Protocol decided to uphold the agreement.'

'*What*! What d'you mean, the *Protocol* decided. *You* are responsible, not the bloody Protocol. That's what tribunals are for.'

'There's no need to take that tone with me, Under-Secretary. I know the Protocol well and we re-ran it four times, as is required.'

'Yes, but that's for a *fault* you idiot, not to decide on something that's clearly beyond the remit of the Protocol. Please tell me she's not died?'

'She was Evented this morning at ten a.m. It all went very well and the paperwork is wholly in order. Would you care to see the paperwork? Every box is appropriately and correctly filled in and countersigned as required.'

'No, I don't want to see the *bloody* paperwork. I would have liked to have been able to see the lady.'

'But, Under-Secretary, there has been no error.'

'What d'you mean, "*There's been no error.*" Someone has died who *shouldn't* have died. That's a *bloody error.*'

'No, there was *no* error. The Protocol was quite clear on the matter.'

'Show me,' shouted Giles as he headed angrily towards the bench on which sat the tribunal chairman's computer.

The chairman brought up the woman's details. The first screen message read, EVENT COMPLETED 10 A.M., and there followed the day's date. The chairman scrolled back through the database. 'Here you are. "Change of circumstance." You see, there is no box for a change of diagnosis so there is no way of changing the outcome.'

'But the change of diagnosis must be registered or the tribunal could not have been called.'

'Yes, but that's here – in the Life Protocol. Section four: Incurable illnesses.'

'Well, there you are. It's clear that there has been a change in circumstance.'

'But that's in one of the Life Protocols, not part of the End of Life Protocol, so cannot be taken into account. That's why the computer disallowed the overrule. The decision was clear-cut.'

'You *idiot*! Why didn't you use your commonsense and just make a decision yourself. It's obvious that the order should have been rescinded. Don't you see?' Giles' whole demeanour was one of complete and utter exasperation.

'Look! Don't you take that tone with me. I know my rights as outlined in the Life Protocol 15; subsection 4: "Interactions with State officials and Channels for complaint." '

'But don't you see? You've done something inherently *wrong* here. Something very bad.'

'No. It's for the best. We can't have every one doing exactly what they want. What would the world come to? There has to be order. We must adhere. Here, let me show you. On the screen it says: ORDER UPHELD.'

'I know what the *bloody* computer says but that doesn't make it right. The computer's an idiot. But *you're* supposed to know better.'

The chairman was now truly out of his depth. He could not understand why this civil servant was not congratulating him on a difficult job well done. He was convinced that he had done the right thing by following the Protocol to the letter. He could not understand how the Senior Under-Secretary, the author of the Protocols, could now be disagreeing with him and implying that he – the chairman of the tribunal – had made a mistake. 'Look, I don't care for your tone. You may be a senior civil servant but I'm chairman of this tribunal and no error has been made. Here, check the paperwork yourself if you want.'

Giles' frustration was boiling over. 'I don't give a toss about your bloody paperwork! You're a complete *ament*.'

'*Right*. That's it. I'm putting in a formal complaint according to subsection four.'

Giles had had enough. For a moment he stood; visibly shaking, then he did something which he knew at the time would have serious repercussions. He hit the chairman. He hit him as hard as he could on the jaw. He truly wanted to hurt this irritating, useless, waste of space and was disappointed when the man didn't even fall over.

As the chairman wobbled and shook his head, Giles nursed his aching hand. For a moment the chairman looked at Giles in disbelief and then, as he registered exactly what had happened and how strongly emotions were running, he turned and ran as fast as he could through the door and out of the courtroom.

Giles stood massaging his right hand which was throbbing painfully. 'Shit, shit, *shit!*' he shouted out loud into the empty room. His fury gradually dissipated as the magnitude of what had just happened became apparent and his emotion turned from anger with the chairman, to pity for the woman who had died, and then finally to annoyance with himself for losing his self-control.

Unless the moronic chairman changed his mind, which Giles knew he wouldn't, (he had met that kind of know-it-all before) his own career was now finished. But as he stood in the empty tribunal room gently massaging his knuckles there came a realisation that there was a much more serious issue at stake than his personal future. This idiot of a chairman had actually thought that he was doing the right thing. *His* protocols, Giles thought, the ones *he himself* had painstakingly written, were being misinterpreted and were now causing actual harm. He had created an unthinking monster and moronic arseholes like this chairman, who normally wouldn't be allowed to make a decision about which what colour of underpants to wear, now had the authority to pronounce on important issues affecting life and death.

Giles slowly walked from the courtroom and returned to the capital, his heart full of sadness.

It was to be a week before the Senior Under-Secretary was summoned to the Minister's office. 'Giles, what's all this about? I've had the most disturbing report from the chairman of the Dorset Tribunal. He says you hit him and called him an idiot.'

If he had wanted to, Giles might have wriggled out of this situation as he well knew how the Dorset chairman was disliked and mistrusted. The Senior Secretary, however, was still outraged and in no mood to be conciliatory and obsequious.

'Yes, Charles, I did. And to be quite honest with you, I wish I'd hit him harder. The man's an idiot. An unthinking, useless, stupid… ' lost for adequate expletives, he simply added, '… *idiot.*'

'Giles, you're not helping your case here. You're probably right about the man but you can't go around hitting officials and calling them names.'

'I know, Charles, but in effect he killed someone: murdered them.'

'Unwise words, Giles. Remember who you're speaking to.'

'I know. But in essence that's the truth.'

'But, Giles, as I understand it, he adhered to the Protocol. Is that correct?'

'Yes. That's the whole problem. He adhered to the bloody Protocol rather than using his miniscule brain.'

'Giles, you and I know that the Protocol isn't perfect, but people like the Dorset chairman don't think for themselves. Good job too, actually; otherwise they might be really dangerous.'

'But he *has* caused some real damage. A woman is dead because of his idiocy.'

'Come, come, Giles. Unfortunate, I agree, but a small price to pay for the stability of a nation. Without the Protocol, people like this could cause real problems – they might try to think for themselves. Lord knows where that might lead. There would probably be civil unrest, perhaps even a war. Thousands might die. Your protocols, Giles, have served the country well.' The Minister paused to think for a moment. 'Giles, would you be willing to apologise to him? He has made the most serious of complaints and unless he withdraws them you know there can only be one outcome.'

'Even if I grovelled, he would not withdraw his charge, Charles. He's that kind of man. I've met them before: small-minded idiots. And to be honest, Charles, if I see him again I'm likely to hit him and this time I'll try to kill him.'

Charles sighed and looked at the papers on the desk in front of him. There could be no going back now, and he signed the topmost document. 'I'm sorry, Giles, but as of now you are no longer a civil servant, and of course your wife will be recalled.'

'I know, Minister.'

'There's a lifelong hostel place held open for you and of course there'll be the usual small bursary as a retired civil servant.'

'Yes. Thank you, Charles. I quite understand.'

Of the two – the loss of his job and the loss of his State sponsored wife – the latter hurt him by far the most. Hers was an official post, a civil service job and she had no say in the matter. That night they talked about her resigning so that they might remain together. They both knew, however, that this would be viewed as a serious protocol violation and dealt with most severely. When the official car drew up to take her away, they both promised to keep in touch, but Giles knew that would never happen. He was an insider and understood how officials' wives, after a tour of duty, were desensitised and that after this short programme she would no longer remember him as anything other than an ex-colleague. No: the pain would be his, and his alone, as would his desolate future.

# SIX

'This is amazing. How fast d'you think we're going, old man?'

'I've no idea. Maybe seventy, possibly more.'

'I wish this journey could go on forever, don't you?' The old man smiled at the boy's childish enthusiasm. 'Yes, I agree that would be good but all journeys must come to an end – otherwise it wouldn't be a journey.'

They sat opposite each other and stared out of the carriage window at the quickly changing scenery. On the seat beside the old man were two plastic bags, now bulging with their belongings and food for the trip. 'Would you like another sandwich?' asked the old man, and he passed one across. 'Here, finish off this juice.'

'Thanks,' said the boy, accepting the food without taking his gaze from the window. His eyes were wide with awe and his whole face suffused with excitement.

Gradually the drab urban landscape with its endless succession of peeling skyscrapers gave way to the greens and browns of farmland, with only observation towers breaking up the skyline.

'How long are we going away for?' asked the boy.

'About six months.'

'Wow, that's great. What will we do when we get to Dalriada?'

'Well the first thing we have to do is decide where we want to go. I thought it would be good to see a mountain, find somewhere quiet; maybe stay in a cottage in the hills. What d'you think?'

'That's fine by me. I'd love to climb a mountain. Perhaps we'll even get to see an eagle?'

'Maybe. Yes, that *would* be special.' The old man looked at the boy. He still didn't know his name, his age or anything about his past. He didn't want to. He was fighting a losing battle not to become emotionally attached to him. The cynical youngster he had met just a few weeks before had now reverted to being a child: the youngster that he might have been, if the system had not expunged the youthfulness from him.

He was now a bright, inquisitive young boy, maybe thirteen or fourteen years old, figured the old man. Most importantly, he was a thinker. His mind had not yet been emasculated by the system, the mindless Protocols that controlled everyone and everything. 'Not that protocols are inherently wrong,' reasoned the old man to himself. He had been in the vanguard of the process and had even helped to introduce some of them many years ago. To begin with, they had been an invaluable asset to government, ensuring consistent and high-quality decision-making across all the different departments and disparate administrations which had sprung up across the land after the disastrous wars of religion. Advice on all matters: from conception to deception; from vaccination to education; and from housing to lousing was now explicit and consistent the length and breadth of the State.

The problem was that those protocols had now become an end in themselves rather than the means. They now existed in their own right as a goal to be achieved rather than as a tool to assist. He had watched in horror as the hydra-like monster had taken on a life of its own, and when he attempted to tame the beast he'd been decried for his actions. The leviathan had bitten the hand of its creator. He had tried to explain to his seniors that these protocols were intended to guide rather than lead, but the new generation couldn't see beyond the words, the chapters and the subsections. They were now slaves to the content and blind to the spirit. They were so reliant on those documents that they'd lost the ability to think for themselves. If anyone challenged the Protocol it was seen as challenging the State itself, the very fabric of society – and punishable as such. A generation of unthinking protocol fundamentalists had been born. If a problem couldn't be solved by the Protocol, they simply created a new one or wrote an amendment. 'Idiots,' thought the old man. 'The problem is that I was instrumental in the conception of the monster, midwife at the birth of this moronic dinosaur.'

He gazed fondly at the boy. Surely this was at least one good thing he had done in his life: salvaging him from the system, possibly even from death. The boy was still naïve and should stay that way. 'I will leave him in Dalriada and return to my fate alone,' thought the old man. Dalriada was as good as anywhere for him to begin his new life. Certainly it was primitive and no place for the elderly, but an enthusiastic youngster could readily carve out a future for himself there. He decided not to tell the boy of his plans and his need to return to Nowton until the end of his terminal holiday. Having returned the boy to the naïvety of youth, he didn't want to destroy his new-found innocence any sooner than was absolutely necessary.

'Look, old man what's that? Look! Over there.' The boy was pointing excitedly to the opposite window where a broad expanse of the North Sea was visible.

The old man grinned broadly. 'That, my boy, is the sea.'

'Gosh. Where does it go?'

'To the foreign world. Out there are whole countries, entire continents, decimated and destroyed during the Wars of Religion. To avoid this virulent contagion, the island on which we live dissociated itself from the world across the water to avoid being torn apart in the name of theism.'

'How do you mean?'

'Well, it seems amazing now but people believed in different gods and everyone considered that theirs was the only true god: a sort of ideological greed – theistic tunnel vision. So they fought each other for more than thirty years. Millions of people were killed, whole countries were ruined and a large part of all civilised society was destroyed. It goes without saying that no one really won. Over there, son,' said the old man, pointing at the water, 'are vast tracts: whole countries of uninhabitable, burned, radioactive land – completely ruined. Our country was only saved because we were an island, and largely left alone.'

'Gosh!' was all the boy could say. 'What about where we're going? Is that safe?'

'Yes, as safe as it can be. Dalriada was spared because no one thought it was worth attacking a poorly governed, fragmented and rather backward state.'

The boy fell silent in contemplation as the land rushed past and the flatlands gave way to the foothills of Dalriada.

They stayed on the train until it reached the end of the line. There, in the early dawn, they alighted and the old man and the boy stood alone on the platform, looking in wonderment at their new surroundings.

Motionless, they stared into the huge expanse of restless cloudy sky and saw a bright halo where the still-hidden sun heralded the warmth of an early spring day.

'Right, son, we'll go to a café and get ourselves a hot meal. Then I'll find a nice place for us to spend the next six months.' The old man said this authoritatively and with genuine enthusiasm. He seemed less stooped than he had been in Nowton and appeared invigorated by the situation he now found himself in. They entered a café on the platform and after eating a pie and drinking his coffee the old man left the boy to read a magazine while he went to the booking agent's office. Just under an hour later he was back, clutching tickets and some glossy literature. He beamed with excitement as he made his way to the table where the boy sat reading.

'You look pleased with yourself,' grinned the boy.

'I am. I have just rented us a cottage near a mountain and next to a loch. It's about a mile from the nearest village where there are shops and a school. It looks absolutely idyllic.'

'Well done, old man. That's great. When are we going?'

'In ten minutes, so drink up.'

Later that day, as the sun was dipping towards the horizon, they reached their destination. The taxi dropped them outside the door of an isolated single-storey stone cottage. In front of it was a loch and behind a mountain. It was a proper mountain, the closest of a whole range of hills extending into the distance as far as the eye could see. Its lower slopes were covered with grassland and a few deciduous trees, while higher up were the deep greens of pines and conifers. Above the tree-line a purple haze of early-flowering heather was discernable and at the summit lay a sprinkling of snow.

They both stood spellbound and gazed in wonder at the scene. It was some minutes before the old man broke the silence. 'Well, this is our home for a while, young man. Like it?'

'It's unbelievable. It's like one of those picture postcards. Wow!' The boy looked around again to take in the whole view. 'And look – is that a real mountain?'

'It is indeed. It's over two thousand feet. That's for you to climb. They say that golden eagles have been seen there on occasion.'

They went inside the cottage and after a brief exploration of its interior the boy chose the bedroom at the back of the house, looking out on to the mountain range, leaving the other, which looked down into the darkness of the loch, for the old man. Exhausted after their long journey they both fell quickly asleep.

As March turned to April and April became May, the boy climbed the mountain and the old man fished the loch. An explosion of colour sprang from the ground as the nights grew shorter and the days warmer. The boy was welcomed into the local academy and took to attending classes on the many subjects that interested him, while the old man shopped for essentials and tended his small garden.

'Why don't you come up the mountain with me?' asked the boy one evening as they sat in the porch outside the cottage.

'It's too high and I'm too old,' replied the old man. 'The mountain's there for you – the loch's for me.' His gaze wandered from the mountain to the loch. 'You reach an age, son, when your rôle is to encourage others, people like you, to do things rather than do them yourself.'

'But it's lovely up there. The views are amazing.'

'I know they are.'

'How do you know if you've never been up?'

'I can see them through your eyes,' said the old man with a smile. 'At my age I can only walk on the flat. Hills and mountains are no longer accessible, so you must climb them for me.'

'I'm not sure I understand what you mean,' said the boy with a frown.

'I'm not sure that I understand what I mean either,' said the old man. They both laughed loudly and affectionately, content in each other's company.

One day the boy brought a girl home with him from the academy. 'Old man,' he shouted as they entered the cottage. 'I've brought a friend home.'

The old man bustled into the living room in a state of confusion. In front of him standing in the doorway he suddenly saw the boy in a new light. There he stood, willowy, but now straight and handsome and next to him was a pretty dark haired-girl of a similar age. She wore a coarse woollen jumper, denim jeans and heavy walking boots on her feet. Her face was cheerful, engaging and extraordinarily pretty. Her shiny chestnut hair was drawn back in a ponytail while her brown eyes were bright and alert. Everything about her was vibrant and natural. The pair of them stood together in the doorway, filling the room with their unspoiled youth and enthusiasm.

'Old man, this is Ruth. I thought you might like to meet her. She's at the academy.'

The old man stood silent, stunned, rooted to the spot. It had never occurred to him that the boy, *his* boy, would ever want or need anyone other than himself. For a fleeting moment he felt jealous; yes, actually jealous that having grown so close to him, the boy had now found another friend.

'What's the matter, old man? Are you all right?' The boy looked at him with concern. The old man recovered quickly. 'Sorry,' he said. 'You caught me by surprise.' He walked up to the girl and shook her hand warmly. 'How lovely you are. Please come in. You are most welcome.'

'I thought I'd take Ruth up the mountain tomorrow. She's never climbed it.'

The girl smiled. 'You know how it is when you've lived somewhere all your life,' she said. 'You don't notice the beauty of what's on your own doorstep.' She looked up at the boy who was standing straight and proud beside her. 'It takes an outsider to point out the things around you that you've previously taken for granted.'

How true that is, thought the old man and instantly warmed to her. 'You're absolutely right, young lady, and both of you would be wise never to forget that. Do you want something to eat or drink before you go?'

'No thanks,' replied the boy. 'We're going for a walk along by the loch and just thought we'd drop in to say hello.'

'I'm glad you did, son. You enjoy your walk. I'll see you for supper.'

'She's a lovely girl,' the old man said to the boy that night.

'I thought you didn't like her. You seemed quite put out.'

'Not at all, I was just a bit surprised and... ' the old man hesitated for a moment '... a trifle jealous.'

The boy chuckled. 'There's life in the old man yet. I'll see if I can find an attractive old woman for you,' he said, tucking into his meal.

The boy has a point, thought the old man to himself. 'I am jealous, on *both* counts. Of the boy's youth and of him befriending such a lovely girl. Life was dull and meaningless before we met but certainly much simpler.' He smiled at the boy with affection. 'Looking after you is all I can manage at my age,' was all he said.

June faded into July and the warmth of August soon arrived. The girl became a regular visitor and the boy grew in confidence and stature. In a short time he had physically grown and become a thoughtful teenager. He maintained that beautiful, engaging naïvety, but now there was a thin, patchy veneer of masculinity becoming apparent.

The old man knew the time was drawing near when he would have to tell the boy that they must part. As the months progressed he had begun to enjoy life again in a way that he had never before thought possible. Although at first somewhat jealous of his boy's burgeoning relationship with Ruth, he now took great pleasure in it, the pleasure of a surrogate relationship which filled a gap in his own existence, making him feel both contented and fulfilled. The boy had now become the focus of the old man's life, cherished as though his very own. But there could be no avoiding it: he had to go back to Nowton – back to the studio. Mandy had already been in touch. A message had been sent to the cottage. 'Looking forward to seeing you on the 28th August,' it read and it was signed, 'Mandy, ACE. Senior Euthanasia Practitioner.' It was a polite, thinly-disguised threat that if he didn't attend he would be taken south compulsorily. 'How *do* they find you?' he wondered to himself.

# SEVEN

Doreese had done well for herself. At the age of only fifty-five she had been appointed chair of the Nowton and District Euthanasia Tribunal. Her rise had been steady rather than meteoric and she had managed her career astutely. With competition for all jobs so intense, particularly prestigious state positions such as the one she now held, Doreese had known that her chances of success were minimal unless she could improve the odds in her favour. Equal opportunities legislation had burgeoned over the last few decades, resulting in minority groups of every size, shape and form being represented on all statutory bodies. This requirement meant that membership of such groups on committees – and in the civil service in general – far exceeded that commensurate with their relative proportion of the population so that in effect they were grossly over-represented.

The disparity between men and women in every walk of life had long been eliminated, but lesbians were still under-represented. Doreese was essentially heterosexual, or more probably asexual, but by virtue of a brief yet well documented lesbian affair she had been appointed to posts ahead of far better qualified rivals who were unable to claim a similar minority status. In addition to this she had successfully established a middle-European lineage in her family – which ticked another box. However, most important of all she wasn't *too* bright. It wasn't that she was stupid, far from it, since she had used considerable guile to work her way up the civil service ladder. It was just that many years ago she had lost the ability to think for herself. She believed implicitly in the official dogma, and its systems, but above all in The Protocol. She could recite vast tracts of it by heart and possessed that infuriating ability to quote from it verbatim to support any particular point of view she might be making. The fact that she was wholly unable to interpret the written dogma was irrelevant (indeed desirable) making her a safe pair of hands for a sensitive position such as chair of a tribunal. She could be trusted not to rock any boats unless there was a specific protocol to instruct her on how and when to do so.

Doreese's complete lack of any original thought or interpretative ability had served her well. Originally a secretary, she had risen slowly but inexorably to become a tribunal member, then senior adviser and now chairman. She revered the Protocol with an almost religious fervour. Of course she wasn't a theist herself; to be so would be professional suicide and would have required careful consideration and a conscious decision, something of which she was incapable. In effect she was what others told her to be. Religion wasn't banned but it was crystal-clear that it was socially and politically unacceptable; and if you were known to be a practising theist you were unlikely ever to obtain work. After the religion-fuelled wars and violence of the twenties, which had led to such cruelty and millions of deaths, a decision had been made to neutralise such influences and accordingly theists were one minority group not represented in the state administration. Another such group comprised State orphans – how could they be represented as officially they didn't exist? Doreese didn't even recognise that there were such people. They were outside the protocol and therefore beyond consideration.

'Good morning, ladies and gentlemen.' Doreese looked down the long table at the members of the tribunal seated around it. It was her first meeting as chairperson and she felt a sense of destiny that she had reached a senior position and was now leader of this important group. If all went smoothly, after a few years, who knows where she might end up, perhaps heading a department of her own or even occupying a Cabinet position.

'Good morning,' she repeated as the hubbub in the room died down. 'It is a pleasure and indeed a privilege to open my first meeting as chairperson.' She looked down the room and smiled, her head slightly tilted with sincerity and self-importance. 'I have indeed been fortunate to be appointed to this post and yesterday had my first meeting at the Department of Intelligent Euthanasia.' She looked up from her notes and gazed along the table to emphasise that she was now moving in the higher échelons of government well beyond the reach of others in the room. 'I am of course unable to tell you all that was discussed, since much of it is of national importance and classified,' she declared with a sigh, an unsubtle indication that she was now privy to important information and that the burden of confidentiality was almost *too* much to bear. 'I *am,* however, allowed to say, that Charles congratulated me on my appointment. In fact I had a rather lengthy meeting with him, longer than most so I'm led to believe, and I took the opportunity to share with him some of my own ideas. Charles… ' and she paused once more to ensure that everyone was listening, '… *Charles,*' she emphasised the Minister's first name again, 'was complimentary about my work thus far and said that he personally had recommended me to the Prime Minister for this post.' She muttered the words 'Prime Minister,' in hushed tones.

'Now we ought to get down to business. Charles has asked me to pilot some protocol amendments here in Nowton. This, I need hardly say, is a great honour and I assured him that we would be proud to do so.' She paused for approbation. There were positive-sounding grunts and murmurs from around the room and one or two members tapped their hands on the table to indicate approval.

'The Department has noticed that there is an anomaly in the membership of this tribunal. Now; has anyone any idea what that might be?' She looked at her colleagues awaiting a response, but none came. There was silence while members either simply looked away or shuffled their papers. 'Well, I'll tell you. We have no orphan in the group.' Once again she stopped to give full significance to this bombshell. She looked around the table as if challenging her committee to explain how this situation had been allowed to arise. For a moment she said nothing, then with an expression of exasperation continued, 'I would be interested to know how *on earth* no one has noticed this before?' She removed her glasses and let them dangle by a chain on to her ample bosom. One or two members looked up at the new chairperson and shook their heads as though astounded at their own stupidity.

Then, from the far end of the room there came a cough: 'But, chairlady, theists and orphans have always been excluded; that's what the Protocol states.'

Doreese sighed, the deep sigh of a schoolmistress with a pupil who doesn't quite get it but refuses to be quiet. She put on her 'I'll try to be patient' expression. 'Thomas, I think you'll find that in protocol two, section four, subsection two, it is clearly stated that the tribunal must be fully inclusive and representative of society as a whole.' She smiled down the length of the table towards the rather shabbily dressed representative for Process Integration, Science and Sociology, 'and not having a State orphan is clearly in contravention of that. The Minister wishes the membership changed to include at least one orphan.'

'But we have always been told that in effect they don't exist and should not be of any concern as they fall outside the protocol. Madam chairperson, you've said so yourself in the past.'

'I think you'll find, Thomas, that I've always said that the tribunal should be inclusive and Charles has identified a gap.'

'Yes, I understand that, but orphans are disenfranchised by definition, so in effect they don't exist. We don't even know how many there are or where they live, so by definition they cannot be part of a formalised structure such as this.'

The new chairperson sighed even more deeply, a sigh which said more clearly than words: 'You really are a stupid man and beginning to annoy me.' 'The answer is obvious,' she replied. 'We will create a pool of orphans to serve on our various committees.'

'But once that happens they will no longer be disenfranchised, and will not, by definition, be orphans and therefore will be unable to represent the very group they are supposed to. It's a piece of bureaucratic nonsense.'

'Really, Thomas you do make things so much more complicated than they need be. We will simply create a few orphans, just enough to fulfill the requirements of the inclusiveness protocol. It's quite simple really.'

Thomas was not happy. He knew that by challenging Doreese he was almost certainly committing professional suicide but this latest piece of box-ticking idiocy had annoyed him even more than the last one. He was also feeling slightly unwell: he had a touch of indigestion and a slight headache, almost certainly related to a celebration he had attended the night before. In general alcohol was severely rationed for the good of the people but last night there had been ample and he had drunk more than his fair share.

'Does anyone else have any comments?' enquired Doreese.

'Seems like a good idea to me,' replied Percy, the representative for the disabled. He himself wasn't disabled of course because the medical problem from which he had suffered had long ago been cured but he was the nearest the committee could come to having a properly disabled person.

'Thank you for that, Percy.' Doreese looked at Thomas to indicate that this was what an appropriate response sounded like. 'Does anyone else have anything to say on this item?'

But Thomas was not finished. 'Look, I know that the protocol, God bless it, states that we should be wholly inclusive, and I'm all for that, but all this does is to create a new group of representatives who essentially represent no one.'

Doreese put on her patient look, with a hint of a smile on her slightly tilted face. 'I don't think you quite understand, Thomas. The Protocol demands inclusivity and this group is not represented. If you look at subsection two you will see it is *quite* clear on the issue.'

Thomas was growing more and more frustrated. He realised that Doreese was either stupid or obfuscating: probably both and that he was alone in his challenge to her proposal. He tried to control his emotions but it was obvious to all that he was becoming angry and this was causing unease among the other members of the committee who avoided confrontation at all costs. 'Yes, yes,' Thomas continued, 'I know. Look, I'm not stupid but you've missed the point. The fact is that this will not resolve the issue. Now if you were to say that we should re-enfranchise the orphans so that they are integrated into society I would be shouting from the tree tops, yes, do it, but this is just a fudge.'

'Really, Thomas, I think your behaviour is becoming inappropriate. You know the protocol doesn't allow that – it's in section four. Here: I'll read it to you.'

'No! No! *Please* don't read it to me. My point is that this slavish adherence to the Protocol is stopping us from intelligently addressing the issue.'

This was *too* much. There were gasps from around the table and the other members looked away in an endeavour to dissociate themselves from the perpetrator of those comments. Doreese took up the challenge, 'Are you saying that we, your colleagues, the other members of the tribunal, are not intelligent? Really, Thomas, I think you're the one who isn't listening. The Protocol clearly states… '

'I don't *care* what the bloody Protocol states! The whole point is… Oh, forget it.' Thomas knew that he had now blown the whole of his future in one slightly bad-tempered outburst.

'Well, Thomas, I think you'll find I'm right, I have been on this committee for a very long time and am very experienced in these matters, you know.'

'Yes, chair, I apologise for my outburst. I think I must have eaten something that disagreed with me.'

'I think perhaps you should go on one of our, *how to behave in committee courses.*' Doreese was quiet, she had won hands down, her authority once again absolute and unchallenged.

'We're all agreed then. We will introduce a new member representing the non-members of society at our next meeting?' The committee acquiesced. 'Very good. Thank you, ladies and gentlemen. An *ad hoc*, short term, working sub-group will be set up to change the Protocol accordingly.' The chairperson carefully moved the papers at the top of her pile to the right, revealing those relevant to the next item for discussion. 'Now then, there has been another protocol amendment which is not at all controversial. We are now required to sit at a round table rather than at long narrow one such as this,' and she indicated the long bench around which they were now seated. 'It is part of the communication protocol, section twenty-two: tribunal management and meeting arrangements.'

The Member for Statistics raised his hand. Doreese nodded for him to proceed. 'Chairman, an excellent idea, but the reason we have a long thin table is that the room itself is long and thin. A large enough round table would need a much bigger room, about twice the width of this one.'

'That's a very good point indeed: one which I have already considered.' The new chairperson smiled knowingly, '*That* is why we will have four small semicircular tables placed down the middle of the room. I have been reassured that that will fulfil the protocol requirements without us having to extend the room.' Interpreting the complete silence as agreement, she continued, 'Well, thank you, ladies and gentlemen. I think that constitutes a most satisfactory conclusion to our first meeting. Remember: the first tribunal is next Wednesday and there are four cases for review. The papers will be with you soon, but they seem quite straightforward.' She then turned attention to the member for P.I.S.S. 'Thomas, may I have a brief word, please?'

# EIGHT

The old man had amazed himself. Only six months before he couldn't have cared less, but now he wanted to live. He knew he couldn't live forever but he wanted it to be for as long as possible. He was desperate to see his boy grow up into an adult, to stay close to this charming young girl; maybe even in a few years bear witness to their children, his surrogate great-grand children: *his* family. He had almost forgotten that neither was related to him, that there were no blood ties: that the boy was just one of many disenfranchised waifs and strays, one of life's many losers whose short existence, had they not met, would have been that of an itinerant. It now dawned on the old man that the battle to remain objective and not to become emotionally involved was lost, and that the boy was no longer the stranger whom he had met outside a suicide shop just five months earlier. The old man had still not told the boy that he would soon have to leave him but that night the opportunity arose unexpectedly.

'Ruth and I went up the mountain again today, she loves it up there,' said the boy as the two of them sat by the open front door looking across the loch, towards the distant hills on the far side. It was a warm, calm evening, without a breath of wind and the surface of the loch reflected a dark image of the hills as clearly as any mirror. 'I love it here. Can we stay?'

It was the ideal opportunity for the old man to explain to the boy what must happen, yet he hesitated. '*You* can,' he said eventually, then adding after a long pause, 'but sadly I cannot.'

The boy turned to look at the old man with a frown. 'Why not? We're a team. We go everywhere together.'

'Not this time, I'm afraid.'

The boy's face now registered real concern. 'What d'you mean, old man? You're not leaving me, are you?'

Tears formed in the old man's eyes. 'Look, son. D'you remember the first time we met outside the Euthanasia Studio and you asked me if I was thinking of doing it?'

'Yes!'

'Well… ' there could be no sweetening the blow, 'Well… I signed up and these last few months have been my terminal leave. I have to go back soon.'

The boy was stunned. It was as if he had been hit by a thunderbolt or punched hard in the solar plexus. In the excitement of the travel and in the sheer beauty of the place, he had forgotten the circumstances of their first meeting. Everything had seemed so natural. It was as though they had always been together, but now the past flooded back. He felt an emptiness in his stomach, an excruciating agony penetrating his very soul. '*No*! Surely not! You *can't* leave me, old man.' The boy's voice rose as he pleaded, 'You're not ready to die. You've lots more to teach me: more hills to climb, lochs to fish, paths to walk. For god's sake, old man, you *can't* go.'

'*You* can stay,' said the old man lamely. And then, in an instant he regressed to the man he had been. The past became the actuality, exploding into the present and making the unreal, real. In an instant he reverted from the man he had become, comfortable in a cottage by the loch, to the hopeless, directionless old man living in a Nowton hostel. He was speechless. He felt that he had not only let himself down, but the boy as well. Once more, what he'd done with the very best of intentions had backfired spectacularly. No sooner had the boy grown to trust and love him as a grandfather than he would have to leave him forever. History was repeating itself. Once again an act of pure altruism had gone sour. What was to have been a decent holiday for himself and a new start for the boy had become far more and now there was everything to lose for them both.

For a few moments there was silence in the room and then suddenly the boy stood up, rushed to the door, slammed it shut behind him and ran up the path heading in the direction of the mountain. The old man made no attempt to follow him but sat staring into the darkness of the loch for what seemed an age before attempting to find some solace in sleep.

When the old man awoke next morning the boy was already up, dressed and sitting drinking coffee. 'Old man, you're not doing it. I've been thinking and I'm not letting you.'

The revelation of the previous night and how it had affected the boy had so completely demoralised the old man that he could think of nothing to say. He simply sat staring through the window into the middle distance.

'I went to see Ruth last night. Her family knew someone in England who had issues with the Euthanasia Protocol some years ago. She says that you can appeal and so that's exactly what we're going to do. We'll go south, register your appeal – that has to done at least a week before your Event Day – and then appear before the tribunal.' The boy had spoken fluently and with confidence. He stopped to look at the old man who sat, tired and passive: the worn-out shell of a once-proud man. 'The grounds for the appeal are that you now have a dependant – that's me, by the way.' The old man lifted his head slowly and realised that his future was now in the hands of his protégé. The boy was focused, knowledgeable and confident.

'When is your Event Date, old man,' asked the boy.

'The twenty eighth,' he replied quietly.

'Well then, we've no time to lose. I think we should go south on Friday. That would get us back to Nowton in plenty of time to register our appeal. I presume you've enough money to get us both back?'

'Yes, I have plenty of money.'

The boy's enthusiasm and optimism were infectious and the old man began to believe that the plan might actually work. Central to the appeal was the ability to repay the pre-mortem financial award. This he could do. The two of them had been living well, but cheaply. The awards had been calculated to attract people who wanted a final expensive fling, a taste of the high life: perhaps expensive hotels in faraway, exotic places. In fact the old man still possessed the award in its entirety and over the next few days his pessimism began to lift as the two of them drew up their plans. Ruth visited regularly and was as much a part of his family as any daughter. The old man went with her to the academy library and reviewed the Protocol himself. Ruth was correct: there certainly appeared to be grounds for an appeal.

Ruth wanted to come south with them but she was at an important stage of her studies so the boy and the old man persuaded her that she should stay behind. Thus it was with some optimism that, the following week, the boy and the old man stepped into a taxi and began to retrace their steps back to Nowton.

* * *

'How nice to see you again,' said Mandy with a welcoming smile, her head tilted slightly. 'And who is this handsome young man?'

'This is my great-nephew,' said the old man, as Mandy shook hands with the boy.

'Is he to be the beneficiary?'

'Well, yes and no. He would be, but I'd like to lodge an appeal. That's why we've come back a week early.'

The smile instantly disappeared from Mandy's face. Appeals were a nuisance; they wasted time, upset her timetabling and if upheld (which was unusual) meant a loss of commission.

'Oh! – You'd better come into the office then,' and she led the way to a small backroom which the old man had not been shown on his previous tour. The old man and the boy took the seats indicated as Mandy settled herself behind a desk on which stood a computer screen. 'Let me just bring your details up,' she said. 'Ah yes. I remember. Short-term prognosis. Not a *huge* point in appealing, is there?' She tilted her head once more and the professional smile flashed briefly across her face only to disappear immediately. 'And you would, of course, need to have very good grounds for an appeal and be able to return the pre-mortem payment.'

'Yes, I understand that.'

'So you're adamant then?'

'Yes. We have grounds and I can repay the award.'

Mandy looked at the old man. Her face was now expressionless, her lips thin and her eyes hard with annoyance. Detecting no change in the old man's intent, her gaze returned to the screen. 'Okay then, if you *insist*.' She sighed. 'For me to lodge an appeal with the tribunal on your behalf, I'll need a few details.' She worked at her keyboard quickly and efficiently until the relevant page of the Protocol came up and then she moved the screen so that the old man could also see it. They went through the items one by one until they reached the key questions.

'Now then. What exactly are your grounds for an appeal?'

The boy and the old man had carefully rehearsed their response to this question. The old man answered: 'It's sub-section four in the Change in Circumstance clause, in Annex three.'

'Oh! We *have* been busy haven't we?' she said crossly. The boy bit his tongue. The old man had warned him not to lose his temper.

'Right, could you please tell me what is your change in circumstance.'

'I now have a dependant,' said the old man.

'Let me guess,' she said as she looked at the boy, slowly shaking her head. 'That'll be you.'

'Correct,' said the boy. He had a glint in his eye that the old man had not seen before. A hint of aggression and of passion which somehow filled the old man with a real sense of pride.

'We will naturally need evidence of your relationship. Will you give me your code please?' Mandy said this without taking her eyes from the screen. Potentially this was the stumbling block, the weakest part of their plan and the old man and the boy, with the help of Ruth, whose raw intelligence had staggered the old man, had long wondered how best to surmount this hurdle.

'It's not a blood relationship,' said the old man, 'but he is dependent on me as he has no independent means and I have been looking after him for the past six months.'

Mandy peered at the screen. 'I'm not so sure about that. That doesn't appear to fit our criteria.'

'I think you'll find in section sixteen that this definition does conform to the dependency criteria as laid down in the Protocol.' The old man was now actually beginning to enjoy himself. If the outcome hadn't been so critical he would have relished this interchange as much as he had enjoyed such verbal contests years before. The trouble was, he thought to himself, back then he'd won the debate, but had started a war.

'We *have* been busy haven't we,' she repeated. 'Let's see. Mmm. Yes, here it is. A non-sanguine dependant must confirm in writing that that there has been a dependent relationship, as defined in Annex twelve, for a minimum of six months. I'll need evidence of that, obviously.'

The old man handed over a signed statement confirming the boy's dependency on him together with a letter from Ruth's father corroborating this fact.

Mandy was hesitant, unsure as to the validity of this request. 'Well, I'm not sure this is sufficient, you know. Firstly this letter is from someone in Dalriada and the Protocol doesn't say that's allowed. And,' she continued, looking at the boy, 'I'm unable to find your registration.'

'That's because I'm not registered,' said the boy with a steely gaze and firm voice.

'If you're not registered you can't really be a dependant, can you?' she said with a triumphant little giggle.

'Yes, I can. For reasons that I don't understand, I appear to have been de-selected. That is the very reason that I am now dependent on this old man. Before de-selection I was in the state school, here in Nowton.'

'Oh!' Mandy's eyes widened. This was unknown territory to her, 'I'm not sure about that. If you're not registered, you can hardly be a dependant. The system doesn't allow for that.'

'But don't you see? That's exactly why I *am* a dependant. That's why this old man had to rescue me. Without him I would almost certainly have died.'

'No, no. That's not possible if you're unregistered.' She smiled triumphantly. 'It's quite simple I'm afraid the Protocol will not allow you to appeal.'

The boy was becoming more and more frustrated by the inflexible idiocy of this woman. 'Look, you obviously don't understand. I *am* dependent. Listen to me, Miss. I have nothing in the world. I am completely dependent on this old man.'

'That's not what the Protocol says and there's no need to take that tone of voice with me. I am not stupid. I'm an expert in this field and the Protocol will not allow an appeal. Look.' She turned the screen to the boy, 'See. It says, NO GROUNDS FOR APPEAL – INFORMATION INSUFFICIENT.'

'I don't care what the computer says, it's wrong.' The boy's voice had grown steadily louder until he was almost shouting; he was breathing heavily and his emotions were beginning to get the better of him.

The old man, who had remained silent during this interchange, put his hand gently on the boy's shoulder to calm him. 'Mandy,' he said, 'I think you'll find that the Protocol has gone into a default mode because there is insufficient evidence to approve an appeal immediately. But that doesn't *necessarily* equate with the appeal not conforming to the criteria.' The old man spoke slowly and carefully while maintaining eye contact. 'Under those circumstances an appeal should be allowed on the uncertainty principle laid out in Protocol one.' The old man was quoting an opt-out clause, for which *he* had been responsible. It was in a Protocol which actually pertained to conception but, due to a composition error by the typesetter, appeared as an annex to the whole document rather than just the protocol to which it had been intended to refer. Not many people knew this and the document had never been corrected.

'Protocol one? That's ancient!' squeaked Mandy as she busily looked at her screen and searched for the relevant document. 'But that's about *conception*!' She looked up. 'What on earth has that got to do with it?'

'If you read Annex one you'll see that lack of complete information is not, *per se,* a reason for refusing an appeal.'

'But Protocol one applies to conception!'

'Yes it does, but as the opt-out is published as an Annex to the State Protocols it therefore applies to all of them, including the Euthanasia Protocol.'

Mandy was exasperated. This was clearly nonsensical, but the old man was correct; the annex was there. 'Well, you seem determined to get your appeal so I will refer your case to the tribunal. I personally think you are wasting their time but there you go.' She paused as she punched a few keys on her computer before continuing brusquely: 'The tribunal sits next Wednesday and I've booked you into a vacant slot at ten-thirty. Pending the outcome of your appeal, your Terminal Event will remain booked for a week on Friday. Here's a leaflet about the tribunal and where it's to be held. *Goodbye.*' She didn't even attempt a smile but simply stood up and opened the door to allow the pair to leave the room and make their way outside.

'Well done, old man!' said the boy as they walked back to their hotel. 'How did you know about all those old Protocols?'

'Because I wrote many of them,' he replied with a smile. 'And you, young man, must learn to control your emotions.'

'I know. But that was the first time in my life that I have come across such crass stupidity.'

'But sadly it won't be the last,' replied the old man. 'You'll have to get used to it, I'm afraid.'

'Anyway,' continued the boy, 'thanks to you, we certainly won that time. I loved the look on her face when you quoted Protocol one.'

'Yes. We've triumphed in that initial skirmish but the main battle is yet to come. The tribunal is likely to be much less amenable to my powers of persuasion than the lovely Mandy. We have one week to prepare.'

# NINE

The tribunal was held in what used to be the courthouse. There were very few court cases now as almost all crimes against the State were managed by the legal Protocol and judgement pronounced by computer in one of the thousands of Law Studios across the land. Only in extraordinary cases was an appeal considered and a case heard in person. In fact, almost all day-to-day events were dealt with by one of the hundreds of Life Protocols and only rarely were human beings required to pronounce on any matter of importance. That was the reason why they had become so inept at the process. The ability to make commonsense decisions had become extinct. De-skilling begins the instant a person ceases to function in any particular arena, physical or mental, and accelerates rapidly. As the old man had said to the boy many times, 'If you don't use it, you'll lose it.'

Doreese sat at the bench where, decades ago, a judge would have pronounced. Below her, at a suitably deferential level, sat the rest of her tribunal (which consisted of the same membership as when she had acceded to the chair with the notable exception of Thomas who was in rehabilitation) and facing them in the otherwise empty room was Mandy. She was sitting nervously in a solitary, lonely chair, with her legs neatly crossed and both hands in her lap. Dressed in her professional blue two-piece suit, her makeup perfect, she was composed but bore a less than content expression on her face. To have to attend a tribunal was an embarrassment, a criticism of her management. Cases required to be selected carefully and there should rarely, if ever, be the need for an appeal. The government target for appeals was one percent and this was her second appearance in two years. To have an appeal sustained would almost certainly be the end of her career in the highly competitive field of euthanasia and it would be nigh on impossible to obtain another post with such a stain on her C.V. Her future hung on the day's proceedings and she sat uneasily in her chair.

The appeal document which Mandy had prepared was now on the screens in front of the tribunal members. Doreese removed her reading glasses and let them dangle on her chest. 'Mandy,' she said, 'thank you so much for preparing the documentation for this appeal.' She switched on her smile, which disappeared as quickly as it had appeared. 'I must say I find it difficult to understand why this appeal has been brought before us. The Protocol clearly states that there is not enough information for an appeal.' The smile came and went in a flash. 'Perhaps you could explain why you have brought this case before us today.'

Mandy began nervously. 'Thank you, chair. I must first apologise for submitting this appeal but my client demanded that I should do so. I explained to him that it was a waste of the tribunal's time but he insisted. It's really not my fault; the old man was quite adamant.'

'I understand. Please give us the grounds for this appeal.' Doreese looked at her watch.

'The old man wants the order overridden on the basis of a change of circumstance – that he now has a dependant. The problem, essentially, relates to the status of his dependant who is a State orphan.'

'Well, that's ridiculous! Such a person cannot be a dependant. Strictly speaking, State orphans do not exist.'

'That's *exactly* what I told him,' Mandy said in a tone indicating that she was as exasperated by the whole issue as was the chairman. 'I explained that to the old man and even showed him the computer's response, but he quoted an opt-out clause from Protocol one which he claimed applied to all subsequent Protocols, including euthanasia.'

'That's ridiculous. Protocol one relates to conception.'

'I know. *I know.* I told him that.'

'It's amazing how stupidly some of our fellow human beings behave in the face of clear facts and logical conclusions.'

'I know. *I know.* I told him it was ridiculous to disagree, but he insisted.'

The smile, this time sympathetic, flashed once more across Doreese's face. 'Poor you. How distressing. Some people have simply no consideration for others. Sometimes I think the appeals system should be abolished altogether when I see it abused in this way.' She then peered over the bench in front of her, towards the tribunal members. 'Are there any questions for Mandy before we bring the appellant in?' There were a few murmurs indicating that the case should proceed. 'Right, thank you. Mandy, would you come and join us, as you are a co-opted member of the tribunal for the duration of this hearing?' Doreese then turned to the court porter who, clad in a regulation brown overall, was standing discretely near the door. 'Would you ask the appellant to enter, please?'

The porter reverently responded with a slight bow before opening the door to the courtroom and ushering in the old man and the boy. He escorted them to the well of the court, where two chairs had now been placed facing the tribunal.

The chairperson once more removed her glasses before addressing the old man. 'Right. I have the background to your appeal here, and I must say it seems like a piece of nonsense to me. Can you explain yourself, please?' There was no smile on Doreese's face now, as she glanced once more at her watch. The old man stood up. He no longer looked either tired or exhausted. His posture was erect and his carriage commanding. There was now a sparkle in his once-dull eyes and his voice was sonorous and even.

'Thank you, your ladyship.' The old man used the official, old-fashioned form of address. There was no visible change in Doreese's demeanour but the title rang pleasantly in her ears. 'Your ladyship?' she thought, 'that sounded most appropriate.' 'Carry on,' was all she said.

'It's quite simple, your ladyship,' continued the old man, 'I'm appealing on the basis of a change of circumstance. I now have a dependant.' Mandy turned to look at the chairman and rolled her eyes in despair.

'My dependant is here with me and it is because of this change in circumstance that I wish to appeal the euthanasia order.'

'That's all very well, but the boy's a State orphan and as such has no rights. He has no right to be dependent on you or anybody else.' There was now just the hint of a smile on Doreese's face, the smile of someone trying to explain a very simple concept to a rather dull child. 'It's quite simple,' she added.

'But, with respect, it is exactly *because* he has been deselected, through no fault of his own, that he *is* dependent.'

'What do mean? Are you insinuating that the deselection was somebody *else's* fault?'

'I can only assume so, your ladyship, or perhaps it was a fault with the system.'

She looked up and made a sound which could only be described as a snort. 'I *beg your pardon*. Are you saying that there has been a fault in the system, a fault with... ' she paused, disbelievingly, '... with The *Protocol*?'

'Yes, your ladyship, quite possibly. But how this situation has come about is not of relevance. My point is that, for whatever reason, I now have a dependant. Something which I did not have when I entered into the Euthanasia Contract and on that basis this is clearly a valid appeal and should be sustained.'

'Let me remind *you*, old man, that it is for *me* to decide what is and what isn't pertinent and whether or not this is a valid appeal.' Doreese looked sternly at the man standing before her, a polite smile on his face. The chairman then replaced her glasses, tilted her head back so she could peer through them and punched at the computer keyboard with both her index fingers. 'No, I thought as much. It's not possible,' she said in a matter-of-fact way as she looked up from the screen. She then removed her spectacles once more and pronounced, 'Here, see for yourself. The computer says, NO GROUNDS FOR APPEAL – INSUFFICIENT EVIDENCE.'

'I know what the computer says, your ladyship. I don't need to read what's on the screen as it's no longer relevant. For reasons Mandy and I have already discussed it *is* appropriate for an appeal and that is why we are here. The only issue that needs to be decided now is whether or not this youngster is dependent on me or not and I have submitted the necessary evidence to support that supposition.'

'It's for *me* to decide what is what, old man. This is most complicated and I am the expert here, not you.' Doreese grunted with frustration. Mandy looked up at her, a matching expression of despair on her face. There was a tentative cough, and the very able Representative for the Disabled looked at the chairman, 'Your ladyship. If I may?'

'Yes, Percy. What have you to say?' said Doreese irritably as she looked at her watch again.

'You will remember that that we were going to have a representative of the State orphans on the committee to help with difficult cases such as this. I wonder if we could enlist such help?'

'Yes. *Yes*! I know,' responded Doreese. 'It was discussed but proved to be impossible as no one knew how to identify such people, so the Protocol change was never activated.' The chairman paused and then added with a complete *non sequitur*, 'Which just goes to prove that the Protocol is correct in this case.' Percy looked confused while Mandy stared at the old man, her expression being one of, 'I told you so.'

'Old man, I see no reason whatsoever to sustain this appeal. Do you have anything else to say?' The old man remained silent and sat down.

'*I* do,' said the boy as he stood up, tall and straight, his shoulders pulled back. His handsome, youthful face was set and thoughtful, his presence such that the room fell silent as his gaze settled on the chairman of the tribunal. 'Madam chairperson,' he began, 'it strikes me that this discussion, this debate, if you can grace it with that term, is absurd. This whole case hinges on whether or not I exist. It must be plainly obvious to all of you who can see beyond your computer screens that I do. It appears to me that because I am not on your Protocol database I have suddenly became invisible, or what you call a State orphan. There can be no doubt that I am dependent on this old man and yet you won't use your common sense and admit that the Protocol cannot cope with the complexities of this case.' The boy hesitated for a moment and then, sensing the mood of the chairperson, decided to soften his approach and try flattery. 'It is in situations like this that we need the wisdom of people such as yourself and your colleagues to pronounce on issues far too complex for a mere computer.'

The chairperson was now flustered. One moment the boy was openly attacking the Protocol – *that* she could cope with – but the next he was attributing to her skills which she simply didn't have. She tilted her head forward, removed her glasses and reacted in the only way she knew. 'Young man,' she began, 'be careful what you say. I am an expert. I am highly trained and I've been on over twenty courses relating to euthanasia. It is not easy to become chairperson of a tribunal, you know.' She sat back in her seat and replaced her glasses, belatedly adding, 'You're far too young to understand.'

'Over twenty courses and you *still* get it wrong. Can't you see beyond your idiotic, slavish, unthinking adherence to a system, this nonsensical thing you call a Protocol. Can't you use your common sense?'

'Young man, that is *enough*. I'm beginning to see why someone might have wanted to remove you from the database.'

The boy shook with anger, 'The Protocol is an ass. You're behaving like the Emperor and his new clothes, hiding behind a governmental administrative system which is unthinking and deeply flawed; and no one dares to tell you so because they're all fawning, gutless puppets.' He paused, registering the open-mouthed, aghast expressions on the faces of the tribunal members. Then, lost for further words, he simply ended with, 'Thank you. That's all I have to say.'

The boy then sat down and stared disconsolately at the floor. He was worried how the old man might respond to this suicidal diatribe which he knew had undoubtedly ruined any remaining chance, however small, of a successful outcome to the hearing. Despite the old man's advice to control his emotions the boy had become angry and he now regretted the outburst. He was apprehensive: scared to look at the old man, fearing censure. As the boy eventually raised his gaze from the floor to look at his friend, he was expecting to see an expression of annoyance, sadness, resignation or even condemnation. In fact he saw none of those emotions: the old man's head was thrown back and he began to roar with laughter. This was no resigned chuckle at the inevitability of the outcome of the hearing. His whole body heaved and tears were streaming down his cheeks as he rocked to and fro, struggling for breath between great guffaws. The boy, puzzled at first, began to grin and then, his anger dispelled, gradually and ever more loudly joined in the old man's merriment.

Then, between spasms of laughter, the old man cried out: 'The woman's an idiot, a complete ament,' before bursting into fresh peals of laughter, the boy following suit.

'I'm glad you find this funny, old man.' Outraged, Doreese glowered at the pair of them. 'I could charge you with wasting the tribunal's time and even with contempt, a very serious crime and one which carries a custodial sentence.' On hearing this, the old man slapped his thigh as both he and the boy dissolved into fresh fits of laughter, while a smile could even be seen on Percy's face – and that of at least one other committee member.

'You should be ashamed of yourselves. This is selfish behaviour. What would happen if everyone wanted to change the rules just to suit themselves? It's a good job we've got the Protocol. If we changed the rules for you we would have to for everyone. What if everyone appealed like this? The whole fabric of society would crumble and we would become uncivilised and deregulated.' Doreese then removed her spectacles, looked at her watch and pronounced firmly: 'Appeal rejected.'

The chairman gestured to the porter who then began to step into the middle of the courtroom and approach the old man and the boy, both of whom had already stood up.

The old man dabbed at his eyes with his red silk handkerchief, 'Thank you, your ladyship,' he said, pausing briefly to get his breath, 'for the best parody, the best laugh I have had in all my years.'

Ignoring this, Doreese continued. 'According to the rules of this tribunal you will now return to the studio and have the Euthanometer attached and timed to your Event as prescribed, which is?' She raised her eyebrows and looked at Mandy.

'Midday on Friday, your honour,' responded the Practitioner.

'We expect you to attend the studio for your Event but if you choose to abscond it will activate at the prescribed time wherever you happen to be. Now the porter will take you to the studio for Mandy to complete the paperwork.'

As the door closed behind the old man and the boy, Doreese peered down at her team. 'Well, I never! What are things coming to? I'm amazed at such lack of respect. Well, ladies and gentlemen, another example of the Protocol successfully resolving society's problems. Now let's look at the next case.' Doreese sighed, 'Someone wishes to increase their post-mortem award because the client was Completed with the wrong End of life scenario. Apparently he was given a view of the Andes, rather than winning the four hundred metres hurdles.'

# TEN

Back in the court's anteroom the old man whispered to the boy, 'You return to the hotel, while I finalise the details with Mandy.'

'I'll come with you,' replied the boy.

'It's best that I go on my own,' said the old man with a wink which he hoped Mandy wouldn't notice. 'I'll be back very shortly and we'll go to the café for tea.'

'Okay, old man,' acquiesced the boy on seeing the wink. 'But don't be long.'

The old man walked the short distance to the studio escorted by Mandy and the porter whose job it was to witness the euthanometer settings. Mandy had regained her confidence and professional veneer, but was not sufficiently sensitive to realise that this was not the right time to chatter – which she did incessantly. The relief of having the appeal rejected and therefore of keeping her job was immense and so she prattled all the way to the studio. Even the porter became irritated by her banal babbling but neither he nor the old man said anything, both of them ignoring her as best they could.

At the studio, all three of them went into the waiting room, which the old man recalled from his visit all those months before. Mandy walked across the room to the desk, reached into a drawer and withdrew the watch-like instrument that was the euthanometer. 'Now,' she said looking at the old man and then at the brown-coated porter, 'are we agreed that the Event Time is midday on Friday?'

'That is correct,' said the old man and the porter nodded and set the instrument.

'And now the payment details, please.' She looked at the old man.

'I'd like a coded cash pick-up please, rather than a bank transfer.' Mandy frowned. Somehow she suspected that the old man was pulling a fast one, but his request was entirely legitimate as many beneficiaries didn't have bank accounts.

Having verified the time of activation and the post-mortem

payment the porter attached the instrument to the old man's forearm. 'There,' he said, 'is that comfortable?'

'Just fine,' replied the old man.

'Sure it's not too tight?'

'No, it's just right, thank you.' The old man smiled at the irony in the conversation.

'Now – have you decided on your final Event Pathway?' asked Mandy with a smile.

The old man hesitated, 'Well I'm in two minds. I'm swithering between having sex with a donkey at the top of the Eiffel Tower, or dangling naked from a power cable over a cesspit full of scorpions.'

Mandy had not been concentrating and looked up puzzled. 'I don't think we've got… '

The porter exploded with laughter.

'I'm sorry?' Mandy's eyes flashed with a mixture of incomprehension and annoyance.

'No, *I'm* sorry,' said the old man. It's not fair on the poor girl, he thought; she just hasn't got a clue. 'Just joshing,' he said, and then with an effort he wiped the smile from his face and added with a serious expression, 'The truth is, I haven't made up my mind yet. Is it all right if I come a little early on Friday and tell you then?'

Mandy looked relieved, having thought the old man might still have had one last trick up his sleeve. 'That's fine,' she said. 'Now, you know that this will activate at midday this Friday and that, once it has, the post-mortem payment will automatically be released for collection on production of this code from the payment depot?'

'Yes. I understand.'

'If it's not collected within twenty-one days the money will automatically revert to the State.'

'I understand.'

'Fine!' She looked at the old man and gave him her best smile, 'I look forward to seeing you on Friday then. Is eleven-thirty suitable?' she added, her eyebrows raised.

'Yes, that's fine. I'll look forward to that.' The sarcasm went unnoticed and the old man rose to leave.

Once the old man had left and the porter had returned to the courthouse, Mandy still felt concerned. The old man's behaviour was not what she had come to expect in this situation. It was true that most clients seemed contented and at ease with the inevitability of the event, but this old man seemed to be smiling, even laughing. Laughing at *her*: as though *he* would have the last say in this strange series of events – that *he*, somehow, would have the last laugh. 'At least I've still got my job,' she thought, 'and my commission.'

Back at the hotel the old man went straight to the boy's room and sat down. 'Young man,' he started, 'I want you to listen to me for a few moments and then we'll go out for tea and not talk about this any further.' The boy sat quiet and expectantly. He implicitly understood that this was not a time to plead, to argue or to remonstrate but simply to listen. 'In this bag,' the old man went on, indicating his plastic carrier bag, 'are all my belongings. They are for you. Most importantly, after The Event, you must go to the payment office and give them this slip with the euthanometer code. The award transfer will be activated at midday on Friday and you must go and pick up the money. I have arranged it this way because I don't want any problem with the fact that you are not registered. You will be given cash. A lot of it. It is imperative that you do this. I do not want the State receiving the reward for my demise.' The old man was speaking quietly but with an intensity that the boy had not heard before. 'Also in this bag is the pre-mortem payment along with the rest of my cash. As you know it has barely been touched since we lived such a frugal life in Dalriada. It's not a king's ransom, but it is enough to set you up somewhere, maybe to learn a trade or buy a plot of land. It's not for me to tell you what to do but try to use it wisely for your own benefit and don't let it slip through your fingers. If I were you I would seriously consider going back to Dalriada. You'll be able to register there as a citizen and open a bank account. I imagine they would welcome someone young and bright like yourself. It's your decision however.'

The old man stopped speaking and looked around the bedroom thoughtfully. 'On balance, while I would love you to be there, I think it would be best if I go to the studio on my own on Friday. I'm concerned that the harridan Mandy might take issue with the payment if she sees you there with me. Between us, you and I have given her a hard time and I suspect she's one to bear a grudge.'

Throughout all this speech the boy had remained silent, staring at the floor between his knees. 'Old man, I'm not happy about this. Is there nothing we can do?'

'No. The die is cast.'

'I don't want your money.'

'I know that, but you *must* take it. Before I met you I had no one to pass it on to but now I have you. I *insist* you take it. If you don't, it will simply line the pockets of the aments in charge. I would lie uneasy if that were to happen.' The boy nodded and wiped his eyes. 'I'm not one for sentiment,' continued the old man, 'yet you, boy, have given me something to live for during these last six months so I'm sorry to leave. But I am old and would soon be shuffling off this mortal coil anyway. You must take up the mantle of commonsense in an idiotic world. Your life is a continuation of mine – I will continue to live through you – that's what you must always remember. You are my surrogate; you must continue to retain some rationality in the senseless world in which we live. Once, long ago, I was in a position of authority and challenged the idiocy of the Protocols, the very systems that I had been integral to developing. But having created the monster, I couldn't control it, and those that took over from me, rather than taming it, just willingly let *it* control *them*. I'm not saying that you should start an insurrection – that would be wrong – but you could be what in spy circles was once called a 'mole' or a 'sleeper', a sensible person who still thinks for himself, ready to be activated and in due course able to take on the mantle of leadership in this insane world. In the meantime you are safer out of the country.' The old man thought for a while. 'The interesting thing is that in a bizarre way you are completely protected. As someone who is not registered, you can come and go as you please. You are invisible to the authorities. You do not exist, you are a spectre. Unlike the rest of us, you cannot be traced, cannot be summoned: you are 'off Protocol'. The Euthanasia Protocol, for example, does not apply to you. You are a ghost in your own country. As long as you are careful, you can come and go with a freedom that is just not possible for the rest of us.'

The old man paused and put his hand on the boy's knee. 'Now let's get some tea. I'm hungry.'

The boy said nothing but rose stiffly from his seat. The old man gave the boy his carrier bag, 'Take care of that,' he said. The boy grasped the old man's arm and they left the hotel to head for the café.

Later, back at the hotel, the old man announced that he was not feeling too well and wanted an early night. 'The excitement of the past few days is catching up with me,' he said. 'Think what you want to do tomorrow. It will be our last day together.'

'Good night, old man. Sleep well.'

'Goodnight, son. See you at eight for breakfast.' And the old man returned to his room.

Next morning, after sleeping only fitfully, the boy rose early and was dressed well before eight, waiting for the old man to knock – his call for breakfast. At eight fifteen, when he had still not arrived, the boy walked along the corridor to the old man's room and knocked at the bedroom door. 'Old man,' he shouted, 'are you awake?' There was no response. He tried the door which was unlocked and opened it a fraction. Not wishing to invade the old man's privacy, he called again. 'Old man. Are you there? It's me. Can I come in?' Still there came no reply so, hesitantly, the boy entered. The room was in darkness, that unnatural half-darkness of a room into which the bright sunlight outside is desperately attempting to penetrate through closed curtains. The boy let his eyes adjust to the dimness of the interior of the room and saw that the old man was still in bed. The boy sighed with relief. 'Old man, you can't lie in bed today. We have lots to do. It's a beautiful day. Wake up!' He pulled back the curtains with a flourish and the August sunlight flooded the room. There was still no sound from the bed and the boy went over to waken the old man.

'Old man, it's breakfast time... ' The boy sensed something was wrong. What it was, he wasn't sure, but he intuitively felt that something wasn't right. He took a step back from the bed, tense and anxious, his heart beating faster. 'Old man, wake up,' he called more loudly and then without further hesitation he advanced and threw back the bedclothes. There, now exposed and lying on his back, was the old man: quite still and quite dead. The boy stood still for a moment then very calmly crossed the room to close the bedroom door. He returned to the bedside and, gingerly at first, then more confidently, felt for the old man's hand and grasped it. It was cool, not cold, but stiff and unyielding. In death the old man's face wore a benign, calm expression – one of being at peace.

'The bloody meter's gone off early!' The boy said quietly to himself and he began to roll up the old man's pyjama sleeve. There was the meter, still counting down and set for the following day. The boy frowned, then suddenly it dawned on him what had happened. The old man had died in his sleep. He had died of natural causes. The boy's face gradually creased into an ever-widening smile. 'You old codger,' he thought, 'you've beaten the system after all.' The boy started to laugh out loud. 'You – old man, against all the odds have avoided the studio death, the euthanasia pathway, your own Final Event.' The boy chuckled to himself, shaking his head slowly from side to side. He brought a chair from the end of the room and placed it at the side of the bed and there he sat, holding the old man's hand and staring into his partially-closed eyes.

'Well done, old man. You've beaten the system by just twenty-four hours. You old devil, you.' The boy didn't cry: instead of sadness he felt an overwhelming sense of elation. This was success, not failure. The old man had won the final battle. He had beaten Mandy and the aments, the idiots with their Protocols, the slavish supplicants to the altar of systems. How simple, he thought, how easy it is to beat the system: you just need to die naturally, what's laughingly called a pre-mortem death. That must be the worst oxymoron ever, thought the boy. Then he remembered the context in which he had heard the phrase. 'In the event of a pre-mortem death then the post-mortem payment will not be awarded, but returned to the State.' Yes, someone had said that – maybe it was Mandy or maybe it had been the old man. But he definitely remembered hearing it. 'I don't want the State to benefit from my demise. *You* must have the money, I insist.' Various words and phrases whirled around in the boy's brain, all muddled and conjoined. 'That's a shame,' thought the boy. 'The award will now return to the State.' He didn't care about the money. He would always be able to look after himself, and in the plastic carrier bag there was more that enough to live on for a year or two if he was careful, but he felt let down that the State would win this final skirmish, score this last-minute goal at the end of extra time as a result of the old man's early demise.

For a while, as he sat next to his friend, the boy's mind wandered and then he began to consider what he must do. He needed to inform the authorities: to inform Mandy of the old man's death so that the body could be disposed of. The boy glanced at his watch: it was eleven-thirty. He had been holding the old man's hand for over two hours. Eleven-thirty. Just twenty-four hours before he's due at the studio, thought the boy.

He rose from his bedside seat, closed and locked the door to the old man's room and then returned to his own room. He donned his leather jacket and stepped out of the hotel on to the warm pavement and set off for the studio. It was a glorious midsummer day and he wished the old man could be by his side, and then it occurred to him that in less than twenty-four hours the old man would have been euthanased. Who was to know that he was already dead. He walked along the same warm and balmy streets, which had been deathly cold when he had first met the old man just six months before. His mind was muddled and it aided his concentration to keep walking. He couldn't take a dead body to be euthanased, Mandy was daft but not that stupid. 'Does it matter?' he asked himself. 'Well, yes it does. The post mortem payment would be lost.' Uncertain as to what to do, he went back to his room and searched through the plastic carrier bag that the old man had given him. Along with a few books was an envelope full of money and there also was the coded certificate that would allow him to collect the post-mortem payment. He read it. It was for cash. The old man had gone to great lengths to ensure that he, not the State, should receive the money.

\* \* \*

The following day Mandy was preparing for the old man's Final Event. She had now come to terms with his behaviour and indeed with that of the boy. They were just not quite in tune with the system, didn't appreciate how important it was that the Protocols should be adhered to. 'Probably chronic Protocol violators,' she said to herself. As eleven-thirty came and went she became concerned. She had expected him to arrive on time as ultimately he had seemed quite content with his situation. He had even taken great care with the details of the post-mortem payment. At ten minutes to twelve she went to the front office, opened the door and looked up and down the street. 'Well,' she said to herself, 'he's cutting it very fine, I wonder if he's absconded.' She frowned, knowing that it happened occasionally. This was not the first nor would it be the last time that a client failed to attend for their final event. The end-of-life pathway would be completed and she would still get her commission but now it might occur in a public place and give someone a nasty fright. 'Selfish,' she thought aloud, 'we have all the technology here, the best in the country, for a perfect Event and he chooses to do a runner.' She looked at her watch. Two minutes to twelve. 'Well, there's nothing I can do about it now,' she murmured and went back inside. At midday precisely the indicator on her central console went red, indicating that the old man's euthanometer had been activated. Although the process had now been completed, somehow Mandy was uneasy. She had a sense of foreboding as though this saga was not finished and the story was destined to continue.

'Oh well,' she said, 'I've done my bit. It's not my fault that he's lying dead somewhere.' She sat pensively at her desk. 'I must inform the retrieval team so that they may trace the body – but that can wait till after lunch.'

As the meter reached midday there was a quiet, almost tuneful beep and the screen message on the euthanometer read: ACTIVATED. The boy watched it for a while longer, and then the message changed to: AWARD PAID.

'Thanks, old man,' said the boy out loud. 'Thanks for everything. You cheated the system and now I'm going to collect the payment as you wanted. I'm sorry that I shan't be here when you're picked up, but I know you'd understand. Goodbye, old man, Goodbye. You saved me several times over. Saved my body from freezing, my mind from stagnating and my soul from the lunacy of this society and its so-called experts. Thank you, old man. *Thank you.*' The boy then grasped the now cold, stiff hand for one last time and as he did so he felt the old man's gold signet ring. It slipped off his shrunken finger easily and, after glancing briefly at the engraved 'G' on its face, he placed it carefully on the little finger of his own left hand. He then let himself out, leaving the door of the old man's last resting place unlocked. Back in his own room he gathered up his belongings, put the slip of paper with the authorisation and euthanometer code in his trouser pocket and headed for the payment office.

Just one hour later he was at Nowton Station. The boy recalled with affection the excitement both he and the old man had felt on that cold and windy day six months earlier when, on the brink of their holiday, they had stood expectantly on the same platform. He was now alone but he knew what he had to do. He would proceed as the old man had suggested. At the ticket office he pushed some money across the counter to the man behind the small wicket. 'Dalriada, please,' said the boy.

'Single or return, young man?'

'Single,' said the boy without hesitation. He then picked up his ticket and as he headed for the waiting train there was just a hint of a smile on his face.

# PART 2

## INVERNEUAGE

# ONE

Two weeks later Mandy received a summons to attend the tribunal. It was a formal letter requesting her attendance at the old court house the following Tuesday. Although phrased as a request it was clear that attendance was mandatory. *If you are unable to be present at this time please inform the chairman immediately in order to rearrange the appointment,* it stated.

Somehow she suspected that this had something to do with the old man and the boy. After the old man's non-attendance she had informed the retrieval squad but had heard nothing subsequently. She continued to feel uneasy, however, and somehow felt that the saga of the old man was not yet over. He'd had the nerve to laugh at her – as though he were superior in some way: in control. He had called her an ament, a mindless idiot. Not only that, but all the members of the tribunal had been abused in the same way and the chairman in particular had been outraged by his behaviour. The boy had also behaved shamefully, implying that the system was wrong and that the Protocol could somehow be challenged: violated, to suit him and his friend. What idiots they had both been to imagine that they could beat the system. And *then,* when they had lost their case, instead of being contrite and chastened, they had laughed: actually laughed out loud in front of the whole tribunal. It had been the worst behaviour that she had ever encountered in all her time as a Euthanasia Practitioner.

The letter had unsettled her. Although there was no indication as to what the meeting was about she suspected that it had to do with this case. She had been lucky to avoid demotion after the appeal as she had now exceeded the Government's target of one percent, or one appeal per hundred thousand of population per year, whichever was higher. Any further misdemeanour and there could be no doubt that she would lose her job *and* her studio. She was roused from her thoughts by the sound of the studio door opening. Glancing up Mandy saw her first client of the afternoon, an elderly lady, accompanied by a man and a woman, struggling through the entrance. She walked across the reception area to welcome the little group.

'Good afternoon, madam. Welcome back to my studio.' Mandy put on her warmest smile. 'Happy Completion Day,' she said. The old woman she was addressing looked at her uncomprehendingly. She was a frail, wizened old creature, dressed in her Sunday best. She was wearing makeup and her hair was newly styled. With the aid of her zimmer frame the old lady stumbled into the studio, assisted by her relatives who were both neatly dressed and smiling widely.

'Thank you, Mandy,' responded the younger lady who was the client's daughter. 'As you'll remember, Mum doesn't understand much these days.'

'Yes, I remember. Shame. Did you have a good terminal holiday?'

'Oh, yes. It was lovely. We went to London and stayed at the Savoy. We saw several shows and then travelled around the south coast. Of course Mum wasn't able to do much but I think she enjoyed it.' She turned to the old lady and raised her voice, 'Didn't you, Mum.' The old lady stared blankly ahead of her.

'Lovely,' said the practitioner, her head tilted at the required angle. 'Would you come through? We need to complete our paper work.' Mandy led the way into the reception room and helped to settle the old lady on a settee. 'Now, I take it you are representing your mother,' she asked the younger woman, while arching her finely-plucked eyebrows.

'Oh, yes. She's unable to think for herself now.' Once more she turned her attention from Mandy to the old lady. 'Aren't you, Mum?' The daughter then settled herself on a chair at the desk facing Mandy.

'Now, I think we agreed the post-mortem payment of 25,000. Is that right?' Mandy looked up from her paperwork, pen in hand.

'Yes, that's correct.'

'And can you confirm your bank details for the post-mortem payment, please.' The daughter checked the form that Mandy had passed across to her.

'Yes. They're correct.'

'Now – the pathway. You chose the Christmas scene, and for the music, *Troika* by Prokofiev. Is that still your choice?'

'Yes, definitely. It was her favourite tune and she used to love

Christmas-time, bless her. Didn't you, Mum.' The old lady continued to stare blankly at the wall.

'Right. Well, I think we're ready for the Event. Shall we go through?' Mandy stood up and started to head across the room.

'Come on, Mum. It's time for Christmas.'

The old lady's son-in-law and daughter helped her to her feet and nudged her in the direction of the event chamber. Slowly she manoeuvred her zimmer across the room. Mandy looked at her watch. This was taking longer than she had allowed for. She preferred her clients to be either fully mobile or in wheelchairs.

As they entered the room they were transported into a Christmas scene. They found themselves inside a cottage. There was a blazing log fire to their left, a decorated Christmas tree stood in the corner of the room and through the window a forest floor was covered with a thick layer of pristine snow.

'Oh, that's lovely!' The daughter looked around, her mouth open in amazement at the scene. 'It's just perfect!'

Her husband stood respectfully two paces behind. 'Lovely,' he acquiesced.

On hearing the familiar music, a brief hint of recognition appeared in the old lady's eyes, only to be extinguished immediately. The old lady was then seated in a comfortable armchair with wings to support her head and when she was settled Mandy gently attached the euthanometer to her arm, left bare for the purpose. Mandy then stood back, positioning herself just behind the daughter and her husband who stood gazing at the old lady, benign loving smiles on both their faces. The daughter's head was tilted to the left and a tear dropped on to her cheek which she wiped away with a tissue.

'Well, I think, if we're all ready, we should complete the Event.' Mandy said quietly. The daughter nodded and Mandy pressed the red button on her remote control. There was no immediate visible sign of anything happening but then, about thirty seconds later, there was a gentle movement of the old lady's head which came to rest on the wing of her chair, while her eyes became glazed and half-closed.

'That's it,' said Mandy quietly, as she moved to usher them out of the room.

Slowly, hands grasped in front of them, as though in a funeral procession the two relatives walked towards the exit and back to the reception room.

The daughter was the first to speak. 'Oh, Mandy. That was lovely. Just perfect. I'm sure she loved it.' Her husband nodded in agreement.

'Thank you. Yes, that was *particularly* special.' Mandy always said this to her clients as it seemed to be well received. 'That's a very popular pathway.' Briefly, Mandy recalled how the old man had asked to have sex with a donkey on the top of the Eiffel tower as his pathway. 'How disgusting! How ungrateful,' she thought. 'Now; is there anything else I can help you with?'

'No. Thank you so much, Mandy. That was just perfect. It's just what she would have wanted.' The daughter brushed away another tear and Mandy gently but firmly directed them to the door, where another old lady was waiting.

'Good, at least she's in a wheel chair,' Mandy thought, as she put on her most welcoming smile and headed towards the little family group.

* * *

'Mandy, I'm disappointed to have to summon you here, but there appears to have been a serious Protocol violation concerning one of your cases.' As she heard these words Mandy's blood ran cold. She knew there must be a major problem when she had received the summons but couldn't for the life of her think what it might be. On entering the courtroom Mandy had been surprised to find that the only person present was the tribunal chairman and there she was, sitting opposite her: well, not quite opposite, since Mandy was seated in the well of the court where the boy and the old man had been just three weeks before, while Doreese was in her customary position on the bench two tiers above.

'You will no doubt remember the case of the old man who had his appeal rejected.' Doreese looked intently at Mandy who simply nodded. 'Well, as you know, he didn't attend for his Completion.'

'Yes, I know. I was very surprised, but you'll remember how rude he was during the hearing; not just to me but to you as well, chairman.'

'Yes, yes, I can recall it clearly. The behaviour of both the old man *and* the boy was quite reprehensible.' Doreese hesitated for a moment. 'Well the thing is that the retrieval team found his body in a nearby hotel – in fact at the same place he and the boy had been staying for the last two weeks.' Mandy was puzzled, for the significance of all this was lost to her. 'Don't you see what that means, Mandy?'

'I'm not quite sure, chairman.' Mandy was at her wits' end. She didn't understand what the tribunal chairman was alluding to but it was clear from her manner that she was going to be critical of her management of the case.

Doreese removed her glasses – an indication that she was clearly annoyed. 'That means that the old man did not abscond, and we have to ask ourselves *why*. Don't we, Mandy?' Doreese was peering intently and cruelly down at her prey. She had been informed of those facts a week earlier and had immediately realised that this episode, if it were ever to be discovered, would reflect badly on her. She had decided that the best way to protect her own reputation would be paint herself in the role of someone who was surrounded by incompetents and deflect any criticism by firmly laying the blame for this mistake on the Practitioner, who was now squirming in the well of the courtroom below her.

Mandy's eyes were wide. 'He was an awkward customer. Maybe he just wanted to cause as much inconvenience as he possibly could. I'm sure he didn't like me, although I gave him no cause.'

'For heaven's sake, Mandy, are you completely stupid?' Doreeses' eyes widened as she stared at Mandy who had begun to shake visibly. 'Don't you see? He died before his appointed euthanasia time.' She paused briefly for emphasis. 'It was a *pre-mortem death*.' The tribunal chairman then fell silent as the awful truth dawned on Mandy. Why hadn't she thought of that possibility. She knew what the next question would be.

'*Why*? Why on earth did you agree to a cash post-mortem payment?'

'H-He requested it as he didn't have a bank account,' stammered Mandy.

'Oh yes, he did.' Doreese removed her spectacles. '*But the boy didn't.*'

Things were going from bad to worse. It now dawned on Mandy

how she had been duped into allowing the boy to pick up the cash. But surely there was no way that anyone could have predicted that the old man would die of natural causes before his completion date. Mandy regained some of her composure. 'It was a legitimate method of payment, chairman. And how can we be sure he died pre-mortem.'

Doreese replaced her glasses. 'Our tracker indicated he hadn't moved for twenty-four hours before his completion time. That surely tells us something, doesn't it, Mandy?'

Mandy said nothing.

'Since you appear to be speechless, I'll fill you in with the rest of the details. Just after your authorisation, a boy picked up the cash and has not been seen since; nor can he be traced.' Doreese stared at the practitioner in front of her. 'Why do you think that might be, Mandy?' She didn't wait for a reply. 'Yes, it's because that boy's an orphan and doesn't officially exist. But he still took the money – rather, *your* money – didn't he, Mandy?... ' she paused briefly then continued more loudly'... *Didn't he, Mandy*?' The chairman's face was now flushed with anger, and her voice had grown louder and louder during this outburst. Slightly more quietly she continued, 'I will *not* – and I repeat – will *not*, let *your* incompetence ruin *my* chances of promotion. I have been shortlisted for a job at the Ministry working directly under Charles and so far, news of this unfortunate episode has gone no further. But you *must* find the boy, and bring both him and the money back as soon as possible. Needless to say you are no longer a Practitioner, but you may use the title Euthanasia Monitor to give you authority to pursue the boy.' The chairman paused. 'You haven't said much, Mandy.'

Mandy was having trouble keeping up with her ever-worsening situation and was still not absolutely clear what she was being accused of. 'Chairman, I'm still not clear what I've done wrong.'

'You've given a significant amount of State money to someone who doesn't exist. *That's* what you've done wrong, Mandy. *That's* what you've done wrong. And that's *fraud.*'

'But I followed the Protocol.'

'Mandy; just retrieve both the money and the boy and you will have your job back. If you fail, I will invoke protocol 24 against you – and you know what that can lead to, don't you?' The tribunal chairman once more removed her spectacles and raised her eyebrows, 'Enforced euthanasia.'

Mandy had gone pale and was wholly speechless. She now realised why there had been no witnesses to this interview and it was clear that Doreese was absolutely serious in her threat.

* * *

Back in Dalriada, the boy retraced the steps that he and the old man had taken only six months before but which now seemed like a lifetime ago. He alighted on to the same platform and proceeded to the canteen where he had waited while the old man had made the arrangements for their holiday. He entered timidly and surveyed the cakes and sandwiches on sale.

'May I have that cake and a can of juice please?' he asked the distrustful looking woman hovering behind the counter, as he pointed to a chocolate cup cake.

'You on your own?' The lady snapped.

'Yes,' replied the boy.

'Show me your money then.'

'I *can* pay. Here.' The boy delved into his hip pocket and produced a small-denomination note. 'Here,' he repeated. 'Is that enough?'

The woman's face softened. 'That's fine, son. But you never know these days, I've been ripped off by boys younger than you, believe me.'

As the boy collected his snack and pocketed his change, he suddenly became acutely aware that he was now utterly alone in a strange land. He had already taken the trouble to hide the bulk of his money inside some clothes in his bag, carrying only a small amount on his person, but he felt unsettled: exposed and threatened. This canteen, previously so friendly and exciting, now had a depressing: an almost threatening atmosphere and as soon as he had finished his refreshment he left and bought a ticket for the final leg of his journey.

When the train arrived he took a seat in the rear carriage and settled down, his two bags carefully wedged between himself and the side of the compartment. He hadn't cried for many years; in fact he couldn't remember the last time he had shed a tear, since he had always been a loner, able to care for himself. He had no time for sadness: there was no point in self-pity when you needed all your emotional energy simply to survive. But now he wept. Suddenly all the pressures and tensions of the past few weeks – no, probably the last eight months – welled up inside him and he sobbed. Silent tears ran down his cheeks as he gazed mistily out of the carriage window at the ever-increasing undulations in the landscape beyond. He felt alone, vulnerable and imperiled. He was carrying more money than he had ever dreamt of owning, which gave him a pleasant sense of independence; yet over a short period of time he had come to depend on the old man and now he was missing his presence. Yes, he acknowledged to himself, he was deeply missing him. It was a sensation, an emotion, the strength of which he had never previously known.

He had intended to go directly to see Ruth and her father as soon as he arrived at the small village but instead he walked to the cottage where he and the old man had lived for six months. The small house was in darkness and as the early autumn light was fading he was about to return to the village when he decided to try the door. It was unlocked. Gingerly, he pushed open the door and entered the silent front room. It was exactly as they had left it, 'How long ago was that?' the boy asked himself. Though it seemed like an age, in fact it was just three short weeks since they had departed for Nowton, their hearts buoyed with optimism. The boy stepped timidly forwards into the dim interior. On the kitchen table he found an envelope propped up against a small glass vase, beside which lay a bunch of keys.

The boy looked at the envelope for a moment then rather hesitantly picked it up. Written in ink on the front were three words: *To my Boy.*

The boy tore it open and inside found two sheets of paper covered in the old man's neat handwriting.

*Dear Boy,*

*If you're reading this it means that I haven't made it back and our appeal must have failed. If my plans have been successful then you should now have a significant amount of money, enough for you to live comfortably for a few years and also to pay for an education, which I strongly urge you to do. You're a clever lad and will soon make up your missed years in school – but start as soon as you can and get the best tuition you can find.*

*The rent for the cottage has been paid for a year, so you are entitled to live here till mid-February and I have made sure that you will be able to renew the lease if you so wish.*

*I feel I've let you down somewhat by leaving you, just as we were getting on so well, but I think you should consider me as an aged grandfather who has died, as all grandparents eventually do. You made my last six months extremely enjoyable and thank you for that. I will always treasure your friendship.*

*Look after yourself and never forget to use your commonsense. Do challenge the existing dogma and the status quo, but always do so in a quiet, thoughtful way: not through ill-educated ranting but with intelligent reasoning. Stand up for your beliefs but be prepared sometimes to bend before the wind of opinion. Never feel ashamed to change your mind in the light of new information or after careful reflection.*

*Take care and enjoy your life.*

*With all my love*
*Your Old Man.*

*PS Ruth and her father are good people. Don't hesitate to seek them out as they are very fond of you.*

*PPS To you I will always be an old man, but I was once young and my name was Giles.*

The boy sat down at the table and re-read the letter. At first he was saddened but then he remembered the old man's demise, how he had successfully beaten the system, and now the boy realised that the old man had planned it all. He had done everything he could to ensure the boy's future.

The boy rose rather wearily from the chair and crossed the room to close and lock the door. He flicked on the light switch and the space was illuminated. For about half an hour he wandered throughout the cottage until, utterly exhausted, he fell asleep on his bed, in his old room facing the mountain.

Mandy was furious. It was quite clear that she was being made a scapegoat for the failure of a system over which she had no control. She had followed the Protocol to the letter. She could not understand exactly what had happened. The euthanometer had been activated – that was clear – and subsequently the authorisation for the post-mortem payment had been received. The money had been picked up by someone – presumably the boy – who had the correct code. What was the problem?

'The problem is,' she thought to herself, 'that the body was found nearby, with no indication that the old man had tried to abscond, and that he appeared to have died twenty-four hours before his completion time.' She wondered what could have happened. 'Either – by an extraordinary coincidence – he had died naturally or he had committed suicide. Either way, the payment should not have been made. But why would he kill himself and thus endanger the completion payment?' she asked herself. She grudgingly acknowledged that, whatever else he was, the old man wasn't stupid.

The more Mandy pondered, the more confused she became. If he had died of natural causes, then that was a failure of one of the Life Protocols and had nothing to do with her: that was someone else's problem. The Health Protocols were there to keep everyone fit and well until an individual entered the End of Life Pathway at the appropriate and designated time. This was not a problem with the Euthanasia Protocol: not *her* responsibility. And why was Doreese so angered by this? She had been furious and clearly held her responsible for the whole episode. Mandy could only assume that Doreese's job was threatened and, if the retrieval team let it be known that this was a pre-mortem death, then strictly speaking, as chairman of the tribunal she held some responsibility for the events which had followed.

'It's that boy's fault,' Mandy thought to herself. 'That precocious, outspoken little brat. He's the one who got me into this mess by questioning the system, calling me an idiot and the Protocol an ass. And *then* implying that all those courses – the endless lectures and seminars – were worthless. "Twenty courses and you *still* get it wrong." ' The barb that had been aimed at Doreese, but applied to all those who worked in the Euthanasia Service, including herself, still echoed painfully in her ears. 'That unspeakable boy, what did he know? He's not even registered as existing. He doesn't deserve to live, let alone criticise upstanding members of society like me: good, upstanding followers of the Protocol. And as for the old man, he seemed to think he was above the Protocol: somehow exempt. At least *he* was dead. There could be no doubting that.'

Mandy's thoughts whirled around, flitting from one scenario to another. How on earth was she going to trace the boy and retrieve the money. He could be anywhere. Normally it was easy to track a miscreant, but the boy wasn't on the database, did not have an electronic chip, and could wander freely around the country undetected. Even the old man had been traceable. She had sent him her usual friendly reminder one month before his completion date.

She thought for a moment. 'Wait a minute! He must have been with the boy at that time and I could track that message.'

It was a long shot, since there was nothing to indicate that the boy would return to the same place but it was the only lead she had. The boy was only young, maybe early teens, she thought, and he might have made friends locally. It was worth a try anyway. She decided to check out the records of that call the following day.

In fact it was to be two months before she could trace the call. She discovered that it had been made to Dalriada where the electronic tracking network coverage was relatively sparse. Eventually she was given an area of about fifty square miles anywhere within which the call could have been received. With this information, she asked to see Doreese again to obtain the necessary authorisation for her attempt to trace and retrieve the boy.

On this occasion when she entered the courtroom it was immediately clear to Mandy that the situation was very different to her interview two months earlier. The tribunal was in full session and its chairman was relaxed and smiling. 'Take a seat, Mandy,' she said with an expansive wave of her arm, 'I believe you have some information regarding the events surrounding an unauthorised post-mortem payment.'

Mandy was caught off-guard for Doreese had said this as though their previous meeting had never occurred. Mandy had expected another confidential one-to-one encounter. Now clearly the whole tribunal had been informed of the events surrounding the old man's demise. Most of them remembered his court appearance vividly and at least one member, Percy – although he would never admit it – recalled it with amusement. The chairman continued: 'Mandy, I'm about to hand over the chair to our new tribunal chairman following my promotion. I shall be taking over from Charles as Minister responsible for the Department of Intelligent Euthanasia.' Doreese positively simpered as she imparted this information and observed the complete discomfiture of Mandy sitting two tiers below her.

A nondescript weasel-faced man in a coarsely-knitted woollen jersey coughed. 'Thank you, madam past-chairman. It is a privilege to take over from you and, if I may say so, it will be hard for me to fill your shoes.' Doreese nodded her agreement to the new chairman's assessment of her rôle, while the weaselly man turned his gaze upon Mandy. 'We have been informed of the shortcomings of your service and of how you falsely authorised a post-mortem payment costing the State a significant amount of money. My understanding from our previous chairman,' and here he nodded in the general direction of Doreese, 'that she – I must say very generously in my opinion – has given you an opportunity to retrieve the situation by tracing both the boy and the money. That is, if he hasn't spent it yet.' There followed a gentle ripple of laughter from the other members of the tribunal. 'My personal opinion is that we should immediately proceed to a judicial enquiry into your conduct, but I will not revoke the agreement made with you by our previous chairman.'

Mandy realised that she had been completely out-manoeuvred by Doreese but, with her back to the wall and with nothing to lose, she proceeded to put forward a convincing argument why she should be allowed to go to Dalriada and try to find the boy.

'It seems rather a long shot to me,' the new chairman said, 'but as the previous chairman has offered you this option I am obliged to support it. We will supply you with the services of a Protocol Enforcer and essential expenses. Is everyone agreed?' The were grunts and nods of approval while Mandy, with a final look at Doreese who was grinning widely, stood up and left the courtroom.

# TWO

The following day, after a deep dreamless sleep, the boy awoke refreshed. He breakfasted on food that had been left when he and the old man had departed: cereal with water, some stale bread and jam followed by a mug of black coffee. His appetite satiated, he decided that before he did anything else he needed to climb the mountain – his mountain. He started up the path behind the house, now '*his* house', he thought to himself as he glanced back at the cottage before setting off along the track he knew so well. Above the tree-line the ground became dry and rocky and he began the steepest part of the climb: a deep gully between two cliffs. Once through this, and now panting slightly, he broke out into the open and then, in bright sunlight, strode the last two hundred yards up the gentle incline towards the summit. As his breathing settled, he gazed at the vista surrounding him: from the range of mountains disappearing in the northern mist, east to the loch where the old man had fished and then south to where he could see the village and just identify the house where Ruth and her father lived. He knew he would have to see them but for the present he was content to be on his own. For the time being he alone knew the events of the last three weeks: of the old man's fate, of his own relative wealth and possession of the little cottage; and that knowledge empowered him. But the old man was right. Ruth and her father were good, honest folk who cared about him so the boy started back down the path intent on visiting them.

As he emerged below the tree-line and walked down the gentle path back to his cottage he heard snatches of a girl's voice carried on the breeze and then, peering ahead, he saw Ruth running up the hill towards him.

'Boy! Boy!' she shouted. The boy halted and waited for her to reach him. She threw her arms around him and then, after a moment, stood back. 'Boy. I heard you were back. Someone saw a light in your cottage last night and I thought it must be you. Are you all right? You should have called in to see us. We were worried about you. Where's the old man? What has happened?' After this torrent of words she grew quiet and simply looked questioningly into his eyes.

'Ruth, I was just on my way to see you. I would have come sooner but I needed some time on my own.' The boy hesitated for a moment before saying quietly, 'The old man's dead.'

Ruth eyes widened, 'Oh, no! But the appeal? The appeal, didn't it work?'

'No it didn't, but that wasn't the problem. It wasn't the Protocol' The boy smiled. 'The old codger died of natural causes – of old age. He beat the system. Here, I'll tell you and your father all about it.'

They ran: skipping down the foothills and across the fields towards the village, then walked to Ruth's house where the boy told his tale.

'I think the old man's right, boy,' said Ruth's father. 'You should enrol at the local academy. The autumn term starts soon and that would be an ideal time. I don't think they'll have any problem accepting you particularly if you're willing to pay.' The boy nodded his agreement. The man continued. 'You should come and live with us. We have a spare room.'

The boy had anticipated this suggestion. Although grateful for the offer, he had been complete in his independence far too long to suddenly favour the idea of being integrated into a family, even one as loving and supportive as that of Ruth and her father. 'Thank you. That's very much appreciated,' he said, 'but I think I'll stay at the cottage for the time being as the rent is paid till February and I don't want to put you out.'

'Okay, if you insist. But the offer remains open and it would be good to have another youngster in the house. Ruth would like it, wouldn't you, Ruth?'

'It'd be great fun, but if boy wants to stay at the cottage that's fine too. I can go up there to play, climb the mountain and fish, can't I, Dad.'

Her father paused, aware that the boy was probably about the same age as Ruth, who was just fifteen, and that this now innocent relationship could soon change. 'Yes, of course,' he said. 'Tell you what,' he added, 'if you supply us with fish from the loch and berries from the hills, I'll buy other essentials such as bread and milk for all of us.' And so it was agreed.

* * *

The boy was assiduous in his studies and learned quickly. At the end of two terms at school he had all but caught up with the rest of the class. He was helped by extra tuition from Ruth's father and from Ruth herself – a star student. The living arrangements worked well and when the lease on his cottage expired the boy renewed it for a further year.

During the spring half-term break the boy decided to go on a walking expedition to explore the area further. His plan was to walk north along the ridge of the mountains with the aim of finding the head of the loch and then to return along the loch side or if possible hire a canoe or dinghy for the return journey. The boy thought it would be fun if Ruth came along but her father was adamant that she should remain at home with him.

On the eve of his adventure the boy packed his rucksack, taking the money which he habitually kept hidden in the cottage. Ruth's father had felt that it might be risky to open a bank account in case anyone was trying to trace him, so he had split his money three ways. One third he habitually carried on his person and of the rest, half was hidden in his cottage and half in Ruth's house. Finally he made ready his hunting knife and fishing gear and set his alarm clock for an early start.

Later that same evening there came a knock at the door of Ruth's house. Ruth answered and observed what at first she thought was a tramp: a down-and-out begging for money or scraps. On closer inspection, however, she noted that this was a woman; her head was covered by a tartan shawl which obscured her face and below her long, rather soiled, raincoat she wore a pair of mud-spattered rubber boots. Her accent identified her as being a foreigner. 'I'm sorry to trouble you, young lady,' she said, 'but I wonder if you can tell me where I might be able to stay for the night.'

'There's a bed and breakfast two streets down, on the left. There's a sign in the window,' Ruth replied.

'Thank you,' said the women and as Ruth made to close the door she noticed that several yards behind the woman, waiting at the gate, was another figure: a short plump man, also wearing a dirty raincoat, his face obscured by a floppy tweed hat. As she closed the door those two apparitions faded back into the night.

'Who was that, Ruth?' shouted her father.

'Just some travellers looking for a place to stay,' she replied.

Mandy – for it was she who was seeking shelter – walked back down the path to where the man was waiting. 'Apparently there's a hostel just down the road,' she said and, without waiting for a response, set off in the direction Ruth had indicated. The Euthanasia Monitor was miserable, tired, dirty and inwardly consumed with anger, furious that the boy had brought her to this condition – little more than a tramp trudging from one place to another accompanied by an idiot who styled himself an Enforcer. 'This must be the twentieth village in this godforsaken country that we've visited searching for that brat and his money,' she thought to herself.

Following Mandy's demotion it had taken a further two months to obtain the necessary permissions from the tribunal and the Border Control agencies to authorise her pursuit of the boy. Then there was the Protocol Enforcement Officer. There was no doubt she needed someone to assist and accompany her on this mission – but she had been landed with an incompetent idiot. When she had first been introduced to him she had noted a thirty-something year old man, short and overweight but most noteworthy was his inability to communicate in anything other that monosyllables.

'Hello, I'm Mandy, a Euthanasia Monitor,' she had said at their first meeting, while offering her hand.

He had stood still, gazing at the ground in front of him. 'Yes, Miss,' was all had to say.

'We're going after an absconder, so will have to work closely together.' Mandy gave him one of her most endearing smiles, of the kind that had been so successful with her clients.

'Yes, Miss.'

Since then she had had to put up with the company of this automaton for almost six months while they had trawled through every town and village they could find within the area she had identified. Luckily, the pre-completion call she had made to the old man had been received in a remote part of the country and the fifty square miles contained no large conurbations, only towns and hamlets. But there were plenty of those, and transport between them was often poor. That day they had walked nearly twenty miles from a town where, once again, they had discovered no evidence of the boy. As she led the way to the B & B, she glanced back at her minder now in his customary position some ten yards behind and she sighed, 'At least he carries the bags, and if we *ever* find the little brat I'll need some muscle to apprehend him.' Having said that to herself, she acknowledged that he was more fat than muscle. She then sighed to herself in the knowledge that the next day she would have to begin her interminable door-to-door questioning – yet once more.

Early the following morning, after a hearty breakfast, the boy put on his walking boots, shouldered his rucksack and set off up the mountain. When he reached the gully halfway up, the early morning mist cleared and bright spring sunshine burst through a gap in the clouds, lifting his spirits and warming his soul. He loved the hills, the moors, the loch; and on trips like these he had become a competent backwoodsman. On the summit he knew so well, the boy set a compass course which would take his along the ridge of the mountain range roughly parallel to the loch. He felt at ease with his situation, enjoying the freedom of being alone in the outdoors, independent and at one with the world around him. He walked quickly, not through any sense of urgency, but because he wanted to explore further than he had ever been before: territory far away, beyond his previous horizons and he was acutely aware that he had only a week before the new school term started. The boy had no maps of this area: he wasn't sure if any existed. He was reliant solely upon his compass and on his natural skills which had been finely honed since he and the old man had first discovered this beautiful land.

Ten hours later, as the sun dipped towards the horizon, the boy pitched his tent in a sheltered area on the leeward side of the mountain and settled down for his first night out of doors. Although sunlight still touched the tops of the hills the valley below was in stygian darkness. He looked into the murky depths towards the loch and estimated he had probably covered twenty miles as the crow flies.

For the next two days Mandy pursued her door-to-door enquiries.

Then, for the first time since she had left Nowton, she felt a glimmer of hope that she might be on the right track. Yes, there had been a lone boy living just outside the village; and yes, there had been a new boy from out of town attending the local school. Apparently he was friendly with Ruth, a bright girl who lived with her father in a house on the main street.

Mandy did most of her investigations on her own since her "minder" (as she called him) annoyed her; thus she was alone when once again she trudged up the path to Ruth's house. This time Ruth's father answered the door. On the doorstep he beheld a pleasant-looking woman, but one who seemed as if she had fallen on hard times. She no longer looked like a down-and-out but her clothes were crumpled and dirty and she still wore a scarf to cover her tangled hair.

'Good morning,' she said. 'I'm sorry to trouble you, but I'm from an English agency trying to trace a young boy who we think might be staying here in this village. I gather that such a boy has been friendly with you and your daughter. Is that true?'

The assertive tone of this question annoyed the man, who had suspected that he had not heard the last of the old man's battle with the euthanasia authorities.

'By whose authority are you asking?' His manner was polite yet firm and he made no attempt to invite her into the house.

'The Department of Intelligent Euthanasia in England. I'm investigating a serious case of fraud. Here are my documents. This is authority from the D.I.E.' Mandy held up a letter typed on official-looking headed notepaper. Ruth's father scrutinized it briefly before handing it back to her.

'I think you'll find that you have no jurisdiction here,' he said.

'I have the all the appropriate and necessary permissions from the Government of Dalriada to seek out and apprehend this boy.' Mandy's voice was firm, her manner official.

'The Government has little authority up here in the highlands,' the man informed Mandy. 'What did you say your name was?'

Mandy had deliberately not volunteered her name because if the boy *was* in the vicinity this would immediately ring alarm bells. 'Sara,' she said.

'Well, Sara, all I can say is that I am not aware of any such boy here in the village and we certainly have no one staying here. Thank you for your enquiry.' And without waiting for a response he gently closed the door.

Mandy was not at all disappointed by this interview because she now knew she was finally on the boy's trail. The man was lying: she knew that from what she had been told at the school, by the headmaster no less. What she didn't want to do was set the hare running – if indeed this was the hare she was after. It was well known that Dalriada was home to many outcasts and outlaws: escapees from England – Protocol violators who had not adhered to one or other of the myriad regulations and guidances laid down in these documents. But there were few, if any, who matched the boy's description. For the first time in months Mandy wore a satisfied smile as she walked back to her hostel.

She found the landlady in the kitchen preparing the evening meal. 'It's a lovely place you have here, and the scenery's just wonderful,' she began nonchalantly. 'I would like to spend more time in the area. Do you know of any properties nearby for leasing? You know – holiday homes. I had heard that one had been rented recently by an old man and his grandson.'

'Oh, that'll be the crofter's cottage up the burn about a mile away. But it's not vacant as it's being leased at the moment.'

'Oh, that's a shame; I'd have been interested in living there for a while. Do you know who lives there?'

'A young lad, the old man's grandson. Nice boy: very polite.'

'I don't suppose you know how long he's rented it for?' asked Mandy.

'No idea.'

'I suppose I could ask him how long he plans to live there. Whereabouts is the cottage?'

'Just a mile away. Follow the road to the burn and then walk up the hill for a few hundred yards. Will you and your friend be in for dinner tonight, Miss?'

'Yes, I think we will, thanks.' And Mandy then went in search of her minder.


'Ruth. I've just had a woman at the door who seems to be looking for the boy. She said her name was Sara. Can you remember? Was that the name of the Euthanasia Practitioner that the old man was battling with?'

'No,' Ruth replied. 'Her name was Mandy. What did she want?'

'Well, I don't want to frighten you, but she's after the boy: to take him back to Nowton to face charges of fraud and she seems to have the authority to do so. She hasn't found him yet but is bound to discover his whereabouts sooner or later.'

'Oh, no! But the boy hasn't done anything wrong.'

'Maybe not. But would you trust the justice system in England to think the same way that we do?'

'What can we do?'

'Where is the boy now?'

'He's gone walking and might be anywhere. I only know that he planned to go north to see if he could reach the head of the loch.'

'That's good. It gives us a bit of time. You and I need to go to his cottage and somehow stop him from returning there.'

It had been a very long time since Mandy had felt so positively excited. The boy, the brat who had discredited her, was now within her grasp. She would take great pleasure in serving him with a warrant for his arrest and taking him back to England. A successful outcome to this mission might actually serve her well. She would call it 'field-work' on her CV. Not only would she get her old job back, or so she had been promised but with this experience she might even be considered for promotion. With careful handling and support from Doreese, she could be appointed to the tribunal: a first tentative step up the government ladder towards a secure future. It was with such optimistic thoughts that she prepared for the short walk to the cottage. She turned to her minder who stood dawdling outside the hostel kitchen. 'I've discovered where the brat's living. Come on, we need to get there before he gets wind that we are after him.'

'Yes, Miss.' He donned his tweed hat and they both set off down the road in the direction of the burn.

Although tarmacked, the road was overgrown and quite hard to traverse in places but they reached the stream quickly and set off up the hill across open meadowland. The sheer beauty of the situation was wasted on Mandy whose one overwhelming objective was to reach the cottage and finally to see and arrest the object of her hatred. For hatred it had now become. She loathed this boy for what he had done to her but also for his lack of adherence to the rules, the system and the protocols: why on earth should *he* be different and not have to conform in the same way as everyone else? If everyone behaved in that way and did exactly as they wanted, there would be chaos: civil unrest, maybe even war. Who knows what would happen? He *had* to be found and brought to book. She strode on through the fields and saw the cottage in the distance.

'Right. We need to be careful now.' She glanced at her minder. 'This is what you're here for.'

'Yes, Miss.'

'You skirt round to the back of the property. I'll give you ten minutes to take up your position and then I'll approach from the front and knock at the door. When the boy sees me he'll try to escape out at the back and then you can arrest him. I don't mind if you're a little rough.' She gave her minder a knowing look.

'Okay, Miss.' The Enforcer then set off to walk around the right-hand side of the building while keeping out of sight as much as possible. Ten minutes slowly dragged by and then Mandy, openly and noisily, began to walk along the path to the front of the cottage. She barely noticed the neat vegetable patch and perfumed flowers as she strode impatiently up to the front door. She rapped loudly on the door and peered into the adjacent window. When there was no response, she knocked again. Just then her minder appeared from the side of the house.

'I told you to stay at the back,' she shouted angrily.

'Yes, Miss, but there's no one there. I've looked through all the windows. The place is deserted.'

'It *can't* be.' Mandy had been so consumed by her passion to arrest the boy and buoyed up by having found his house that it had simply never occurred to her that he might not be at home. '*Damn!* Damn that boy!' While her minder sniffed the scent of a climbing rose she wondered what to do next. 'Well, he might not be in now but he's bound to come home soon.' She would just have to wait.

While Mandy was deciding how best to observe the cottage and wait for the boy to return, she was totally unaware that she herself was being watched from the scree-covered slopes of the mountain. From there, Ruth and her father had observed the approach of Mandy and the Enforcer and seen the minder peer through each of the windows for any traces of occupancy.

'Dad, I think they're going inside,' Ruth said to her father as she continued to observe the scene below through her binoculars. Sure enough, the minder had found an open window and having clambered indoors had opened the front door to let Mandy enter. She had decided that the best and most convenient way to catch the boy on his return was to wait inside, rather than outside his house, and she had no qualms about a little housebreaking if that were necessary.

After checking that the cottage was indeed empty, Mandy returned to the main parlour, moved a chair to one of the windows at the front of the house over-looking the village, then sat down and addressed the Enforcer. 'Right. What we'll do is spend the daytime here at the house, and just return to our digs in the evening for supper. You'll need to come back surreptitiously after dark in case the boy returns at night. I'll have to stay at the B & B so that no one suspects we've broken in. School's back on Monday so he must return before then.'

'What'll we do, Dad? Now they're inside they'll catch the boy as soon as he returns.' Concern registered in Ruth's voice.

'Not if we find him first they won't.' Ruth's father had been considering the options. 'There are only two routes back for the boy – that is, assuming he sticks to his plan. One is to come down from the mountain, though that's less likely as he planned to return on the loch, and the other and more likely way is for him to approach from the loch-side or even on the loch itself. We'll need to watch both paths and catch him before he reaches the cottage; I'm assuming he'll only be travelling by day and won't return at night.'

And so, from early morning till after sunset, Ruth's father settled himself in the heathery scrub at the tree-line from where he could survey the surrounding area without being seen, while Ruth walked along an old secluded rail cutting, out of sight of the house, to the loch-side where she found a sheltered place from where she could observe that approach to the cottage.

# THREE

After his first and rather uncomfortable night on the hills the boy followed the mountain range north to its highest point. On reaching the summit he found himself enveloped in a thick clinging mist and barely able to see ten yards ahead. The drizzle ran in little rivulets down his waterproofs, making him feel damp and cold, and he began to question how wise he'd been to persevere with the climb. As the boy peered into the thick whiteness that enveloped him, suddenly the mist grew less dense, the sky became brighter and then, as though a curtain had been drawn back, sunlight burst through and streamed over him. He watched spellbound as the clouds slowly thinned, separated and disappeared, one by one, revealing a panoramic view of a seemingly endless landscape. He could now see for miles around. Below him to the west lay the loch, now small and insignificant, glistening like a puddle on a country lane; at its head he could see a small hamlet with some boats moored off shore. To the south from where he had come the loch faded into the horizon while to the north-east he saw something that he had not seen since he travelling north for the first time with the old man – the sea. On the horizon he could see the sun glinting on water and he could just discern where the sea became sky. He wondered to himself how far away the coastline lay. He tried to compare it with the distance he had already travelled – maybe thirty miles as the crow flies. The sea was further away than that, maybe forty miles, but definitely within walking distance if he had sufficient time.

As quickly as it had cleared, the sky clouded over again and the warming sun disappeared leaving the boy once again chilled and damp; he decided to head for the hamlet that he had espied at the head of the loch. From his vantage point he had taken a compass bearing and identified a route down the mountain. The paths were wet and slippery and after a difficult descent he reached the outskirts of the village by late afternoon and, tired by the walk, he decided to treat himself to a night indoors, a hot bath and a proper meal. He knocked on the door of the first house he came upon. A young woman opened the door just enough to see who was there.

'Yes?' was all she said while peering round the half-open door.

'Hello. I'm looking for somewhere to stay for the night. Do you know anyone that would put me up?' asked the boy.

'Try number six,' she said and then banged the door shut.

'Thank you,' said the boy politely to the now closed portal. He walked further down the street until he reached a green wooden gate on which a number six was prominently painted in white and repeated his query, this time to an elderly man. On this occasion the door was open wide and the man bore a welcoming smile. He was thin and wiry, with grey hair and a weather-beaten face.

'Come away in,' he replied cordially.

'Thanks very much,' said the boy before easing the rucksack off his shoulders and untying his sodden boots.

'You'll be off the hills, then?'

'Yes, it's half-term so I thought I'd walk along the ridge and try to return along the loch side.'

'Where have you come from?'

The boy gave the name of his village.

'You've done well to get this far. It's been a while since I walked the whole range myself but it's a beautiful view from the top. Did you reach the summit?'

'Yes. Before the weather closed in there was a wonderful view.'

'Aye, you have to watch the weather here. It can be treacherous.'

'Yes, I reached the top late morning, I even thought I could see the coastline. Is that possible from there?'

'Aye, that would be the estuary, beyond which is the sea.'

'I thought so. Anyway, suddenly the clouds swept back in so I thought I'd better get off the hill before the visibility got any worse. I was thinking that I'd treat myself to a night indoors before setting off down the loch.'

'Well, I'm more than happy to put you up. We used to look after many walkers – hikers and climbers – in the old days, but you're the first for years. You look quite young to be out on your own.' The man eyed the boy up and down.

The boy responded nonchalantly. 'Oh, I've been walking the hills and fishing the loch for years now.' In fact the boy had no idea how old he was. He thought he was probably a similar age to Ruth and would have said he was fifteen if pushed for an answer.

The man just seemed genuinely pleased to see him. 'Well, you're very welcome. I'll show you to your room and when you've washed and changed come down and sit with me. I'd love to swap stories with you and hear about your trek.'

The boy and the man spent the evening talking. The man's wife, a handsome woman with greying hair and an open and honest face cooked supper, which they ate together, while the man reminisced about his days at sea and his treks around the highlands. At the end of the evening the man took a bottle from the mantelshelf and poured a measure of amber fluid in to a glass. He took a sip. 'Will you take a wee dram, son?' he asked.

'I've never drunk alcohol, if that's what you mean. I was warned against it,' said the boy.

'Aye, it's dangerous stuff if you're not careful – but in small amounts it can be life-enhancing. It's a bit like dynamite in that respect. It can render obstacles surmountable, but handled incorrectly, it'll blow your heid off.' The man chuckled at his counsel and took another sip. 'It's not for me to lead you astray but try a wee dram, wi' water if you'd like.'

'Okay. Thank you.'

The man took another glass from the cupboard and poured a small amount of whisky, topping it up with an equal quantity of water. 'It's years since I've shared a dram with another outdoor person like yousel'. Here. Here's to the great outdoors and the sea beyond the hills.' He passed the tumbler to the boy who swallowed a large gulp. As the fiery liquid hit the back of his throat he began to cough and splutter.

'Whoa, boy. Sip and savour, that's no' juice you're suppin'.'

The boy was not impressed by the taste of the whisky but it certainly gave him a warm inner glow.

'How are you travelling south?' asked the man once the boy's coughing fit had subsided.

'I was meaning to follow the east side of the loch,' he replied.

'You could do that but it'll take you more than a week. There's no loch-side path and there are steep cliffs and waterfalls to cope with. You'll be up and down like a mountain goat.'

'How about the west side then?'

'Similar. It's flatter, but it'll still take you the best part of a week as it's a lot longer. No, there's only one way you'll get back in time for school and that's by boat. With a decent wind you'd be back in a day.'

'That's fine but I don't have a boat and I've never sailed.'

'Would ye like to learn?'

'Absolutely. I'd love to.'

'Tell you what then. In the morning I could teach you to sail. You're welcome to stay here tomorrow night and listen to me blethering on about the past and I'll lend you my boat to return in.'

'But how will I get it back to you?'

'I trust you, son. I'll no' be needin' it. On your next holiday you can sail it back. It'll take you longer, mind, as you'll have to tack all the way. The prevailing wind is a northerly blowing down the length of the loch.'

'Well, if you're sure. That would be marvellous,' said the boy as the deal was sealed with a handshake.

The following day the two of them went sailing. The man's boat was a masted skiff, a wooden, clinker-built open craft twelve feet long, with a single gaff-rigged mainsail. She was the perfect boat for a loch: she could be rowed *or* sailed, while her build and fixed keel meant that she was relatively stable. Also, as she only drew a foot of water, she could sail into the shallows near the loch-side. Throughout the day the man taught the boy the rudiments of sailing to all points of the wind and in the evening they returned, tired and sunburnt, hungry for their supper.

'Well, son, it's been a real pleasure meeting you. There'll be a fresh northerly tomorrow, which is perfect for your trip. Sail a broad reach: just let the sail three-quarters out. Don't get too close to the shore and you should be back in six or seven hours. Watch out that you don't gybe though, particularly about half way down the loch where there's an island and the wind shifts and becomes more easterly.'

'Thank you very much. It's been great staying here and thanks for the loan of the boat. I expect I'll bring it up during the Easter holidays.'

Next day, with his rucksack stowed safely in the stern of the boat, the boy rowed out on the loch, where he raised the mainsail. As the canvas caught the wind the boat tilted slightly then surged forward cutting a neat furrow through the water as it headed south. As their images faded into the distance he waved to the man and his wife, their arms around each other's waists, as they stood on the rapidly disappearing shoreline behind him.

With the water gurgling under the bow of the boat, and the wind whistling in the rigging, the boy sat back, raised his face to the early morning sun, and thought how wonderful everything was. As he sailed he could feel the old man's presence, viewing this new world through *his* eyes and he was excited at the prospect of relating his adventures to Ruth and her father who would be eager to hear of his travels and to learn about the northern reaches of the loch.

Mandy and her accompanying Enforcer had got into a routine. They spent the day in the boy's cottage, keeping out of sight as much as possible, awaiting his return. In the evening they went back to their lodgings for supper and then the Enforcer returned to spend the night in the little house. After three such nights, Mandy became concerned. Where on earth could the boy be? she wondered. Had he gone away somewhere for the half-term break? She knew that the girl and her father would know but had resisted the temptation to ask them. Clearly the boy was liked by the villagers and, although she had the authority to arrest him, the locals could certainly make things difficult for her and her companion if they so wished.

Similarly Ruth and her father had grown into *their* routine. Keeping out of sight of the cottage, Ruth would patrol the loch-side from early morning, often walking several miles in the hope of catching a first glimpse of the returning lad. Her father took up his post on the mountainside in what was, in effect, a small hide at the tree line. Here, in relative comfort, he could scan the mountains and the southern reaches of the loch with his binoculars, while also monitoring Mandy and her companion at the cottage. He had been tempted to challenge the outsiders about breaking into the boy's house but on reflection thought that this would only exacerbate the situation and he recalled how he had denied all knowledge of the boy's existence when Mandy had questioned him. From his hideout on the hillside he could watch for the boy while keeping an eye on Mandy and her chum. Thus the watchers watched the watchers, both desperate to catch first sight of the returning adventurer.

The man had been right, thought the boy. Right about several things. The wind *had* been a steady northerly and *yes*, he had made good time sailing down the loch. But the man had also been correct about the change in wind direction half way down and he had accidently gybed the boat, causing the boom to crash round, narrowly missing his head and almost causing the boat to capsize. After this initial surprise the boy was able to steady the boat, reset the sails and now, two hours later, was beginning to recognise familiar stretches of the shoreline. The man had also been correct about the impossibility of walking along the loch-side. At regular intervals, crashing waterfalls cascaded down the steep rocky cliffs that edged the northern half of the loch. There could be no doubt that the best, no the only, way to travel was by boat. After a further hour he could just identify the shore near his house and the place where the old man used to fish. There was no jetty and the boy decided that the best way to come ashore was simply to beach the boat.

The wind was now strengthening and whistled through the rigging, yet as he drew closer he thought he could hear a cry. He looked around but saw nothing, so he shrugged and was preparing to let the sail down when he heard the sound again; this time there could be no doubt – it was Ruth shouting his name. He peered at the shore where now, in the deepening gloom, he could just discern Ruth jumping up and down while waving her arms wildly and shouting excitedly. Unable to hear what she was saying, he waved back and pushed the tiller to starboard in order to bring the boat closer to shore. Once he thought himself to be within shouting distance, he yelled against the noise of the increasing wind. 'Ruth, you'll never guess what! I've just sailed all the way down the loch.' The boy smiled and waved again but Ruth continued to gesticulate, pointing to his house while attempting to make herself heard above the ever-increasing racket of wind and flapping sails. As his boat crunched on the gravel beach and tilted slightly, the boy stepped into the shallow water to greet Ruth. His expression changed from a welcoming smile to one of concern as

Ruth grew closer. She was clearly agitated, shouting and pointing in the direction of his cottage.

Finally within hearing distance, Ruth yelled, 'Boy, you must go away! Mandy is after you. She's in your house, with an Enforcer. They want to arrest you and take you back to Nowton.'

'*What*? Mandy here?'

'Yes! Quick! You must leave.' Ruth pointed towards two figures that were now visible some three hundred yards away, running down the path from the cottage to the beach on which Ruth and the boy were now standing. This was so unexpected that initially the boy had difficulty comprehending the situation but as soon as he recognised the familiar figure of Mandy the truth of the matter dawned on him.

'*Damn*! Help me get the boat off again, Ruth. Quick!'

By now the wind had strengthened considerably with powerful gusts blowing down the loch from the north. Luckily the boy had beached his boat on the east side of the loch and not further south where he would have been stranded, trapped by the on-shore breeze. Ruth and the boy pushed the bow of the boat until the little skiff slid off the beach and back into the water. As she floated free, the wind caught the boat abeam and, rocking wildly, she started to drift toward the foot of the loch and the lee shore. The boy leapt aboard at the very last moment and began to raise the sail. As boat and boy floated away, Ruth flung a plastic bag into the boat shouting, 'That's your money. Take care, boy.' She then waded back to land and directly into the arms of Mandy who grabbed her wrist angrily.

'You little shit,' hissed Mandy, dropping Ruth's hand in disgust. Breathlessly she turned to her minder and yelled, 'Go after him, you moron! Go on! *Quickly*. He's getting away.' The Enforcer waded into the cold water without enthusiasm but by now the boat was a good twenty yards off shore and already in deep water. All three watched as the boy struggled with the main halyard while trying to turn the skiff into the wind. Eventually, with the mainsail raised and sheeted in, the little boat, after the briefest of pauses, suddenly caught the wind and skipped across the loch, heading away from the lee shore and in the direction of the opposite bank. The stiffening breeze was blowing Mandy's yellow tipped hair wildly in all directions as she glared in fury at the vessel while the boy pushed the tiller to port and started to sail northwards along the loch.

For the first time since re-launching the boat, the boy now had a chance to look up and take his bearings. He was on a starboard tack heading north-west and now about a hundred yards away from those on the beach. The boy then realised that he had to say goodbye to Ruth and so he turned the boat about, on to the opposite tack and headed back towards the little group on the beach. As he drew within shouting distance he stood upright, waved to Ruth and yelled, 'Thanks, Ruth. Take care.' Then, without thinking, added, 'I love you.' As he prepared to go about once again and sail away he stared directly at Mandy and saw the blazing anger in her eyes. 'Bye, Mandy,' he yelled and waved cheekily as his boat pulled away.

Ruth's father, having seen those events unfolding from his vantage point on the hill, now arrived and, still panting, put his arm around his daughter's shoulders. Together, they both waved triumphantly at the rapidly disappearing skiff, broad smiles of relief on their faces.

The boy's last memory of this extraordinary scene was of Ruth and her father waving gaily, pleasure etched on their faces, while only five yards away stood Mandy, yelling furiously and waving her fists in his direction, her hair now blown horizontally across her face. Standing a safe distance away to her left, ankle deep in the shallows was the luckless Enforcer, hands deep in his pockets as he kicked at the water listlessly. As this picture faded into the dusk the boy's last image was of Ruth jumping up and down, waving and shouting; her words whisked away by the wind long before they could reach him.

# FOUR

'Good morning, ladies and gentlemen. I think we should now start.' The Prime Minister coughed loudly and the buzz of conversation gradually faded until there was quiet in the Cabinet room.

'All stand, please,' said the P.M. and there followed a scraping of chairs as those around the table stood, clasped their hands in front them and bowed their heads. On the table sat five neat stacks of red, leather-bound tomes and the Prime Minister, having placed his right hand on the topmost book of the pile in front of him, pronounced in subdued tones, 'We ask that the Protocol will allow us to make wise and righteous decisions at our meeting today.'

All standing around the table then recited, 'Bless The Protocol. May it serve us well.'

The opening catechism complete, the P.M. then said, 'Please be seated.' After his colleagues had settled once more, he continued. 'Right. Firstly, it is a great pleasure to welcome our new Cabinet member to her first meeting: Doreese.' The P.M. smiled in the direction of the new head of D.I.E. while polite applause rippled around the table. Doreese flushed with pride as she nodded to all the other members of the Cabinet.

'Right, Doreese, I don't like to drop you straight in at the deep end but I should be grateful if you would present your report on how the euthanasia project is proceeding.'

Doreese was dressed in her most extravagant finery. Flowing robes of red and green all studded with jewels, shimmered and shone, while her hair, newly permed, glistened as she rose to her feet. 'Prime Minister and esteemed colleagues,' she began. 'It is indeed a proud moment for me as I join your ranks around this hallowed table. It is a privilege to assume the post so ably held by Charles until his unfortunate accident.' The new Minister placed her glasses carefully on the end of her nose and glanced momentarily down at her notes.

'It is clear to me, that since the end of the disastrous wars of theism thirty years ago, we have regained social stability by introducing an atheistic culture, central to which are, of course, the Protocols. Initially merely a guidance for government, these have evolved into something much more and are now the very essence of our advisory structure. We have an algorithm for all eventualities from birth, indeed pre-conception, to death and beyond. Since its introduction, the Euthanasia Protocol has been enormously successful: reducing the average age of the population by a whole decade and the cost of care for the elderly by over a trillion. An additional benefit has been a commensurate increase in those in employment, as the network itself employs thousands of skilled workers; through the ranks of which I myself have risen.' Doreese removed her glasses so that she could glance around the table.

'Thank you, Minister,' said the P.M. 'I think we may once and for all say goodbye to the ridiculous religious interference which had such a negative effect on society. Are there any questions for our new Minister?'

Lady Carter, the Minister for Babies, raised her hand. 'Yes, Prime Minister, if I may?'

The P.M. inwardly groaned. 'Why haven't I been able to get rid of her?' he thought to himself as he nodded his approval for her to speak. Doreese, similarly, took a short intake of breath. She had been warned that Lady Carter could be a troublemaker and was rather too much of a free-thinker.

The Minister for Babies rose to her feet. 'Can you confirm or deny the reports that there has been an alarming number of cases of enforced euthanasia?'

'Such cases are very rare,' Doreese responded, 'but on occasion there is no alternative. There are still some people out there who feel that they are above the Protocol. There remain those who are of the opinion that they do not need to adhere – they are the chronic violators. On those rare occasions we may have to invoke Protocol 24. I have indeed come across such a case myself when I was chairman of the Nowton tribunal.'

'Just remind us, Minister, what *is* Protocol 24.' Lady Carter, now seated, looked enquiringly at the new head of D.I.E. She knew exactly what Protocol 24 referred to, but wanted it stated aloud so that it would be minuted.

'It is the Supreme Protocol, to be invoked when all attempts to adhere have been refused by an individual.'

'Supreme Protocol: by that do you mean capital punishment?' As Lady Carter delivered these words sharp intakes of breath could be heard from around the table.

Doreese's face registered her amazement at this suggestion. '*No!* No, of course not. Capital punishment was abolished years ago. This is entirely different.'

'Tell me, if you would, in what *way*, exactly, is this entirely different?'

Doreese was flabbergasted. Here was a member of the Cabinet challenging the Supreme Protocol. Had she *no* idea how the system worked. 'Lady Carter, surely you understand that this is wholly different.'

'Remind me if you would, Minister, just *how* this is *wholly different.*'

'Well, this is not a case where a mere individual decides on a whim and a whisper that someone should be executed for a misdemeanor. No! This is an integrated protocolised decision, made by the Protocol, for the Protocol. No human being is involved at any level. It is *entirely* different to the old system. Before we had Protocol 24 we were totally dependent on the vagaries of highly fallible individuals – the judiciary.'

'Well, in that case why have there been so many cases where Protocol 24 has been invoked?'

Doreese was flustered. She had no idea how to answer the question and responded gruffly, 'Well that's not *my* problem – you'll have to ask the Protocol.'

'Ah, yes. Bless the Protocol,' Lady Carter sighed.

No one else had been listening to this interchange but on hearing these words there was a reflex murmur, 'Bless the Protocol. May it serve us well.'

Taking the opportunity that the subsequent silence offered the P.M. brought the discussion to a close. 'Thank you, Minister. Are there any other questions?' There was continued quiet. 'No? Well there is *one* other associated issue which I would like to debate while we are on the subject and that is our aid to foreign countries, particularly those which have made no attempt to control their ageing populations. For example, in certain areas of Dalriada the median age is well above ours, at one hundred and fifteen, and *we* are giving *them* aid. I gather there are even worse examples overseas. I know these countries are backward but it occurs to me that we should withdraw all financial assistance unless they commit to an active euthanasia policy such as our own.'

The Science Minister took up the baton, 'Well said, P.M. We cannot carry on funding countries which have made no attempt whatsoever to control the age of their population.'

'Right then. If that's agreed, I'll bring it up at the next meeting of the World Age Group. Thank you.' The P.M. glanced down at his agenda and then looked over the top of his spectacles at the new Minister for Disasters. 'Now, Gerry, what's the climate doing this year? Getting hotter or colder?'

'A bit of both, I'm afraid, P.M.'

\* \* \*

A gentle rain had begun to fall and Mandy's hair dripped and clung to her forehead and cheeks as she stared at the boat now fast disappearing into the deepening gloom of the loch. 'The cheeky brat,' she said quietly, almost to herself. Then she raised her voice, shook her fist once again and yelled with all her might, '*You cheeky bastard. I'll get you. Just you wait, I'll be after you.*' Her face screwed up with hatred as she realised that the boy was now out of earshot. 'You tried to kill us, you did – but I'll get you,' she shouted across the unhearing loch.

Ruth and her father were visibly relieved when they saw the little craft catch the wind and sail into the dusk but they were puzzled by this latest abuse from Mandy who sensed their disbelief. 'Yes he did,' she shouted. 'You saw it. He deliberately drove his boat directly at us. He tried to kill us. That's attempted murder.' She paused briefly and then looked at Ruth. 'And *you*, young lady, are an accomplice.' Mandy's minder was still standing ankle-deep in the loch, hands in his pockets. 'You saw that. He tried to kill us, didn't he?' she shouted in his direction.

'Yes, Miss,' replied the Enforcer without looking up.

Ruth's father had had enough. He had no wish to get into an argument with this woman, now crazed with hatred, so he grabbed Ruth's arm and turned to go. 'You're not going anywhere until I say so,' Mandy snarled. 'You're an accomplice too. *I could arrest you.*' Then she stood stock-still, both arms at her side, lost for words. '*Ugh!*' was all she could utter, her voice now hoarse from trying to be heard above the noise of the wind.

Ruth's father slowly turned around to face Mandy. '*You*, madam, have gone well beyond the authority invested in you. I could report you for house-breaking. A serious crime in these parts, particularly for an outsider.' He led Ruth away from the scene of the boy's escape, up the path to the road where they headed for the village and their home.

'You haven't heard the last of this, d'you hear? *I'm going to get you,*' Mandy shouted at their departing silhouettes. In a final gesture of frustration, she stamped her foot hard on the damp grass by the foreshore, splashing her legs and skirt in the process. She then spun round to face the Enforcer, stared at him and crossed her arms in frustration. 'Why didn't you get him?' she hissed, slowly and poisonously. 'Just wait till I tell the Tribunal how useless you were. He was in our grasp. You were *useless.*'

'Yes, Miss. Sorry, Miss.'

She stomped back in the direction of the path where she could see Ruth and her father disappearing into the distance. 'Ugh,' she grunted again, then still more loudly, '*Ugh!*'

Back at their hostel, an hour later and after a bath and a change of clothes, Mandy had simmered down considerably and had grown more sanguine about the day's events. 'Well,' she remarked to her companion, 'despite your incompetence I suppose things could be worse. We have a positive identification of the boy. We know where he's heading. He won't get far in this weather. We just need to keep on his tail. And now,' she added quietly, looking at her bare feet and wiggling her toes, 'we can add attempted murder to the charges.' On seeing her minder's eyebrows raised in disbelief she continued: 'Don't you look at me like that. You saw it. He drove that boat straight at us. If I hadn't shouted at him he would have killed us both. There's no doubt in my mind that he deliberately tried to kill me.'

'Yes, Miss.'

'You know what that means, don't you?'

'What's that, Miss?'

'It means, *Mister Enforcer*, that we can enlist help from the local constabulary to arrest him. Until now his crimes were purely an English affair, but his attempted murder was on Dalriadan soil, so the police are now obliged to help us.'

Mandy smiled to herself with satisfaction, then shivered slightly. 'If I've got a chill from standing out there in the rain, that boy will pay for it.' She rose from her seat. 'Right, I'm going to contact the local enforcement agencies so that they can chase him up the river or whatever they call that bit of water up there. He can't get far in that floating pile of rubbish he was sailing.'

In fact the boy had travelled quite a long way but not in the direction he desired. In the strengthening wind the boat had sped through the water, however, with the rain sheeting down in the ever-darkening evening, visibility was now only a few yards and he was travelling far faster than was safe. The little skiff careered wildly across the loch until he could see the trees on its eastern slopes and then, when only a few feet away, he spotted the rocks that edged the loch. He slammed the tiller across just in time, realising that if the light skiff hit the rocks at the speed it was travelling it would break up like matchwood. He sailed his boat back therefore across the loch until the opposite shore was in sight where he repeated the process to avoid the steep cliff face. As he neared the eastern shore again he recognised the landscape and realised that, because of the strong prevailing wind, he was tacking to and fro across the loch without making any significant headway northwards. He considered dropping the sail and rowing but realised that he would make little progress against the wind, and the choppy water was now causing the boat to rock wildly when not under sail. The boy spent the next hour performing two further tacks across the loch with each sighting of the shore confirming that he was making no significant progress up the loch.

He wondered what to do for the best. His instructor had told him how to sail in a gentle wind up and down the loch but not how to manage in gale force winds in the middle of the night. He considered trying to beach the boat but each time he came close to the shore all he could see were rocks, cliffs and cascading waterfalls. He decided there was only one safe course of action and that was to sail all night, keeping the boat in deep water. He knew that if he stopped tacking he would be blown to the south of the loch and into the arms of Mandy and her Enforcer whom he assumed would be waiting for him there. He began to regret his cheeky wave, as he knew how greatly that would have infuriated Mandy, yet he smiled to himself at the memory.

His decision made, the boy settled down as low as he could in the boat in order to have as much protection as possible from the elements and, with one arm on the tiller, steered his boat back and forth across the loch. The rain became still heavier and the wind angrily whipped the water into crested waves which splashed and spluttered over the skiff's leeward gunwale making him still more damp and cold. Six hours after waving farewell to the little group on the shore, he caught his first fleeting glimpse of dawn. The southern end of the loch became grey, then luminescent yellow as the golden rays of the new day beamed between the dark cliffs that surrounded the loch, chasing the shadows of night northwards across the surface of the water.

As suddenly as it had arisen the wind dropped; the rain became lighter until it ceased altogether and a few minutes later the boy watched with amazement as a beautiful spring morning exploded on to the landscape.

In the dying breeze the boy could now relax his grip on the tiller. He rubbed his hands and shrugged his shoulders while looking around to take fresh stock of his situation. He was surprised to find that he was still within sight of his cottage and the beach where he had landed the previous night. He had been tacking to and fro across the foot of the loch, making only about a hundred yards in a northerly direction, but it had been the correct decision as it had kept both him and the boat safe and out of reach of his pursuers, of whom there was no sign.

Now was not the time to hang around, he thought, and so, in the lighter and more favourable wind, he turned the skiff north. His boat was not designed to sail close to the wind, but as the wind shifted slightly to the east he began to make progress up the loch and by midday had reached the island half way along its length. He began to recognise landmarks from his voyage the previous day and was confident that he would reach the head of the loch by the evening.

He had now finished all his provisions, but that didn't concern him as he was used to going for long periods without food, sometimes days on end, and the loch provided him with fresh water from the hills. Every now and again his eyelids would begin to droop and he would then try to waken himself by slapping his cheeks, but undoubtedly he drifted off to sleep a number of times. On one occasion he was startled into wakefulness by the spray from a waterfall and was horrified to see a cliff face directly in front of him, only a few feet away. He had sailed far too close to the shore and only just managed to turn the boat about before it would have smashed into the jagged rocks at the water's edge. This startled him and from then on he decided to stand while helming the boat.

The sun was now streaming down and its comforting heat dried and warmed him. He removed his waterproofs and basked in its rays while making his way steadily north. As the afternoon wore on the sun, now well past its zenith, slipped lower in the sky; then, just as it was beginning to grow cooler, he had his first glimpse of the hamlet at the head of the loch. After that desperate night-sail he had made good speed up the loch and the slight shift of the wind to the east meant that for most of the trip he had been able to sail off the wind rather than close-hauled. As he grew closer to the beach by the hamlet he began to discern the figure of a man standing there, binoculars held to his eyes. When he was about a hundred yards away the figure waved and the boy realised that it was the man who had loaned him the boat. He waved back and a few minutes later dropped the sail and rowed the boat to the shore. His friend grasped the bow and pulled the skiff further up the beach where he tied the mooring rope to a metal hoop attached to a large concrete slab half buried in the sand.

'I've been expecting you,' he said as he checked his knot.

'Why? I wasn't due back until Easter!'

'It's all over the news.'

'What is?'

'Quick. You'd better come inside. There's no time to lose.'

The boy picked up his bags and peered into the one Ruth had thrown into the boat at the last moment. Yes – there it was, a little damp but intact – his copy of *Brave New World*. Good old Ruth, he thought as he jumped over the gunwale and landed on the sand, stumbling as his numbed legs briefly gave way under him. The man led him back to the loch-side road and along the main street to the house where his wife was waiting by the open front door.

'Here, quickly. Come inside,' she said as she closed the door firmly behind him.

'Wife,' said the man handing over the binoculars, 'you watch for the police, and I'll brief the boy.'

The boy was confused, unsure why the pair of them were sounding so melodramatic. 'How did you know I'd be back so soon?' he asked.

'It's all over the news. You're a wanted man.'

'*What!*' The boy was flabbergasted.

'Yes, its been all over the emergency information channels. You're wanted for attempted murder.'

'*Attempted murder?*' The boy's eyes widened in an expression of surprise and disbelief.

'Yes! Attempted murder.'

The boy could scarcely believe what he was hearing. 'This is a mistake. It must be someone else. I've never tried to murder anyone.'

'There can be no doubting it's you they're after, son. The bulletin stated that a boy fitting your description and wanted for fraud had attempted to murder a Euthanasia Monitor and an Enforcer before making his escape by sailing up the loch. You did well to get back in those conditions last night.' The boy just shook his head in amazement. 'I presume you didn't try to kill anyone, boy. You don't look like the type.'

'No, of course not. I just don't believe it. I didn't get within ten yards of her.'

'Her?'

'Yes: that besom, Mandy.'

'Look, son, you don't have much time as the local police are involved and will be along soon. This is the only other inhabited place around the loch and they'll guess that you'll be here, so you must leave as soon as possible. But you'll need something to eat, and if you want to tell me what this is all about, that's fine. If you don't, that's fine as well.' The man passed the boy a bowl of hot soup and a crust of bread.

The boy started to eat voraciously. 'You deserve an explanation,' he said between mouthfuls and then, while he ate his supper and drank a beer, he told the man his story from the very beginning.

The man listened, speechless throughout and, when the boy had finished, he sat thoughtfully for a minute. 'Aye,' he said. 'Up here in Dalriada society has disintegrated. We have civil unrest and an ineffective government. The place is a haven for criminals of all kinds. We certainly have our problems but in England you have a totally different problem: unthinking overregulation, where the whole country is run by a computer programme.' The man paused for a moment, thoughtful. 'Look, I wish you could stay here, but you can't, for your own safety and for ours. The police here are ruthless. You're as likely to be summarily executed for the bounty money as to be handed over to the English authorities and I should think that would suit Mandy and her pal just fine.' The boy looked at him intently and shivered with the realisation of the danger he was now in. 'If I were you,' continued the man, 'I'd head over the hills. Although violent and undisciplined, the police here are soft and not at all comfortable in the wild. They prefer their home comforts to stomping around in the hills and will only make a pretence of following you. However, never forget that in urban areas they *will* hunt you down. There is a price on your head and you would be betrayed within hours.' The boy nodded unbelievingly. The man continued, 'If I were you I'd head east. There's a seaside hamlet on the estuary, the one you saw from the summit the other day. It's cut off as the main access was over a bridge, which collapsed long ago, so it's difficult to reach and the authorities tend to leave it alone. The downside is that it's probably a haven for outlaws and miscreants, so watch yourself.'

'What about you? You'll be in trouble for helping me,' the boy asked, obviously concerned.

'We'll say you took the boat without our knowledge, so don't be surprised if the theft of a boat is added to your list of misdemeanours.'

'Husband, they're coming,' the man's wife whispered urgently. 'There are four of them and they're armed. They're coming down the road from the west.'

'Right, son, you must leave. Go directly up the hill behind this house and when you're at the top turn right. It's a moonlit night, so keep below the skyline but you'll be able to see well enough to travel. The police won't follow for more than a few miles and you should be able to put twenty miles between yourself and them before dawn. Good luck.'

'Here,' said the wife. 'Food for a day or two.' She gave him a hug, then brusquely pushed him away before adding, 'Take care.'

The man opened the back door of the house quietly and with quick handshake and a whispered, 'Farewell,' the door was closed behind him and the boy was once more alone. He set off up the hill as fast as he could, and when he reached the top turned for a brief glance whence he had come. He was startled to see the shadowy figures of four men, all holding rifles, at the base of the hill about a hundred yards away. Just at that moment one of the policemen looked up and, on seeing the outline of the boy in the moonlight, shouted, 'There he is: up there at the top. Come on!' The men glanced upwards to where the boy was standing and one of them unslung his rifle, dropped to one knee and took aim.

# FIVE

Mandy had ascertained that the local policeman lived at the other end of the village but decided to phone him rather than brave the stormy evening to go round in person. She introduced herself as a Euthanasia Monitor from England who, with an Enforcer, was on the trail of an absconder and related the events which had taken place on the loch-side only two hours before. 'The point is,' she said, 'that this is now a case of attempted murder and I therefore need to enlist the help of the local authorities.'

The policeman, like most of the population north of the border, was somewhat in awe of the euthanasia squad, or 'death unit' as they were known locally. However, it was beyond his authority to initiate a manhunt so he referred Mandy to his superintendent, head of the regional force, based in a town some twenty miles away. Mandy related her story yet again to this senior officer who, although sympathetic to Mandy's request, was not one to act in haste and to her frustration would only agree to come over to see her the following morning.

True to his word, early the next day, the superintendent parked his battered Land Rover outside the house where Mandy and her companion, the Enforcer, were staying. After introductions, he unrolled a map of the local area and pointed at the south side of the triangular shape that was the nearby loch. 'We are here,' he said, pointing to the foot of the loch. 'Although the loch is large, there are in fact very few places where you can safely land a boat because of its steep rocky sides.' The superintendent glanced at Mandy and her companion, before continuing. 'There are only two beaches, one here and the other at the head of the loch where there's a small hamlet.' The officer pointed to the relevant spot on the map. 'I think *that* is the place to start our search.' He looked at Mandy and the Enforcer, a satisfied smile on his face.

Mandy nodded. 'How do we get there?' she asked.

'I'll have to drive us up. The problem is that the roads are poor and it will take some time so I've radioed ahead to alert the local police and I've also put out a public warning on the emergency channels.' The superintendent was relishing the excitement. There hadn't been a serious crime, anything to really get his teeth into, for over ten years since an old man had gone berserk, taken off all his clothes and set a house on fire.

Mandy and the Enforcer threw their bags into the back of the Land Rover, jumped inside and, pausing only to switch on its blue flashing light, the superintendent drove off as fast as the vehicle would allow.

The journey north was arduous. The roads were poor and the occupants of the car were severely jostled as it negotiated the hilly roads. They had to skirt around the eastern edge of the mountain range, then take a thirty mile detour before turning west through a valley which took them to the head of the loch. It was thus late afternoon by the time they drove through the village and along its main street to where they were to rendezvous with the local police. There, sitting on a bench by the side of the road, smoking cigarettes and chatting, were four men dressed in khaki, their rifles propped against the wooden bench. As the car halted, and the superintendent stepped out, they all rather wearily rose to their feet, stubbed out their cigarettes and stood loosely to attention. The superintendent looked somewhat disapprovingly at the rather motley group. 'Who's in charge?' he asked.

One of the men, a tall lanky individual who had a badge of rank on his tunic, took a step forward. 'I am, sir,' he said and saluted.

'Any luck yet?'

'No, sir. None, so far. We've checked that end of the village.' He then indicated the road heading west, out of the hamlet, 'and we're about to continue with the rest.'

Mandy then stepped forward from behind the officer, her eyes wide with fury. 'Well, get on with it, for god's sake.' She stared wildly at the little group, 'What are you waiting for! Get on with it!' she yelled while stamping her foot repeatedly.

The four policemen looked at her in surprise. 'This,' said the superintendent officiously, nodding towards Mandy, 'is the Euthanasia Officer from the south, and that,' he looked in the direction of her minder, 'is an Enforcer.' The khaki clad group shuffled uneasily.

'Okay, sir… Ma'am,' replied their leader and the four of them set off down the main street. The superintendent then turned to face Mandy.

'May I remind you, madam, that I'm in charge of this operation – *not* you.'

'Well in that case make them get a move on. This boy has already slipped through the net once and I don't want him to escape this time.'

'That is, *if* he is here,' replied the policeman.

'He'll be here. He would have made it, the little brat.' Mandy had developed a grudging respect for the boy's ingenuity.

'Maybe. Let's see if the boat's here.'

The three of them walked to the beach where Mandy was the first to see the skiff lying on its side in the gravel, its mast at an angle, its mooring rope snaking to the heavy anchorage point.

'*That's* it. *That's* the boat. He's here.'

'Are you sure?'

'Yes. That's definitely his boat. He's *here*.'

'What do *you* think?' the policeman asked Mandy's minder. The Enforcer was bemused. During the journey up he had been reminiscing. He'd had a difficult life. He was a product of the great Protocol vision: born in a place he wasn't aware of, to parents he'd never met, he had spent his early life in a State home. He'd always been a bit of a loner and was bullied at school. He had attempted to abscond on several occasions, only to fail and be brought back – humiliated. As he grew older he learned that the way to survive was to work with the system rather than try to change it and once he had discovered that, he had flourished. After leaving school he joined the local police and then became an Enforcer for the Euthanasia Retrieval Squad. He wasn't particularly successful in his job, because he was essentially a mild-mannered man unsuited to chasing absconders and bringing them to book but his overriding talent – which was to do exactly what he was told – saw him through.

This lifelong principle of following instructions was, however, being sorely tested by his current boss. He had never come across such a vindictive and poisonous woman. To see four armed men hunting a teenage boy and clearly intent on killing him, seemed outrageous. Although he had only seen the boy for the first time the previous night and from a distance, he felt a certain affinity as the lad reminded him of himself when he had been that age, only a more intelligent, more self-confident version. 'Yes, I think so.' was all he said.

'Right. Well let's follow the policemen.'

They walked down the road behind the armed policemen who were proceeding along the street knocking on each door along the way. Eventually they came to a gate on which a number six was painted in white. From a distance Mandy saw a lady came to the door and shake her head in response to a question from one of the khaki clad policemen. As the man turned to leave, the superintendent who had followed him up the path stepped forward. 'Can you tell us who owns the little skiff on the shore?' he asked.

She hesitated before replying, 'Oh, that's my husband's.' Mandy, now within earshot, heard this and burst through the little group on the doorstep, pushed the woman aside, and ordered the policemen into the house.

'He *must* be here,' she shouted. 'Go in – search the place.' The men shuffled past the old lady into the house where they separated, going from room to room in search of the boy.

It was their lanky leader who first reached the passageway at the rear of the house where he encountered the owner standing at the back door. The man appeared alarmed by the disturbance and the presence of strangers in his house. 'What are you doing here? You've no right in my house,' he said, maintaining his stance in the doorway.

The superintendent stepped forward. 'We're searching for a boy who's wanted for attempted murder, sir. I'm the senior police officer in charge of the search. We believe he sailed up the loch in a boat which apparently belongs to you.'

The man had regained his composure and was trying to play for time. 'Yes, we have a boat, it's on the beach. I'm a fisherman. But I wasn't aware that it had been stolen.'

'Indeed. Have your seen… ?' The superintendent was interrupted by one of the policemen who had been peering into the dusk through a window to the rear of the house.

'There's someone at the back, sir,' he said.

The fisherman was roughly pushed aside as all four policemen rushed through the back door. In the gloom they couldn't see anything at first but as their eyes adjusted to the dark one of them saw the figure of the boy at the top of the hill and shouted excitedly, 'There he is: up there at the top. Come on,' while another knelt down to take aim. The kneeling soldier was a marksman: a hunter who had shot deer from much greater distances than this and he knew that the boy was as good as dead. For just a moment the boy hesitated, staring at the scene below him, long enough for the marksman to bring his gun to bear. As he saw the boy's young face appear in his telescopic sight the sniper whispered to himself, 'Got you, boy,' and squeezed the trigger. As he did so there was a gentle nudge against his arm and the shot went wide of its mark.

'You *idiot*.' The sharpshooter didn't look up as he said this but started to reload his rifle as rapidly as possible to take a second shot. But when he peered through his sights again, his prey had vanished. He looked around to see what had caused him to miss and briefly saw a shadowy figure slip quietly back into the darkness.

The boy felt the shot before he heard it. A puff of air passed his head and a split second later there was the crack. '*Bloody hell!*' he said as he flung himself down to the ground on the opposite side of the hill below the horizon, and then, getting to his feet once more, he sprinted across the ground, along the side of the hill to his right. He was weighed down by his rucksack and his walking boots were not designed for speed, but he ran as fast as he could. He knew that for the first time his life was in real danger. He ran without a break for about fifteen minutes and only then stopped for a brief backward glance. 'Yes, there they were,' he thought, 'three, no, four of them.' They were making their way along the ridge while looking down into the valley on its far side where they presumed he had disappeared. He could hear them talking, but they were too far away to decipher what they were saying. Then one of then waved and the group disappeared from the ridge down the hill on its opposite side.

On seeing this, the boy breathed a little more easily. It was now crucial that he didn't give his position away so he began to jog, as quietly as he could, along the side of the hill below the skyline. He was fit and so kept up a steady pace heading east. It was hard going as he dared not risk using the path that ran along the ridge and he had to contend with a steady upwards incline. For the next couple of hours he would glance back every few minutes but once he saw no further sign of his pursuers he was able to keep up a steady jog for an hour without resting. By now he was skirting around the summit of the mountain he had climbed four days before, and at that height there was still a faint glint of light in the southern sky. He still didn't dare rest as he knew if he stopped he would fall asleep and it was vital to put many more miles between him and Mandy's squad before he could relax. He settled down therefore to a fast walk, striding out just below the tree line where deer paths allowed relatively easy going.

The man with whom he had stayed had been correct: the bright full moon now lit up the landscape and visibility was better than it had been in the middle of the day when he had last been on this mountain. All night the boy continued to walk and, as the first rays of daylight began to pierce the darkness of the pre-dawn, he climbed to a vantage point and wearily laid down his rucksack. He was risking being seen but he needed to take his bearings. He had checked his compass several times and knew that he had maintained an easterly course but in the excitement of his escape had no true idea of how far he had travelled.

He looked back whence he had come and in the distance identified the loch. The road which led into the hamlet was obscured by the range of hills surrounding it and of his pursuers there was no sign. Of course they might be anywhere but the fisherman had said that they wouldn't follow him for long and he reckoned he'd put about fifteen miles between himself and the hamlet.

He pondered for sometime, considering whether or not to set up his tent and rest. He vividly recalled the sound and sensation of the speeding bullet. These were men who would shoot first and ask questions later. Mandy had become more than just an unthinking automaton: she now wanted him dead. 'This is not the time to take a nap,' he thought as he tried to shake off his drowsiness.

Refreshed by having something to eat and warmed by the rising sun, the boy decided to press on, accordingly he continued east along the north side of the mountain range while still avoiding the ridge.

By midday his legs and shoulders were aching and he felt completely exhausted. He couldn't remember how long it had been since he had last slept. He persevered for a while longer, walking ever more slowly, and then in front of him he caught his first glimpse of the estuary glistening in the sun, a mere ten miles or so away. He staggered forward for a few more minutes until, utterly worn out, he slumped on to the heather and fell into a deep sleep.

The boy dreamt that someone was poking him in the chest and shouting, 'Hey! You. Get up.' Then he heard it again, 'Get up.' It was even louder this time and the prodding grew more persistent. He wearily forced his eyes open and found himself looking at a man who was poking him with the barrel of his rifle. Suddenly the boy was wide awake and realised that there were three other men peering down the barrels of their guns which were levelled menacingly at his chest.

* * *

Ruth's father was furious when he saw the bulletins next morning. He couldn't believe how the events of the previous day had been so grossly distorted. The boy had been dubbed a dangerous escaped criminal – a desperado on the loose. 'Do not approach or try to apprehend,' was the warning, 'Inform the authorities immediately.' He feared for the boy's safety. His first concern was whether he had survived the night in his boat and if so, had he made it safely ashore somewhere. Then he was fearful that Mandy and her cronies would now stop at nothing to capture him, including killing him if they had the slightest excuse. Dalriada was a wild country, lawless in many parts, and the law-enforcers were little better than the law-breakers; indeed in some instances they were the same people.

'D'you think they'll catch him, Dad,' asked Ruth over breakfast.

'To be honest, Ruth, I really don't know. There's a streak of vindictiveness in that Mandy woman that's worrying. However, the boy's a resourceful kid. He knows how to look after himself.'

'He's very clever, Dad. You should see him at school.'

'I know. It's a shame his education will be disrupted yet again.'

'Can't we do *anything* to help him?'

'Ruth, we've done everything we can for the time being.'

'Are you sure, Dad?'

'Absolutely sure. We've even put ourselves in some danger. You heard what that woman said.'

'You mean about being accomplices.'

'Yes.'

'D'you think they'll arrest us?'

'No I don't, Ruth, because that woman knows we would refute her accusation of attempted murder. The best we can do is to keep quiet and get on with our lives. Next term you have your exams and hopefully after that we'll be off to the capital so that you can go to university.'

'*Oh no!*' The boy shook his head and closed his eyes in disbelief. 'How could they have caught up?' was his first thought, 'The man had said they wouldn't follow me across the hills.' The boy shook his head and as he peered unbelievingly at the men. Then he noticed that they were dressed differently from the policemen whom he had glimpsed briefly the night before as he had made his escape. One was wearing an old army greatcoat, another an anorak and the other two were clad only in thick woollen jumpers and dirty jeans.

'It's him all right,' said one of them, lowering his rifle.

'D'you reckon, Ted?'

'Hey, boy, get up,' said the man who had been poking him with his rifle while warily stepping back. The boy slowly rose to his feet.

'Gently, now. Apparently you're dangerous.'

The others laughed. 'He don't look dangerous to me,' said the one called Ted. The boy bent to pick up his rucksack.

'We'll take care of that,' said the man who had prodded him as he lifted up the heavy bag.

'Right, boy, you're coming with us,' said the one called Ted.

One of the men then tied a rope loosely around the boy's waist and then looped the other end around his own wrist as a deterrent against escape. To the boy's surprise the group then set off in an easterly direction, towards the estuary which the boy could now see was quite close.

'Are you the police?' the boy asked.

There was a roar of laughter. '*Us*, the police? Yeah, of course we are,' said one.

The boy decided to keep silent, not sure into whose hands he had fallen. He was coming to the conclusion that these were neither the police nor enforcers. Firstly, he was being marched in the wrong direction for him to be handed over to Mandy; and secondly this quartet looked more like a group of rebels than an official force like the police, however disreputable the latter had become. As they marched east they began to descend slowly until they entered a broad valley. The hills were now behind them – and ahead a new vista gradually unfolded until the open flatness of the estuary filled the evening landscape. To his right, tucked closely against the foothills, was what had once been a village; the houses now lay mainly derelict, while at the water's edge was a small stone-walled harbour, within which, now high and dry, a solitary boat lay on its side in the mud. The boy was amazed by the grandeur and beauty of the scene; even the broken and rusted stanchions of the old bridge had largely been reclaimed by nature and couldn't detract from its loveliness. Then, flying low across the water and heading inland there appeared three swans and, as these servants of Apollo wheezed overhead, the boy halted in his tracks completely overwhelmed by the place and the moment.

'Come on, lad. Never seen a swan before?' asked one of his guards.

'Sorry,' replied the boy. 'No, I've never been this close to the sea.' And as he walked on, he thought, 'This is it – the village that the man had talked about.' The boy had escaped the clutches of Mandy and the Enforcer but was now in the hands of those outlaws for whom this lovely place was home. 'Out of the frying pan,' he thought to himself as the group walked along the main street of this decrepit village.

\* \* \*

When she heard the shot, Mandy had thought it was all over and that her mission was complete; but it then became apparent that the marksman had missed the boy. Mandy had a feeling that the boy would escape. Ever since she had first met him – when he returned to the Studio with the old man and they had requested an appeal – he had proved to be elusive and cunning. Then there was that humiliating outburst in front of the tribunal. She still did not fully understand how the old man had died pre-mortem and how the boy had claimed the payment which *she* had authorised. If it were not for the boy she wouldn't be in this godforsaken place: she'd be in her Studio doing what she enjoyed and did best. It was all *his* fault.

She urged the policemen onwards, up the hill after the boy but when they returned two hours later, empty-handed, she was annoyed but not surprised.

'I'm afraid he's away, sir,' said the lanky one to the superintendent, and then, on seeing Mandy, added, 'Ma'am.'

'But can't you follow him?'

'Not at night, Ma'am. Too dangerous. Never know what could be out there: animals and all sorts.'

'*Ugh!*'

'He'll be well away by now. There's no point in chasing him.' This said, the superintendent walked through to the sitting room in which the man and boy had swapped yarns just two nights before.

'Care for a whisky, gentlemen of the constabulary?' asked the man. He had already had a few drams to calm his nerves and now that he knew the boy was safely away he had become slightly tipsy.

'No thank you, sir, not while on duty,' said the senior officer.

'I will, if you don't mind,' said the lanky one, who then added on seeing the disapproving look shot at him by his senior. 'Perhaps I'd better not – on duty, you know: health and safety and all that.'

'You realise of course, that you've been harbouring a known criminal,' the superintendent continued

'I had no idea. He simply knocked on the door and then disappeared out the back just before you arrived.'

The officer shrugged. He knew there was no point pursuing that line of questioning and there was nothing to gain by interrogating the man or his wife any further. Mandy, however, was not finished. 'We could arrest you, you know.'

'Could you?' the man answered, a smile on his lips as he took another sip of his single malt.

'You must have *some* idea which way the boy went.'

The man considered laying a false trail but thought better of it. 'I've absolutely no idea, ma'am,' he said.

'*Ugh!*'

'Well, Mandy,' continued the superintendent, 'where do we go from here? My men won't attempt to pursue the boy tonight. I suggest that we try to pick up his trail tomorrow.'

'*Ugh!*' was all Mandy could utter once again.

The following day they did indeed pick up the boy's trail and it was clear that he had gone east, for there were footprints and patches of crushed undergrowth in that direction. They followed the trail for sometime but after three hours the weather began to close in and the policemen returned.

Back in the village the lanky one explained. 'It's getting pretty nasty out there and there's no doubt he'll be heading for the estuary.'

'*So!*' screamed Mandy, 'Go out there and get him.'

It was the superintendent who replied. 'Dangerous area, ma'am. Full of outlaws. It's pretty much a no-go area for us police, I'm afraid. Our only hope is that he is picked up by the banditti who live around that area. They'll hand him over for the reward.'

'How will they know?'

'Oh, *they'll* know. They listen to the emergency bulletins as much as anyone else – more, probably as it's their early warning system. I think we should return to headquarters and wait for an approach from the outlaws. I've dealt with them before. They'd kill their own parents for a few hundred quid.'

# SIX

'Prime Minister; I've been thinking about the Overseas Aid issue, particularly with regard to Dalriada.'

'Oh, yes, Doreese.' The Prime Minister looked at the head of D.I.E. with interest. They were in his private rooms where they were meeting at her request.

'Well, it strikes me that as you said yourself at the last cabinet – most eloquently if I may say so,' simpered Doreese, 'It's completely unrealistic for foreign governments to expect aid from us here in England if they are making no attempt whatsoever to control their ageing population.'

'Well I'm glad you agree, Doreese. I think it's outrageous but of course politically it's a highly-charged issue.'

'Yes I know, but it occurred to me that, with the government in Dalriada being in such turmoil, this might be a good time to address the problem. Apparently the country has returned to a type of clan-based rule with everyone fighting each other, and the capital's administration is not in overall control. I think that this might be the ideal time to introduce the protocol system of government – including the Euthanasia Protocol.'

'Well, of course it was inevitable that once it became a separate country they would revert to their old ways. It's happened to every other country following independence – sooner or later. We really *must* learn from the past. Machiavelli got it right, hundreds of years ago. It's all in *The Prince.*'

'Absolutely, Prime Minister: and what a great singer *he* was,' said Doreese, who had no idea who the P.M. was talking about, and thought he might be referring to Mantovani. The P.M. looked puzzled as Doreese continued, 'Anyway, I think that with a little gentle diplomacy we might convince the Dalriadan government of the benefits of protocol rule and then persuade them to introduce their version of D.I.E.'

'But surely they're *far* too unruly up there. There needs to be a structure already in place to introduce protocolised government – as *we* did after the wars of religion.'

'P.M., the *Protocol* itself will be the structure. I believe there are enough disenfranchised people up there willing to seize the opportunity of attaining security and safety that only a protocol system of government can bring.'

'Well I have to say, Doreese, that I admire your enthusiasm but I'm not convinced that your goal is achievable. How would you envisage going about it?'

'The first step will be to open negotiations with their central government in the capital. Although they don't have overall control of the country they do still run several important agencies including the police. My intelligence source there tells me that the President is using aid money, charitable funds for heaven's sake, to ensure that the police and other key agencies remain on side. Otherwise there would have been outright civil war years ago. What we should do is offer *more* money, not less, but this would be tied into a programme of reform to build the infrastructure necessary for the countrywide introduction of the Life Protocols.'

The P.M. nodded. 'Go on,' he said.

'As has been our experience here, the Protocol will create jobs, thus reducing unemployment; it will decrease the age of the population and give a tax-free handout to those with elderly family members.'

'I see your logic, Doreese, but our track record of working with Dalriada is really not at all good. What would make it any different this time?'

'Well, P.M., I think the time is now ripe. For a while now I have been obtaining regular reports from my agent up there: a Euthanasia Monitor who has been tracking an English absconder for some time. From her, I have had a first-hand account of a society desperate for change: a fractured, disenfranchised community which would welcome a return to firm management from a strong government.'

'Mm. How do you suggest going about this?'

'What I'm proposing is that I should lead a small delegation to the Dalriadan capital. I would require you as P.M. to authorise this with the President who, so I'm led to believe is a weak man and then, with the help of my agent there, open negotiations. I would also approach those clan leaders with whom my agent has made contact. Hopefully as an outside independent agency we will be able to achieve what their own leader cannot. Gradually we would then introduce the Protocol system much as we did here forty years ago.'

'Well, I'm happy to support you, Doreese. Certainly the department here is running smoothly and will be able to operate without you for a while. Take a couple of your best people and head north. I will contact the Dalriadan President and explain that I'm sending a small delegation to discuss matters of mutual interest. How's that?'

'That's perfect, P.M. Thank you so much.'

'If you pull this off, Doreese, you'll certainly be up for a gong.' The P.M. smiled, 'But I won't put your name forward just yet.' He then shook her hand, said, 'Good luck,' and ushered the head of D.I.E to the door and out of his office.

* * *

The following year Ruth did well in her exams and was accepted into the capital's university. The curriculum had been slimmed down over the years and even the Principal, who was aged ninety-two, could barely recall those days when medicine, law and theology were the most popular subjects. Although Dariada had chosen not to follow the example of England with regard to Protocols, they had absorbed some elements of the legal and medical administration systems so that there was a diminishing requirement for lawyers and doctors.

Ruth had in fact initially hoped to read law or medicine, but her father had pointed out that both those subjects were now effectively moribund and would soon be of no practical use, and only required in backward countries. 'As soon as health and legal protocols are nationwide – which they will be soon – there will be no requirement for doctors and lawyers,' he said to her. 'You remember what the old man said about what happened in England. The same will happen here, there can be no doubt about that.'

Ruth accepted her father's advice and opted to study politics. Political theory had been expunged from most university courses in

England, but one thing about being a backward-looking nation was that topics disapproved of elsewhere were still being taught, indeed taught well, in Dalriada. Extreme theorists had of course been banned and exiled, but it was still possible to get a good grounding in politics, some sciences and even religious studies. Ruth opted for politics with the history of religion as her second subject as she thought it would be enlightening.

Her father worked in the capital's fish market in the old port of Leith doing what he knew best and the two of them lived in a small flat at the top of an old tenement near the docks.

Ruth's course covered political philosophy from ancient times to the present. She read Plato, Marx and Hitler, amongst other writings and of course studied all the early works pertaining to Protocol theory. In her religion classes she learned of the religious conflicts from pre-Christian times through to the disastrous wars of the twenties.

'How could any one be so stupid as to fight over a belief in something that didn't exist?' she thought. 'How idiotic were my ancestors.' She remembered the Protocol discussions she had had with the boy and the old man all those years ago. She realised that the Protocol governmental model offered stability and, although not perfect, at least didn't result in mass murder in the name of a god.

Ruth worked hard, played well, grew in knowledge and confidence and after three years of study passed her exams with excellent grades. Once graduated, she was appointed to a prestigious post as Junior Adviser in the government's policy-making department. Occasionally she would wonder what had happened to the boy. She'd received no news since that evening on the loch-side and after the initial outcry surrounding his escape everything had gone quiet. Her father advised her that it was best to keep silent about the whole episode and not to ask questions.

* * *

There was no approach from the banditti so Mandy and her Enforcer colleague once again scoured the country in search of the boy. Interestingly, Doreese from the Department, had been in touch with Mandy and far from being angry about her lack of success in apprehending the boy seemed unconcerned. She asked Mandy to continue her search but at the same time to meet local leaders and discretely obtain information about how the country was run and whether or not the time was ripe for the introduction of a protocolised form of government. Indeed, Doreese had been quite friendly towards her. She did not seem to mind that the boy had escaped and she gave Mandy and her Enforcer a generous allowance to pursue their research. Thus they travelled around the country, speaking to local communities, clan leaders as well as government officials, and then Mandy reported their findings to Doreese on a weekly basis. Mandy never forgot about the boy and was still intent on finding him; but with adequate funds and the new authority invested in her she became reasonably content with her situation. She even grew to tolerate her minder.

# SEVEN

The four men chatted happily as they led the boy down the main street of the derelict fishing village. During their short trek they had seemed in good humour, joking and laughing, so the boy considered that they didn't pose a physical threat to him so long as he behaved himself. It was now late afternoon; behind them the sun had disappeared below the hills and ahead the estuary was beginning to grow dark as it merged imperceptibly into the sea beyond. While they walked along the street the boy couldn't help but think how pleasant the little village appeared. It was like a picture from one of his history books. He noticed that the houses were stone-built, with paint of varying colours flaking off the walls and most looked uninhabited. On the front of each house was a single flight of external stone steps leading to its entrance which was on the first floor. The ground floor frontage was largely open and in some of the cottages the boy could see large nets hanging from the ceiling. 'Fishermen's cottages,' he thought to himself.

The little group strolled rather than marched along the street, which ran parallel to the shoreline, then half way along they turned right up a steep hill heading away from the harbour. By the time they had reached their destination the men were panting slightly from their exertions. The single-storey building they had arrived at looked like an old warehouse. It was long and narrow, low and squat, with only a few small windows along its length, all of which had bars on the outside. The wide wooden doors were heavy and solid, with cast iron hinges and locks.

'Right, son, this is your home for the night,' said one of his captors, the one called Ted, who appeared to be in charge. When they entered, the boy was immediately overwhelmed by a rich smoky smell, pleasantly infiltrated with the odour of fish. The boy noticed hooks hanging from the low darkened beams above him as the men led him through the middle of the large, bare, barn-like room to the far end where there were a series of rooms, each with its own door. The leader selected one, looked inside, switched on an electric light and ushered the boy inside.

'It's not luxury but it's warm and dry,' said Ted. 'There's a toilet over there.' He pointed to a wooden partition. 'But there's no way to escape; so I wouldn't bother trying.' The man looked at the boy. 'Believe me, I tried, many years ago!' He smiled, while the others laughed.

'Settle in, son. Get some rest. I'll be back tomorrow morning and we'll have to decide what to do with you.'

Throughout all of this the boy had not uttered a word. He was still physically exhausted after his three sleepless days in the open, first on the loch and then in the hills; but more than that, he was mentally shattered. So much had happened in such a short space of time that he was unable to take it all in.

'Thank you,' was all he said.

'We'll keep your rucksack, and your money,' said one of them. 'But don't worry, they'll be quite safe. We're not thieves here.' The door was then banged shut and the boy heard the sound of a padlock being snapped closed. He wasn't concerned by the loss of the rucksack or indeed of his money. After being apprehended he had been searched and his money bags and hunting knife confiscated. Somehow, for reasons he didn't fully understand, the loss of these items hadn't troubled him. The events of the last few days had taken his life in a wholly new direction and those possessions now belonged to the past, a previous existence from which he had moved on. Also, for some inexplicable reason, he trusted these men when they said his belongings would be safe.

The boy looked around his new accommodation. In the corner was a sink and behind a wooden screen there was a flushing toilet, while there was a bunk bed against the far wall. The single small window, made up of four glass panes and covered with sturdy iron bars on the outside, was set firmly in the thick brick wall and it didn't even occur to him to search for possible ways of escape, since he implicitly believed what his captor had said. He took off his waterproofs, then his boots and socks, and took great pleasure in washing his face and feet before crawling into bed where he immediately fell into a fitful, restless sleep.

The boy was wakened by the first rays of dawn as they crept though the small window into his cell and then, as the he recalled the events of the previous day, bright sunlight began to beam in to his cell, warming and heartening him. Somewhat refreshed from his sleep, but stiff from the exertions of the previous days, he washed, more thoroughly this time, then dressed and when he heard the rattle of the padlock, he was ready, sitting expectantly on the one chair in the room.

Ted, the leader of his band of captors from the previous day then entered. 'Good morning, boy,' he said jovially, 'what a beautiful day.' As the man smiled, deep creases around his eyes and cheeks came alive. The boy now looked at his captor inquisitively, as though for the first time. He saw an extremely thin man, less than six feet tall, wearing faded blue jeans which hung limply from his hips, while a loose-fitting T-shirt was visible underneath his well-worn leather jacket. However, it was his face that demanded attention. Although the boy thought he was probably only in his mid-thirties, his face appeared to be older than the rest of him. This was a lived-in face: deeply lined with a bluish swelling over his left cheekbone below which a small, pale scar was just visible. His nose was slightly misshapen while thick curly-brown shoulder-length hair gave him a slightly piratical appearance. This was a man who'd had an interesting and difficult past, thought the boy.

'You don't say much, do you?' the face asked.

'Sorry,' said the boy, jerked suddenly from his musings. 'I didn't mean to be rude, but the last few days have been a strain. I'm totally confused as to what's going on.' The boy then glanced at the window, 'but you're right, it does look like a nice day.'

'I understand,' replied his captor. 'I was in a similar position to you many years ago. I'm afraid I can't tell you much – that's for the chief to do – but I *can* tell you that you are now in Invernueage. An independent city state.'

'Oh. What's that?'

'You'll find out soon enough. I'm going to take you to our leader. He's variously called a clan chief, chairman, bishop, village elder, or leader of the council, depending on where you come from and how you define our administrative system. But whatever you call him, he's in absolute charge. That's all I can say for now; apart from the fact that he's a fair man.'

That said, Ted led the boy out of the old salmon smokehouse – for that's what the building had been – and on to the street. The boy glanced at his watch: it was still early but there were already one or two people out and about. He saw one man sweeping the street while another appeared to be placing cans of some fluid on the doorstep of each house. The boy was not restrained in any way yet felt no urge to try to abscond. As he proceeded up the hill, passers-by stared at him; some smiled, while others looked away – yet all seemed intrigued by his presence, aware of whom he was and keen to catch a glimpse of the person branded a dangerous murderer and thief.

At the top of the hill, on the very edge of the village, the boy caught his first sight of a strange-looking building. It was built of grey stone and was in much better condition than the others. It was double-fronted and at its centre was a large, ornate wooden door on either side of which were long, narrow gothic windows. Most noticeable, however, was a tall structure emerging from the centre of the building. It wasn't a chimney, thought the boy, because it rose to a point. He wondered if it was what people used to call a spire.

'Welcome to the City Health, Utility and Recreational Civic Hall,' said the man as he unslung his rifle. 'It's a bit of a mouthful – has to be, not to offend anyone. We normally just call it, "The Hall." '

'It looks like what used to be called a church,' observed the boy.

'In a way it *is* a church but that term has historical connotations with religion and the wars of the gods, so it's a term we don't use,' replied his captor. 'In fact it's much more than a church. It is the heart, the very soul of our city state.'

Once inside, the boy gazed at the interior in amazement. It was not a large building but crammed inside were all sorts of shining artefacts. Colourful material clung to every wall and pillar. Benches and chairs were draped with rich tapestries and at the opposite end of the building was a broad table on which were shiny cups of silver and gold. Every inch of the floor was covered with brilliantly-coloured rugs of different shapes, sizes and patterns and the whole scene was illuminated by the bright sunlight that streamed in through a large arched window at the far end of the room.

'Quite impressive, ain't it,' stated his guard.

'I've never seen anything like it,' replied the boy.

The man led the boy around the periphery of the room to the east end where, directly behind the large table on which stood silver and gold cups, was a door on either side of which was a chair.

'Take a seat, son. These are the council offices and you'll be summoned shortly.'

The boy did as he was instructed while his guard remained standing beside him.

After a few minutes the door opened and a young, nervous man: balding, bespectacled and wearing a creased suit, poked his head out.

'Good morning,' he said nervously as he looked about. 'Ah, Ted, it's you. How are you?'

'Fine thanks, clerk. I've brought the boy along,' replied the boy's captor, nodding towards his charge.

'Excellent, excellent.' He turned and looked at the boy in a short-sighted fashion, 'Do come right on in,' then, turning to the guard, added, 'You'd better come as well, Ted. Is he dangerous?'

'No, clerk. Hasn't given us any problems at all.'

'Good. Good. Come in, young man,' and the clerk flung the door wide and held it open while Ted and his captive entered. Inside, the boy hesitated for a moment, registering the large open room which reminded him of the courtroom in Nowton where he'd sat next to the old man and listened to the farce that was called a tribunal hearing. In front of him was a raised dais, on which was a long table behind which were placed thirteen chairs, the middle one, rather more ornate than the others, was occupied by an elderly man. As Ted and his detainee walked into the room the man looked up, smiled and beckoned them forward. The boy thought he was dressed strangely, rather like the old man used to dress. He wore what looked like a hairy jacket, underneath which was an old-fashioned shirt and tie. His hair was white, as befitted his age, while his face was round and jovial. The boy thought that he looked as though he might burst out laughing at any moment.

'Chairman, this is the boy we apprehended last night,' announced the clerk.

'Thank you, clerk.' A benign smile creased the old man's face as he gestured for Ted and the boy to be seated. 'Now, boy, what's your name?'

'I've always been known just as "boy", sir.'

'Oh, come on. You must have a name. Everyone has a name.'

The boy was at a loss. He genuinely had never been aware of being called anything other than "boy", or "son". He glanced at the signet ring that he wore on the little finger of his left hand, the one he had removed from the old man's cold body. There, just discernible, was the letter 'G'.

'Giles,' he said.

'That's better. We can't keep calling you "boy" now, can we? Now, Giles, how old are you?'

'Fifteen, sir.'

'Good. Well, Giles, we know you're on the run from the Euthanasia squad. Tell me how you've managed to land yourself in that unenviable situation, if you will.' The boy hesitated. 'Look, Giles,' the man continued. 'In situations like this, when we come across someone with a price on their head, we normally hand them back to the authorities and take the money. You need to persuade me that we shouldn't do that.' The leader of the council paused and looked directly at the boy. 'Now, tell me your story, please.'

The boy sensed that this was not a time for obfuscation and realised that once more he was fighting for his life, so he started to talk, omitting nothing from the moment he had first met the old man in Nowton right up until the time he escaped from the police and been apprehended by Ted and his squad. During the boy's rendition the leader occasionally interrupted with a question for clarification but essentially he listened attentively, simply making the occasional note on a pad in front of him from time to time.

When the boy had finished his tale the leader put down his pencil, sat back in his chair and sighed. 'How very interesting,' he said. 'Things down south are worse than I thought. They have certainly deteriorated since I left. Your story has the ring of truth about it and I have no reason to disbelieve you.' The man sighed again before continuing. 'You see, Giles, all of us in this community are outlaws from society for one reason or another. Most of us have escaped persecution: some religious, some academic, while others, like you, have just found themselves on the wrong side of the law through no fault of their own. Many have simply fallen foul of the government of the south, and have had to escape from the tyranny of the Protocol.'

'But I was told that you were all bandits and violent criminals here. Outcasts from society.'

The man chuckled. 'Well, in some ways we are, and it's an image that suits us. It means that the authorities generally leave us alone. Isn't that so, Ted?'

'In general, sir, yes.'

'But my point is,' continued the leader, 'is that in *this* society we must all have a purpose, a function, to be able to perform a task that is useful to the community at large. Simon, our clerk here, is an experienced administrator. Used to be a senior civil servant in the capital until he began to question the system and challenge those in charge. He fulfils the council's requirement for a scribe and information expert. Ted, who brought you here has, I think he would be the first to agree, a chequered past but is an excellent guard: essentially he and his team make up our police force. And as for myself: well, the community seems to think that I am able to run things in a fair and open fashion and they can vote me out whenever they get fed up with me.'

'Don't you have any protocols?' asked the boy.

'No. None. However, that doesn't mean we don't have any rules, it's just that ours are laid down by the elders, or the council, as it is sometimes known. Human beings, not computers, make the decisions here.'

'So you use your experience and commonsense, not just a book of rules or a computer programme.'

'Indeed. You seem to know a lot about this, Giles.'

'I read a lot and the old man I told you about was deeply saddened by the protocolisation of society in England. It is easy to see the nonsense that the Protocols can perpetrate. It has led to generation of unthinking automatons who rely totally on a computer to make every decision for them. The more difficult the decision the more they seem to rely on it.'

'Yes, indeed. I think you are very much in tune with the views of this community. But to remain here you must still have a role: a function. You said you could sail. Is that correct?'

'Yes, sir.'

'Have you ever sailed at sea?'

'No, just on the loch.'

'Okay, Giles, the final decision is yours. No one is going to force you to stay here. But escape, as you will know from your overland trek, is difficult: no impossible, if we are intent on stopping you. In fact, no one has absconded in the thirty years that I've been here.' The leader of the council put the tips of his fingers together and sat back in his chair. 'I will advise the council that, if you wish, you may stay here on the understanding that you join our education programme, and become our fisherman. Unfortunately we are without one, following his death during a violent storm last year and our diet has suffered as a result. Sadly, we have no one within our community with the aptitude to handle a sailing boat. However, we do have those with knowledge of the tides and all that sort of thing and they would educate you in those matters. Or, if you decide that you don't want to stay we will hand you over, unharmed, with all your possessions – including the considerable amount of money you had on your person – to the authorities in the capital and take the reward.'

The boy barely hesitated. 'I'll stay if I may, sir.'

'Good decision, Giles. I have a feeling you'll like it here. This issue is of course not entirely within my gift, but I will advise the council accordingly when we meet this afternoon. In the meantime I'm afraid we'll have to keep you under lock and key in the old fish-smoker. Any questions?' The leader looked at him and smiled.

'No, thank you, sir.'

'Okay, Ted. Take him away. You might like to show him around the town.'

'Yes, chief,' Ted nodded.

'And bring him back at the same time tomorrow if you would, please.'

The clerk rushed to open the door and Ted escorted the boy out of the council chamber and back into the main hall.

'Right, Giles. I want you to promise that you won't try to run away. As the council leader said, you'd not get far. If you promise, I'll not restrain you and we can have a pleasant day looking at the sights of Inverneuage.'

'I promise,' said the boy with a smile.

The pair of them left the church and turned left up the hill. The boy wondered where they were going as they seemed to be heading out of the village, but as they breasted the hill there appeared below them a shallow valley in which there was a small town hidden from both the sea and the land. It consisted of two main streets running parallel to one another along the sides of which was an eclectic mix of buildings. Unlike the houses in the old derelict village, these were newly built, from whatever materials were available and were sprawling one or two-storey constructions – no two being the same. In front of some were stalls on which were spread a variety of goods on sale including clothes, food and books. On seeing the last of these the boy's eyes lit up. 'Gosh,' he thought, 'There are books here – *openly* on sale.' However the overwhelming sensation was one of activity: of bustle and noise. The streets were buzzing with swarms of people, the pleasing racket of human beings, men and women of all ages jostling and shouting; of children playing while weaving their way through the mingling throng of people laughing and bargaining. It was a scene of boisterous, noisy humankind, unconstrained and unfettered. There was something else quite different and for a while Giles couldn't quite put his finger on what it was. Then he realised – there were very few old folk. One or two elderly men and women mixed with the rest of the crowd, but this was quite unlike Nowton, where the grey, lassitude-ridden oldsters moaned and creaked their way along the dispiriting streets, hunched against their zimmers. This place was bright, noisy, colourful and vibrant.

'Gosh!' The boy stood on the brow of the hill and gazed in amazement.

'What are you staring at, Giles?'

'The people. They're, they're... ' the boy was lost for words '... well. They're *happy*.'

'Ah, yes. I forgot that you've been in the south all your life. Yes, I noticed that when I first arrived. Don't worry, you'll soon get used to it,' Ted explained, almost apologetically, as he waved to a woman who then joined them at the side of the street. 'Maisie, come and meet Giles.'

'Hello, Giles. Are you the desperate criminal we've all been 'earing about? Don't look like much of a desperado to me, Ted.' The woman smiled and chuckled. 'How many of you did it take to catch this little sprat. 'E's tall, mind.'

'Giles, this is Maisie. She's my woman. We've been together nearly twenty years now.'

'Nice to meet you.' The boy shook her hand.

'Hopefully he'll be staying, if the Council agree.'

'Well, welcome young man. Giles, you say? That's a posh name. Any'ow, Ted, I must rush. I need to get some bread. See you later. Byeee,' she sang and was gone, swallowed up by the milling, swarming throng.

Captor and prisoner then followed, gently pushing their way along the street, where every few yards Ted would meet with an acquaintance. 'Here, Charlie, this is Giles.' 'Oi, Richard, meet Giles,' 'Giles, meet Michael.' And so it went on.

'Right, it's time for lunch.' Ted led Giles out of the sunlight into the gloom of one of the houses. Inside there was a pleasant smell of cooking: of garlic, spices and fresh bread. The guard escorted the boy to a long table where they sat alongside several other diners.

'Daisy, this is Giles. He's a violent criminal so you'd better give him something nice to eat, smartish.' The boy was quite overcome by all this bonhomie and could only sit and grin.

'Don't look much like a murderer to me,' she answered with a laugh. 'Has 'e got an 'ome yet?'

'No. You volunteerin'?'

'Well, me eldest has moved out, so I've got a spare room and I could do with the rent. Bear it in mind.' Ted ordered them something to eat and a beer each, which they consumed while Ted swapped pleasantries with the other diners. When they had finished he bade his farewells.

'Thanks, Daisy. I've got to take him back to jail now,'

'Oh. Poor soul. D'you 'ave to?'

'Yes, until tomorrow, but hopefully he'll be freed then.'

'Okay, Giles. Good luck! I 'ope to see you again.'

They walked up the hill and back into the most derelict part of the town. 'You see, Giles, from the sea the whole village looks quite uninhabited, so no one troubles us. We have to guard it, mind. That's the job for me and my men. There are a few inhabited buildings here and they are largely for the administration. I have an observation post here so I that can watch the estuary. The hall and council building you've already seen and then there's the old smoker-cum-jail which you know.'

They wandered down the hill towards the smokehouse. 'You see that house, the one with the nets?' Ted pointed to a cottage near the shoreline at the foot of the hill. 'Well, that's the fisherman's cottage. That would be yours if you became our boatman.'

A moment later they reached and entered the smoker. 'I'm afraid I'll have to lock you up again, Giles as I've now got to do my rounds but I'll drop by later to check you're all right. 'Bye for now.' The door of the cell slammed shut and the boy found himself once more alone, yet feeling more contented and positive than he had done for as long as he could recall.

# EIGHT

The council of elders, or synod as some called it, ruled that the boy should be allowed to stay and he rapidly settled in to his new life at Inverneuage. An exiled lecturer in astronomy taught him navigation and how the tides were created, while with the help of some local tradesmen he renovated the fishing smack and mastered how to sail it. He learned at what state of the tide he could sail his boat in and out of the harbour, while on his trips he charted the position of sandbanks and other hazards that he had to contend with when sailing. The estuary was broad and with a spring-tide range of over twenty feet the currents could be fast and treacherous. Thus twice a day the sea swept in, transforming the muddy, landlocked harbour into a calm sanctuary in continuity with the sea some ten miles away. The boy calculated how long he could stay out before having to wait for another tide to be able to sail back in and, with the help of his friends, even drew up some basic tide tables. Initially he was often caught out, finding himself high and dry in the middle of the estuary miles away from home. But his boat simply sat on the exposed mud and he whiled away the hours reading until the sea flooded in once more and he could continue his journey.

As the boy grew in experience and confidence he fished further away and his catches became larger. As soon as his smack with its heavy red sails was spotted approaching, willing helpers from the village would descend on the harbour with their barrows in order to transport his catch up the hill to the town. There, some would be distributed immediately, the rest being sold from a stall on market day. He made no money directly but in return for his fish he would obtain items that he needed from the other shops and stalls: food and clothes, or trinkets and ornaments as well as his beloved books. He lived alone in the fisherman's cottage from where he could follow the tides and watch the weather rolling in from the east; it reminded him of his house at the foot of the loch. The vagaries of the tides and his fishing trips meant that his attendance at classes – which were held, as was everything else, in the City Hall – was sporadic. That, however, was not in any way detrimental to his education, since within this strange and eclectic community were many academics whom had been expelled from their posts during the secularist revolution. They came mainly from Dalriada and England but amongst them were others with strange guttural accents who hailed from across the sea. Their expulsion had not merely been about religious reform but due to the total annihilation of free and independent thought: a sort of 'Dalriadan Darkenment,' as one of his teachers had labelled it. The extraordinary thing was that, through these people, knowledge was welded into the very framework of this strange community. Those senior academics taught the boy history, politics, philosophy, religion, information technology and the basic sciences. In effect this young fisherman was receiving one-to-one tutorials with some of the finest minds in the world; and the boy's enthusiasm and his thirst for knowledge, linked to his natural intellect, made him a delight to teach. While he absorbed information like a sponge he never forgot the old man's advice: to challenge the dogma and question the *status quo.* On more than one occasion his clear analytical thinking had his tutors struggling to justify their own beliefs.

The boy's education was broad and balanced, with no fixed curriculum or constraints such as there were at the few remaining universities across Dalriada. He usually fished alone, since most of the community were townsfolk and not readily at ease in boats but when required he would also ferry people, mostly council members, across the estuary from where they could travel as far as the capital if they wished. In this way the community was kept informed of what was happening in the outside world.

Thus, as fisherman, ferryman and scholar, the boy grew tall and strong. His voice broke, he grew a beard and by the time he was eighteen he had matured into a healthy, muscular young man. He also began to see girls in a different light. There was a strict code of sexual conduct in the community to reduce the risk of inbreeding and although he himself came from outside the village he had to await his turn before being allocated a girlfriend.

One feature of this otherwise idyllic, epicurian culture that he found difficult to comprehend was that of religion. He couldn't quite make out if this was a religious community or not. Some of his friends and seniors appeared to possess a faith and to observe certain traditions but it took an unidentifiable form. One old man, for example, seemed to worship the estuary and the birds which flew across it, while another offered up prayers to the village council itself. At the close of one tutorial he asked his teacher how it worked.

'Well, Giles, we don't have religion here, as such. Theism *per se* is banned. But what we *do* have is freedom of expression, freedom to pursue our own particular beliefs.'

'Surely that's the same as religion,' observed the boy.

'No. Not at all. We do not have individual religions such as Catholicism, Buddhism, Islam, or people who claim to be Jains, Sikhs or Jews. That is not allowed. History tells us that this type of sectarian theism results in ideological greed and *inevitably* leads to conflict. It seems to me to be a crass piece of nonsense that one group of individuals, who happen to believe in one thing, attempt to annihilate another group, just because they believe in something quite different. It beggars belief that this was once commonplace and resulted in the misery of the Wars of Religion. The problem continues to exist, however, because many people do need to believe in *something*. So here we let them believe in anything they want, within certain behavoural guidelines.'

'I still don't see how that can work.'

'In essence we have thrown all beliefs, religious, secular, pagan – whatever – into one pot. We have the village hall, which looks a bit like an old-fashioned church but has features of all the old religions, and at the same time is part of our secular administrative structure. All our beliefs are inextricably combined. Our administration is our religion and our religions are our administration. Our city council is our synod, and the bishop is our council leader and clan chief.' The boy's teacher searched for words to explain the concept further. 'Here, you see, secularists and radical atheists can pursue their beliefs in the same space and at the same time as theists of all types. There are those for whom belief in the council is their religion and there are even some Protocol fundamentalists – although there are few of those in this community.'

'Is this a stable mix?' asked the boy.

'Yes, essentially. Everyone is allowed to follow his or her own path – or faith as it used to be known. There are some who pray to their own particular god; others, like the orthodox councillists, believe that our clan leader is a kind of elected prophet, almost a deity in his own right. That's why we have several names for the ruling group. Clans are an old Dalriadan institution, so those of us from the south are more familiar with the concept of a City Council. The important thing is that it doesn't matter, as long as it works. Some go up to the table, called the altar, and say prayers; others bypass the altar and enter the church beyond, to what some call, "the chancel," others call it "the council chamber," while some kneel on the rugs.'

'And there's no friction?'

'We don't allow any. The overriding rule, the law above all laws, is that *no one*,' and he paused to emphasise his point, '*No one* may try to convert another to their belief: that's the key. People can talk about it as much as they like but must never criticise anyone else.'

'And what happens if someone tries to convert another to their own belief?'

'They are given a warning and if they persist they are then expelled from the community. It is the only way to maintain peace and stability. We can all live happily together as long as we do not try to insist others become like ourselves. As soon as that happens then chaos and violence is inevitable.'

'Tell me why protocols weren't introduced here.'

'After the wars of the great religions, when much of the continent was laid waste and millions were killed, most governments, including the one in England simply banned religion and many introduced protocols in their place. Here, following the separatist movement nearly a hundred years ago, the fabric of our society fractured, resulting in fragmentation, and we returned to an ancient clan-like feudal system. This culture resisted national protocols as no one could agree, and so little village and city states like our own have grown up.'

'So what on earth does the capital's government do?'

'Some would say, "Not a lot." ' The teacher smiled to himself. 'Although it's called a government, it represents less than a third of the population, and then only those in the south-east of the country. There they have incorporated some of the features of protocolisation, particularly in health and in law, but not others such as the Euthanasia Protocol which you fell foul of.'

'And as a result of that, people like you were expelled.'

'Exactly. We had to conform or leave. My understanding from our trips to the capital is that over the last few years there has been a resurgence of interest in national Protocol government and that a delegation of Protocol fundamentalists from England is working with the President and his government to resurrect the concept.'

The boy was thoughtful. 'It strikes me that protocols and the enforcement of them do provide stability and longevity; but result in misery. Whereas here, where people become ill, die young, perish at sea, and are ruled by the vagaries of human beings, things can go badly wrong, but the people are happy.'

'I can see you as a future member of Council, Giles, my son,' said the professor as he smiled. 'I think that's enough for this evening.'

'Yes, I've an early tide to catch tomorrow, that is, if you want fish for your supper!' And the boy wandered back down the hill to his cottage.


But not all was happy in this little corner of Dalriada, the garden of Inverneuage. Some became envious of the boy's success and the green-eyed monster that is envy began to surface. The boy's good looks and intellect, along with his popularity marked him out in the small community and there were those who began to resent him.

'He doesn't have a religion,' whispered one young man to another.

'I think he's a spy, a Protocol fundamentalist, sent from the capital,' said the other.

'He's got a price on his head.'

'So have I.'

'Yes, but not for murder.'

'Has he murdered someone?'

'Apparently.'

'Gosh!'

'I was told he killed several people. There was a battle, down in England, and he killed a whole family.'

'Gosh!'

'So he escaped up here. He's an absconder and the death squad are after him.'

'Gosh!'

# NINE

It was with considerable pomp and ceremony that Doreese and her delegation were welcomed to Dalriada. The capital's station was decorated with bunting and as she stepped off the train a throng of press and public surged forward to catch a glimpse of the first English politician to visit Dalriada for over two decades. Waiting on the platform to welcome her, at the head of a small party of local grandees, was the President himself and as Doreese approached he bowed his head a trifle before shaking her hand enthusiastically.

'Minister, welcome to Dalriada,' he pronounced fulsomely, before turning to a tall, pretty young woman who was standing behind him. 'I would like you to meet my Junior Under-Secretary for Protocols, Miss Ruth. She'll be looking after you during your stay.' Doreese looked at the attractive, soberly dressed young woman who had stepped forward. Her thick chestnut hair tumbled heavily on to her shoulders and as Ruth moved forward to shake her hand the Minister registered her bright intelligent eyes and wholesome appearance.

'A pleasure to meet you, Minister. Welcome to Dalriada,' the young woman said warmly and without affectation.

Doreese smiled and shook her hand but there was something about the confidence, the ease, the artlessness of the girl that instantly made her feel uneasy. Somehow – in the time it took to shake her hand – the girl had effortlessly managed to establish her superiority – her position on the intellectual and moral high ground. In an inexplicable way Doreese felt belittled, somehow threatened and inferior. 'Thank you. It is indeed a pleasure to be here,' she replied with a fixed, sardonic smile on her face.

The party then proceeded along the platform towards the exit and Doreese, in a way that she she'd seen royalty do on old newsreel films, smiled and waved at the applauding throng which lined the route. Suddenly she wished she'd worn a hat and between waves she whispered to her aide, 'Roger, see if you can get me a hat, would you.

You know, something wide, maybe with feathers. That sort of thing.'

'Certainly, ma'am,' came his reply.

The first meeting of the delegation with the capital's cabinet was held the following morning. Roger had a slightly sore head, having inadvertently drunk too much of the national drink the previous evening at the welcome reception. His memory of that evening was rather vague but he was almost sure that he had propositioned Ruth, the pretty Junior Secretary and, so far as he could recall, he had been politely but firmly turned down. As he settled in his chair he glanced at the fresh-faced woman who was sitting opposite him next to the President. 'No hangover there,' he thought as he looked at the neat tidy hair and the bright intelligent face. As their eyes met, Ruth smiled, an open, engaging and confident smile.

The Dalriadan leader hit the table with his gavel. 'Ladies and gentlemen,' he began, 'I would like to welcome the Minister for Age Control and head of the Department of Intelligent Euthanasia to this Cabinet meeting of the Dalriadan government. She and her delegation are here to work with us with the object of expanding our existing protocols and introducing new ones. Members will be aware that, although we have introduced a number of these including the Health and Legal Protocols, their uptake has been only partial at best and they are by no means consistently adhered to across the whole of the country. Indeed, there are areas and communities which are beyond the reach of central government.' The President paused for breath. 'The Health Protocol has worked well here in the south-east but, as has been observed elsewhere, it has resulted in an age crisis. Here, as in England a few years ago, we have a non-viable population with an *average* age of nearly one hundred and twenty. The problem is that in those communities where protocols have *not* been introduced, although the people die at an acceptably young age, their behaviour tends to be unpredictable. As such they pose a security risk and are a threat to the rest of society. They are a lawless, unregulated bunch and this is clearly unacceptable. We therefore have a dilemma.' The leader stopped, looked at his guests and then turned to Ruth. 'I would like my Junior Secretary to fill in the background details before we open this up for debate.'

Ruth rose to her feet. 'Thank you, Mr President. I have been asked to present some historical data to inform our discussion.' Ruth spoke clearly and confidently. 'As our leader has said, in the regions where we have incorporated the English Health Protocol there are now ageing populations which are economically unsustainable, but where there are few, if any, health problems; the main issues being those of housing and nutrition. Conversely, there are many other areas across the country over which the government has little influence: where there are no protocols whatsoever and people are dying of curable diseases – illnesses which could, and *should*, have been wiped out years ago. There are so-called city-states where avoidable accidents are allowed to happen almost on a daily basis and even some where theism is still practised,' Ruth looked around the table before continuing. 'It is surprising that there hasn't been more civil unrest. My research would indicate that that a similar approach to that taken in England is the best way to manage this problem. The first element is to roll out the whole gamut of protocols widely across the country. They would be based on the English model but adjusted where necessary to suit the local population. The second element is to introduce an age-control policy of one sort or another. I personally find it morally difficult to justify the introduction of the English Euthanasia Protocol in its totality but we do need to have a debate about how best to manage this issue.' Ruth put her notes down, turned to her left and said, 'Thank you, President,' before resuming her seat.

Roger had been staring intently at Ruth during this speech. He hadn't registered a word of what she had been saying as he was still feeling decidedly queasy, but he had been mesmerised by her vivacity and beauty. As she finished he began to clap but stopped when no one joined in and dropped his gaze to the floor. Ruth looked at him, a slight smile playing upon her lips.

When the meeting broke up for lunch, Roger sought Ruth out. 'I say,' he began, 'that was a jolly good speech.'

'Thank you,' replied Ruth.

'Absolutely spot on. Hit the nail right on the head, I'd say.'

Ruth smiled at him and thought, he's a good-looking lad. Not too bright but well-educated. 'How are you feeling?' she said, 'You had quite a lot to drink last night,' she added with a chuckle.

'Not top-hole, to be honest. You see, we're not allowed to drink much back at home and I got a bit carried away. Hope I wasn't embarrassing or anything.' Roger smiled ruefully. 'To be honest I can't remember much about it.'

'No, not at all. Although you did ask your Minister to go to bed with you!'

Roger's jaw dropped and his eyes widened, 'Oh, no. *Please, no*! Tell me I didn't. Please tell me I didn't.'

Ruth smiled at his complete discomfiture and couldn't be cruel for any longer. 'No you didn't,' she laughed, 'I just made that up.'

'Oh, thank *god* for that.' Roger's whole demeanour relaxed.

'Here, come and have some lunch.'

On hearing this, Roger briefly hesitated and then without a word made a dash for the toilet. Ruth smiled to herself and joined a friend in the queue.

At the top table Doreese was sitting next to the President. 'Your Junior Advisor seems very knowledgeable but rather too independent in her thoughts for my liking. She's not a free-thinker is she? That would never do.'

'She's young, very bright, truly believes in the systematic management theory of government and is an enthusiastic supporter of protocols. Yes, is in a way she is a free-thinker but of course we are well behind you in England in that respect. Sadly, we still have people here who think for themselves: that's why we need help – urgently.' The leader smiled at Doreese then addressed his plate once more.

'Well, President, I must say I'm slightly concerned but if she's the best you've got I'll just have to work with her, I suppose.' Doreese had been disturbed and wrong-footed. In Ruth, she saw everything that she herself was not: intelligent, knowledgeable, thoughtful, innovative and, of course both confident and pretty. 'Roger!' she looked around the table for her aide then addressed the other member of her delegation on the opposite side of the table. 'Where's Roger?'

'I think he's a trifle unwell, ma'am. A touch of food poisoning I believe.'

'Well, when you see him ask him if he's got my hat yet.'

After three days of discussions between the delegation and the capital's government, a framework for collaboration was agreed. Crucially this included an age-limitation clause which would allow Doreese to reassure the P.M. that aid to Dalriada could continue, thus avoiding a major and potentially inflammatory international incident. That evening she summoned Mandy to her hotel.

Mandy had been informed that her presence would be required at some stage and so, after nearly three years of traversing the country in search of the boy as well as gathering information, she had returned to the capital.

Roger ushered Mandy into the spacious and elegant reception area of the Minister's suite. 'Mandy. So nice to see you. Gosh, you're no longer blonde,' said Doreese on first seeing her. 'Otherwise you haven't changed a bit.'

As Mandy advanced she couldn't help but notice the extraordinary artefact that sat on the Minister's head. Perched rather precariously there, squashing her coiffure, was an amazing construction resembling a large bird's nest with bits of twig and straw seemingly growing out of her head and what looked like a bunch of grapes dangling from one side. 'Minister,' she said and gave a little curtsey, barely able to take her eyes off the hat.

'No news of the brat, I suppose?' asked Doreese.

'No, none. But we'll get him eventually.'

'Never mind. That's not the main issue now, although I *would* like him caught. It would send out the right signals. Particularly now we're going to introduce the Euthanasia Protocol here.'

'Oh, good!'

Doreese was thoughtful for a moment before adding more quietly, 'Although not *everyone* has signed up to that yet. In fact, Mandy,' continued Doreese, once more at her strident best, 'apprehending the boy and subjecting him to the machinery of the Protocols would be a superb opportunity to promote the new policies. I think we should increase the reward for him. Just a thought.' The Minister gave Mandy a knowing look.

'Good idea, I'll do it straight away, Minister.'

'Now, Mandy, I have a key job for you. It won't be easy but the situation is that we have negotiated an agreement with the Dalriadan government to introduce the whole protocol programme, which as far as I'm concerned includes euthanasia, across the length and breadth of the country.' Doreese paused briefly. 'I want *you* to lead this project.'

'*Thank* you, Minister.' Mandy felt an inward glow. This was good news – better than she had dared hope for.

'I can't think of anyone better placed to do this. You know the industry inside out and have local knowledge. Will you accept this challenge?'

'Of course, Minister. Delighted.'

'Good. I'm pleased we're on friendly terms again after those problems of a few years ago. Now you can recruit your own staff. Probably best to do that from the local community I would think. Ostensibly you should report to the Junior Secretary for Political Organisation, or whatever she's called.' Doreese dropped her voice, 'but in actuality you will report directly to me. You will of course need to keep the Under-Secretary informed, but to be honest I don't trust her. She seems to me to be far too independent, a bit of a free-thinker.' The Minister hesitated for a moment, lost for words, 'You know – the kind of person we used to have in England until we got them under control – awkward and argumentative.'

'Ugh! I know the type.'

'A bit like the boy and the old man, in a way. Anyway, you'll need to keep her on side but I'd play your cards close to your chest if I were you. Maintain your distance.'

'Understood, Minister. What's her name?'

'She's a woman called Ruth.'

'Okay, Minister. Thank you for this opportunity.'

'Pleasure. We're off, back to England tomorrow.' They shook hands. 'By the way; d'you like my hat?'

'Very impressive, Minister.'

'Oh good! I think I'll wear it at cabinet next week.' She turned to her aide. 'Now, Roger, we've got packing to do.'

'Beg your pardon, Minister?' Roger, having celebrated the success of the mission with a few glasses of the national drink earlier on that evening, had been concentrating on the Euthanasia Monitor's rather trim figure and had not kept up with the conversation.

'I said, Roger, that we've got our packing to do.'

'Oh yes, of course, Minister.'

'*Do* concentrate, Roger.'

Mandy was delighted. Not in her wildest dreams had she thought that she would be charged with managing a national programme. With even just a modest degree of success this would rehabilitate her into the service and ultimately, who knows, perhaps lead to a senior post in the department. Doreese seemed to have forgiven her for the debacle surrounding the old man's death and the boy's escape. Mandy had made many contacts during her time in Dalriada and now she would activate this network to introduce the national protocols. It would take a few years but she would hit some soft targets first. She had fostered contacts in a number of small communities with an elderly population, where there was discontent and a dysfunctional local government. With some judicious bribery she could introduce the protocols with little resistance. Her priority, however, was to find the boy. There was always the danger that he might become something of a national celebrity, which could make him dangerous. While he was at still at large, the system that Mandy represented lacked credibility. After his disappearance rumours had abounded about his whereabouts and stories of his escapades were beginning to acquire legendary status. If she could arrest him and put him on trial, with some imaginative publicity, it would be an excellent start to the programme while enhancing her authority both in Dalriada and England. 'Everyone has their price,' she thought, 'I just need to put a big enough price on his head and someone will hand him over.' She called her minder, who was in the adjacent room, 'Mister Enforcer.'

'Yes, miss?'

'I think we should put a price on the boy's head of half a million.'

The Enforcer gasped, 'But that's… '

'Shut up. *I* do the thinking, and *you* do my bidding,' she snapped, then added more quietly, 'Yes. That'll get him, the little brat.'

'Yes, miss.'

'Tomorrow I want you to put out an all-station emergency statement. Make sure it reaches every corner, every nook and cranny, every crevice of this lousy country. Say that the boy is violent and considered to be a major risk to the public; that it is essential he be apprehended and that the reward for his capture has accordingly been increased. Give your contact details and don't inform that secretary here. I want to sort this out and hand that Ruth woman a *fait accompli.*'

'Yes, miss.'

* * *

'Giles, sit down, would you.'

'Thank you, chief.'

'I thought I'd better get you along for a chat.'

The young man and the chief, as Giles liked to call him, had got on well over the years and the clan leader had watched the boy grow and mature with the pride and pleasure akin to that of father and son.

'Giles, I have some worrying news which I thought I should share with you.' The young man raised his eyebrows. His tanned face was framed by wild, bleached hair which fell to the collar of his wide-sleeved, coarse cotton shirt. He had only just returned from a fishing trip and was wearing the shorts and sandals which he customarily used for sailing. 'I have learned that some weeks ago there was an all-station warning regarding you, stating that you are dangerous and that the reward for your capture has been increased to half a million.'

'Crikey!' said Giles, 'I'd hand *myself* in for that.'

'Sadly, Giles, this is no joking matter. I had thought that the hullabaloo around your escape had settled down and I don't understand why this has happened now. But it's a real threat to you. For a reward like this it's highly likely that someone will betray you.'

'What d'you think we should do?'

'Well, Giles, it's your decision. I'm saddened by this because you've been a great asset, bringing humour, intellect, honour and good nature, not to mention fish, to our community. I personally see you as a potential future chief, but I'm truly concerned. If you're arrested, anything could happen. I was speaking to Robert,' and the chief referred to the senior lawyer from England who had settled in Inverneuage a decade before, 'and he couldn't predict what the outcome of any trial might be. He's kept up to date with the English legal protocol and ran a simulation of your situation on his computer. If commonsense prevailed you should be reprimanded for taking the post-mortem payment and sent on your way, but as we well know, commonsense *doesn't* always prevail and the protocol model he ran made the decision that the old man's euthanasia should be completed.'

'But that's ridiculous. They can't kill the old man. He's been dead nearly four years.'

'True. But they can kill *you*!' The chief paused for a moment before continuing, 'We have to realise the vindictiveness of this woman, Mandy. For her, it seems nothing could be too severe a punishment for you. And of course she has raised this ridiculous charge of attempted murder. All in all, I am very concerned that this could go horribly wrong for you. It is clear that the legal protocol would find you guilty, although one would expect an appeal to be allowed. That then brings us to the vagaries of the euthanasia tribunal.' The Chief looked Giles directly in the eye. 'It's all very messy.'

Giles was silent and thoughtful for a while. He stared at the ground, his broad hands clasped in his lap. 'There seem to be three options,' he said, looking up, his clear blue eyes intent on the chief. 'The first is to carry on here as normal in the hope that no one will turn me in, though I would be inclined to agree with you, that the money will be far too tempting and it's highly likely that I will be betrayed. The second is to hand myself in to avoid any adverse effect on our community. Once in custody I would be found guilty and would receive a sentence that could range from a slap on the wrist to execution.' The chief winced at the old fashioned term and the boy noticed his expression. 'Yes, not a nice word but appropriate, I think. The third option is for me to go on the run to protect myself and this society which I have grown to love.' Giles stopped and sat back. 'Have I missed anything, Chief?'

'Sadly, no. As always an excellent summary of the situation, Giles.'

'You're the chief,' continued the boy, '*You* tell me what you want me to do. As leader, it's your responsibility to recommend what's best for the community at large, not simply for me. I'll do whatever you instruct, chief. If you tell me to, I'll hand myself in today.'

'I know you would. You're well liked here and most would never dream of betraying you but I'm concerned that there are some factions who have been put out by your popularity and success. Ted tells me that there is also some evidence that protocolism is gaining support in our community and that's a worry.' The chief sighed, 'I need help with this. I shall discuss it with the council as soon as possible. Can you come back at the end of the week, Giles?'

'Of course, chief. Thank you.' The young man rose to leave.

'Giles,' said the chief, 'you're a fine young man. This whole situation pains me. You understand that, don't you?'

'Yes, chief. I understand.'

# TEN

'We have a response! *We have a response.*' Mandy almost screamed with excitement. 'Mister Enforcer, I told you that for enough money someone would betray him.'

Mandy and her companion had remained in the capital to set up the networks that were needed to introduce the web of studios and personnel required for the introduction of protocol-based government. That morning she had received a communication informing her that the boy was residing in a place called Inverneuage. 'Get the map,' she shouted at her minder.

'Yes, Miss.'

The Enforcer spread a tattered map of the country on the table and after a while they identified the village where the boy had been reported. Mandy was puzzled. 'That's not far from the loch where he tried to kill us.' She looked at her companion. 'Why didn't you search there?'

'It's bandit territory, Ma'am. The local police wouldn't pursue him; if you remember.'

Mandy looked at the Enforcer, spite in her eyes. 'For years we've been searching for him and here he is, just a few miles from where we last saw him.' Her voice rose. 'You idiot! You imbecile!'

'Sorry, Miss.'

'Well, we've got him now.' Mandy's voice softened. 'What we need is a trap to entice him out of the village so that the police or soldiers, or whatever they're called up here, can apprehend him without starting a war. *You*, Mister Enforcer, are going to set this up but you must do exactly as I say. I want to be here to welcome him back to civilisation – if you can call this place civilised – and to justice.' She paused for a moment. 'What was the name of that girl who was on the beach when he tried to murder us?'

'Ruth, Miss.'

'Yes, that's it. Ruth.' Mandy was silent for a moment, a puzzled expression on her face. 'That's strange,' she said quietly to herself. 'Not a common name either.'

'Pardon, Miss?'

'Oh, nothing. Nothing.' She turned her attention back to the minder, 'Go to this Inver… whatsit place with as many policemen as you can muster and set up an ambush. Send the boy a message that this Ruth woman wants to meet him. If he doesn't fall for that, then you and your men are entitled to go into the town and arrest him, using whatever force is necessary. D'you understand?'

'Yes, Miss.'

'Once you've got him, let me know and I'll arrange a reception committee for him here.'

It was to be the best part of a week before the crude trap could be sprung, but sprung it was and as the arresting party waited, hidden in a small copse, the Enforcer instantly recognised the boy as he appeared on the path below, striding masterfully up the hill directly into the ambush. 'How he's changed,' he thought, as he registered the tall, muscular young man: tanned and athletic with long, tousled fair hair. The Enforcer was surprised that Giles had been deceived, but when the soldiers stepped out and he showed no sign of surprise the Enforcer realised that the young man had known all along that he'd been betrayed. 'I wonder why he deliberately walked into this paltry trap,' asked the Enforcer of himself.

When Giles received a note purporting to be from Ruth requesting a meeting at a location just outside the city he was fairly sure that it was a trap. He considered that it was just possible that Ruth did want to meet him but he hadn't heard from her since he had sailed away that stormy evening and all his instincts told him that this was an ambush: that he had been betrayed. However, he decided to attend this tryst. His logic was that if it were a trap and he didn't go, that might result in an attack on the village. Such an action could quite possibly escalate into violence as he knew many in the village would not allow him to be arrested without a fight. If his suspicions proved unjustified and Ruth was waiting for him then he would be pleasantly surprised.

But a trap it was. As he left the village and climbed out of the valley to the designated meeting-place, four soldiers came out of the trees, their rifles levelled at his chest. For a moment the boy thought he might be shot. He raised his arms high.

From behind the armed men came a senior officer who simply looked at the boy and asked. 'Is this him?'

The boy then noticed two further men, one of whom was the Enforcer, short and fat, who merely said, 'Yes, sir.' The second; also short, but scrawny with a thin face and sunken cheeks, was a man he recognised as being from the village. 'Yes. That's him,' said the betrayer, without raising his gaze from the ground.

'Thank you, gentlemen.' The officer then addressed the boy. 'You, sir, are under arrest for crimes against the English Life Protocols, most particularly the Euthanasia Protocol. You are also charged with a number of other crimes perpetrated on Dalriadan soil, as yet to be defined but which will be explained to you on arrival in the capital.'

And so the boy was handcuffed and the little group marched nearly twenty miles to where a truck was waiting to take them to the capital.

Back in the Capital, Mandy could barely wait to parade her prize before the irritating Junior Secretary who had already started to make life difficult for her. Instead of supporting Mandy in her endeavours, Ruth had raised all manner of concerns about her plans for a network of Euthanasia Studios. This raw, young civil servant was demanding a host of checks and internal controls that were wholly unnecessary. Doreese had been correct – she was far too much of a free-thinker. She seemed to imagine that that the policy of voluntary euthanasia was still up for debate and in the event that it was introduced should only apply to those over a certain age and *then* be subject to the clients full consent. She simply didn't understand that folk of that age could not be allowed to make decisions of such importance for themselves and that the State needed to act on their behalf. Ruth had suggested that the financial agreement amounted to coercion and if there was to be any monetary gain it should all be paid pre-mortem. 'What sort of an incentive was that? That woman, Ruth, had no idea. She was too big for her boots by a long shot,' thought Mandy. Never mind, this success would give her an immense amount of kudos in Dalriada *and* back at home. As had been agreed, she informed the English Minister first and then composed a communication to the Junior Secretary:

*Dear Ruth,*

*I'm sure you will be as pleased as I am to confirm that joint forces from Dalriada and England have apprehended the dangerous escaped criminal called Giles. He is wanted in England for crimes against the Euthanasia Protocol and here for attempted murder.*

*He is currently being brought, under guard, to the capital and I wonder if you would like to share in celebrating his capture and join our welcoming party. I'm sure it would be beneficial to our joint initiative if this event were given maximum media coverage and I am therefore arranging an all channel statement.*

*Yours sincerely,*

*English Protocol Adviser for Dalriada.*

'That will shock her,' thought Mandy who, after savouring the moment, pressed the send button on her computer.

Ruth was becoming ever more confused and disillusioned. Her remit *had* been clear: she was to advise on the introduction of protocolised government across the whole of Dalriada. She understood that the country needed to be governed centrally and this required rules and structures which could be enshrined in protocols. Ruth also realised that increasing longevity was a problem which needed to be managed sensitively and selective euthanasia, in exceptional cases and with the individual's agreement, *might* therefore be necessary. But here was this woman from England who seemed to imagine she had *carte blanche* to introduce the English system throughout the country without recourse to, let alone any discussion with her. They had never met and Mandy always referred to herself as 'The Protocol Adviser for Dalriada.' Now in front of her, on her screen was Mandy's letter. This was news to her. She had not been informed that the adviser had been going after a criminal called Giles and she herself had no prior knowledge of his existence.

Ruth felt out of her depth and was suspicious of Mandy's proposal for a reception to welcome a captured criminal. It seemed hardly appropriate to greet a prisoner in this way so she decided to seek advice from the President. However, after several failed attempts to obtain an audience she felt that she had no choice but to attend the reception and so three days later she prepared herself for this bizarre event.

The press briefing was to be held in the Old Palace and Mandy stage-managed the whole event down to the smallest detail. On the evening in question she dressed carefully, as she had done when she had been a Euthanasia Practitioner. 'Appearance is important,' she thought to herself as she applied her makeup and dressed her hair. Pleased with the result, she then made her way to the large reception room where the event was to be held. There she checked the sound systems, welcomed the media and, as the door opened glanced up expecting her first sight of the boy for nearly four years. Suddenly she froze, stunned by what she saw. Heading towards her was a statuesque, handsome young woman wearing little make up and dressed simply. Then, with just a few feet separating them, they stared at one another, neither believing what they were seeing.

'Ruth?' asked Mandy.

'Yes,' the young woman replied, puzzled. 'Are you the Protocol Adviser?'

'I am.'

Ruth peered at Mandy for a moment, a thoughtful expression on her face. Then, suddenly her face lit up with understanding. 'I recognise you.' She looked at Mandy intently. 'You're the Euthanasia Monitor from England. You're... ' Ruth hesitated trying to recall the name... '*Mandy.*'

'I am indeed.' Mandy was annoyed that she had never considered that this Junior Under Secretary was the same girl who had helped the boy escape from the banks of the loch that stormy night. But then they had never met and, as Doreese had advised, she had kept communication to the barest minimum always using an intermediary; and she'd never used her own name, simply signing missives with her title.

For a few seconds they simply stared at each other, both of them trying desperately to come to terms with the significance of what was happening, before the media, as one, turned their attention to the doorway and camera shutters began clicking as they caught their first glimpse of the arresting party and their prisoner. Flanked by four armed soldiers and firmly handcuffed to the overweight, balding

178

Enforcer was a relaxed-looking, tall, handsome young man.

As they advanced into the room, for the second time in five minutes Ruth could not believe what she was seeing. This Giles, this violent escaped criminal, was *the boy*: her childhood friend whose last words, barely audible above the noise of the storm had been, 'I love you.' She remembered shouting the same words back, aware that he would not hear them above the din of the wind. That had been four years ago, but there could be no doubting that this was him. It was not so much his appearance, which time had altered, but more his demeanour. On his face remained a trace of that cheeky grin which she had recalled so often over the years since she last saw him.

Mandy was also staring at the boy, a self-satisfied smile on her face. She strolled forward and stood directly in front of him.

'Hello, *Giles*,' she said silkily, 'you've grown.'

'Ah, Mandy,' replied the boy in a rich baritone. 'I thought you must be behind this particular piece of nonsense. You've not learned anything, have you?'

Mandy's smile evaporated and her face became suffused with anger on hearing this. How dare this boy behave in such a superior fashion when this was *her* triumph. *She* was the victor; the boy was beaten and outwitted. He should be cowering and begging for mercy, not lecturing her on morals, the little brat. 'That's what you think, do you, *boy*? Well, you are going to pay for what you've done to me.'

'It saddens me to see your vindictiveness. It's an ugly emotion, Mandy.' This statement, delivered in calm and measured tones, infuriated Mandy even further. Suddenly her anger boiled over and all the frustrations of the past four years exploded. She stood on tiptoes and slapped the boy's face as hard as she could.

Ruth had hung back during this interchange, trying to order her thoughts. She had been expecting someone called Giles, a dangerous criminal. Gradually the pieces of this jigsaw began to fit. After the boy's escape, Mandy must have stayed in the country and now she was the authority behind the introduction of Protocols. *She* was the nameless English Protocol Adviser. Now she realised that the crimes that the boy was accused of made sense, even the so-called attempted murder that had annoyed her father so much. She advanced slowly towards the young man and as their eyes met she said quietly, 'Boy?'

'Ruth?'

After the instant of recognition, Ruth advanced, gently nudged one of the guards aside and put her arms around the boy who hugged her with his one un-manacled hand. This awkward embrace complete, they separated and she smiled at him. The media were now going wild. Not only had the Protocol Advisor to Dalriada, a Euthanasia Monitor no less, slapped her prisoner, but now a junior government official was embracing the criminal as though they were long-lost friends.

'I presume you're not responsible for this reception, Ruth.'

'This is the first I was aware that you'd been arrested, boy.' Ruth hesitated, 'Sorry – Giles. It'll take me a while to get used to calling you by your new name.'

'Boy's fine by me, Ruth.' He smiled and rubbed his cheek. 'She's got quite a right hook,' he said glancing at Mandy.

'And quite a vicious tongue.'

'Okay, sir. It's time to take you down.' The Enforcer gave a gentle tug on his manacle and the armed guard turned and began to usher the boy through the entrance.

'You're in trouble, Giles. I'll do all I can.'

'Thanks, Ruth.' Then he repeated his farewell from four years before, 'Love you,' he said as he raised his eyebrows while the cheeky grin once more spread across his face.

Ruth flushed with pleasure, 'Me too,' was all she could think of to say as the tall figure of the boy was escorted from the building.

Once her fury had settled, Mandy began to smile to herself. 'Things could not have worked out better,' she thought. 'I can now destroy both of these little brats at the same time.' She called the room to order. 'Thank you, ladies and gentlemen.' She paused for a moment until the hubbub had settled, 'The criminal called Giles will now be held in secure accommodation overnight and the legal enforcement protocol will decide on his case tomorrow. You will all be most welcome to attend the hearing tomorrow morning at ten o'clock.' Then without a backward glance, Mandy pushed her way through the buzzing throng of journalists to the door.

# ELEVEN

By the following day the reception room of the old palace had been transformed into a temporary courtroom. A platform had been raised along one side of the room, at the end of which now stood a dock and about two hundred chairs arranged in rows, facing the magisterial bench.

When the doors to the courtroom opened at nine that morning there were already over a hundred people awaiting entry. The press coverage of the boy's arrest, and the reporting of Mandy's and Ruth's very different responses to the boy's arrival the previous day, had ensured that press and public were jostling for seats for what was likely to be the most interesting public event in the capital for decades.

By five minutes to ten, when the boy arrived, the room was packed and those who couldn't find a seat were standing several rows deep around the periphery of the room. As an official representative of the government, Ruth had a front-row seat and alongside her was the chief legal adviser for Dalriada. 'What's the remit and authority of this court?' Ruth had asked him when he'd arrived.

'God knows. Everyone is completely confused by the process,' the legal eagle admitted. 'That Mandy woman has taken over the whole proceedings on the basis that the primary crime occurred in England and she is therefore using the English legal protocol. However, she is of course on foreign soil so I suppose we could challenge her authority.'

'Surely whatever happens the case will have to go to tribunal.'

'Only if there is an appeal.'

Just then there was a commotion as the boy entered, manacled to one of the four guards. The boy looked bright and relaxed as he was escorted to the dock where, still wearing handcuffs, he sat down to await the start of proceedings. Suddenly the doors at the opposite end of the long room were thrown open, and through the grand main entrance there emerged a small procession. Leading was the stout Enforcer who carried a red velvet cushion with tassels on each corner on which was placed a computer. It was the size of a small briefcase and was coloured black. As he entered the room, the Enforcer announced loudly: 'Please be upstanding for the Protocol Adviser and Euthanasia Monitor for Dalriada.'

Behind him walked Mandy. She was wearing a gown reminiscent of those worn by academics in past times. Behind here marched four policemen in their full dress uniforms walking two abreast.

'I don't believe it. What a pompous ass,' whispered Ruth.

'I agree, but in England this process is commonplace for serious crimes,' responded the legal adviser.

'But she's got no authority here. Who said she was the Monitor for Dalriada?'

'She did.'

'You can't just go around giving yourself titles like that.'

'Apparently our President agreed.'

'Late in the evening, was it?'

'I expect so.'

Ruth simply nodded her head.

With great ceremony the Enforcer then laid the computer on the makeshift bench and plugged it in, while Mandy seated herself ostentatiously behind it. The policemen then took up their positions on either side of her.

'You may be seated,' stated the Enforcer, who seemed to have taken on the rôle of master of ceremonies.

After the clatter of scraping seats had died down, Mandy opened the hearing with great *gravitas*. 'Good morning, ladies and gentlemen. We are gathered here today to hear the Protocol pronounce on the crimes of Giles, previously known as "the boy". With the authority invested in me by the Prime Minister of England, as head of the Dalriadan Department of Intelligent Euthanasia and as Protocol Adviser and Euthanasia Monitor, I hereby open these proceedings.' Mandy looked around the room and then respectfully intoned the words: 'Bless the protocol. May we serve it well.'

There arose a murmur around the room as those in the know repeated the mantra, 'Bless the Protocol. May we serve it well,' while others simply muttered, 'Bless the Protocol.' One old man, confused by the process, simply said, 'Amen,' and then coughed loudly to disguise his error as those seated nearby looked at him in dismay.

Mandy then continued, 'Mister Enforcer, please read out the charges.'

Ruth knew that none of this was necessary as proceedings such as these were normally enacted in legal studios where the data were entered, the programme run and the sentence pronounced, all within the space of a few minutes; but Mandy wanted to maximize the theatricality of the moment and her minder duly read out the list of alleged crimes, including theft of government money in the form of a post-mortem payment, theft of a boat, attempted murder by the use of said boat in an aggressive fashion likely to endanger life and lastly: escaping from police custody. As each of the offences was read out she entered the data into the computer on the bench in front of her. There was a large image of the computer screen projected on to the wall behind her so that all those in the room could view the proceedings as they unfolded.

Mandy was in her element. It was what she had been trained for; what she was good at: entering data and then implementing what the computer told her to do.

Once the coding and data entry were complete, she pressed the key marked VERDICT. An alert sign came up on the screen, followed by the message VERDICT REACHED.

Mandy very deliberately pressed another key on the console in front of her. There was a pause before the single word GUILTY appeared in large letters. A gasp went round the room and there was a ripple of applause.

'No surprise there then,' whispered Ruth to her companion.

Mandy smiled. 'Thank you,' she said, looking at the computer. 'Now for sentencing.' Mandy manipulated the mouse and moved into the sentencing programme. Then, once more, with a flourish she pressed a key, this time the one marked SENTENCE.

Now the on-screen alert sign read: SENTENCING PROGRAMME RUNNING. After some ten seconds, the screen became red in its display and the message now read, EUTHANASIA COMPLETION. Mandy could not disguise her pleasure, for this could not have gone better, she felt. With a broad smile on her face she turned her attention to the dock. 'Giles, do you have anything to say?'

The boy stood up, shaking his head slowly in disbelief. After a moment he looked directly at Mandy and said calmly and slowly, 'I do not recognise the authority of this court. I do not recognise the findings of the computer nor its sentencing. In fact I do not recognise a computer as a legitimate tool to pronounce on anything that requires even a modicum of intelligence.' A sharp in-drawing of breath and gasps of disbelief could be heard in the room. Surely the boy had gone *too* far.

'So you do not recognise the Protocol as enshrining the rules, the very structure of our society?'

'Not at all. The Protocol is an ass.' Another gasp and some muttering could be heard.

'Do you accept the judgement?'

'No! I most certainly do not. I wish to appeal.'

Mandy had a sense of *déjà vu*. 'On what basis?' she asked.

The boy thought for a moment. 'On the basis that these allegations are unproven.'

'But you have seen for yourself the computer's decision based on the evidence available.'

'I have seen *no* evidence to support *any* allegation,' riposted the boy.

'Its all in the *computer*.' Mandy's voice rose in frustration. Didn't he realise that the computer had pronounced and that meant it was true? 'You saw me enter the data yourself. The whole room saw it. How can you argue with that?'

'I don't care what the computer says. It's an ass. And you're an idiot for not realising it.'

'That's blasphemy. You must retract that statement at once.'

'Don't you realise you cannot blaspheme against a computer or a Protocol, any more than you can blaspheme against a teapot? You're behaving like some sort of theist, as though that useless piece of junk is a God, something sacred. Don't you realise how stupid that is?' More gasps came from around the courtroom. This was indeed a vicious exchange; the boy was well out of order.

'I will ask you again. Do you accept this judgement?'

'And I will answer again. *No!*'

'But you can't challenge the Protocol.'

'Then why are you asking me?'

'Ugh!' Mandy was losing her patience. The boy just did not understand. He was deliberately being awkward but somehow he seemed to have gained the upper hand in this interchange and once more appeared to be laughing at her and making her look stupid.

In the brief silence that followed, Ruth rose to her feet. 'Monitor,' she said, addressing Mandy. 'I would agree that the allegations are unproven. For example, the charge of attempted murder is quite unsubstantiated. In fact I was witness to the event and there was never any attempt to cause injury, let alone loss of life.' Ruth sat down.

Mandy smiled inwardly. 'Got you!' she thought, before replying, 'Junior Secretary, firstly, may I remind you that are here as a government representative and that you have no official standing in this courtroom other than that of an observer; and secondly that you yourself were involved in the incident that helped the boy escape. Therefore you are scarcely unbiased and charges will be brought against *you* for aiding and abetting a wanted criminal.'

Ruth was outraged by this arrogant reply but realised the difficult position in which she was now placed. 'I refute those allegations absolutely, Monitor,' was all she said.

Mandy turned once more to the boy. 'For a final time, do you accept this judgement.'

'And for a final time, *no*! *And* I wish to appeal,' replied the boy.

Mandy was furious She didn't even bother to respond but simply rose and stormed out of the courtroom, leaving the Enforcer to conclude proceedings. Surprisingly confident, he stepped forward. 'Ladies and gentlemen,' he began, 'these preliminary proceedings are concluded and the Protocols verdict and sentence have been challenged by the defendant. This case will therefore be referred to tribunal.' This said, the Enforcer followed Mandy out of the room and noisy chatter broke out as press and public conferred.

Giles was led away before Ruth could reach the dock, but their eyes briefly met, and Ruth saw the defiance in his eyes soften into a cheeky smile as he was led away.

The next day Ruth was summoned to an audience with the President. As she entered his office she noticed that he looked tired and drawn, as though he hadn't had much sleep. He waved her to a chair on the opposite side of his desk and then, focusing his slightly reddened eyes on Ruth said angrily, 'Ruth, what on earth did you think you were doing. I'm beginning to think that the English Minister was right, that you're a radical: a free-thinker. You've totally lost control. What *on earth* did you think you were doing?'

Ruth had been expecting some feedback concerning the events of the last few days, and indeed was hoping for some support from her leader, so this extraordinary, wanton criticism came as a total surprise, a thunderbolt out of the blue. She was puzzled, amazed at how the interview had opened. 'How do you mean, President?' was all she could say.

'Have you no insight? Don't you realise what you've done?'

'No, Leader. I presume you're referring to events surrounding the débacle that was called a trial by that idiot from England, Mandy.' As soon as she'd said this, Ruth was annoyed with herself. She was generally restrained in her comments but the frustrations of trying to work with a woman who had stopped thinking many years ago had now got the better of her. 'Sorry, Leader. I didn't mean to be rude but the so-called trial was just a sham, a showcase.'

'It conformed to the Protocol legislation and as such was completely legitimate; consequently its findings have to be respected.'

'But it's a piece of nonsense!'

'You mustn't say that. The Protocol has evolved over many decades, it has a mind of its own and... ' the leader paused, then quietly added '... it's wise.'

'No it's not. It's just a piece of hardware, like a radio or a vacuum cleaner. It's no wiser than a *kettle*. To give it extraordinary powers is ridiculous. It does not possess supernatural powers.' Ruth's voice had risen in anger, 'We must challenge this piece of nonsense.'

The leader sighed and changed tack. 'I have had a formal complaint about your behaviour from the Monitor.'

'Oh, I see.'

'She said that you harboured a known criminal, were party to the attempted murder of her and the Enforcer, then aided and abetted the boy's escape.'

'What absolute rubbish.' The leader looked at Ruth enquiringly, so she continued, 'Certainly, when the boy arrived in our village my father and I made friends with him. At that time he was accompanied by an old man who was fighting a Euthanasia order. When the old man died, the boy returned and we went to school together. Then Mandy and her puppet arrived to arrest him and he escaped. That's all there is to it.'

'That's not what she says.'

'Who are you going to believe? An idiotic, unthinking, vindictive witch – or *me*?'

'She is an extremely powerful woman.'

'No she's not. She's just given herself some airs and graces and a few titles to which she has no right.' Ruth looked directly at the leader. 'How on earth did she get appointed to be Monitor for Dalriada?' she asked.

The leader looked uncomfortable, 'It was a request from the P.M. in England, I seem to remember,' he replied somewhat evasively.

'So, did you agree?'

'I had to.'

'*Why*?'

'Look, Ruth, I don't have to answer your questions. The fact is, you are in trouble and the accusations come right from the top.'

'So, what are those accusations?'

'As I've said, they relate to aiding and abetting the boy's crimes.'

'But that's nonsense. I was there when the alleged attempt at murder was committed. It's a complete fabrication.'

'That's not what the computer says.'

'*What*!' Ruth was stunned. 'What d'you mean, the computer? *What* computer?'

'You've been found guilty. The Monitor has entered all the data: the events of the night in question along with all the relevant background information; and the computer has given a verdict of guilty.'

'But I haven't even been charged.'

'You don't have to be.'

'But that means I've been found guilty before I knew I'd been charged. That's outrageous.'

'It's the new system. Mandy said you were behaving in a rather reactionary fashion, and I can now begin to appreciate why.'

'Leader, you can't support this.'

'Ruth, I have no choice. The Protocol has pronounced.'

'But it's a piece of hardware!' She searched for words adequate to express her feelings and could only think of the boy's outburst, 'The Protocol's an ass.'

'Careful, Ruth you're not doing yourself any favours.'

Ruth regained her composure, 'How has this women suddenly gained so much power?' she asked.

'That's none of your business. Now you had better leave, I've got a migraine coming on. I have given my guarantee that you will not try to escape while awaiting your hearing. Do you agree to that?' Ruth just nodded her head in disbelief while the leader continued. 'You realise that this has reflected very badly on me. A member of my department, consorting with the enemy as it were. It puts the whole programme at risk.'

'What programme?'

He hesitated, 'Oh, I don't know – the usual stuff.'

Ruth was becoming angry with the leader's evasiveness. 'What usual stuff?'

'Oh – aid. That sort of thing.'

Suddenly Ruth understood. 'So that's it,' she thought. 'Why on earth didn't I think of that before. It's all about the aid programme. About money.'

She had made enquiries about this financial aid in the past on many occasions when trying to obtain grants for her own projects but no one had ever acknowledged that they knew anything about it. The fund-holder was the President and its distribution was solely within his gift.

'Yes, Leader, I promise I'll not try to escape but I'm bitterly disappointed by your lack of support, indeed by your total lack of insight into what's happening in your country.'

'That's enough. Now I'm off to lie down for a while. The boy's tribunal will be held here in the capital and the Minister is coming up from England to preside. I have taken the liberty of putting in an appeal on your behalf, although I must say I'm beginning to wonder why. Anyway, Mandy has accepted it.' Ruth simply looked at the leader in disbelief. 'We might as well hold them both at the same time. Cheaper that way.'

The President then rose, groaned quietly and left his office, leaving Ruth stunned and uncomprehending. As he left, a policeman entered. 'Miss Ruth,' he said, 'I've been instructed to apply a tracer.' Ruth looked up at the man, questioning, 'Just so we know where you are, Miss.'

Wearily Ruth offered up her arm for the device to be attached.

* * *

Having had been escorted out of the courtroom, Giles was taken to what was to be his prison for the next five days. Only one tower of what was once a magnificent palace remained and it was in a small room half-way up that he was incarcerated. The boy recognised the architecture to be ancient and the building material as stone, the walls being about two foot thick. He surveyed his cell for any possible means of escape. There was one small window which, like in the fish smoker in Inverneuage, was barred on the outside and he calculated that his cell was located nearly a hundred feet above ground level. Within the semi-circular room was a small bed, a single chair and a bucket for toiletry purposes. 'These facilities are not as good as my last prison,' Giles thought to himself as he lay on the bed and stared at the ceiling.

In the middle of the afternoon there came the rattle of keys. The door opened and the Enforcer entered carrying a briefcase. 'Hello, Giles,' he said brightly, as the door was closed and locked behind him.

The boy raised himself to sit on the edge of his bed. 'Hello. You're Mandy's sidekick, aren't you?'

'I'm a Euthanasia Enforcer. I work for the Department of Intelligent Euthanasia in England.'

'Then maybe you can you tell me what on earth is going on here?' asked the boy.

'Well your request for a tribunal hearing has been accepted and it is to be in five days' time.'

'That's quick.'

'We do like to get things done as efficiently as possible,' the Enforcer said, placing his case on the table.

'But that doesn't give me enough time to instruct a lawyer.'

'What d'you mean – a lawyer?' The Enforcer looked puzzled.

'The lawyer who will be defending me against these ridiculous accusations.'

The Enforcer looked incredulous. 'Are you suggesting that the computer might be wrong?'

'No, the computation won't be wrong, but the data that it has processed most certainly is, as is the protocol it follows.'

There was an expression of non-comprehension on the Enforcer's face as though the boy had been speaking in an alien tongue. 'That's impossible.' He frowned as though the boy was a dim schoolchild. 'Anyway, I've been instructed to inform you that there is a defence programme that you may wish to avail yourself of.' He opened his briefcase and began to extract a small computer.

'Oh, good!'

'I've brought it along.' The Enforcer then placed the computer on the table opened the lid and pressed a few buttons. After a moment he smiled and turned the screen to face the boy. 'There you are. I think you'll find *this* is your lawyer.'

The boy peered at the screen where written in large letters were the words, DEFENCE PROGRAMME.

'Don't I get access to a real lawyer? You know, one who can walk and talk.' The boy pretended to search his mind for the correct terminology, 'Yes – that's it! It's called a human being.'

'*This* is your lawyer. I suggest you access the defence programme. You fill in these little boxes here. Look, it's quite simple.' The enforcer demonstrated how to use the cursor. 'And then these new data are fed into the legal protocol – which of course includes the prosecution programme and the computer does the rest. Hey presto – and Bob's your uncle.' The Enforcer looked at the boy triumphantly.

'You seem quite jovial today,' said the boy.

'Well, Giles, to be honest, I'll be pleased to see the end of this saga. I've been stuck with Mandy now for over four years and it's not been easy.' The Enforcer looked tired and worn-out so that the boy began to feel some pity for this unfortunate who had been defeated by the system, a system where Mandy was in charge.

'What happens if the verdict is upheld and I'm found guilty?'

'Well, then the sentence will be reviewed in the light of your defence data.'

'What if that is unchanged as well?'

'What? The sentence of Euthanasia Completion.' The Enforcer looked at the boy, 'You *know* what that means!'

'It's the death penalty.'

'No, no, no. *No.*' The Enforcer looked horrified. 'It's quite different. That was banned years ago. Things were so backward in those days, so uncivilised. This is a life-completion process, not a... ' and he hesitated '... a death penalty. *Wholly* different. No comparison.'

'It's *exactly* the same, it's *execution.*'

'Shush. You mustn't say that. The computer's running.'

'I don't care if the bloody computer's running, it's execution.'

The Enforcer tenderly closed the lid of the computer as though it might be offended by the conversation.

'You really are making it difficult for yourself, you know.'

'But I'm fighting a bloody machine.' The boy made a half-hearted grab at the computer but the Enforcer, who was closer, seized the machine and placed it carefully under his jacket.

The boy settled back on the side of his bed. 'Sorry,' he sighed. 'It's not your fault. Mustn't shoot the messenger.'

The Enforcer relaxed, sat down again and replaced the machine on the table. 'When you're found guilty... ' and hearing this the boy shook his head with resignation '... you'll have the choice of going back to Nowton or staying here for your Event.'

'And do I get to choose the pathway?'

'Of course. You can have any one you want.'

'Including having sex with a donkey on the top of the Eiffel Tower?' The boy smiled grimly.

The Enforcer looked bemused, then recalled that in a loose moment Mandy had told him the story of the old man and his bizarre request for his Final Event. After a moment he chuckled at the recollection. 'That must have really confused Mandy,' he said. 'She doesn't have a sense of humour; it was surgically excised at birth.' He looked at the boy, who was also smiling, and they laughed together at Mandy's expense. 'No! We still don't have that particular pathway, I'm afraid.' The Enforcer paused and thought for a moment. 'You know, Giles, I really would like to help you.' He deliberated for a moment, as though choosing his words carefully, then added, 'You remember that night when you were nearly shot?'

'Yes.' The boy looked at him, intrigued, unsure how the Enforcer knew about those events.

'Well; let's just say it was fortunate that I stumbled and nudged the sniper just as he pulled the trigger.' He gave the boy a knowing look. 'Here, Giles, I'll leave the defence computer with you. If I were you I would use it, as it's your best – no, your *only* – chance.' The Enforcer stood and turned to leave.

'Thanks,' said the boy as the keys rattled and the Enforcer left leaving him alone once more.

# TWELVE

Ruth was now under house arrest. She had been suspended from work and forbidden to leave the confines of her flat or to have visitors. She felt in desperate need of advice as her normally well-ordered mind was in turmoil. The events of the past few days whirled around in her head, becoming ever more confused and illogical. Commonsense told her that nothing harmful could result from this show trial. Clearly Giles was innocent of all charges. Even though he had taken the post-mortem money, fraud had not been proven: he had simply followed the old man's instructions, which couldn't possibly constitute a capital offence, *and* moreover he was a minor at the time. She would testify that the charge of attempted murder was complete nonsense and surely Giles would then be released. Yet she had discovered over the past few months that this new world could no longer be construed in that fashion. Logic did not automatically prevail: the protocols and computers held sway. She could no longer trust the system in which she had previously believed. The structure, which she had helped to introduce and had considered to be fair and honest, had now been shown to be demonstrably and fundamentally flawed, yet no one would challenge it. She began to worry that a Completion Order would be delivered. That seemed unthinkable but the populace was so blinded by the system that they no longer questioned its legitimacy. The right to challenge the Protocol had long ago been abrogated and the concepts of human rights and civil liberties relegated to the dustbin of history. Completion was not a death-sentence but merely a computer pathway: part of a programme over which humanity could hold no sway. It constituted '*The will of the Protocol.*'

The President was useless. She had always suspected that he was ineffective but now it was clear he was out of his depth and meekly doing what he was told. She suspected that the foreign aid received had gone into his coffers and that he was now, in effect, being blackmailed by the English authorities. Certainly he could not be relied on to help *her* in any way; that much was now apparent. Ruth wished that her father was still alive to discuss those matters, for he had always been a sympathetic and wise counsellor.

It was during these ruminations late that afternoon that the there came a knock at the door to her flat. She opened the door and standing there, to her complete surprise, was none other than Mandy.

'Hello, Ruth,' she said silkily and then glanced at Ruth's wrist. 'Nice bracelet.' Ruth started to close the door. 'Aren't you going to invite me in?'

'Why should I? We've nothing to discuss.'

'I want to help you, Ruth. You're in trouble and I'm the only person who might be able to assist you.'

Ruth had no wish to talk to her but the events of the past few days had weakened her resolve and she simply didn't have the energy to argue. She held the door open and Mandy pushed past her.

'Now, Ruth, let's cut to the chase. You're in trouble. The charges against you are serious.'

Ruth had been worrying about the Giles. She had never taken the charges against herself seriously. 'They're complete nonsense. A total fabrication – and you know it,' she said.

'Ruth, you just don't seem to understand, do you? It's what the Protocol says that's important, not what you, or even I, may think. Mere individuals like us don't need to worry about what's right and wrong, anymore.'

'That may be the case in England but it doesn't apply up here.'

'Ah – but it does, Ruth. You see, your Leader seems to think that the Protocol should apply equally up here just as it does in England and is as keen as we are to use it on high-profile cases, and the boy's and yours are ideal.'

'The charges against me are unproven and, even if they were upheld, wouldn't carry a custodial sentence.'

'Ruth, dear. You've been reading your history books again, haven't you? Because all this proven, un-proven malarkey is in the past – it's ancient history.' Mandy gave Ruth a look of pity. 'I actually ran your case through the Legal Protocol just to see what might be the outcome. It's pretty serious actually. Complicity with a known criminal carries a sentence of deportation. You'll know from your studies that in

England for many years now we have deported all our troublemakers. It's been a successful policy: they can't cause a problem from the other side of the world.'

'I don't believe that. It's… ' Ruth was lost for words '… *ridiculous*.'

'You'd *better* believe it, because in four days time you're going to be in the dock and the tribunal will not be as helpful as me.' Mandy looked at Ruth knowingly, 'I understand the Minister is keen to make an example of you both. She is still smarting from the boy's behaviour all those years ago. And *you* are now part of her irritation. There is no doubt that she has every intention of punishing both of you as severely as is possible.' Mandy paused and put on her best Euthanasia Monitor's expression, a mixture of sympathy and sorrow. Then she continued quietly. 'However, there is, just possibly, a way to get yourself out of this mess.' Mandy smiled as Ruth looked at her questioningly.


'Morning Giles, sleep well?'

'As well as can be expected, thank you, Mister Enforcer.'

'I've brought you some cake.'

'How kind. Thank you,' the boy replied as he accepted the wedge of sponge cake offered. 'You seem to be in extraordinarily good spirits this morning.'

'Indeed, I am. Mandy has said that I can have my old job back when we return to England.'

'What: not working for her?'

'Got it in one, Giles. No more being Mandy's punch-bag.'

'Congratulations, that must be a relief.' The boy looked at his piece of cake and then asked, 'Are you to be a witness at my trial?'

'Not allowed to say. Classified – you know.' The Enforcer took a mouthful of cake and chewed for a while before adding, 'But – yes.'

'Ah. For the prosecution, I presume.'

'Of course. Now eat your cake. It really is excellent.'

'You realise this trial is a complete sham, don't you?'

'Of course it is. But the Protocol must prevail.' The Enforcer took another bite of cake and ate quietly for a moment. 'Mmm, nice cake, don't you think?'

'Yes, delicious.' The boy smiled. 'You realise that I might, in fact *probably* will, die as a result of this nonsense.'

'Without a doubt. But it's for the greater good. As is clearly stated in the Protocol: every now and again someone may have to suffer for the benefit of the rest of society, or *pro bono publico*, as Mandy likes to say – again and again. In a way you're doing a great service for the rest of us. In fact you should consider it a privilege to die for your country.'

'*Dulce et decorum est, pro protocol mori.*'

The Enforcer looked at Giles perplexed.

'It is sweet and fitting to die for the protocol,' Giles said and smiled at the Enforcer. 'Personally, I'm not convinced.'

'Doreese and her gang are arriving tomorrow and the show, I mean the trial, is set for the following day.' The Enforcer wiped a few crumbs from his mouth. 'Should be a good turnout by all accounts. It's completely sold out.'

'What d'you mean – *sold out*?'

'All the tickets have been sold. Mandy thought she'd make a bit of money out of the event. It's really all gone very well. I don't think you realise how famous and popular you are.'

'Obviously not. Nice cake, thanks.'

'Now to business, Giles. Have you completed your defence programme?'

'Yes. I think I've done all I can. I'm confident it will make a difference to the proceedings,' said the boy as he reached for the computer.

'Good. I told you it would be worthwhile. I'll just take the computer and then I'll load it up for the big day.' The Enforcer stood to leave. 'Now, is there anything else you want? Happy to get you anything you need; within reason of course.'

'No, thank you. I've all the creature comforts I need,' he said looking around his sparse cell, 'unless you can lay your hands on a donkey.' The boy grinned and the Enforcer laughed.

'See you tomorrow.' And the door slammed.

'Roger, I'm *so* glad you've come back with the Minister as I was hoping to meet you again.' Ruth was dressed elegantly and ever so slightly seductively. 'May I come in?'

'Gosh!' was all Roger could utter as he opened his hotel room door.

'When you were last up here you left before we could say goodbye properly.' Ruth smiled and Roger's face flushed a vivid shade of pink.

'I say, it's good of you to come round. Sorry about leaving so abruptly but if the Minister says jump, we just jump.'

'I quite understand, I'm in a similar position myself. I hope you've recovered from your hangover.' Ruth giggled.

'Gosh! Yes thank you. That national drink of yours is the business – but does carry quite a kick.'

'I know. Here, I've brought you a bottle to welcome you back.' Ruth handed over a bottle of whisky. 'Have you any glasses?'

'Gosh. I say, that's most awfully kind of you.' Roger poured out two large measures and handed one to Ruth. 'Well, cheers, bottoms up, chin-chin, and all that.' Roger took a large swig of the golden liquid. 'Now tell me, Ruth, why have you come round?'

'To see *you*, of course. We never got to know each other at your last visit and I wanted to make sure I didn't miss the opportunity this time.'

'But I thought that you were on the other side as it were. I'd heard that you'd been arrested yourself.' Roger glanced at Ruth's arm. 'Where's your tracer?' he asked.

Ruth looked at her wrist where the tracer had been. 'Oh, Mandy and I had a little chat and let's just say – we came to an agreement.'

'Excellent. *Excellent*. Because it would look bad for me to be consorting with a known criminal.' Roger snorted loudly, the nearest he ever got to a laugh.

'So, now that I'm a free woman, maybe you can tell me what your plans are for the next few days and, if you're not too busy, possibly spare a bit of time to spend with me.'

'Gosh! Yes that would be J.T.J.'

'J.T.J.?' Ruth looked quizzical.

'Just the job.' Roger snorted loudly and a fine jet of spittle sprayed from his mouth. He took another large swig from his whisky glass and topped it up from the bottle. 'All being well the trial should be over by lunchtime tomorrow and we are scheduled to go home immediately after.'

'Oh.' Ruth looked disappointed. 'That doesn't give us much time to get to know each other. What's the rush?'

'Well, strictly speaking I'm not allowed to say, but now you're no longer a criminal I can probably confide in you.' Roger took another gulp from his glass. 'The Minister wants to take the Giles back to England for Completion, since she and Mandy think it would be appropriate for that to be carried out in Nowton. Trial here – Completion in England – sort of brings our two countries together. It's rather neat, don't you agree?'

Ruth was thinking as fast as she could. 'Yes, very neat,' then after a pause asked nonchalantly, 'So when are you actually leaving with the brat?'

'Well, 'tween oursel's, straight after the trial.' Roger was already beginning to slur his words a little.

'That's a shame; because after all the trouble he's caused me I really would have liked to see him, face to face, to give him a piece of my mind.'

'Well, why don' we go together: after the hearing.'

'Could you get us access to the prison?'

'Mos' definately.' Roger took another large swig, 'You can tell 'im what you think of 'im, and then we can get to know each other. Know wot I mean?' Roger attempted a knowing smile, which turned out to be a leer before taking a step towards Ruth, who neatly dodged his clumsy advance.

'Roger, it's a dreadful shame but I really must go now. I'll see you tomorrow after the trial. Don't forget, will you?' She gave him a peck on the cheek and let herself out, a smile on her face.

As Mandy prepared herself for the Minister's reception, she was filled with pleasurable anticipation. She gazed at her reflection in the dressing-table mirror in front of her and smiled. '*I'll* show them,' she thought. 'Thought you could get the better of me, did you? Well, tomorrow we'll see who's won *this* particular battle.' She turned her head a little from side to side. 'Not bad-looking. So I've lost a few years, but the day after tomorrow I'll be back at home and placing the euthanometer on that brat. I wonder what scenario he'll choose?' She applied a touch of lipstick. 'What was it that the old man had wanted?' She frowned as she tried to remember. 'It was something perverted. Something to do with sex and an animal,' she seemed to recall. She hadn't been concentrating at the time, as she had been furious with the way the old man and the boy had affronted her: laughed at her in the courtroom in front of everyone *and* they'd insulted the Protocol. 'But who's going to be laughing tomorrow?' she said aloud to the image now smiling back at her. 'Who'll have the last laugh? *Me*, that's who. Ruth's evidence will clinch it.'

In truth, Mandy had been surprised that Ruth had given in so easily. 'She's not as clever as she thinks she is,' thought Mandy as she pulled a comb through her hair. The mere threat of deportation had been enough and she had agreed to give evidence against the boy in exchange for indemnity. 'Everyone can be bought,' she said to the mirror. 'Everyone has their price. Okay; for now the girl's got off, but it's worth it to see the brat punished.'

Mandy was aware that the evidence for some of her allegations was flimsy and that the outcome of the trial could have been unpredictable but for Ruth's evidence. Even with careful handling the Protocol didn't always come up with exactly the verdict or sentence one desired and she knew that the case for attempted murder in particular was weak. Luckily, the only other witness to the event, apart from the Enforcer, was the girl's father who Mandy had discovered had died some two years earlier. 'Typical of what happens if you don't adhere to the Health Protocol.' Mandy sighed at her own image in the mirror. She then applied a touch more make up, finished combing her hair and, wearing a slightly flouncy, deep-blue cocktail dress, set off down the corridor of her hotel to the Minister's suite where Doreese and her team were holding a small reception. 'I do hope Roger's there,' she thought. 'With this trial in the bag and the help of someone close to the Minister, who knows how far I might go?'

# THIRTEEN

Once again the courtroom in the old palace was packed and the clamour of laughter and chatter so loud that those in the room had to shout to be heard. Reporters, politicians and the general public all jostled for seats or even space to stand where they might have an uninterrupted view of the proceedings. Many carried plastic cups filled with one of the selection of drinks on sale outside. Coffee, beer and the national drink were all available for purchase in the courtyard, along with sandwiches and fried food in buns. Business had boomed as people waited for the start of the trial and by the time the boy was led in to the dock, to the accompaniment of whistles and jeers, many had been drinking for quite some time. Then, slowly and mysteriously, the great doors at the end of the room opened and there, framed in the entrance, appeared the Enforcer. Cradled in his arms was the tasselled velvet cushion on which lay the black computer.

'Please be upstanding for the Tribunal procession,' called out the Enforcer and, as silence fell, he led the procession slowly and sedately into the room. Immediately behind him was the Minister. She was wearing a deep-purple gown with long flowing sleeves edged with gold, while around her neck was a chain of the same colour. Her feet were shod in scarlet slippers embroidered with a coronet, but the attention of those in the room was drawn to her head, on which sat what appeared to be a flying saucer. It was grey in colour and every bit as broad as her shoulders, while on one side there appeared to be a small tree on which was perched a stuffed bird.

As Doreese slowly processed across the room towards the bench, she graciously waved her gloved hand, while the crowd in the courtroom responded by cheering and raising their drinks in a toast. Behind her walked Mandy, wearing her dark blue academic-styled gown over her very best work clothes. She too had wondered about wearing a hat and had hoped to ask Roger's opinion at the reception the previous evening but he had suffered a bout of food poisoning and was too unwell to attend. Also, on reflection, Mandy thought that it might be wise not to upstage the Minister so she had deliberately dressed down – simple, yet smart and formal.

As Doreese took her seat the Enforcer placed the computer in front of her, while Mandy occupied the seat to her right. The four policemen then took up their positions at either end of the bench.

'Please be seated,' called the Enforcer.

As the acclamation settled, Doreese smiled to the assembled crowd. 'It is a great pleasure to be with you today on this momentous occasion.' She nodded to acknowledge the applause of the audience. 'Today we are witnesses to the beginning of a great collaboration and friendship between our two countries. With our help, I'm confident that Dalriada can be saved from the deprivations of many decades and can be brought back from the brink of social breakdown and barbarity to a standard of civilisation not far removed from our own in England.' The Minister paused for effect, and looked around the room. 'This trial is an example of how the Protocol operates in England and could, if introduced fully, work here in Dalriada.' She reached forward with her gloved right hand and placed it upon the computer, 'Bless the Protocol,' she pronounced, her voice heavy with *gravitas.*

From all around the room rose a murmur, a rumble of voices, and from those who were civilised enough to know the catechism, came the response; 'Bless the Protocol. May we serve it well.'

The Minister then opened the formal proceedings. 'Now, we all know that we are gathered here to find the defendant guilty. Giles, previously known simply as "the boy", has been charged with numerous heinous crimes but has decided to appeal. In its goodness, the Protocol has permitted him to do so. We have fresh evidence for the prosecution and also a case for the defence. These data will accordingly be entered into the computer and then I shall then ask the Protocol to pronounce.' The Minister looked at the dock and then to her right. 'Mandy, you have the prosecution data ready for entry, I believe?'

'Yes, Minister. The girl Ruth has confirmed that the boy deliberately tried to kill both me and the Enforcer by driving his boat directly at us with the intention of doing us bodily harm. It was only by virtue of our swift and nimble reactions that we avoided serious injury and almost certain death.'

A gasp went round the courtroom. Someone shouted, 'Shame!' and the boy, who had been staring at the floor of the dock, looked up in surprise. He was puzzled. Although he'd had no contact with Ruth, he'd assumed she would defend him against the ridiculous allegation of attempted murder. He looked all around the courtroom and initially failed to see her in the mêlée but then, tucked away in a corner, he identified her standing next to a tall thin man who was drinking from a paper cup, while swaying slightly. Ruth herself seemed to be staring at the floor. 'That's it!' thought the boy. 'I'm done for.' But then he considered: 'But I was done for anyway. Perhaps Ruth had to protect herself.' He knew that Mandy had it in for her but inwardly couldn't help but be disappointed by what he had just heard. 'Might as well go out with a bang,' he thought and sat back resignedly on his chair and smiled to himself.

'Thank you, Mandy,' said Doreese. 'Please enter the new evidence.' Mandy operated the keyboard efficiently and, when she pressed 'enter', the words, PROSECUTION DATA ENTERED appeared on the huge screen on the wall behind her. There were nods and grunts of approval from around the room and someone called out, 'God bless The Protocol,' in a slightly drunken fashion.

Another shouted, 'Send him down.'

'Quiet, please,' cried the Enforcer.

'Now, Giles, I believe you have some defence data to offer,' continued the Minister.

'Yes. I submitted it to the Enforcer yesterday.'

'Thank you,' said Doreese with a smile, before adding more quietly, 'Though a fat lot of good it'll do you.' The Enforcer then handed a plastic data card to Mandy who inserted it into a port on the side of the computer. Then, with flourish, she pressed the 'enter' key and the big screen mounted on the wall behind the bench flashed with numbers and symbols until, after a few seconds, the message DEFENCE DATA RETRIEVED appeared. 'Well, I suppose we might as well see what the defendant's got to say,' said the Minister. 'Can you show us please, Mandy.' Then, with great pomp, Mandy pressed, 'display defence data'. Doreese and Mandy then stared at the screen in front of them in disbelief at the image which had now appeared. In a panic, Mandy swung round in her chair to look at the large screen behind her, hoping against hope that the image there would be different, but it wasn't. There – larger than life – was an animated picture of two donkeys copulating, their lips drawn back over their teeth, while in the background there was an image of the Eiffel tower. And if that wasn't bad enough the action was accompanied by the sound of enthusiastic he-hawing.

What happened next was probably the result of many members of the audience having had a few drinks. After a moment of stunned disbelief some burst out laughing then others followed suit until the room was in uproar. After a moment a voice could be heard above the turmoil, 'Do not laugh. He has defiled the Protocol. He must be punished.'

Then from the other side of the room came the cry: 'This is blasphemy. Death to the blasphemer. Death to the defiler.'

Gradually the debauched laughing faded. Doreese and Mandy, once they had recovered from their stupefaction, both simultaneously reached for the computer but the donkeys continued to copulate and to he-haw happily – refusing to be erased.

'*Do something*. Get those animals off my screen,' screamed Doreese.

Mandy was now panicking and pressing any key that she thought might stop the animals cavorting behind her. 'The programme won't stop,' she yelled.

It was the Enforcer who saved the day. He was stifling a smile as he suggested that Mandy should press the 'verdict' button to move the programme on. As soon as she did so, the donkeys instantly disappeared and VERDICT AWAITED appeared in their place. A moment later a second message appeared: DEFENCE DATA NOT VALID, followed by VERDICT – GUILTY.

With some semblance of order now restored, Doreese adjusted her hat, which had become somewhat askew in the excitement, and instructed Mandy to proceed to sentencing.

Mandy was still completely unsettled by the image of the donkeys copulating and realised that once again the boy had seized the upper hand. She hadn't grasped the significance of the images but somehow she knew that it reflected badly on her. Once more, the boy seemed to have gained the moral high ground, and the proceedings hadn't turned out to be the satisfying catharsis that she had hoped for. She pressed the 'sentence' key and as the words EUTHANASIA COMPLETION came up on the screen she heaved a deep sigh of relief and allowed herself a smile. She looked at the dock where the boy was now standing to receive his sentence, a broad smile on his face.

How could he possibly smile? she thought. He's due to be Completed. Mandy shook her head in disbelief. She simply did not understand this boy.

Doreese coughed loudly and called, 'Order. *Order!*' Then, more quietly, she continued. 'The Protocol has found the boy, Giles, guilty of the offences as charged and his sentence is an End of Life Completion. This will be carried out in Nowton, where his first crime was committed. He will be taken there tomorrow. Normally, I would ask if the defendant has any thing to say but after his appalling behaviour and defilement of the Protocol I am withdrawing that privilege.'

Doreese stood and, after again adjusting her headgear which once more had taken on a dangerous tilt, led the procession out of the court following which the boy was escorted back to his cell.

As the noise in the room settled and people drifted towards the exit, Ruth looked at Roger. 'Serves him right,' she remarked.

'A'solutely. Jolly good result.' Roger was once again clearly the worse for imbibing the national drink.

'Let's celebrate.'

'I sh' say so.'

'You said you'd spend some time with me.'

'Loo'ing forward to it, I sh' say so.'

'We haven't got long but remember, you said you'd take me to see the prisoner before he's taken away.'

'A'solutely, fine by me. I sh' say so.' Roger took another large swig from his paper cup and swayed dangerously. Ruth grabbed him by the arm and steered him towards the door from where, once safely negotiated, she nudged him in the direction of the prison tower. If her plan was to work, Roger had to be drunk – but not too drunk or it would fail and if that happened, not only would the boy be taken south for Completion but he would also die thinking that she had betrayed him.

When Mandy had visited her two nights previously, Ruth had been in a state of turmoil. Although she didn't trust Mandy, she suspected that she was correct about the possibility of deportation but that hadn't been her main concern. The problem was that while she was under house arrest and tagged there was no way she could help the boy. She had learned enough about Mandy and the English Protocol to know it was inevitable that he would be found guilty, even if she could testify on his behalf. Moreover, now that she herself had been charged, she was not allowed to give evidence. Mandy had been clever in her machinations. When she had first been offered indemnity provided she acted for the prosecution, Ruth had been appalled but then she realised that this might be the only way she could help the boy, so she had agreed. Central to her plan had been Roger. She knew that he was attracted to her and was senior enough, as the Minister's aide, to help her gain access to the boy's cell. The problem was that after a few of the national drinks he was unpredictable and she therefore had to get the dose just right. He was now far more intoxicated than she had intended him to be.

'Come on. Take some nice deep breaths.'

'Orright,' he mumbled as she guided him, step by step, across the now empty courtyard.

'In – out. In – out. That's very good.'

'Think I'm a b – bit drunk. Zorry!' Roger peered blearily at Ruth and in so doing stumbled, only managing to regain his balance with her assistance.

'That's okay. You and I are going to say goodbye to the brat. When we reach the door you must tell the guards that you're here on official business. Tell them that you're here to take the boy to England.' In truth, Ruth hadn't formulated a detailed plan. She knew that the first essential was to gain access to the boy and once that had been achieved she thought that some possibility might present itself. At the back of her mind was the fact the boy and Roger were of a similar height, if not build, and the possibility of an identity swap had crossed her mind. As they approached the tower she began to realise how flimsy all her ideas were and the enormity of her task now became apparent. To console herself she thought that even if she were unable to free the boy she would at least be able to speak to him and explain her actions.

By now they were approaching the doorway to the tower outside which stood two armed police officers. As they drew closer, Roger (to Ruth's great relief,) managed to straighten up and in a reasonably commanding voice explained that he was chief aide to the Minister and that he was there to interview the boy before extradition. Ruth explained that she was a government advisor working with the English Department for Intelligent Euthanasia. This explanation proved enough to persuade the guards to unlock the door and allow them entry.

'Up three flights and turn right,' said one, as he locked the door behind them.

As Ruth guided Roger up the narrow stone spiral staircase it occurred to her that it was strange that neither of the guards had accompanied them. With a combination of pushing and cajoling, Ruth managed to steer Roger up the three steep flights and by the time they reached a small landing they were both quite breathless. From there they turned into a small passageway to their right and, as they did so, Ruth could hear laughter. She recognised Giles' voice and he appeared to be chatting convivially with someone. Her heart sank, 'Oh, no!' she thought, 'I didn't anticipate there being a jailor in the room with him.' The seriousness of the situation suddenly dawned on her. 'What on earth can I do now?' she wondered as she peered along the narrow corridor ahead of her. Roger was stumbling noisily forward and there could be no turning back – they were committed to entering the cell. As they approached, the voices grew louder and the passage curved slightly to reveal a room, its door ajar, from where the laughter emanated.

Roger stumbled through the low doorway, hitting his head on the lintel as he did so. 'Mornin'', he declared as he entered the cell. When Ruth followed him her worst fears were realised. There in the room, sitting with the boy and looking with surprise at the two unexpected visitors, was the Enforcer.

'Roger. How unexpected,' said the Enforcer as he rose to shake his hand. 'And to what do we owe this pleasure?'

On seeing Ruth, the boy had also stood up. He didn't know whether to be angry or pleased to see her but noticing the alarmed expression on her face decided to remain silent.

Ruth was now unsure what to do. Her original plan, already flimsy, had totally collapsed once she had realised that the Enforcer was guarding the boy. She had reckoned that with a bit of luck she might have overcome the drunken ministerial aide, but with the Enforcer present, that wasn't going to be possible. Trembling and without conviction she began to deliver her prepared speech. 'So there you are. D'you realise how much trouble you've caused me, *Giles*.' She tried without conviction to sound angry. 'I've lost my job, been arrested and threatened with deportation all because of you.'

The boy was completely bemused. 'Sorry!' was all he said with a frown.

The Enforcer, having helped Roger to a chair, now turned to Ruth. 'Surprised at *you*, Ruth, giving evidence for the prosecution,' he looked questioningly at the girl. 'I suppose Mandy got to you.' Ruth never subsequently understood why it was then that she broke down. She had been prepared for the boy to insult her and accuse her of betrayal but for the Enforcer to criticise her came as such a surprise that it was his comments that cracked, what had up until then been, an unpenetrable façade. She bit her lip to try and control her emotions but then burst into floods of tears. 'Thought so,' continued the Enforcer, 'that's just what I was telling Giles here.' He turned to the boy, 'Told you it would be Mandy's doing, didn't I?'

The boy just nodded, stepped forward, put his arm around the girl's shoulder and for a moment the cell was quiet apart from the sound of the girl's sobbing. Roger was rocking gently on his chair, opening and closing his eyes in an attempt to maintain his balance and focus.

It was the Enforcer who broke the silence. 'What are you doing up here, Ruth, and why have you brought the chinless wonder with you?'

Ruth wiped her eyes with the back of her hand, like a little girl who had been told off for behaving badly. 'I wanted to say... goodbye.'

'Then why give the boy a hard time?'

Ruth hesitated. She couldn't admit to the Enforcer that she had been intending to help the boy to escape. 'To get Roger to help.'

'To help with what?'

'Get me in here to... ' she stammered, '... *say – goodbye.*'

The Enforcer then said something to the boy that initially Ruth failed to understand the significance of. 'That's messed things up, Giles,' then he added in a whisper nodding in the direction of Roger, 'what are we going to do with him?' then looking at Ruth, 'and her.'

The boy thought for a moment while Ruth scrutinised him, unsure what was transpiring. 'They'll just have to come with us,' he said.

'What d'you mean, "come with us?" ' Ruth's eyes were wide with incomprehension.

'Well,' said the boy, 'Mister Enforcer and I were about to take our leave of this pleasant little cell and head north before the escort party came to cart me back to Nowton and what is charmingly called "Life Completion". Now you two have come along and upset our little plan.' He glanced at the girl. 'Ruth, you look puzzled.'

'Yes I am.' Ruth's response to these rapidly unfolding events was to become angry. 'Are you telling me, boy, or Giles, or whatever your name is, that Mister Enforcer here, Mandy's minder; is going to help you... *escape*?'

'Yes, indeed. It seems that four years in the company of Mandy has convinced him that his future lies up here in barbaric Dalriada and not back in the protocolised world of Mandy clones.' The boy paused briefly. 'It appears he has already saved my life once. When I was escaping from the village at the head of the loch he was the one who nudged the sharp-shooter, causing him to miss. The final straw came yesterday when Mandy announced that she actually enjoyed working with him and that she wanted him to continue to be her personal Enforcer for the foreseeable future.'

'But, I'm confused. *I* came here to help you escape.'

'Excellent! So you're *all* trying to help me escape.'

'Apart from him,' said the Enforcer, looking at Roger.

Some of this conversation had filtered through to Roger's befuddled brain and he'd registered that there was a conspiracy in the room and he needed to make his exit. He managed to stand and then attempted to walk in the direction of the door but before he had completed his first unsteady step the Enforcer had placed his forearm around his neck in a loose stranglehold and his other hand over Roger's mouth. This unexpected activity unsettled his stomach and a plume of vomit sprayed from between the Enforcer's fingers in the direction of the door.

'Bloody hell! Why did you get him so drunk, Ruth? He's a liability.'

'I needed him to help me get past the guards,' said Ruth as the Enforcer guided Roger back to his seat before wiping his hands on a towel.

'Okay! Here's the plan,' Giles announced in a clear confident voice. 'Ruth, we were just waiting for the extradition party to arrive when you came along with the vomiting wonder. They're due any minute so we don't have much time, and in the light of developments I think we need to move quickly. We'll have to take Roger with us: the gorillas downstairs will smell a rat if you two don't come down with us.' The boy glanced at Ruth and his new friend. 'Mister Enforcer, you'll escort me, handcuffed, while Roger and Ruth can follow us. Ruth, here's a knife. If Roger does anything untoward just jab him in the ribs with it, but try not to kill him.' The boy turned to Roger. 'Roger, do you understand that you must come with us and do exactly what we say or we'll stab you? If you behave yourself we'll let you go unharmed when we've reached safety.' Roger, now slightly more sober, nodded his understanding.

'Ruth,' continued the boy, 'you'll have to come with us to the port but after that we can release you as well; that is, unless you want to come with us.'

'Where are you going?'

'We plan is to sail back to Inverneuage.'

'But that's a barbarous community.'

'Not as barbarous as this one.'

'What about the police? They'll follow us. Mandy and the Minister will go mad.'

'Probably. We need to slip out of the port and sail north before they know we've escaped.'

'But they'll kill us.'

'Not if they can't catch us. Look, Ruth, *I've* nothing to lose. Mister Enforcer here knows that if he goes south Mandy will make his life hell. Roger? Well, he can do what he wants once we release him, but you, Ruth, have a choice. We can let you go and you can say you were taken hostage; or else you can come with us.'

Ruth thought for a moment: of her weak, alcoholic leader, of her lost job, of how her beliefs in a system of government, one which she thought, might help the society in which she lived. All her hopes had vanished, leaving her alone and disillusioned. She considered how, if unchecked, the thoughtlessness of those like Mandy and Doreese would ruin the lives of people like her and Giles as they had the old man; of how the inevitable advance of protocolisation, in the name of civilisation, threatened the freedoms of everyone. All she longed for was a return to her pleasant childhood in the village at the foot of the loch.

'I'm in,' she said.

'Good. Let's do it.' The boy held his hands out. The Enforcer placed the manacles around his wrist but did not click them locked. He then pulled Roger to his feet and the little procession then descended to the bottom of the spiral stairs. There, the Enforcer shouted to the guard: 'We have brought down the prisoner to meet the extradition party.' They little group then heard the scraping of keys and the door swung open on to the courtyard which was now bathed in pleasant afternoon sun.

'The transport's not here yet, sir,' said one of the guards.

'Damn,' said the Enforcer, as much to himself as to the policeman but then, as he looked at his watch, a police van drove into the square and pulled up by the tower where the driver and his companion jumped out and opened the rear doors. The boy was then hustled into the back of the van and the door locked behind him.

'Right, we'll take it from here,' said the Enforcer to the driver. 'Thanks for coming.'

The driver looked at him with surprise. 'But we're driving you to the border, sir.'

'No need. The Minister's Aide here has said that I must take the boy south.' The Enforcer nodded confidently at the policemen.

'But those aren't *our* orders, sir.' The driver and his companion looked more confused than suspicious.

'English jurisdiction, apparently.' The Enforcer turned to the Aide, 'Isn't that right, Roger?'

Ruth nudged Roger who was looking terrified. 'Spot on. A'solutely.' Ruth addressed the policemen, 'As the Enforcer has explained, this is the Minister's chief Aide and it is his personal responsibility to deliver the prisoner to the Euthanasia Studio in Nowton. This transfer is now under the direct control of the Euthanasia Squad.'

As Ruth had anticipated, the mere mention of the death squad was enough to erode any remaining resistance the driver and his companion had. 'Certainly, Miss,' they said in unison.

'Thank you,' said the Enforcer, 'you've done a good job.' Then with Roger sandwiched between himself and Ruth in the cab the Enforcer engaged first gear and steered the van out of the courtyard, through the surrounding park and headed towards the port, leaving the driver and his companion talking and smoking with the guards outside the now empty prison.

# FOURTEEN

'Personally, I am very disappointed in your behaviour. However, it is not for me alone to judge your actions.' The leader of Inverneuage Council looked at the scrawny man who was seated before him. The Council Chamber was full to capacity with men and women of all ages. Those present – a cross-section of the community – were all desirous of expressing their opinions on the actions of the man who had betrayed Giles and the atmosphere in the room was accordingly tense. Ranged on either side of the chief was the full complement of twelve village elders. Their leader once again addressed the betrayer. 'What do you have to say for yourself?'

'Chief. Giles was a criminal. He was wanted by the police in both England and Dalriada. In my opinion his presence in this city was becoming an ever-greater threat to our community. He was attracting the attention of the authorities and by informing them that Giles was here I was performing a great service to this society.'

'Why didn't you speak to me, or to one the elders, so that *we* could deal with it?'

'I knew that you would protect him.'

'Why should *you* know better than *us* what was the right course of action?'

'You, *sir*, were too close to him. You didn't appreciate how dangerous he was.'

'You know that in this community we protect and care for each other. It is an unwritten rule that we do *not* betray people to the outside world.' The Chief was aware that his anger was becoming apparent. He paused to compose himself before resuming in more settled tones, 'That is how we have survived successfully for so many years.'

'But the boy was an outsider, a criminal, not part of the community.'

'He was not alone in that respect.'

'He had strange ideas. He challenged the old order. He was

dangerous.' The betrayer, his face sullen and his eyes dull, fell silent.

A voice then came from the body of the chamber. 'Chief, may I speak for the defendant?'

'Yes, Professor.'

An elderly academic rose to his feet. 'The defendant felt that he was doing the correct thing for his fellow-man and for the community at large. He was putting our society as a whole before the individual: something that has been central to all civilisations since the dawn of history. Surely that cannot be considered a crime.'

'But, Professor, the problem, as I see it, is that he acted in isolation. The correct course of action would have been to see me, or to petition the Council. We would have debated the issue and we might well have expelled Giles had we felt that was the wisest course of action. I had already called an emergency meeting when Giles was arrested.'

'My understanding is that the defendant considered the issue to be of such an urgent nature that there was no time for discussion and that action had to be taken quickly and decisively for the safety of the community.' There was a moment's silence, 'I think we should be applauding this man rather than pillorying him. He has done us all a service and in my view this so-called Council has recently taken a rather autocratic stance on how it manages our affairs: it has become what Plato described as an aristocracy.'

'Thank you, Professor.' The Chief removed his spectacles and looked at the speaker. '*We*, of course, are elected by the community, and so we are hardly the same as an autocracy. Anyway, our local politics are scarcely relevant to this debate.' The Chief replaced his spectacles. 'Is that all?'

'Yes. Thank you, Chief.'

'Does anyone else have anything to say?'

'I have, Chief.' The café owner stood up.

'Yes, sir. Please go ahead.'

'To my mind this betrayal of a respected member of our community was abhorrent and indefensible. I would like to ask the betrayer how much money he was paid to do this.'

The Chief addressed the man seated before him. 'Well?' There came no reply. 'How much were you paid to hand over Giles?'

Still the betrayer, sullen and menacing, refused to answer. 'Well,' continued the Chief, 'we all know how much the reward was and unless you tell us otherwise we must assume that was the amount you received.' Still there came no response. The Chief continued, 'It seems clear to me that the defendant perpetrated this act: betrayed a respected member of our community for financial gain rather than for the benefit of the community.'

'The Chief's right!' came a shout from the back of the room.

'Does anyone else wish to argue the case for or against the defendant.'

'He had no religion,' shouted one.

'Nor have most of us, but that is how we live. We respect each other's beliefs – or lack of them.'

'I think he was a secular fundamentalist,' came another voice.

'I believe he held no fervent religious opinions but *that*, to my mind, is an irrelevance. We are here to decide whether this act was justified and, if not, what punishment is appropriate.' The Chief gazed around the room.

The greengrocer rose to his feet. 'Giles was a good man. He supplied us with fish and cared for others in the community. It doesn't matter what his beliefs were.'

The boy's tutor then stood. 'He had an exceptionally enquiring mind and would have been a great asset to our society, a wise head on young shoulders. He will be missed.' The tutor paused for a moment then continued. 'The loss will be ours of course, as he most certainly will be executed if and when he is returned to England. But that is not the point. The fundamental question here is whether or not the defendant acted appropriately. It doesn't matter if the victim of such an action was an exemplary member of our community or someone who brought little or no value to this society; whether he was liked or disliked. The question is simply this: was the action morally defensible? Does our community – our City State – allow such individualistic behaviour for monetary gain?'

'It was to save our city. They would have invaded and arrested us if he hadn't been handed over.'

'He was betrayed for money. No more, no less.'

'He was stupid to fall into such an obvious trap. I'd say he can't be that clever.'

These and other comments then popped up like firecrackers, bouncing and snaking around the room.

One of the elders then joined in the discussion. 'He was not one of us and therefore does not deserve to be treated in the same way. Now if it were one of us here on the bench that had been betrayed – well, that would be different.'

'But you cannot have two sets of rules for different members of our community. That's a recipe for disaster.'

So the debate continued. The Chief was an astute and experienced chairman and he knew that both his own standing and that of his elders was on trial as much as the fate of the defendant. He allowed the discussion to continue for two hours before announcing in a moment of quiet, 'I think we have heard all relevant opinions and I thank you all for taking part in this frank discussion. I believe it is fair to say that this is an important day in the evolution of our society, with consequences for how we police our community and for the behaviour of its members. How we set out guidance as to what is, and what is not acceptable, is fundamental to any society. There are, as we all know, many different models. You must now trust your elected elders to discuss all the matters raised today and reach a decision on two issues. The first is whether the defendant's behaviour was acceptable, even commendable, or whether he acted against the spirit of our community. The second issue – *if* we find his behaviour to be unacceptable – is what punishment is appropriate. The rule of twos applies here, so please return in two hours. If by then we have not come to an agreement then we will reconvene in two days. Thank you, ladies and gentlemen.'

With this, the chamber slowly emptied as the audience drifted away. Some headed over the brow of the hill to their homes and businesses, while others waited outside chatting and continuing to discuss the case. Two hours later they returned and once more crammed themselves into the council chamber and the Chief called the hearing to order.

'This has been a most difficult task,' he began, 'and I should say that, although we have reached a consensus, it has by no means been a unanimous decision.' The Chief looked around the room before continuing. 'We are obliged to accept that the defendant felt that he was acting in the best interests of the city, and we are cognisant of the fact that Council might well have made the same decision if we had been allowed to debate the issue. We do, however, find it repugnant that the defendant has accepted a significant reward for his action – which raises the suspicion that he might, at least in part, have been acting for his own personal gain.' The Chief paused once more. 'On balance, we feel that we cannot condemn the defendant for his actions but, since he claims that he acted purely for the benefit of the community rather than for personal gain, the remuneration he received should also benefit the community and we therefore order him to hand over the reward monies to the Council to be used in the best interests of the city.'

The Chief glanced up from the jottings in front of him. The council room was quiet, then from the back came a shout, 'Good decision, Chief.'

Then another, 'Seems fair.'

And another, 'Hear, hear! We should all benefit.'

'Defendant, do you accept the verdict of the council?'

'Yes,' said the weasel-like defendant in a quiet, malevolent tone; adding after a pause, '*Chief*.'

'Thank you, ladies and gentlemen. That concludes this hearing.

* * *

Once well away from the old palace the Enforcer parked the police van in a lay-by. 'Right,' he said. 'Let's get Giles out of the back and swap him with Roger here. Out you get,' he added looking at the aide. Then, holding Roger tightly by the upper arm, he led him to the back of the van where he opened the door and helped the boy to step out.

Roger was in no fit state to argue and needed little encouragement to enter the back of the van. 'I say, wha' you going to do w'me?' he asked.

'Just taking you along with us for a while as an insurance policy,' replied the Enforcer. 'Once we're away, we'll let you go.'

On hearing this Roger started to nod and then, after retching a couple of times, he vomited copiously on the floor of the van before finally settling himself on a seat.

With Giles in the front and the Enforcer behind the wheel, they set off once more and headed north in the direction of the coast road where he turned the van westward.

'Where are we going?' It was the first time that Ruth had spoken since they'd left the old palace.

'Well, I'm not exactly sure,' answered the boy, 'but Mister Enforcer here says that there are some yachts in a harbour near here and the plan is to steal one and sail north.'

'But they'll follow us.'

'Only if they guess what we're doing,' explained the Enforcer. 'I don't think anyone will anticipate that we'll try to escape by sea. Sure, they'll be blocking all the roads, but they'll not think of the river as a potential escape route as no one uses it any more. It was considered too dangerous years ago and sailing was banned in the Risk Averse Act.'

The boy took up the narrative. 'We plan to find a boat tonight, then sail away under the cover of darkness. We should be well away by daylight.'

'Isn't that dangerous?' asked Ruth.

'A bit. But I've been sailing and fishing the waters further north for several years; though it's true I never came this far south.' The van rattled on as Giles continued, 'I think we should be at the Inverneuage estuary in about twelve hours, wind and weather permitting.'

'Well, there's no going back for me,' said the Enforcer.

'Nor for me,' added Ruth. 'What shall we do about Roger?'

'We'll let him loose when we're ready to leave. It'll probably take him ages to find his way back to the capital and raise the alarm,' the Enforcer said with a smile. 'They'll be after us long before then. Giles was expected to be at the border around six o'clock and when he doesn't arrive all hell will break loose. We need to have found a boat and hidden this van by then.'

Those in the cab then fell silent as the Enforcer drove along the road towards the harbour. There was little traffic and they made good progress but the police van was extremely conspicuous and Giles thought that it couldn't be very long before it was reported. The police would then add two and two and realise that they were planning to escape by boat.

217

Two other things were worrying him. Firstly, the tide was out and they would have to wait until it had turned before they could escape. Secondly, the weather was looking ever more threatening, with storm clouds darkening the evening sky. 'This is not going to be easy,' he muttered to himself. He knew that neither Ruth nor the Enforcer had ever sailed before and leaving a tidal harbour, under sail, in a gale force wind were not ideal conditions for a first sailing lesson.

To avoid detection the Enforcer had chosen a small unguarded harbour, where he had seen several fishing boats, rather than the much larger commercial port with its barbed wire and security systems. It was about seven in the evening and heavy drops of rain were beginning to fall when the little group reached the outskirts of the capital and halted the van at the roadside opposite the old harbour. Its walls of massive grey stones glistened with the damp as they stretched out into the river, like two arms embracing a basin of mud, stones and the debris of a thousand tides. At the very tip of the northern wall stood a small white lighthouse, long unlit, its paint peeling and its wrought-iron badly rusted.

'Wait here,' said Giles as he opened the door of the van and set off to examine the boats. When the boy saw the craft lying at crazy angles on the mud his heart sank. All were small and most looked to be quite unseaworthy and initially he couldn't identify a single one which was close to being adequate for their purpose. He needed a boat sturdy enough to weather the brewing storm, yet fast enough to get them out of harm's way by dawn. Then he spied a yacht by the far wall of the harbour, semi-hidden in the fading light. It was moored near the entrance and he had to scramble through a hole in a vicious barbed wire fence to reach it. Like the other boats, the yacht was sitting on the mud, but its bilge keel meant that it was relatively level. From his vantage point the boy could see that water was now beginning to enter the harbour and he estimated that it might be two or three hours before it was deep enough for there to be a navigable channel to the open river. He examined the harbour bed, making a mental note of obstructions and hazards and the best way to exit.

Giles then looked at the boat below him and judged it to be about thirty feet long and rigged in such a fashion to be manageable without an experienced crew. He scrambled down the metal rungs of the ladder encased in the stone harbour wall and stepped on to the deck. He checked the rigging, noting that both main and jib sails were in place and ready for use. 'It's essentially a pleasure craft,' he thought, 'one of those now banned for safety reasons.' He then found the government logo in the cockpit. 'Ah, that's why it's in such good condition: it belongs to the River Police. That means it may have a tracking device on board.' He pondered for a moment about the wisdom of stealing a police boat, before saying to himself, 'But it's the only craft suitable, so we haven't any choice.' The main hatch was locked but, as with most boats, the lock was flimsy. He easily broke it and descended the steep ladder into the main cabin.

Once inside, he carefully noted the layout: a chart table to his left, the small galley on the right; then two seats, which doubled as berths, on either side of a drop-leaf table. He walked the length of the cabin and opened the small door to the forepeak. Here there were life jackets and some flares. At the stern was the main double berth and a small toilet.

'Perfect,' he said to himself. 'This will do very nicely.' He identified the engine controls but there was no sign of an ignition key. 'No time to mess about trying to start the engine,' he thought. 'We'll just have to sail out.' He looked up at the sky: it was now getting dark and water was beginning to slap against the twin keels. 'A bilge keel will serve us well,' he thought, 'just like my fishing smack.' The wind was now coming from the north-east and steadily increasing in strength. Giles looked towards the harbour entrance which faced north-west. 'With a bit of luck we should be able to sail out,' he concluded. Having thought things through as thoroughly as he could he returned to the van and climbed in to escape from the now heavy rain.

'Right,' he said to Ruth and the Enforcer. 'I've found a suitable craft. We won't be able to leave for another hour or two but we might as well go on board and get ready.'

'What about Roger?'

'He'll have to come with us for now but we'll release him before we leave.'

'And the van?'

'We'll need to hide it down a side street.'

Giles led Ruth and Roger along the harbour wall while the

Enforcer drove the van round a corner, off the main road, parked it out of sight and then followed them. Once through the barbed wire they started to clamber down on to the deck of the yacht.

'Okay, mind the metal rungs. They're slippery,' advised the boy as Ruth descended, followed by Roger and then himself. Finally the Enforcer joined them having disposed of the police van.

Giles then took charge. 'Now, listen everyone. This is going to be quite a tricky manoeuvre. Ruth, you first. I'll show you what you'll need to do.' Giles rearranged the mooring ropes so that they looped from the on-board cleats, around the huge metal bollards on the harbour wall and then back to the boat. Tied up in this fashion, Ruth could release both bow and stern lines at the same time from the deck of the yacht.

'Now, Mister Enforcer, I'll need you to help me get the sail up and fend off if we get too near the harbour wall.'

'Anything you say, Giles.'

Having made as many preparations as was possible there was nothing to do but wait for the tide. With appalling slowness the sea gradually filled the harbour. All those on board kept their eyes on the road and harbour entrance, expecting at any moment to see police cars and vans screech along the wall towards them.

Just across the border Mandy and her deputation had been waiting patiently in anticipation of escorting the boy and his minder on the second part of the journey back to Nowton. As the expected time of their arrival came and went with no sign of them Mandy began to fret. Once again she felt uncomfortable; somehow she knew that the boy might have a card up his sleeve. When the van was thirty minutes late she phoned the police department in the capital only to be informed that the escort sent had been dismissed by a government official, that they had set off with the prisoner hours ago and should have arrived for the border exchange on schedule. Mandy didn't bother to reply but simply slammed the phone back in its cradle, marched into the main office of the police station and addressed the sergeant who was drinking tea with two of his men. In a surprisingly calm voice she said, 'The prisoner has escaped and taken three hostages. I need you to drive me back to the capital immediately.'

'But that's outside our jurisdiction, Miss. We have no authority to enter Dalriada.'

'You have, *now*.'

The sergeant began to remonstrate.

'Just do it.' Mandy's eyes were like diamonds and her voice of cut glass. 'I need as many men as you can muster. I know where he'll be. The Dalriada police are incompetent idiots and they'll never catch him; he's far too clever. However, I know him. I've been tracking him for years. I just *know* what he'll do.'

'But I'll need written orders, Miss.'

'I think you'll find that a Euthanasia Monitor's instructions are authority enough. Let's just say that it will be in your best interests to do as I say.' Something in the way this was said made the sergeant shiver. 'Right away, Miss.' And within ten minutes Mandy was seated, along with the sergeant and three other police officers in a police car, its blue light flashing eerily in the dusk of early evening, heading at speed in the direction of the capital

The water was now lapping around the hull of the boat but there needed to be at least another foot in depth before the boat would begin to float. The boy did a quick calculation, 'Another hour should do it,' he said as much to himself as to Ruth and the Enforcer, who were standing alongside him in the cockpit. Thank god Mandy was in England. She would be aware of his escape by now, and he dreaded to think how furious she would be.

'Okay, everyone; let's run through the procedure once more,' and for the fourth time Giles rehearsed how they would cast off and make their escape. It was now quite dark and the harbour mouth was becoming difficult to identify, but the boy reckoned that there was just enough moonlight to navigate by. Then, finally, they felt the boat lift off the harbour floor and start to rock.

'Right, let's go,' said the Enforcer,

'Not yet, I'm afraid. We need at least another foot of water underneath us to sail or we'll run aground on the sand spit at the harbour mouth. We'll have to wait a bit longer.' The boy had managed to set the instruments working and was monitoring with some concern the increasing wind speed, which was now gusting up to twenty-five knots. 'No point in showing signs of alarm,' he thought. 'We have no choice.' He felt a gentle pressure against his side. It was Ruth.

'Giles, do you think we'll make it?'

'Yes. It should be fine.'

'I can tell that you're concerned about the conditions.'

'Yes. A bit,' he conceded. 'But remember the last time – not dissimilar as I recall.' He looked at her and smiled.

She chuckled. 'Then I had the dreaded Mandy hanging on to my arm. At least she's nowhere near this time.'

'Don't count on it.' They both fell silent and alternately watched the height of the water, willing it to deepen, while surveying the road for any sign of pursuit. Thirty minutes later the boy noted a vehicle stop on the coast road. A door opened and a man emerged who, after peering in the direction of the boat for a few moments, spoke urgently through an open window to those in the car. Suddenly the vehicle reversed, a blue light started to flash and it headed down the uneven harbour wall, the beams of its headlights flashing wildly like searchlights seeking a target.

'Shit! That's the police,' shouted the boy. 'Right let's go! *Go! Go! Go!* Enforcer, let the jib out, but don't sheet in,' he yelled. 'Ruth! Get ready to cast off. *But not yet.*' The noise of the flapping jib now added to that of the shrieking wind and the lashing rain so that the boy had to shout at the top of his voice to be heard. 'Right, get the mainsail half up and then jam the halyard. *Quick* ! *Quick!*'

With the mainsail half-raised, the boat was now straining against its moorings, held there by the lines Ruth was holding. The police car had now stopped on the opposite side of the barbed-wire fence and the occupants were scrambling out. The boy instantly recognised the female figure now running towards them.

'*Right,*' the boy yelled to the Enforcer. 'Sheet in the jib. Hold on, Ruth. The boat now tugged wildly against its moorings, like a dog on a leash. 'Ruth, let her go. *Cast off.*' Ruth let go of both mooring lines, which whipped around the bollards on the harbour wall. No longer restrained, the boat then shot away from the quayside and into the middle of the harbour. Giles struggled with the tiller as the yacht swung to port, heading directly for the wall at the opposite side and when just a few feet away he pushed the tiller from him and the yacht went about, crazily lurching from the starboard to the port tack and throwing all three of them across the cockpit as the boat careered in the opposite direction across the harbour. Once again, when only feet away from the wall, he pushed the tiller across and then, after an interminable moment of uncertainty, the wild, flapping, frenzied sails filled, the yacht heeled then began to move forward and, gaining speed all the time, slid through the harbour mouth with inches to spare on her port side.

Once in the river and beyond the relative shelter of the harbour, the full force of the storm hit them and the little craft listed dangerously. The boy tacked twice more until the boat began to head into the river, once more passing close to the harbour mouth. Until then the boy had been wholly preoccupied with leaving the harbour safely but now he glanced towards the little group on the quayside. There, standing in front of four police officers, was the irate figure of Mandy shouting and shaking her fists in frustration, rain pouring down her face, her hair plastered to her forehead and cheeks, her utterances inaudible.

'Just like old times,' he thought as he gave instructions to the Enforcer on how to adjust the sails. Conditions were still very difficult with a heavy swell and high winds, while driving rain stung their faces. Although now safely away from the harbour, they were making extremely slow and uncomfortable progress. With every wave the craft rose only to hang briefly on its crest before it plunged into the trough beyond causing a great plume of spray to crash over the boat and land in torrents within the cockpit, where the trio were clinging to anything that offered security. By the time Giles felt that the boat was reasonably under control, they were in the middle of the estuary, over a mile from the southern shore and the ever-receding harbour. There, he could still just glimpse the small group standing in the rain and wind yelling furiously.

For the first time since casting off, the boy, Ruth and the Enforcer could now take stock of their situation as they huddled together in the cockpit. 'Just like old times,' the boy repeated with a smile. 'Well done, everybody. That was quite exciting.'

Ruth wiped some spray from her face. '*Too* exciting. I thought you said it would be safe!'

'Too much excitement for me,' said the Enforcer. 'It was only the sight of Mandy on the pier that stopped me from jumping overboard and swimming ashore.' He burst into peals of hysterical laughter while the boy and Ruth both chuckled.

'D'you think they'll follow us?' asked Ruth.

'You must be joking,' laughed the boy, 'Only an idiot would go sailing in conditions like these.'

Ruth nodded in empathy before her eyes suddenly widened. 'What about Roger?'

'Oh, shit. I'd completely forgotten about him in all this excitement. We forgot to put him ashore. You'd better check that he's all right.'

The Enforcer disappeared and carefully negotiated the swaying steps down to the cabin. A moment later he returned.

'Well?' asked Ruth.

'No problem. He's being as sick as a dog in the toilet. He won't be any trouble.'

The boy smiled to himself as he set a course that would take him out of the estuary towards the sea beyond.

# FIFTEEN

'Ladies and gentlemen. Order please.' The Prime Minister looked along the table around which were seated his Cabinet Ministers. When the chatter had died down he stood and placed his right hand on the pile of books in front of him. 'Please be upstanding,' he said as he bowed his head and solemnly intoned, 'Bless the Protocol. May we serve it well.'

'Bless the Protocol. May we serve it well,' came the unhesitating response from all across the room.

'Thank you, ladies and gentlemen. Please be seated.' The P.M. then glanced across the table to where Doreese was sitting opposite him, her face largely concealed by a hat of truly enormous proportions. 'Firstly,' he continued, 'on behalf of the Cabinet, I should wish to congratulate Doreese, if I may, on her enoblement.' He tapped the table lightly and murmurs of approval echoed around the room. 'Well deserved, I might add, *Lady* Doreese.' The P.M. smiled beatifically, his profile sleeker than ever. 'The Department of Intelligent Euthanasia has progressed from strength to strength under your ladyship's leadership and we are now rolling out our Protocols throughout Dalriada following your highly successful visits there.' The new Lady of the Cabinet simpered below her millinery. The P.M. then continued: 'I am sure it would be helpful if we might begin our meeting with a brief summary of progress from yourself, Lady Doreese, if you should condescend so to do.'

'Thank you, Prime Minister. and may I thank everyone present for their kind good wishes.' Doreese waved a gloved hand in the general direction of her colleagues. 'I have to say it has not been at all easy but my untiring efforts have succeeded. The leader of Dalriada has agreed – in exchange for our continuing to supply aid to his country – to introduce the Life Protocols across the whole of the land, including, of course, the Euthanasia Protocol.'

Before Doreese could continue, Lady Carter interrupted. 'But they don't *need* a Euthanasia Protocol up there because the inhabitants of Dalriada all die so young.'

Doreese tried unsuccessfully to conceal her irritation. 'Ah, yes, Lady Carter, you seem to have missed the point. Perhaps I failed to make myself entirely clear.' Her facial muscles twitched in a failed attempt to smile. 'The whole beauty of this process is that by introducing the Life and Health Protocols these barbarians *will* live long enough to cause an ageing society and therefore *will* require a Euthanasia policy.' She paused briefly to stare fixedly at Lady Carter. 'With the introduction of the Life Protocols the days of the Dalriadans as uncontrolled barbarians are numbered. Who knows?... ' Doreese chuckled slightly, '... soon they may be as civilised as we are!'

'*Lady* Doreese, it seems to me that you are merely creating a problem in order to solve it!'

'*Lady* Carter, *surely* you are not suggesting that we withhold life-saving and life-prolonging technology from our deserving neighbours in Dalriada. You *must* agree that they have as much right to these Protocols as do we.' Lady Doreese smiled as she attempted to seize the moral high ground.

'But *then*, when they live *too* long you're going to *kill* them!' Lady Carter was unable to conceal her exasperation.

The P.M. now entered the debate. 'Really, Lady Carter, "kill" is hardly an appropriate word in this context.'

'Properly designed and fully integrated, end-of-life management can *hardly* be termed killing,' replied Lady Doreese, 'The Protocol will be in complete control of the whole process, with no human being requiring to be involved at any stage.'

Lady Carter shook her head in disbelief before trying another tack. 'My understanding is that the Dalriadan leader, their so-called President, has no mandate outside the capital, so that the country has essentially reverted to clan rule.'

'Ugh!' Doreese shook her head, amazed that anyone could be so stupid as to not understand her logic. '*Precisely*! That – for heaven's sake – is where the Protocols come in: when they are properly enforced the whole country *will* once more be united.'

'Sorry to appear dim, Lady Doreese, but how can you enforce Protocols in such an ungoverned country?'

Lady Doreese sighed even more deeply. 'We shall introduce a new Protocol *of course*. One which will ensure that everyone follows the *existing* ones.' She glared angrily at her inquisitor. 'I have already given it detailed consideration and I propose that we should call it the Dalriadan Amendment for Total Integration: DAFTI for short.'

Lady Carter, however, was not finished. 'There is no doubt in my mind that their leader is too weak to see this through,'

'Now, *there* I do agree with you,' Lady Doreese smiled at Lady Carter and waved her gloved hand in her adversary's direction as if to say, 'D'you think I'm an idiot and hadn't thought of that?' 'And that is why,' she continued, 'I have instructed my agent in Dalriada, Mandy, to take on the role of managing the whole project. I have every confidence that *she* will succeed where the President has failed.'

The P.M. glanced at his watch and thought to himself, 'Good, nearly time for an aperitif, I wonder what's for dinner.' Aloud, he pronounced, 'Excellent, excellent! Now, tell us about the tribunal you chaired up there.'

'Well, P.M. it went very well indeed and I think that the local leaders were highly impressed with the way in which our systems work.'

'And the outcome?'

'Oh! – guilty of course! There could never be any doubt about that!'

'Good, good.'

Lady Doreese continued, 'The prisoner is, as we speak, returning to Nowton (where, you will remember, the Euthanasia Protocol was first trialled) for completion.'

'Excellent, excellent.' The P.M. glanced at his watch once more.

There was a collective murmur of, 'Good,' and 'Excellent,' from around the room, while a few ministers tapped the table in approval.

'Mandy and her team are bringing the prisoner south and his completion date is tomorrow.'

'Well, I thank you for that, Lady Doreese.' The P.M. looked around the table. 'Clearly our policies are proving popular with the electorate, as the last election showed, but we must never relax: we are only as good as our last success.'

'Or as bad as our last failure,' added Lady Carter.

'Yes, yes! You really are *so* negative at times, Lady Carter. Now, are there any other D.I.E. issues?'

Doreese resumed: 'Well, P.M., our helpline has proved to be enormously successful, with nearly a dozen calls in the last year alone.'

'Excellent, excellent. And Ofdeath?'

'Similarly, very successful indeed. I have received at least fifteen complaints, all of which I have dealt with personally.'

'What kind of complaint?'

'Oh, nothing of any great significance: failure of the pathway, some studios' décor being substandard, the wrong person being euthanased – that kind of thing. Nothing that cannot be readily resolved.'

'Excellent. Well, I think I may speak for all of us when I say that you've done a cracking job.' There were gentle murmurs of approbation from around the table before Lady Carter raised her hand.

'Yes, Lady Carter?' groaned the P.M. as he once more glanced at his watch.

'I am still concerned about the lack of independence – of transparency if you like – of Ofdeath.'

The hat swivelled in the direction of the questioner. 'Absolutely, I couldn't agree with you more, Lady Carter, and that is why I have commissioned an Ofdeath Protocol to be composed. That way the whole process will be managed without human interference, with all its attendant frailties to which…' and Doreese tilted her head slightly, raised an eyebrow and placed a gloved hand on her ample bosom, '… even *I* might be susceptible.'

'But surely the whole concept of Ofdeath is that it embodies a system for appeal if anyone has a problem with the Protocol.'

'Yes, that's precisely why we need a new PAMP, or Protocol About Managing a Protocol, to ensure uniformity.'

'But what if someone has a complaint about *that* Protocol.'

'In that event we shall establish another to monitor it. It's *quite* simple really, Lady Carter.'

The P.M., who was now desperately in need of a drink, decided to press on with the agenda, and enquired, 'Justin, please tell us about the financial aspects.'

'Thank you P.M. Well, as I predicted at the very beginning, it's coming in on budget and doing rather well actually. Essentially it's self-funding. The average USPELY... ' Justin hesitated for a moment... 'that is, as you will recall, the Unit Saving Per Euthanised Life Year, is... '

'We really must find a better acronym,' interrupted the Prime Minister.

'Yes, I wholly agree, P.M. The average USPELY is just over 200,000, the tipping point being 150,000, so we're well within the safety zone.'

'Excellent, excellent.' Well if there are no further questions we should move on. 'Now, Martin. Why on earth do you want to raise the issue of ideological greed? You'd better make it brief.' The Minister for Ideologies nervously rose to his feet.

* * *

As the night wore on and the little yacht sailed eastward the wind lessened, the rain eased and, by the time the first grey light of dawn could be seen on the horizon, conditions were much calmer and the boat with its motley crew had reached the mouth of the estuary. Once the craft had cleared the sand spit at its northern tip Giles asked the Enforcer to free off the jib and main sheets, then he pushed the tiller away from him a trifle turning the bow of the boat northward. The sails filled and a chill but invigorating north-easterly drove them in the direction of Inverneuage. As Giles scanned the horizon and confirmed his compass bearing he saw a sea eagle ahead of them, gliding through the grey sky of a new dawn, and as he watched, it gently banked to its left as if to lead the way.

# PART THREE

## THE PROPHET GILES

# ONE

For some time the eagle flew overhead, soaring and banking – leading the way. Then, after about an hour, as though confident that the yacht was sailing in the correct direction, the massive bird caught the wind, rose high into the sky and was gone. Giles watched it disappear, saddened that it had left him and his crew lonely on the ocean. He shivered, cold after the night's sail but exhilarated by the moment. It was a crisp, clear morning: the sky cloudless and pure, cleansed by the storm. The north-easterly wind, now light, was driving the boat slowly, yet steadily northwards. The Enforcer was standing just in front of Giles, where he had been for most of the night, holding on to the spray hood, silent, lost in his thoughts.

'Not missing Mandy, are you?' asked Giles with a wry smile.

'In a strange way I am,' answered the man, without taking his eyes off the horizon. 'With her, there was a constancy, an absolute certainty that she would be an ever-present, vindictive, annoying, bullying besom. You could rely on it. Now, for the first time since I was a child, I have no idea what the future holds. I am in a small boat, heading lord knows where, to a place which is supposed to be beyond civilisation accompanied by an outlaw, a government official and a chinless wonder from London. It's a strange feeling.'

'It's called self-determination. You'll soon get used to it. You'll find it addictive and you won't want to be bossed around by the Mandys of this world ever again.'

'What do you think Mandy and the aments will do?' asked the Enforcer continuing to peer into the distance.

'I'm not sure,' replied Giles. 'I've been giving it some thought overnight, while we've been sailing. There's little doubt that she's going to be pretty annoyed.'

'That's an understatement. She was *furious*. I'm just glad that we couldn't hear what she was shouting as we sailed away.'

'Yes, she did seem a trifle upset.' The boy Giles smiled at the memory. 'She could make a big hoo-ha: turn my escape into an international incident and get the English government involved. But relations with Dalriada are delicate, at best, and as far as the Dalriadans are concerned I was packed off to Nowton for Life Completion and am now dead, sitting on the top of the Eiffel Tower with my friend the donkey.' The Enforcer chuckled while Giles continued, 'There are no more than a few people who know that we have escaped. The English authorities can only know what Mandy tells them and the Dalriadan authorities think I'm in England. If Mandy has any sense she'll keep the whole episode as quiet as possible.'

'Since when was Mandy known for her commonsense?'

'True, that's a worry. However, although her instinct will be to chase us even into the jaws of hell, she's a scheming old witch and she may – just *may* – realise that it's in her own best interests to keep our escape a secret.'

The hatch to the cabin slid open and the Enforcer moved aside to let a disheveled looking Ruth ascend the short ladder from the saloon up to the cockpit of the little yacht. Giles smiled at her with affection. 'Morning, Ruth, sleep well?'

'Morning, boy – I mean Giles. Morning, Mister Enforcer.' Ruth looked at the empty expanse of sea all around their little craft. 'Yes, not bad; once the storm settled. You must be dead tired. Have you been steering all night?'

'Yes, but I'm fine, thanks.'

'Where are we, Giles? Have we far to go?'

'Well the storm actually blew us in the right direction and, if I'm not mistaken, that promontory there,' and Giles pointed to a vague shadow just visible on the horizon, 'is the estuary. The mouth of the river that will lead us to Inverneuage.'

'How long will it take?'

'Unless the wind picks up it'll take the rest of the day and once we're there it's quite a long sail up the river to the harbour. And of course we may have to wait for the tide.' Giles looked up at the sails and adjusted the tiller slightly. 'Mister Enforcer here has said he was already missing Mandy. How are you feeling, Ruth?'

'Oh, the same as anyone who has just thrown away the fruits of their hard-earned study and a promising career, for a completely unknown future with an escaped convict, a mutineer and a hungover aide to an English minister.'

'So, pretty good then?'

'Absolutely.' Ruth looked at the boy and smiled ruefully.

'How is the chinless wonder?' asked the Enforcer.

'Sleeping,' replied Ruth. 'He stopped being sick when the storm settled and has been quietly snoring ever since.'

'He's good at that,' said the boy.

'What? Sleeping?' asked the Enforcer.

'No – being sick,' responded Ruth. 'Every time I've met him he's ended up vomiting.' She fell silent for a moment – thoughtful. 'What are we going to do with him? Strictly speaking, we've kidnapped him.'

'We could set him adrift in the life-raft,' suggested Giles.

Ruth laughed. 'What? To row all the way back to London?'

'We'll put him ashore as soon as we can,' said the boy, 'and anyway, we might need the life-raft.'

Just then the hatch slid open and Roger's head appeared. 'Morning, chaps. I say, spiffing morning.' Roger looked about him. 'Has anyone got any idea where we are?'

'Morning, Roger. We were just talking about you.'

'Oh gosh! Sorry about being sick and all that but I'm beginning to think I've got a bit of a weak stomach. I'm fine now though.' Roger smiled at the other members of the crew.

'Roger, you do realise that you've been kidnapped, don't you?' Ruth looked enquiringly at him.

'Absolutely, Ruth. Spot on – as always.'

'You don't seem too upset by your circumstances.'

'It's rather fun, now the weather's better. I presume you're not going to kill me, or anything ghastly like that.'

'Actually we were just wondering what to do with you,' said the Enforcer. 'The options seem rather limited.'

'Oh, I say! Well while you're thinking about it, is anyone for breakfast?'

'We haven't got any,' said Ruth, surprised at the suggestion.

'Ah! That's where you're wrong,' responded Roger with a grin. 'I've found a few tins of this and that and can easily rustle something up. Nothing like throwing up for several hours to give one an appetite.'

Roger smiled and went back into the cabin, closing the hatch behind him to keep out the draught while he lit the little cooker.

Ruth smiled in amazement. 'Well, I've never seen him looking so happy. We may as well let him make breakfast for us before we cast him adrift.'

True to his word, half an hour later, Roger reappeared carrying four steaming bowls filled with a mixture of various tinned foods that he had found in the galley. 'Life on the jolly old ocean wave, eh? It's rather fun, don't you think?'

Ruth looked at Giles and then the Enforcer, her face suffused with amusement, 'Roger,' she said, 'you never cease to amaze me.'

'Oh! Jolly good,' came the reply.

\* \* \*

Mandy didn't take long to make up her mind. She could legitimately blame the local authorities for letting the boy escape, but that wouldn't help her much because, as Head of Protocols for Dalriada, she was in effect responsible for the fate of the boy and it would be impossible to distance herself completely from this debacle. As the small yacht, lashed by the wind and rain, bounced and splashed its way slowly towards the sea, she turned and ushered the four policemen who had accompanied her, back to the car.

Once out of the rain she turned to the sergeant. 'You and your men are the only witnesses to the prisoner's escape. Strictly speaking I should report you to your seniors for gross misconduct in failing to apprehend Giles and his companions.'

'But , Miss, it's hardly our fault... '

'*Shut up* and listen. It *is* your fault since you failed to deliver the boy to Nowton as instructed, and that is a Protocol 24 offence, *believe me.*' The policeman was about to remonstrate but, on seeing the look in Mandy's eyes, decided the better of it. 'However,' Mandy continued, 'I see little point in ruining your careers for that little brat, and it's very likely that they'll all drown in this storm anyway, so I have a proposition.' She looked at each of the four policemen in turn to emphasise her words. 'Never, *ever,* mention this episode to anyone and I will report that the boy was handed over to the Euthanasia team in

Nowton. In that way you will escape being tried for gross dereliction of duty.'

There was no response from the officers. 'Right! I'll take that as agreement. Now, drive me back to the capital and then proceed to the border and don't say a word to anyone. I will do my utmost to cover this up but, if you let anyone know what happened tonight, I will have no choice but to have you all arrested and you know what that will mean.' She gave all four officers a meaningful stare. 'Now, *drive.*'

The next morning Mandy sent a message to Doreese.

> *Dear Minister,*
>
> *I am pleased to say that the prisoner Giles has been Completed and I have also managed to solve the problem of the girl – the free thinker – Ruth. Roger has gone native, but that's no great loss. There should now be no impediment to the successful introduction of The Protocol in Dalriada.*
>
> *Your humble servant, Mandy.*
> *Director of The Protocol in Dalriada.*

# TWO

'Good morning, everyone.' The Prime Minister smiled and looked up from his papers as he called the Cabinet meeting to order. Although his hair was now tinged with grey he was still sleek and youthful-looking. His new heart had given him an extra lease of life and he was now back to his old enthusiastic self. When the chatting had ceased, he assumed his most serious expression and said, 'Please be upstanding.' The members of the Cabinet then rose as one, clasped their hands in prayerful manner and bowed their heads. The P.M. placed his hand upon the topmost book of those in front of him and pronounced, in the most resonant and reverential tones that he could muster, 'Bless the Protocol, may we serve it well.'

'Bless the Protocol,' came the resounding response from around the room.

'Please be seated.' The P.M. then relaxed his solemn expression and sat down. Once everyone was settled he continued. 'Welcome to this meeting of the Cabinet. I should like to begin by picking up the theme of age-control in those countries to which we give aid.' The P.M. looked up to make sure that everyone was paying attention. 'Ministers will recall that the Cabinet considered it inappropriate to continue to give financial aid to countries where there was no attempt to control the age of the population. The nearest example of such a country is, of course, Dalriada. You will no doubt recall that last year we sent a delegation, led by Lady Doreese, to its capital.' The P.M. paused for a moment and looked along the table to where her ladyship was seated.

Lady Doreese was now wearing an extravagant gold-coloured coat with cut-glass buttons while, across her ample bosom, flashed a vivid purple sash which terminated in a gigantic bow upon her left hip. Pinned to the sash was a large ceramic brooch on which was inscribed, 'Bless The Protocol'. Her hair was now bright yellow and freshly permed, while half-moon spectacles were perched on the end of her nose. It was, however, her hat, which again caught everyone's attention.

Squarely set upon her head was an enormous straw contraption, larger than any traditional boater, on which sat a bunch of grapes surrounding what seemed like half a melon. At the mention of her name she smiled and graciously waved a gloved hand in that circular motion which she had seen royalty perform in old films.

'Lady Doreese, perhaps, as head of D.I.E. and Minister for Age Control, would you kindly give us an update on the results of your recent trip.'

'Most certainly, Prime Minister,' Lady Doreese gushed, as she rose to her feet. 'Ladies and gentlemen of the Cabinet, I am delighted to say that, after a few initial teething problems, the introduction of The Protocol in Dalriada is moving forward at a steady pace. The President has agreed to support our initiative on the understanding that financial aid continues. The whole project is under the control of our man – or I should say, our woman… ' Doreese chuckled at her little joke '… in Dalriada.' Doreese paused to acknowledge the ripple of laughter from her fellow-ministers. 'The lady in question is Mandy, who has spent many years in Dalriada and knows the country well. I have appointed her "Protocol Minister for Dalriada." She is training a team of missionaries to work their way gradually across the country, converting the population and setting up Protocol Studios as they go.'

There came a cough from one end of the table, 'If I may, Prime Minister?'

'Yes, Lady Carter,' said the P.M. with a sigh.

'Could you inform us about those initial problems, if you would, Lady Doreese?'

Doreese clenched her teeth. Why on earth hadn't the P.M. got rid of that woman, she wondered to herself. She turned towards Lady Carter, the hat following a fraction of a second later, and smiled. 'Merely a few minor inconveniences which I was well able to deal with, Lady Carter.'

'Maybe you could clarify what those, "few minor inconveniences," were?'

'Well, if you insist. But there's barely time to go into details here.' Doreese was flustered as she hadn't expected to be questioned on her mission but merely to accept the plaudits for her success.

'I *do* insist. *Briefly* will be acceptable.'

'Well,' and Doreese took a deep breath to register her annoyance. 'There was a certain Junior Secretary for... ' Doreese hesitated for a moment... ' something or other, who was far too much of a free-thinker to be entrusted with such an important initiative, and consequently she was demoted by the President himself. You will recall that I presided over the trial of that young English delinquent, a brigand wanted by the police who was brought home for sentencing. I must say that went down particularly well, since the local population could then see how the English Protocol operated, and could work equally well in Dalriada if introduced.' Doreese thought it better not to mention the donkey episode and the shambles that had followed.

'And what was the sentence?' Lady Carter looked along the table to where Doreese was standing.

'Oh! I'm not sure I can remember the more trivial details of the case.'

'You seem to have an extremely short memory, Lady Doreese. Let me remind members about the "trivial detail" that was the sentence.' Lady Carter paused briefly while she looked around the Cabinet table, 'It was *execution*.' There was an audible gasp of disbelief from around the room.

The P.M. was the first to recover his composure. 'Really, Lady Carter, that is hardly appropriate. Capital punishment was banned over a century ago. Such barbaric practices have long since ceased.'

Lady Carter was not to be silenced, 'If it wasn't execution, what was it?'

'It was Life Completion,' Doreese responded indignantly. 'Totally different.'

'Ah, yes! Protocol 24.' Lady Carter sighed, and a reflex murmur of, 'Bless the protocol. May we serve it well,' rumbled around the table. She then continued, 'Why was that necessary?'

'The Protocol stated that it was necessary. It was quite clear on the issue. We went through all he appropriate procedures and even entered a plea on behalf of the defendant. The Protocol didn't hesitate for one moment, stating that Life Completion, or rather completion of a previous euthanasia order, was the correct verdict and that protocol 24 applied.'

'And the Junior Secretary. Was she killed as well?'

'Lady Carter, that is *too* much. I must ask you to stop that tone of questioning. Remember that the computer is on and the Protocol is running.' The P.M. looked at the machine in front of him almost apologetically, then back at Lady Carter who sighed and sat back in her chair.

The P.M. continued, 'May I remind Cabinet that there are certain standards of behaviour for these meetings, as set down in the Protocol, *Appropriate Behaviour During Official Government Meetings*, which must be adhered to at all times.' The P.M. let his words sink in.

'Hear, hear,' said one Minister, while another tapped the table in approbation. 'Now, Lady Doreese, that all sounds highly satisfactory. May I presume that when the Protocol is rolled out across Dalriada then the two countries will in effect be administered as one since we will be following the same set of rules?'

'Precisely, PM.' Doreese smiled broadly in the knowledge that she had won the day.

The P.M. looked at his agenda. 'Next item. Ah yes! Gerry. What's all this nonsense about holes appearing in the sky. How on earth can the sky have holes in it?' The P.M. looked menacing. 'This had better be good, Gerry.' The Minister for Disasters rose wearily to his feet.

\* \* \*

'You see, P.M. I didn't want to raise this in Cabinet this morning as it is highly sensitive and, dare I say it, there are some ministers, or should I say *one*, who is not as sympathetic to some of my ideas as she might be.'

'Ah, yes, I know. But we all have our crosses to bear, Doreese.'

They were closeted in the P.M.'s private rooms later that day. It was nearly five o'clock and the P.M. was looking forward to an aperitif, and wondering what was for dinner.

'Well, you see, P.M.,' said Doreese, 'I think the Protocol has become so successful that we need to cement it further into the collective psyche.'

The P.M. was hoping that it would be steak and glanced at his watch. He looked up on hearing these words. 'The *what*?'

'The collective psyche, P.M.' Doreese loved the phrase and had been wanting to use it ever since she'd read of it in an article on women's sexual health some weeks before.

'Ah, yes. What exactly are you proposing, Doreese?'

'Well, millions of people now believe wholeheartedly in the Protocol and the computer that administers it but many are asking where it came from: what is its provenance?' The P.M. was still thinking that it would be nice to have steak for dinner as he hadn't eaten steak for a some time.

'All successful systems of management such as those defined in the works we call "The Protocol" have in the past had a provenance: a clear link with their creator.' Doreese paused, leaned forward and then – her expression loaded with significance – added quietly, 'A Prophet.'

The P.M. looked up, surprise registering on his face. 'A Prophet?'

'Yes. Someone at the centre of that intricate network that is society. Somebody kindly and comforting who adds credence to the system. An image: a person who will soften the otherwise rather austere and uncompromising nature of the hardware – however wise it may be.'

'Mmm.'

'It would also help with the little problems we have with certain members of the public and, if I dare say so, the Cabinet itself. Because then we could introduce a Blasphemy Protocol which would effectively and speedily deal with the kind of outburst that we witnessed this morning.'

The P.M. knew that Doreese was referring to Lady Carter who, as the long-standing Minister for Babies, had been a thorn in the P.M.'s side for many years. The reason that he hadn't sacked her was simple – he was simply scared of her. He didn't want to upset her, but in Doreese he had an ally, and if she could do the dirty work for him, that would be fine.

'Go on,' he said.

'Well the first thing is to *discover* a prophet.

'Ah, yes. That could be quite difficult.'

'Well, not really, P.M., there are only a few candidates.'

'And who might those be?'

'Well, the Minister who designed the service was of course, Charles.'

'Yes – but the accident. That would hardly be acceptable.'

'Precisely, P.M. After him, though I hesitate to say it, there is myself. There has never been a female prophet so I think one is long overdue.' Lady Doreese thought it would be rather fine to be a prophet. It would certainly be one in the eye for Lady Carter and she rather liked the title, *The Most Worshipful Lady Doreese*, or something rather snappy like that. She began to wonder what type of hat a prophet would wear.

'No, Doreese That would never do.'

'Why on earth not?' Doreese looked at the P.M., aghast.

'Well for one thing you're still alive. Prophets have to be dead to be any good. And, like it or not, it's a man's job being a prophet.' The P.M. stroked his chin and creased his brow with concentration. 'Mmm, let me think. Prophet? Prophet?'

Doreese was much put out. Part of the reason for suggesting that there was a need for a prophet was so that she might assume that rôle. Head in hands the P.M. continued to deliberate. Suddenly he looked up, his eyes bright and alert. 'I know! Who was the Junior Secretary who did all the work for Charles. The one who actually wrote the original Euthanasia Protocol.' The P.M. searched his memory, 'Yes, I remember – Giles. It was Giles. He's ideal. He was involved from the beginning and helped to spawn the whole system. His name is easy to remember and, above all, he's dead. He's perfect for the job.'

Doreese was horrified. She remembered his appearance in her courtroom all those years ago. He had actually challenged the system and had called the Protocol an ass. 'But P.M., that's hardly appropriate. He was sentenced to Life Completion himself and died in suspicious circumstances. Hardly good material for a prophet.'

'Not at all. He's ideal. All prophets have to suffer: it gives them credibility. You can hardly have a prophet who simply invents a religion (must avoid *that* word) converts everyone, generally has a jolly good time, and dies peacefully. That's no good at all. They've got to be persecuted, tortured a little and killed for their beliefs. That is what makes prophets special; otherwise we'd all be prophets, for heavens sake. No, Giles is the man for us.'

This was not going as Doreese had anticipated. 'I'm not so sure, Prime Minister.'

'No, he's just perfect for the rôle. Besides, we don't have any choice.

You're still alive and, like it or not, women do not make good prophets and as for Charles, well the accident rules him out.'

Doreese saw that the die was cast, that the P.M. had made up his mind and that further argument was futile. 'On reflection, P.M., I think your decision is very wise. I was being rather foolish in failing to consider Giles as an option. It required your foresight and wisdom to identify the obvious candidate,' simpered Doreese.

'Good. I'm pleased that we see eye to eye on this, Doreese. Now I think the introduction of this concept falls to your department. I'll leave that to you but I think we require some original Gilesian philosophy – the sayings of Giles – that sort of thing – and it would be helpful to know how he dressed. The followers of prophets always like to dress in the same way as I recall. Report back to the next Cabinet if you would, Doreese, Now I must go, I'm sorely in need of refreshment.'

# THREE

The wind did not pick up and the little yacht made painfully slow progress towards the mouth of the estuary. Darkness was falling when they finally reached the entrance to the river that would take them to Inverneuage and Giles made the decision to anchor just offshore overnight as he judged it too dangerous to continue further in darkness. He discovered a fishing line in one of the lockers and caught several good-sized mackerel, which Roger cooked along with some remaining tinned food. The four of them then sat around the small table in the main saloon and ate by the light of an oil lantern on the aft bulkhead which rocked gently on its gimbal in time with the swell.

'Roger, those fish are lovely. You amaze me, I had no idea you could cook.' Ruth looked at the hostage and smiled.

'Gosh. Actually, Ruth, I do a lot of cooking back at home. Living on my own it gives me something to do.'

'Isn't there a Mrs Roger to do that sort of thing?'

'Gosh no! I left home a long time ago.'

'No, I mean; a Mrs Roger – *your wife*.'

'Oh, I see. No. I've not been allocated one as yet.'

'Allocated one?'

'Yes. As a senior civil servant, after a certain period of service, you are allocated a State wife.'

'Can't you marry whoever you want?'

'Well you could, but that would be political suicide. You see, the Protocol tells us who to marry. There is a database of women who have been screened and are considered to be appropriate: we call it the *Dating Database*, rather good don't you think?' Roger wheezed and snorted with amusement.

'Oh!'

Giles looked up from his plate. 'I remember the old man telling me about his State wife. She was withdrawn when he was sacked for challenging the system. It saddened him greatly.'

'Who actually was the old man?' asked Roger.

'I met him years ago, outside a Euthanasia Studio, when I was about fifteen. I was homeless and he saved my life by putting me up in his hostel. He signed up to the Protocol and we spent his six months terminal holiday up here in Dalriada. After he died I took his name.' Giles showed the others his signet ring, 'This is his ring. We stayed in a village not far from where we're now going. That's where I met Ruth.'

Ruth nodded at the memory. 'A lot has happened since then,' she said wistfully.

'Gosh, Giles,' continued Roger, 'how did you ever manage to become a wanted criminal?'

'That's a long story but essentially Mandy and her minder here – Mister Enforcer – chased me around, claiming that I'd tried to kill them.' Giles glanced at the ex-Enforcer, 'But before he responds, Mister Enforcer then saved my life by putting a sniper off his shot as I was escaping. Then, with the assistance of Ruth, he helped me escape once more, this time from the prison – that's where you came in, Roger. But more to the point: what are *you* going to do?'

'How do you mean?'

'Have you forgotten? We've kidnapped you. You, Mister *aide-de-camp*, are our prisoner.'

'Gosh! Yes. I had rather forgotten that.'

'Don't you want to escape?' asked Ruth. 'Most prisoners do. It's sort of goes with being a captive, it's part of the job. If you do, that's fine. We'll just drop you off somewhere nice and safe and you can head off back to London and Lady Doreese.'

'Ruth, I'm not sure I want to go back to being Lady Doreese's dog's body.'

'This is really bizarre,' said Giles. 'You're a prisoner. We, your captors, are trying to help you escape and you're not entirely sure that you want to. How ungrateful is that?'

'Do we have to *force* you to escape?' asked the Enforcer with a broad smile.

'To be honest, I'm really not sure I want to escape. Lady Doreese was not an easy boss being more concerned about her hats than her team. And I quite like it up here with you guys.' Roger looked affectionately at Ruth, who in response put her arm around Giles' waist.

'Well, it's up to you,' said the boy. 'I guess if you want to change your colours, like the Enforcer here, then it's always good to have someone in the gang who can cook.'

The yacht rocked and jerked slightly as it settled on to the seabed and then, for the first time since they had left the capital, it lay steady and still.

'That's us drying out,' said the boy.

'How d'you mean?' asked Ruth.

'The tide's gone out and we're now sitting on the bottom. I used to dry out here and wait for the tide when returning from my fishing trips. When the tide comes in we'll float off and we should be able to set off up the river in the early hours, wind permitting. Mister Enforcer, you and I need to get some rest as it'll be an early start, about 3 a.m.' The boy turned his attention to their hostage. 'Roger, thanks for the meal. As far as I'm concerned we're not forcing you back into the arms of Doreese. Think about it.'

Giles smiled at Ruth, 'I'm off to bed,' he announced and disappeared into the main cabin at the stern of the boat closing the door behind him.

Giles sensed something was wrong as they approached Inverneuage harbour. He and the Enforcer had sailed the ten miles upstream with the incoming tide and had made good progress. At eight o'clock Giles had decided to heave-to in the middle of the river to wait for the water to become deep enough for their boat to enter the harbour. Roger and Ruth had prepared a somewhat unorthodox breakfast of bean stew and tinned peaches along with a side dish of pickled gherkins – all that was left of the food they had found on board and which they had eaten while they waited for the tide. Now, as they approached the harbour mouth, all four of them were on deck. Roger and Ruth were at the bow and stern respectively, each holding a mooring line; the Enforcer was preparing to lower the sails while Giles steered the boat expertly toward the harbour entrance. In days gone by, a crowd would have promptly gathered to help him moor and unload his catch. But on this occasion standing at the tip of the eastern pier there were only four men, all armed with rifles. As they grew closer, Giles recognised two of them: one was Ted, the head of security, while the other, whose name he didn't know, was the scrawny, gaunt-faced man who had betrayed him. The four of them held their rifles at the ready as the yacht approached and there were no smiles of welcome on this occasion.

As Giles nudged the tiller to change direction slightly, he glanced briefly at the Enforcer. 'I'm not happy about this,' he said as he turned the yacht into the mouth of the harbour. 'Right. Drop the main and loosen the jib sheet, please.' Then, as the boat drew up alongside the harbour wall, he instructed Ruth and Roger to step ashore and tie up. They had moored on the opposite wall to where the men had been waiting and so the welcoming party had to walk around the harbour and approached the travellers just as Giles and the Enforcer joined Ruth and Roger on the harbour wall. As the armed quartet came within earshot, Giles shouted, 'Hello! Remember me?'

Leading the party was the man who had betrayed him, his rifle held ready. He halted a few paces in front of the little group from the boat and for a while simply stared at Giles suspiciously, his eyes sullen and malevolent. 'I thought you were dead,' he said.

'I was – very nearly – thanks to you. But you'll be pleased to know that I managed to escape.' Giles looked at the grim-faced men and smiled. 'So fish is back on the menu, chaps.' No one else smiled.

'You don't seem enormously pleased to see me?'

The nameless leader continued to stare sullenly at Giles. 'You're not welcome here,' he stated. 'There have been changes.'

'So it seems.' Giles turned his attention to Ted. 'Ted, what's going on here? Where's the Chief?'

Ted said nothing but simply nodded towards the man with no name.

'I'm the Chief now,' said the nameless one.

'What happened to the old one? I rather liked him.'

'He became indisposed.'

'How indisposed?'

'Terminally.'

Giles was now becoming increasingly worried with the direction in which this conversation was going and was trying to mask his concern with some humour. He was aware that his group was in danger. 'Look, will someone please tell me what on earth is going on

248

here?' he said, looking at each of the men in turn. 'I thought you'd be pleased to see me.' He paused for a moment but there was no response. 'I told my friends here what a fine place Inverneuage was and how we would be welcomed. Told them how this was an enlightened, caring society: open, sensible and well-ordered. Now you threaten us with your scowls and your weapons.'

The nameless betrayer took a step forward. 'I'm the new Bishop. There's been a change in management. Let's say it's been slimmed down. I'm now the Chief, the Bishop, the Council leader.'

'And what happened to the old Chief?'

'He was voted out.'

'Where is he?'

'He refused to adhere to the new order and so was twenty-foured.'

'What d'you mean? – twenty-foured.'

'He was tried and the computer invoked Protocol 24.'

'*What*? You killed him?' Giles was aghast. 'But you don't *abide* by the Protocol here. That's why it's such a sensible, enlightened society.' Giles was exasperated. He couldn't believe what he was hearing. Surely the whole basis of this community couldn't have changed in the few weeks that he'd been away.

'This society was *not* enlightened. It was in darkness. People like you and the old Chief had stopped us from embracing the true faith. Following your arrest there was discontent. The old Council was overthrown and I was elected leader. We have introduced the Protocol and all it stands for and we are now converted – happy in our new beliefs. Before, we had nothing; now we believe. Now we have everything. Bless the Protocol.'

'May we serve it well,' came the response from Ted and the others.

'But what about those who believed in something else? What about the old man who worshipped the tides and the birds that flew over the estuary?'

'They were offered a conversion course but some refused and so had to be Completed. This *was* a society without direction, without faith. *Now* we believe. The Protocol tells us what to do. No need for those interminable discussions, those meetings, listening to people's opinions, like the hearing that made me hand my hard-earned money back to the community. Now that we have embraced the Protocol we need none of that. We simply ask the Protocol and it tells us what to do.' The Bishop then looked heavenwards and said, 'Bless the Protocol.'

'Bless the protocol,' echoed the other three.

The truth was now beginning to dawn on Giles and he realised how he and his companions were in an extremely dangerous situation. His friends had said nothing during this interchange, completely at a loss as to what was going on. Roger was the first to break the silence when he whispered over Giles' shoulder. 'I say, Giles, they don't seem awfully friendly. Not the sort of welcome you'd led us to expect.'

Giles kept his gaze fixed on the man who was the new leader. 'Quiet, Roger. I think you should begin to untie the boat and then you and Ruth get back on board – if you would.'

'Absolutely, Giles! Got the message,' answered Roger who then drifted away slowly to where Ruth was listening, spellbound.

'Oh, I *understand* now,' Giles smiled and looked at the new Chief. 'I quite appreciate your change of direction. Good luck with the new faith. I'm sure it'll go well. Probably best if we just head off now, in view of the past, and everything.' Giles then whispered to the Enforcer, 'Get the sails up and push off, I'll try to keep them chatting and then I'll join you on board.' Giles then turned his attention back to the group in front of him. 'Well, good luck. No hard feelings. The last thing you want is me interfering with the new order,' and Giles turned to go.

'We cannot let you go without interrogation.' The nameless leader said this, but Giles caught a slight hesitancy in his voice.

'Chief,' said Giles, 'think about it. If you take me back to the village, that might destabilise your position. I'm just a wanted criminal and clearly you were right to hand me over to the authorities. We're not the kind of people you want in your new order. We'll just be going on our way.' Then he added, without smiling, 'Bless the Protocol.'

The armed men didn't know what to do and simply stood watching as Giles jumped on to the yacht just as it began to drift away from the harbour wall. Without being told, the Enforcer sheeted in both sails and under the light breeze that was blowing from the south the boat headed steadily towards the harbour mouth.

As they gathered speed and left the safety of the little port, Giles looked up at the foursome standing speechless on the quayside and shouted, 'Bless the Protocol.'

Immediately there came the response, 'May we serve it well.'

Once more in the estuary and out of range of the armed men, Giles turned to his bemused crew. 'Well, that didn't go quite as well as expected. Sorry.'

'So much for the great Inverneuage Enlightenment,' said Ruth quietly. 'Great place to live, you said. Complete freedom of speech, you said. No slavish adherence to Protocols, I seem to recall. The citizens make the rules and use their intellect to make judgements, I think you said.' Ruth smiled, her handsome face creased with rueful mirth. 'Epicurean, was the word you used, I believe. Can't say I'm not a trifle disappointed, Giles.'

'Not half as much as I am, believe me. There seems to have been some sort of seismic change in philosophy at Inverneuage. That soulless idiot who calls himself the Chief was the one who turned me in for the reward. Looks like he's led a coup. There's no doubt it would have been unsafe to stay. Sorry!'

'He's an evil, greedy man, Giles,' said the Enforcer. 'I was there when he betrayed you. He wanted the money and I guess that when he wasn't allowed to keep it he started a rebellion.'

'Well, for whatever reason, we are now officially back at sea.'

'All at sea. *Again!*' added Ruth with a rueful smile.

Roger started to sing, 'Life on the ocean wave, tra-la, and all that.'

'Look, chaps,' said Giles, 'we can either sail out of the estuary, back to sea, or carry on upstream as far as we can get.' Giles looked at his crew questioningly.

'We've no water or food,' observed Roger, 'I vote for upstream.'

'I'm easy, as long as it's a long way from the Bishop,' then after a moment's thought, the Enforcer added, 'and Mandy.'

'And Doreese,' chipped in Roger.

'And the so-called President,' said Ruth.

'Right. Upstream it is,' said Giles as he pushed the tiller away from him and turned the bow of the boat westward.

# FOUR

'Good morning, ladies and gentlemen.' The Prime Minister banged his gavel and silence began to fall in the cabinet room. The P.M. looked different: indeed all the members of the cabinet looked different. Normally sleek and well groomed, the P.M. now appeared unkempt and bedraggled. His once short, neatly-trimmed, dark hair was now grey and dishevelled curling over the top of his ears and the collar of his coat. Instead of his expensive Saville Row suit he wore an old tweed overcoat, threadbare at the cuffs, in the breast pocket of which was a red, silk handkerchief. Underneath his coat was a grubby looking white shirt and an old tie was loosely knotted around his neck. Not visible beneath the table at which he was seated, was a pair of creased corduroy trousers and old black brogues adorned his feet. He seemed to have only shaved half his face and that patchily.

The P.M. glanced around the table at the other members of his cabinet. All the men were similarly dressed and the two women were regaled in a female version of this attire. Both the ladies of the cabinet were wearing a loose fitting tweed jacket and skirt with woollen tights and brown low-heeled leather shoes. In truth, this was how Lady Carter had always dressed, but Lady Doreese was more used to extravagant flowing robes of satin and silk; gold and red were the colours of *her* preference. Only the headgear was reminiscent of her past exuberance. Even this, however, had been toned down in deference to the new order and its dress code. On her head she had a large tweedy structure, its brim frayed to just the right degree, while perched in a crevice could be seen a small bowl of fruit, a few twigs and a stuffed starling.

The P.M. rose to his feet, allowing the string with which he kept his trousers up to be seen. This was his own take on the new dress code and marked him out as the leader of Cabinet. 'Please stand,' he said as he placed his open hand on the pile of books in front of him. Then, when all present had struggled to their feet, he closed his eyes and began to chant. 'Bless the Protocol,' he chanted in a high unmelodious voice.

'Bless the Protocol,' came the response from around the table.

'May we serve it well,' continued the P.M.

'May we serve it well.'

'Bless Giles, the Prophet.'

'Bless Giles, the Prophet.'

'May we serve him well.'

'May we serve him well.'

'May Giles be with us and guide us today. May he assist us, as we invoke his Protocol and its computer to ensure accurate data entry and keyboard usage.'

This last chant totally bemused the rest of the Cabinet as no one had heard it before. The P.M. had been carried away by the fervour of the moment, and no one could remember what he had said.

'May Giles help… ' sang one Cabinet member before his voice drifted away.

'May Giles assist with… ' said another who paused before adding more quietly, '… everything.'

'Please help us use the Protocol… right,' sang someone else while another chanted, 'Bless the keyboard on which we sit,' before realising his error and starting to cough loudly.

The P.M. opened his eyes and sat down. 'Please be seated.' He then looked across the table to the head of D.I.E. who was seated opposite him. 'Lady Doreese, would you kindly open our meeting with your report, please?'

'Thank you, P.M.,' said Doreese as she rose to her feet, 'Bless Giles.'

'Yes of course. Bless Giles,' said the P.M. somewhat curtly. This is all getting a bit out of hand, he thought to himself. The protocol for speaking at Cabinet meetings had not been clearly defined: titles and styles of address required to be tightened, otherwise one could spend the whole day chanting and blessing every object in the room. The new attire he could cope with but, if half the meeting was spent reciting catechism after catechism rather than addressing the business in hand, there was a real danger that the meeting might well erode into his aperitif time. This diverted his train of thought to dinner. He couldn't quite remember whether if it was fish and chips or pancakes that night.

Lady Doreese launched into her report. 'I am pleased to say that Gilesian philosophy has now spread widely across our land. The rule *of* Protocol *by* Protocol is now virtually complete.'

'What do you mean by "the rule *of* Protocol *by* Protocol?" ' asked Lady Carter.

Lady Doreese sighed, and said, 'It's very obvious, isn't it?' In fact she had no idea what she meant but rather liked the phrase and the way it rolled easily off the tongue.

'Well, just remind us, if you would, Lady Doreese.'

'It means the Protocol now runs by itself. It is in complete control. It writes itself and monitors itself, it has become... ' and Doreese looked at Lady Carter, '... *wise.*' Doreese was pleased with her quick recovery and her face now bore a supercilious smile. 'Now, *if* I may continue?' she said with a disdainful glance at her inquisitor. 'As for Dalriada; we are making steady progress. A large team of missionaries, led by Sister Mandy, is crisscrossing the land and, one by one, cities and villages are being converted. We now have thousands of converts and to accommodate them we are building new Studios in all the big cities. As well as housing copies of all the Protocols, including of course the Euthanasia Protocol along with the necessary facilities for End of Life Management, these buildings are now much more than mere Studios. They are places of contemplation: places where our brothers and sisters may meet together to reflect and to bless Giles the Prophet.'

The P.M. looked up from his papers. 'That's jolly good. Excellent, well done.'

Someone said, 'Bless Giles.'

Another added, rather crossly, '*And* the Protocol.'

Doreese continued. 'That brings me to the Blasphemy Protocol.' She paused to add significance to her words. 'There have been disturbing reports of non-adherence to The Protocols and even... ' and she looked around the room, '... yes, *even* some adverse comments about Giles himself.'

'Bless Giles,' said someone at the far end of the room.

'Yes, even Giles. This civil disobedience needs to be dealt with swiftly before it can spread. I am therefore pleased to announce that the Blasphemy Protocol is now complete and has been integrated into the Life Protocols in all our Studios across the land.'

'Could you give us a brief summary of what these involve, Lady Doreese?' Lady Carter once more peered along the table.

The head of D.I.E. groaned. Why did Lady Carter always have to be so awkward: ask questions and want know the details of things – rather than just accept how things were. 'Well, Lady Carter, if anyone takes the name of Giles in vain, or does not adhere to Gilesian philosophy, they will be tried using the new Blasphemy Protocol.'

'Will there be an appeals process?'

'Of course. The Euthanasia Tribunals will serve that function.'

'That implies that blasphemy will be punishable by euthanasia?'

'It's an appalling crime.'

'Hardly as appalling as capital punishment, which is essentially what Protocol 24 is!'

From around the table there came a murmur of astonishment on hearing these words and the P.M., who was still wondering what was for dinner, was roused from his reverie. 'Quiet,' he said firmly. 'That's quite enough of that sort of talk, Lady Carter. Capital punishment was abolished over a hundred years ago, as you well know, and Protocol 24 is simply an adjunct to the End of Life Protocol. *Really*, Lady Carter, you should know better.'

Doreese now picked up on the theme, and was at her most patronising: 'It just so happens that comments such as those, Lady Carter, are in breach of the blasphemy code, section 3, clause four and, strictly speaking, you could now be tried under these new laws.'

'And euthanased?'

'Protocol 24 *could* apply – yes.'

'Oh!' said Lady Carter. 'I'd better watch what I say then, hadn't I?'

'That would be wise. We all have to be careful what we say now that we have embraced the new faith.'

'Mmm. Bless the Protocol,' replied Lady Carter.

The P.M. glanced at his watch. He was ready for a drink but there were several more items to discuss before he could legitimately close the meeting. 'Well, thank you, Lady Doreese. That's all most satisfactory.' He glanced around the table. 'As head of the new Department Of Protocol Enforcement, and the lead Minister for Gilesian philosophy, I have decided that you should have a title to distinguish you from the rest of us, who are merely elected politicians.

Something snappy I think. Does anyone have a proposal?' The P.M. looked around the table.

'What about Archbishop?' suggested the Minister for Disasters. We used to have one of those before the Wars of Religion.'

'Mmm, quite good, Gerry, but it has religious connotations.'

'Okay then. What about Her Most Wonderfulness, The Archvizier?'

Doreese smiled inwardly when she heard this, as it was exactly along the lines that she was thinking herself.

'No. Religious connotations again. Whatever we do we must never return to the bad old days when religion clouded our views and affected our judgement. That would *never* do.'

'A new title for the Head of the Department of Protocol Enforcement.' Lady Carter said thoughtfully. 'Let me think. That's D.O.P.E. for short isn't it?' She stroked her chin and looked heavenwards. 'How about... ' she paused, her brow furrowed in concentration, '... I know, The Archdope.'

'*Brilliant*,' said the P.M., looking at his watch once more. 'Archdope it is.'

Lady Doreese, who had been beaming, pretty pleased with developments up until then, now frowned. 'I'm not sure about that, P.M.'

But the P.M. was ready for his aperitif and there would be no changing his mind. 'No: Archdope is perfect. Just the right amount of *gravitas* and no religious connotation.' The P.M. shuffled his papers, now feeling fairly sure that it was fish for supper. 'Next item. Now, Gerry, what is the climate doing this year?'

'Well, P.M. its rather hot, in a funny, cold sort of way.'

'What, in Giles' name, do you mean by that?'

The Minister for Disasters rose to his feet, adjusted his corduroy trousers and began to address the Cabinet.

\* \* \*

The sail upstream was slow and tedious. The navigable channel was narrow, the yacht dried out at every low tide and they regularly went aground. At such times one of the crew would generally wade ashore to search for fresh water and forage for food, while their fare was occasionally supplemented by fish: but their diet was poor. They used the yacht for shelter and warmth but after a week of very slow progress, when they had only travelled a further ten miles, the boy Giles decided that they had come as far as they could by boat. At high tide they sailed and punted the boat as close as possible to the shore, then he jammed her anchor deep into the mud, it having occurred to him that they might just need to use the boat again. Then, after gathering together all that might be of use to them on land, they bade a fond farewell to the craft that had helped them escape and had been their home for over two weeks.

It was bitterly cold when they set off upon their trek. A freezing north-easterly howled across the snow-covered mountains: conditions far from ideal for a cross-country walk without proper equipment or clothing. Staying on the boat, however, had ceased to be an option as they would have slowly frozen to death on the wide-open, unprotected expanse of windswept water that was the estuary. They had decided to walk along the mountain range, retracing the route that the boy had travelled nearly five years before. Then, however, Giles had been alone, well-equipped and provisioned. Now, there were four of them. Only Giles had any experience of survival outdoors and the others were unfit. They had no provisions and would have to rely on what they could forage *en route*.

It was a difficult and dangerous trek. After three days, they reached the summit where, years before, Giles had first spied the estuary. From that vantage point he showed his companions the hamlet at the north of the loch where he had borrowed the skiff, and indicated the route to the village at the south of the loch where he and Ruth had lived.

'We could be down in the hamlet by this evening if we're quick,' said Giles. 'But once we're there I've no idea if we'll find shelter.' Giles was pensive for a moment. 'The only alternative is to continue. To walk all the way along this ridge to the village at the south of the loch, where there may be someone who will remember Ruth and take us in.' Giles knew that they would not survive the walk south as they were already undernourished, tired and cold and that even one more night on the mountains might lead to one or more of them succumbing to hypothermia, but he wanted the decision to be shared. Ruth was bearing up quite well but both the Enforcer and Roger were cold and tired. Giles looked at his companions, 'What would you like to do?' he asked, then, turning his gaze upon Ruth said, 'Ruth, what's your preference?'

'I don't think we'd survive much longer up here, Giles. I think we *must* find shelter and food.'

'Roger?'

'I'm with Ruth. I'm totally done in, Giles. Sorry but I'm frozen and can't walk much further.'

'Mister Enforcer?'

'I agree. I need warmth and food and the only chance of survival is to get off this bloody mountain and down to the hamlet as quickly as possible.'

'That's unanimous then,' said Giles as he picked up his bag and started to lead his party down the mountainside.

A painful four hours later, as the light was fading, they finally reached the road leading to the handful of cottages which constituted the village. Giles headed for number six. It had been five years since that fateful night when he had escaped only yards ahead of his pursuers, but little had changed. The gatepost was faded and the paint peeling, but the number six was still visible. Giles didn't hesitate. He strode up the path and knocked at the door. Initially there was no response but, after he had knocked a second time, the door opened just a crack and an old lady's face appeared.

'Yes, what do you want?' she asked. Her voice was timid and weak but Giles recognised the woman who, along with her husband, had cared for him all those years ago.

'Old lady,' he said, 'it's the boy who stole your boat and was nearly shot on the hill behind your house. I have returned for more whisky.'

On hearing this, the old lady opened the door wide and flung her arms around the boy's neck and wept.

'Thank god you're all right,' she said. 'I've often wondered what happened to you. I heard rumours, but you never know what to believe. The last I heard was that you'd been sent back to England to be executed, or whatever they call it nowadays. My husband always reckoned that you'd survive. He used to say that he could see it in your eyes.'

'Where is your man?' asked Giles.

'Dead, boy. Long dead.' The old lady wiped a tear from her eye. 'But he always remembered you and hoped that you'd return some day.' The old lady then looked at Giles' bedraggled companions. 'Who are those people?' she asked.

'Let me introduce my travelling companions.' Giles stood aside and waved his hand towards Ruth, 'This, old lady, is Ruth, a good and close childhood friend and until recently a girl with a bright future in Government.' He turned his gaze to the tall shivering figure of Roger. 'This is Roger, He didn't have such a bright future as the chief aide to the English Minister for Protocols and head of D.I.E. He's actually a hostage, but try as we may to encourage him, he refuses to escape.' Giles then turned his attention to the short plump figure of the Enforcer. 'You may remember this gentleman, old lady. He was Mandy's side-kick and came here, with her, to arrest me. He more than redeemed himself by nudging the sniper just as he was taking aim when I raced up the hill behind your house. Otherwise I most certainly would have been killed. He's *never* had a bright future, but is content in the knowledge that he no longer has to be at the beck and call of the besom Mandy.'

Giles then looked back at the woman. 'Old lady, once again I am in need of your help. We are on the run and we are in desperate need of food and shelter.'

'Come in, boy. Come away in, all of you. You are most welcome. I have nothing to fear from the authorities now. I care not what they do. Come, sit in the warmth of the parlour and I'll fetch some food. Later you can tell me of your adventures since you left on that moonlit night.'

Thus they were nourished and loved by the old lady. She shared with them her food, the warmth of her cottage and her dead husband's whisky, while the four travellers told her their stories. After three days they had recovered sufficiently to consider their future.

'Old lady,' said the boy, 'we have to find somewhere to settle. Somewhere safe to live. A place free from protocolists. Perhaps we could stay in your village?'

'You could,' she replied. 'But there are very few people left here. This is a dead village. You and your companions are the future; this village belongs in the past. You're probably best going to the south of the loch, back to where you and Ruth once lived. I believe it is still safe. You can have the skiff to sail down and I'll give you provisions for your journey.'

'Thank you, old lady. Why don't you come with us and share our future?'

'I appreciate your offer, boy. But I must stay here. I have a grave to tend and memories to savour. But – it would be nice if you returned every now and again to visit.'

'That,' said the boy, Giles, 'is a promise.'

So it was that on the following day four fugitives: an Enforcer, a ministerial aide, a pretty young government official and Giles came to sail down the loch heading for a new life.

# FIVE

The Capital's station was packed with the faithful. The platform thronged with hundreds of believers, all dressed quite properly in the style of Giles. Threadbare tweed overcoats were worn over white shirts and baggy corduroy trousers, and everyone sported a red silk handkerchief in their breast pockets. The men were bareheaded but the women all wore hats. Those varied in style but all complied with the Gilesian dress code, being of wool and a dull earthy colour: browns and greens predominating. Some had decorations attached: a piece of fruit, or a small dead animal.

As the train drew in, as one, they chanted, 'Bless Giles the Prophet. Bless the Protocol, may we serve it well.' At the head of the waiting throng was Mandy. She was also wearing regulation attire and on her head was an understated green trilby, a baby hedgehog jauntily attached to one side. As the train drew to a halt she walked forward and opened the carriage door. After a moment, Doreese appeared and briefly paused in the doorway to acknowledge the applause, before stepping down on to the platform. There she stood, magnificent in her flowing tweed jacket and corduroy skirt, her face half-masked by the huge artifice on her head. It was regulation green but was both wide and tall. At its highest point there was a small forest with oak leaves and acorns in abundance while climbing up the side was a stuffed ferret, its mouth open as though snapping at the nearest bunch of nuts. She waved her gloved hand and the cheering crowd gradually fell silent. This was Mandy's cue.

'Welcome to Dalriada, Archdope,' she cried. 'We are privileged to welcome you to this land of Giles. Bless Giles, the Founder of the Protocols.'

A cry of, 'Bless Giles, Founder of the Protocols,' came from all around the station as Mandy took Doreese's gloved hand in her own and bowed her head in a gesture of obeisance.

Doreese waited for silence to descend once more; then she raised her head imperiously and addressed the crowd: 'I am here on a pilgrimage,' she said, looking around as she had observed great orators do in old newsreels. 'I have heard great things about the people of Dalriada and wish to see for myself how far you have advanced.' Once more she paused for effect and now her voice grew deeper and more sonorous. 'I will travel your country – from east to west and from north to south. I will inspect your Studios and your facilities. I will speak to the people of Dalriada.' Her voice now grew louder and higher in pitch. 'You have come far since my last visit, but there is still a long way to go. I believe there may still be some non-believers – those not *yet* of the faith.' By now Doreese was shouting. 'I will seek them out and *Protocol 24 awaits them.*' On hearing this the crowd erupted in cheers and applause, then, above the racket, Doreese screamed at the top of her voice, '*They will be twenty-foured. In Giles' name, they will be twenty-foured.*'

The crowd went wild, '*Bless Giles,*' they shouted. '*Bless the Protocol. May we serve it well.*' Some even shouted, '*Bless Doreese. Bless the Archdope.*'

When the frenzy had settled Mandy guided her mentor through the crowd to the palace where the President himself was waiting to welcome her. His face seemed slightly flushed. 'Welcome, Archdope,' he announced as he adjusted the string holding up his trousers.

As Doreese waved her gloved hand to the adoring crowd and proceeded indoors to a formal reception, she briefly turned to Mandy and said, 'What a wonderful welcome, my subjects seem to appreciate me up here.'

The Archdope (Doreese still hadn't come to terms with this title as she thought it somehow insulting) and Mandy then went on a tour of the country in a specially converted bus. The pilgrimage had been highly stage-managed and they visited only the faithful and the newly converted. They toured the latest facilities, the new Studios and Euthanasia parlours. They were shown the new, official End of Life pathway where those being euthanased had a vision of the old man, Giles the prophet, beaming down at them from the sky above the Eiffel Tower. His iconic symbol: the ever-present donkey, baying in the background.

As the pilgrimage came to its end the Archdope declared herself satisfied that all was well in the new land of Giles.

After supper on the evening before her return to England, Doreese turned to Mandy and asked, 'Whatever happened to those non-compliers?' She searched her memory for their names, 'You know: the boy and that girl, that annoying little Junior Secretary.'

Mandy was suddenly alert. She had hoped that her dealings with those two had been forgotten. 'Dead,' she said nonchalantly. 'The boy, Giles, was completed in Nowton and the girl – I forget her name – was arrested for her part in the boy's crimes but drowned while trying to escape. She would have been twenty-foured anyway. So all worked out for the best.' Mandy smiled, wishing what she had said had been true.

'Good. Good, that's very satisfactory. And Roger, whatever happened to him?'

'No idea, Archdope. The last I heard was that he had gone native and was living in the wild somewhere.'

'I'm not surprised. He had a terrible taste in hats as I recall.'

Mandy looked up at Doreese's current headwear, with its ferret and acorns, 'Yes indeed, Archdope.'

'Tell me, Mandy, is it true that there are still some backward areas where the protocols and Gilesian principles are not embraced?'

'Possibly a few remain, but we are seeking them out one by one.'

'And what happens when you find one?'

'We convert them.'

'How do you do that?'

'We persuade them of the benefits of the Protocol and the value of a good Gilesian lifestyle.'

'Does anyone dissent?'

'No, none. Well, if they do, they are tried under the Blasphemy Protocol and twenty-foured. The very threat is normally enough to ensure conversion.'

'Ah. Very good. Well, Mandy, I think I may report to the Prime Minister that you are managing things up here exceptionally well. I will also suggest that you, like me, deserve a reward – a title – for your unflinching service in the name of Giles.'

'Oh! *Thank you*, Archdope.' Mandy flushed with pride. 'What have you in mind?'

'Well that'll be for the P.M. and his cabinet to decide, but I rather felt that *I* should now be up-titled and in that way you could take my old title of, Archdope for Dalriada,'

Mandy's smile was wiped from her face. 'Thank you,' she said, 'that would be amazing.'

And so Lady Doreese, the Archdope, returned to England and reported favourably on progress in Dalriada and, for her work in the field of Gilesian endeavour, was elected into the Glorious Order of the Defenders of Giles. This came with a large enamelled brooch to be worn over her left breast, emblazoned with the initials, 'G.O.D.O.G.' or good dog as Lady Carter called it until her accident.

# SIX

'Giles, there's someone here who wants to speak to you.'

Giles looked up from the papers on the desk in front of him, puzzled. 'Who is it, Roger?'

'He won't say, Chief.'

'What? Is he an outsider?'

'He's not one of us, that's for sure. You should see how he's dressed. He looks to me as though he's fallen on jolly hard times.'

'Well, you'd better show him in.'

Roger walked to the door and ushered in a man who was quite startling in his appearance. He was of medium height and excruciatingly thin. His face, drawn and sunburnt, had a large bruise on the left cheek below which was a small scar. His long hair was unkempt and he was wearing an old, threadbare overcoat buttoned up tightly against the cold. Dirty green corduroy trousers covered his skinny legs while mud-bespattered black leather shoes, cracked and misshapen, adorned his feet.

As this strange apparition entered the room, Giles stood to welcome him into his office, indicating that he should take a seat. While the visitor advanced, Giles observed him carefully – he looked somehow familiar, but he couldn't quite place where he had seen him before. 'I understand you wish to speak to me,' he said. 'How can I be of help?'

'It is more a question of how I can help you,' said the visitor. 'Are you the head of this community?'

'I am indeed,' said Giles.

'I am a missionary: here to spread the word. The word of Giles the Prophet.'

'Well, you're in the right place,' said the Chief with a smile. '*My* name is Giles.'

There came no smile in response, just a continued dull, soulless stare. 'You are not the true Giles, the one of the Protocol.'

Giles now began to feel disturbed. Since he and his companions had arrived in this community more than five years before, they had heard nothing more about the Protocols and life had been wholly uneventful. Ruth had been welcomed back into the thriving little community and had become a teacher at her old school. The Enforcer, Roger and the boy Giles had all striven to be accepted: and accepted they were. Giles farmed and fished, much as he and the old man had done all those years ago, while Roger utilised his culinary skills by running a small greengrocery and a cooked-food shop. The Enforcer had joined a group called the Community Workers: an amalgam of police force, fire service and general council worker.

The deep affection and respect that Giles and Ruth felt for one another had flourished, matured into love and then marriage. Since her father had died, Ruth invited Roger to give her away: a poor second prize so far as he was concerned, for he continued to nurture an emotion which was more than mere affection for Ruth. However, he decided to remain in the village to be close to both Giles and Ruth rather than abandon the only family he had ever known. Soon Ruth gave birth to a daughter whom they called Hope.

Following the retirement of the Council leader (a harmless but ineffectual nonagenarian) the community required a new chief and Giles' attributes, which were clear for all to see, ideally suited him for the rôle and he was therefore appointed unanimously. With the help of Ruth and Roger, Giles then set about developing a management structure based loosely on that of Inverneuage – before the revolution that had transformed it into a Protocol State.

Giles' style of management was fair, open-handed and transparent. This was welcomed by the community, which flourished under his sagacious leadership. As had been the case in Inverneuage, he imposed no ban on religion, but would not permit individuals of any particular religious persuasion to interfere with anyone else's beliefs. Most in the village were atheists. Some had knowledge of the Protocols but because of its isolation no one in the village knew of the Gilesian philosophy which had swept across the rest of the country, extinguishing any freedom of thought in its path.

Now this man's presence was making Giles feel uneasy. The tattered missionary reminded Giles of the past: of the madness that had engulfed the world outside, the crazy and unthinking automatons in the Capital and in Nowton: of his own early days living on the street: the Studios – a world which he thought he had left behind.

'Why are you here?' Giles asked of the visitor.

'I am here to convert you to the true faith.'

'Well, I appreciate that, but in this community we allow people to believe in whatever they want and all faiths are considered to be equal. Most of us believe in peaceful coexistence and consideration for one another.'

'That is no longer acceptable,' stated the visitor. 'There is only the one true faith: that of the Prophet Giles.'

'Well, I appreciate you coming but here we're quite content with our organisation as it stands: we are not looking to be converted to Giles or anyone else.' Giles was becoming increasingly uneasy: there was something about this man that made him nervous – his unflinching gaze was unsettling and somehow his face still seemed familiar though he couldn't place it. 'I hope you haven't come far,' he continued. 'You're welcome to stay the night before you move on.'

'You are expelling a servant of Giles. Your community will regret this.' Then the man said something strange: something which made Giles' blood run cold. Instead of calling him Chief, or Giles, after a pause the man hissed '... *Boy.*'

Giles regained his composure, determined to remain polite in the face of this overt verbal aggression. 'No: I'm not expelling you, but if I'm being honest we really don't want your style of indoctrination here. We are entirely happy as we are. As I have said, you are welcome to stay overnight but then you must move on.' Giles turned his attention to Roger who had been listening with interest to this interchange. 'Roger, would you please ask Mister Enforcer to look after our visitor overnight. Make sure that he is treated well, is fed and given all that he needs in order to continue his journey tomorrow.'

'Certainly, Chief.'

The visitor stood, his glazed eyes staring but unseeing. 'You will regret this,' he said to Giles as Roger led him out of the room.

Later that night, after they had eaten, Giles related his experience to Ruth.

'I share your concerns, Giles,' she said. 'The past was bound to catch up with us eventually.' She looked across the table at him. 'We've had several good years here, but we have been very much cut off from the outside world. I've heard rumours that Protocol fundamentalism is spreading like an evil virus, strangling free-thought and annihilating all other beliefs in its path.'

'But what is all this nonsense about a prophet called *Giles*?'

'I've no idea.' Ruth smiled at her husband. 'I presume it's nothing to do with you?'

Giles reported the incident at the next Council meeting, expressing his concern about what he perceived to be a threat to their society, and urging vigilance.

'Who is this prophet *Giles*?' asked one of the elders.

'I've no idea,' said the Chief. 'No relation to me, I can assure you.' Giles looked at the group of twelve men and women who, along with himself, made up the governing body of the village. 'In fact, some of you may not know this, but Giles isn't really my name at all. I simply took the name of an old man who had died. An old man who cared for me when I was hungry and homeless.' He glanced down at the signet ring on the little finger of his left hand, at the letter 'G', which was still discernable on its face.

'Well, Chief, you did the right thing to send him packing. The last thing we need here is some outsider trying to change our ways.'

That evening Ruth and Giles entertained Roger and the Enforcer to dinner. After reminiscing about their escape from the Capital and their boat trip north, they fell to discussing local issues – including that of their strangely-dressed visitor.

'I think he was just some jolly old tramp looking for shelter.' Roger had clearly not been disturbed by the visitor in the way that Giles had.

'No, Roger. This may sound melodramatic, but I'm really concerned that he is the harbinger of disaster, the very embodiment of evil.' Giles fell silent and then, suddenly, he shouted, 'I know who it was. *It was Ted*! The missionary was Ted.'

The others looked at Giles. 'Who's Ted?' asked Roger.

'He's changed a lot, but that was definitely Ted.' Giles looked at Roger, 'Ted was head of security in Inverneuage. He found me on the hillside after I had escaped from you and Mandy.' Giles looked at the Enforcer. 'He was a good man. We got on well together. He believed in free-thought and had no strong feelings about anything: that is apart from Maisie, his woman – and when his next meal would be ready.' Giles was silent for a moment. 'That's why he called me "Boy", as I only took the name Giles after my capture.'

'We have no idea what's been going on in Invernueage since you left,' observed Ruth.

'That's true. Its society seemed to change, almost overnight.'

The four of them were silent for a while, in that contented quiet which can only be shared by those who have faced deprivation and danger together – and survived. After a few moments, Giles suddenly raised his head, his brow furrowed, and there was a bemused look on his face. 'What is it?' asked Ruth.

'This sounds improbable... ' Giles hesitated.

'What does?' Ruth's face registered concern.

'No! It couldn't possibly be.'

'*What?*'

'Well, it just occurred to me that this new faith of Giles might be based on the old man.' Giles then shook his head in disbelief. 'No, that's ridiculous. It couldn't be.'

'Mandy used to talk about the old man's slightly bizarre appearance,' said the Enforcer.

'His clothes were just a little old fashioned,' said Giles, '*and* worn out.'

'I suppose it's possible,' said Ruth. 'We know he was the author of many of the early Protocols – and Gilesian philosophy, if that's the right term, seems to be intricately tied into fundamental Protocolism.'

'What a strange irony that would be,' mused Giles quietly. 'I just hope that's the last we see of Ted the missionary. You're right, Mister Enforcer, he *was* dressed rather like the old man.'

'I say, chaps, this is all a bit maudlin. Anyone for another whisky?' Roger held up the half-empty bottle, and replenished their drinks.

They clinked glasses. 'Let's hope that's the last we hear of my namesake, Giles the prophet,' toasted the Chief.

But it was not to be.

# SEVEN

Mandy rose to her feet and the crowd of several hundred who had gathered in the capital's assembly room grew quiet. She was attired in traditional Gilesian fashion but somehow still managed to appear well-dressed and smart. Her tweedy coat had bald patches but they were symmetrical, and the splashes of brown, representing mud, matched those on her bespoke skirt. On her broad-brimmed hat was a neat, well-constructed nest within which a finch resided – colourful in blues and gold. Behind the dais on which she was now standing hung a huge tapestry depicting Giles. His hand was placed on a book emblazoned with the words: *The Protocol,* and in the background were the blessed symbols of the Eiffel Tower and the donkey.

'Bless Giles the Prophet,' she said.

'Bless Giles,' chanted the crowd who had gathered at the studio for the weekly proceedings.

'Bless the Protocol.'

'Bless the Protocol,' they replied.

'May we serve it well.'

'May we serve it well. Bless the Archdope.'

Mandy winced. She hated her new title. 'We are gathered here to thank Giles for all he has given us. For the peace and security that he has provided through his Protocols.'

'Bless the Protocols.'

Mandy paused to allow the crowd to settle before continuing her address. 'Sadly, today we have an onerous task. In our midst there are two who have blasphemed.' There was an audible gasp from those in the room and the crowd shuffled anxiously, wondering if they might be standing next to one of the accused. 'Yes: within this very room there are two who have refused to accept the goodness that is Giles and have not complied with the Protocol.' Mandy slowly looked all around the room, seeming to peer into the very soul of each and every person gathered there. 'Bring them up,' she shouted.

Ten Enforcers then entered the room and pushed their way roughly through the throng from within which they identified two men, whom they dragged, struggling and kicking, to stand in front of Mandy. There they stood, wide-eyed with fright, each held by the Enforcers, pinioned by the arms. They were both ordinary-looking men: middle-aged, slightly overweight and dressed appropriately for the weekly assembly. Their faces, however, registered terror at having been singled out for attention.

'You two,' said Mandy, 'have committed a crime against Giles.' The two men, who clearly knew one another, now looked puzzled. 'You have consorted with non-compliers of the Protocol.' The men looked at Mandy, uncomprehendingly. 'Don't pretend that you don't know what you've done,' said Mandy sternly. The men stood, visibly shaking, horrified by the unfolding events. 'You,' she continued, 'are members of a conspiracy to overthrow the Protocol.'

'I've absolutely no idea what you're talking about, Archdope,' stammered one of the men.

'Oh yes, you do! Don't pretend that you're innocent of this charge.'

'No! *Really*! I've no idea what all this is about,' the taller of the two men, his eyes wide with fear, looked around the hall as though appealing for help, but none came.

'You and your friend met with two spies from the hills in order to perpetrate an insurgency and overthrow the rule of Giles. *That's* what this is about.' On hearing this there was a gasp of disbelief and amazement from those in the room.

Suddenly it dawned on the man who had been doing the talking, what Mandy was referring to. He seemed to relax slightly and his expression of terror changed to one of dismay. 'Oh, *I* know what your talking about now. That was nothing. They were just travellers, hungry and cold, and my friend here and I took them in and fed them. They stayed the night and left the next day. There was no anti-Gilesian behaviour, I can assure you of that, Archdope.'

'That's not what I've been told. The witnesses for the prosecution said that you spent the night plotting to overthrow the Protocol.'

Now both men were totally confused. '*What* witnesses? *What* prosecution?'

'The undercover Enforcers who were posing as travellers, *those* are the witnesses to the crime that you perpetrated and for which you are now being prosecuted,' pronounced the Archdope firmly. 'Our witnesses state that you stayed up all night and behaved in a depraved, anti-Gilesian fashion: drinking alcohol and denouncing the State and its Protocols. What do you have to say to *that*?'

'Well, we may have got a bit drunk, and said some stupid things, but that was all. We didn't mean anything by it or do anything wrong.'

'That's for the court to decide, not you.' Mandy now addressed the room at large. 'Ladies and gentlemen. The legal Protocol has pronounced and these two men are guilty of anti-Gilesian behaviour and crimes against the Protocol. What have you to say to these two reprobates?'

From the back of the room came a shout: 'Twenty-four them.'

Someone else piped up, 'Invoke Protocol twenty four,' and soon the whole room was chanting, *'Twenty four – twenty four – twenty four,'* to the tune of Colonel Bogey.

Mandy's expression remained fixed and stern, but inwardly she was smiling. 'That'll serve them right for having a good time,' she thought. She then proclaimed: 'The Protocol has determined that this crime should be punished by Euthanasia, under the terms and conditions of Protocol 24.'

As Mandy said this, the colour drained from the faces of the two men. They had both been witnesses to similar situations in the past, and had indeed taken part in the proceedings; but now *they* were the hunted, the focus of this crowd: this lynch mob whose blood was up. They knew there was no way out and that they were already as good as dead.

'Take them to the Completion Room,' shouted Mandy above the noise of the chanting and then, turning her attention to the accused, she said, 'You have no right to request a Final Event pathway and so the official Gilesian one will be used.'

'*No*! You can't do that,' shouted the taller man. 'All we did was have a drink and a laugh.' The second man slumped to the ground, sobbing uncontrollably.

'Archdope, please spare us. We will do anything. *Please spare us.*'

'It's too late for that.'

'But all we did was to feed hungry travellers.'

'That's *enough*. Enforcers: take them away for immediate euthanasia.'

The crowd bayed its approval, '*Twenty-four – Twenty-four. Euth – euth – euth,*' they shouted.

As the two men were led away struggling to the Final Event Chamber, the crowd quietened gradually. Mandy spread her arms. 'Bless Giles,' she called out.

'Bless Giles,' came the roar in response.

'Let that be a lesson to us all,' she said. 'No one is above the Protocol. Giles is all-seeing and all-knowing. No one can escape his justice.'

\* \* \*

'I'm sure the Cabinet would be *very* interested in hearing your dream, Lady Doreese.'

'Well, Prime Minister, it wasn't so much a dream, more of a vision: a visitation even.'

'A visitation?' The P.M. looked up enquiringly.

'Yes, P.M. I have been visited by the Prophet Giles.'

'What, in the night? Lucky you!' exclaimed Lady Carter.

'That's enough of that sort of anti-Gilesian talk, thank you very much, Lady Carter.'

'Sorry, P.M. It's just that Lady Doreese seems to have all the luck.'

'Yes, that's true, thank Giles, I have been fortunate,' Lady Doreese replied, glancing at the huge order of the G.O.D.O.G. pinned to the breast pocket of her tweed coat, just below her regulation red silk handkerchief.

'Tell us about your vision,' said the P.M., with a glance at his watch, noting that it was nearly time for a drink.

'Well,' continued Lady Doreese, 'I was in an altered state of consciousness.'

'Just like every other night!'

'I'm warning you, Lady Carter. Any more of that sort of disrespect and I will invoke the cabinet Protocol: appropriate behaviour at meetings, section B, clause 4, and have you expelled.'

'Sorry, P.M.'

'Yes, I was in an altered state of mind and I had the vision of a donkey.' As she began to relate her experience, she briefly adjusted her hat – on which were a few carrots and a small kitten – then her ladyship's eyes closed and her face took on a beatific glow.

'The donkey was grey-coloured, had a sweet face and large teeth.' Lady Carter looked heavenwards and sighed heavily.

'I heard that,' said the P.M.

'Sorry.'

'It was munching on a carrot. I say munching because it was making a great noise. Noisily masticating might be a better description.'

'I didn't know they could do that: lucky animal,' Lady Carter murmured under her breath.

'Then the donkey spoke to me. "Doreese," it said, "you have done well, but listen to my story and learn." '

'Yes, donkey, I replied.'

The P.M. looked at his watch. When he had agreed that Doreese could relate her story at the end of the Cabinet meeting, he'd assumed that it would be a short, pithy anecdote, but Doreese seemed to be settling into a long saga and it was now well past his aperitif time.

Doreese recapped the story so far, 'As I was saying, the donkey was eating carrots – noisily. "Why do we eat carrots, Doreese?" the donkey asked.'

'Because you like them, I suppose, I answered.'

' "No they're rubbish," said the donkey, "It's not for that reason. Think again." '

'Maybe it's because they're good for you, I said.'

' "Not at all. They just make you fart and belch," said the donkey.'

'Well, in that case I don't know why it is that you eat carrots. Why do you? I asked.'

' "Because it beats the hell out of eating sticks." ' Then the donkey burst out into howls of wheezy laughter. "Geddit – sticks and carrots!" When the donkey had stopped laughing and had settled down, it said, "No, just joshing. Actually we eat carrots because we can't buy cakes." '

'What! I said, you like *cakes*?'

' "Yes, why shouldn't we? Just because we're donkeys doesn't mean we can't appreciate the finer things in life, like Palladian architecture,

Beethoven's ninth and fondant cakes. Those little strawberry tarts are my favourite." The donkey's expression softened and he looked almost wistful at the thought.'

'How do you know about these things, wise donkey? I asked.'

' "Because I went to Paris – on holiday." '

'Oh, do tell me more, I said.'

' "Well it was when I was just a young donkey, all he-haws and testosterone, you know – a bit wild. Anyway I'd got a bit cheesed off with doing nothing but eating carrots and breaking wind all day so off I went to Paris. Once there I went up the Eiffel Tower, as you do, and from there I could see for miles around. I saw wonderful buildings and lots of cake shops, or patisseries as they call them there. So I ate cakes, visited galleries, admired the architecture, and took in a show or two." '

'What happened then? I asked.'

' "Oh, I got appalling colicky stomach pains and didn't open my bowels for a week." '

'What did you do?'

' "I went in search of carrots but there were none." '

'So, what did you do then?'

' "I came home, ate a pile of carrots, did a massive poo and was as right as rain." '

Lady Doreese opened her eyes and looked around the table. The P.M. opposite her was fast asleep, snoring gently, his head on his hands. Lady Carter was rolling her eyes, an expression of complete and utter dismay on her face, while, Gerry, the Minister for disasters, could be heard muttering, 'Oh that's lovely. What a lovely story. I wonder what the weather was like.'

'And that, ladies and gentlemen of the Cabinet, was my vision.' Doreese smiled beatifically, 'I like to think of it as the parable of the wise donkey.'

The P.M. awoke with a start. 'Yes! Yes! Absolutely. That was great.' He looked at his watch and his eyes widened as he realised that he should be on his second drink by now. 'Mmm,' he thought to himself, 'Steak pie tonight.' He then looked back at Doreese. 'Very good. Very good indeed. Just remind me, Lady Doreese – the message *is*?'

'Well, I think Giles is telling us that things may *seem* better elsewhere, particularly from a different vantage point, but that is not necessarily the case and we should be grateful for the odd carrot now and again.'

'Or maybe, *just maybe*, it simply confirms what we already know – that donkeys should not eat cakes or they get constipated.' Lady Carter seemed deadly serious. 'Are you sure this was a vision? Had you been eating anything unusual that evening?'

'No. It was definitely a visitation. I can tell a vision from above when I see one, believe you me! Giles is telling me to continue with my mission. With your permission, P.M., I will return to Dalriada. I believe they need me there. Giles is calling upon me to do my duty.'

'Gosh,' said the P.M. 'Gosh, you'd better go then.'

'What was the weather like in Paris?' asked Gerry.

'The donkey didn't say, but in the vision it seemed sunny: good visibility certainly.'

'Thanks.'

Lady Carter could not contain herself any longer. 'What a load of *utter shite!*'

'*Right! That's it!*' exclaimed the P.M. 'You're expelled. You've gone too far this time. You're banned henceforth from attending Cabinet meetings.'

Lady Doreese smiled benignly, 'I shall leave for Dalriada tomorrow.'

# EIGHT

It was six months later that the missionaries returned. All ten of them were dressed in strict Gilesian attire and on this occasion Ted and his companions were armed. Slung over the shoulders of their regulation tweed overcoats were bandoliers of cartridges while all but their leader carried an ugly-looking rifle. Now known as Edward the converter, Ted, as their commander did not shoulder a rifle but instead carried a pistol in a holster at his waist. Few noticed them as they straggled into town early that autumn morning, and those who did were too frightened by their sinister and portentous appearance to take any action. As they reached the main street they split into two groups. The first, led by Edward, marched towards the Council Chamber, while the second headed for the school.

The children were in assembly when the missionaries burst in. One fired a shot into the air while the others levelled their weapons in the direction of the teachers who were seated in front of the children. Ruth and her colleagues were speechless at first and then, after a moment, they rose to their feet as one to remonstrate. A further shot rang out and they were ordered to lie face down on the floor.

One of the men – broad and burly – stepped forward. 'We are missionaries, servants of the Prophet Giles and His Protocols,' he announced. He scrutinised those in the room before nodding his head slowly from side to side. 'We are here to convert you,' he stated. 'To convert you to the true faith.' He paused and gazed at the ground as though disturbed by what he saw. 'You are the children of infidels. But you *can* be saved. It is not yet too late.'

'*Who are you*? What right have you to burst in here and fire your guns? *Get out. Leave at once.*' As she shouted this, Ruth attempted to stand. Immediately three rifles were trained on her and one of the men threw her roughly back down on to the floor.

'*Lie down!*' yelled the burly leader, his eyes wide with the intensity of his zeal. 'Lie down and listen. *You! You*, woman – will be the first.'

Ruth was stunned into silence and slowly resumed her prone position. She could sense, almost touch, the violence, the fervour, the insanity of this man. 'All of you,' and he glared at the children, 'be seated and listen.' After a brief pause, the man continued: 'The situation here is simple. We are missionaries and have come to spread the word of Giles and His Protocol. We *know* you are blasphemers and are therefore subject to Protocol twenty-four. *We* have come to save you. The issue is simple. You can repent: convert and live. *Or...* ' the man paused and looked about the room, '... *Or* die, in order to be reborn a believer. Make your decision carefully and understand that we have the authority, *and* the will, to do this. Even if we have to kill every last one of you, we *will* do this. It is stated clearly in the Protocol: some must suffer for the benefit of the many. Protocol 24 applies. Bless Giles.'

The other missionaries then waved their rifles in the air and started to chant, 'Bless Giles. Bless Giles,' and 'May we serve the Protocol.'

Those in the room, both adults and children, were petrified with fear and incomprehension at this outburst and at the insane fervour with which it was delivered. As the chanting ceased, the room fell silent apart from the pitiful sound of sobbing children.

'Children of infidels – you may die *now*, or be taught the true faith. There will be no more liberal, unfocussed, un-Gilesian teaching for the sons and daughters of Giles in *this* school.'

Meanwhile, half a mile away, Edward had led the second group into the town hall where Giles, the Chief, was chairing the weekly Council meeting. There were gasps of surprise and amazement when the double doors to the Council Chamber burst open and the five men entered. Those in the room, councillors and others who had business to discuss that day, strained to see the cause of this unexpected and unwelcome intrusion.

One old man rose from his seat and turned to face the intruders and shouted, 'What on earth are you doing? You've no right to burst in here. Get out immediately.' There was a single shot and the back of the old man's head exploded on to the wall behind him as he crumpled to the ground.

Edward, the converter, then slowly and very deliberately replaced his revolver in its holster. The room was silent.

Giles had recognised their leader as soon as he'd come through the doors and he knew that his worst fears – his recurring nightmare, was now being enacted in real life. In the eerie silence that followed the gunshot Giles remained silent for a moment, then he looked at the man who had fired the shot.

'Ted,' he said quietly. 'Why have you come to kill us? We fed and cared for you. Why have you returned with a gun in your hand and hatred in your heart.'

For the briefest of moments these words, delivered in quiet, unassuming tones, wrong-footed the commander, but he quickly recovered.

'Boy,' he said. '*Boy*. We are here by the authority of The Protocol. You and your community are blasphemers: even the name you have assumed is blasphemous. You have not followed the true faith – have not adhered to the ways of the Protocol. We are here to enlighten you: to resolve this conflict. You can do one of two things. You can be converted to the true faith of the Prophet Giles, before it is too late, or you will be subject to the Blasphemy Protocol and enter an accelerated End of Life Pathway.'

Giles the Chief looked at his colleagues seated in the room and added dryly, 'To you and me, members of Council, that means being shot.'

'Boy, *you* are behind the paganism of this community. *You* are responsible for the danger they are now in. *You* are the cause of these people's misery.'

'No, Ted. These people are not miserable, but content, and *you* are responsible for the danger they are now in, *not me*. Before you and your soldiers came here with your guns and your malevolence there was no danger.'

'We are not soldiers. We are missionaries. We represent the right pathway: that of goodness over evil. You were warned. When I came, alone and unarmed, you refused to listen to my message and threw me out. Now is the time for retribution and justice.'

'No, Ted. You are mistaken. *You* and your followers are the evil ones. Your moral compass has been corrupted by some malignant force: turning north to south – good to evil. Ted, what has happened to you? We were friends, we laughed and worked together. You were sensible and level-headed. Why have you changed? And your woman, Maisie. How is she?'

For the briefest of moments Ted's diamond eyes softened but then immediately hardened once more. 'That, Boy, is none of your business. You, Boy, are a heretic. *You* are responsible for what happened in Inverneuage: the deaths, the destruction, the carnage that followed your arrest; and now the same will happen here. *You* and those like you are the root of the evil, the cause of all that is wrong, by not following the rules: by not abiding to the Protocol.' Edward the converter, then pointed his pistol menacingly at Giles' head, '*You* are to blame for the bloodshed and the heartache.'

'No. *No!* Wait a minute. *You* are the ones who are causing death and destruction. *You are* the ones with the guns, *you are* the ones who killed the Chief in Inverneuage, and this old man now lying dead on the floor – *not me.*'

'It was the will of Giles because you challenged *his* word, *his* Protocol.'

Giles sighed with disbelief.

'We are missionaries, not soldiers,' Edward continued. 'We are here to help you, so that, like us, you can become part of the body of Giles.'

'Missionaries, mercenaries, what's the difference?'

'No: not mercenaries but crusaders; and in order to save the majority we may have to sacrifice the few.'

'What do you mean by that?' asked Giles, mystified.

'We will convert one of you each day invoking Protocol 24 until the whole community follows the right path.'

Giles was staggered by this statement. 'Let me get this clear. You are going to kill one of us each day until we say we'll abide by the Protocols and swear allegiance to the Prophet Giles?'

'It's rough justice. The way of Giles can be hard but it's in *your* best interests. It's an accelerated End of Life Pathway to paradise.'

Throughout this interchange the others in the room had remained silent, unable to believe what was happening, the future that was unfolding before their eyes. Suddenly all of them began to shout at the same time before a second shot rang out and quiet once more descended on the room.

Edward continued: 'My fellow missionaries have entered your

school and are at this moment converting your children and their teachers.'

This statement prompted another outburst from those in the room, only to be silenced by further shots.

'Ted,' said Giles, 'You and I need to discuss this together as responsible leaders of our two factions.'

'My name is no longer Ted. It's Edward, the converter. If you wish to speak to me, address me thus.'

'Very well, *Edward the converter*, you and I need to discuss this before any one else gets hurt.'

'Boy, It is too late for that. There is nothing to discuss. One of you, either here or in the school, will be euthanased tomorrow. Then one more, each subsequent day, until you see the light. That is the way of Giles.'

'*No it isn't the bloody way of Giles*,' yelled Giles the chief, the boy, the heretic. 'I *knew* him. He saved my life – many years ago. He was a frail, disillusioned old man. True: he wrote some of the earliest Protocols they but they were abused, taken too literally, too seriously. He designed them to *help* men, not to *rule* them. In the end he denounced them. He's the one who called the computer an ass. I know, because I was there. It was in *this* village, in a cottage just down the road that we stayed. I have his letter, written to me just before he died, telling me to challenge the dogma, the *status quo* and all that is wrong.' Giles then held up his left hand, 'Here. *Here*, look! This is his ring. I took it from his finger after he died. You and the Mandys of this world are the ones who are wrong. It was not the way of the old man. This is the opposite of what the old man Giles intended. It is the antithesis of what he stood for.'

'You blaspheme to speak of Giles the Prophet in that way.' For a moment, Edward, son of Giles, fell silent. In the quiet that followed shots was heard coming from the direction of the school. Giles feared for Ruth's safety and for that of her fellow teachers, along with his own daughter and the other children.

For twenty minutes Giles the chief argued and cajoled but Ted simply regurgitated the catechisms, the Protocols and the philosophy of Giles, by rote: unthinking. Then the door of the Council Chamber was once more thrown open. In the doorway stood the stocky missionary. Slung over his shoulder was the body of a woman, and in the crook of his arm lay that of a child. He let both bodies fall to the floor.

'There lie the bodies of infidels, now converted, thank Giles,' he cried out.

All eyes in the room turned to where Ruth's body lay, blood gently oozing from a small hole just above her left ear, her unseeing eyes wide open, staring as though in disbelief. Next to her lay the doll-like corpse of Hope.

'*No! No!*' screamed Giles, rising to his feet.

But it was Roger who lost his self-control and thus certainly saved Giles from being summarily executed. Roger started to walk – trance-like – towards the door and the corpses that lay there on the floor. '*Ruth?*' he said, quietly at first; then again, 'Ruth, *Ruth,*' louder and louder until he was shouting. As Roger stepped slowly forward, Ted very deliberately raised his pistol and shot him between the eyes. Roger dropped and lay still and quite dead, only a few feet from the body of the woman he loved.

Giles was strong and it took all four of the missionaries to hold him as he struggled to reach the bodies of his wife and daughter. For the first time in years he cried, he wept, he screamed and lost all control. He didn't care what happened to him. He had been prepared for a fight, to be defeated, even to lay down his life in defence of common sense – but these men had done something much worse: they had killed Ruth, his childhood sweetheart, his wife and their baby, little Hope. By killing them they had killed him a thousand times over. He struggled as hard as he could screaming, '*Kill me. Kill me.*' He wanted to be killed, he was desperate to die, to be lying on the floor, lifeless, alongside the bodies of Ruth and Hope: to be at one with them in death. He was *willing* the missionaries to execute him yet plead as he might they would not.

Eventually, wholly exhausted by his struggling and his emotions, he fell to his knees, and, now unfettered, begged quietly, 'Please kill me. *Please* kill me.' He began to crawl towards the bodies that lay in the doorway and, as he grew closer, the man who had brought in Ruth's body smiled and kicked the corpses.

Giles looked up at the man and his sorrow turned to anger. He had never been so angry in his whole life. He had never hated anyone so much as he hated that man at that moment. He wanted to strangle the life slowly out of this stupid, unthinking murderer. It would be impossible to hurt him *too* much. No amount of pain and agony would be enough for Giles to inflict. He physically ached with the hatred he felt for this man who had taken Ruth away from him: for the thoughtlessness, the stupidity, the idiocy of his actions. Giles looked at the man, now sneering down at him, and launched himself at his throat.

Throughout all of this, the Enforcer had remained still – quite rigid: stunned into inactivity, unable to make sense of the events of the last few minutes and physically incapable of movement. But then he stepped forward. Slowly and deliberately, just as Giles launched himself forward, he clamped Giles' head in an arm lock. After a brief struggle Giles once more fell to the floor gasping for breath; and as he did so the Enforcer whispered into his ear, 'Giles, we need you. Your people need you. We need you to stay alive.' The Enforcer then loosened his grip, helped Giles to his feet and led him slowly across the room to where the bodies lay. There the Enforcer stood, while Giles collapsed to his knees sobbing, cradling in his aching arms the lifeless forms that had been Ruth and Hope. For what seemed like an eternity the only sound was that of Giles' heart breaking as his tears washed the faces of his wife and daughter and their blood turned his white shirt scarlet.

Realising that all resistance had been broken, Edward the converter, announced: 'The conversion has started. Four of you have now been reborn into the true faith: they have been saved. Bless Giles.' He smiled and even chuckled as he looked down at the grief being enacted in front of him. 'Well, boy, not so sure about your principles now, are you, heretic? Where are your free-thoughts now, *hey*? Your polytheism, your liberalism? Mmm.' He looked around him at the others in the room and shouted, 'Welcome to the world of the Prophet Giles. The world the rest of us have to live in. Not your *bloody ivory towers*,' he sneered. 'Right! That's step one in the conversion process. Step two is tomorrow when we shall repeat the process until you see the light.'

No one wanted more blood spilt, so they buried their dead, swore allegiance to the Protocol and the town was converted. Giles was bereft: his heart and his spirit utterly broken; shattered into myriads of small inconsolable shards which pierced every cranny, every atom of his soul. He buried Ruth and their daughter on the lower slopes of the mountain where they had so often walked together, overlooking his cottage and the loch where the old man had fished. From there, seated on the mound that marked their grave, Giles could view his whole desolate existence in one sad panorama. Roger was laid to rest nearby, close to the woman he had loved but who had loved another.

The missionaries remained to monitor compliance, while Edward the converter, took over as leader of the Council.

# NINE

Conversion was straightforward and the town quickly embraced Protocolism. It needed no Pentecostal moment for the community to realise that it was easier to be told what to do: simply and blindly to adhere to the myriads of rules and regulations that were The Protocol and live, rather than to resist and risk execution. So within weeks the population of this small town had adopted the new faith, dressing and behaving accordingly.

Only Giles, the ex-chief, was not part of this transformation. For three years the heretic mourned, alone and inconsolable. Giles wanted to die, to embrace eternity, but the missionaries would not oblige and kill him. They did the opposite – they kept him alive. He was excluded from this new order, as an exemplar of failure, disillusion and un-Gilesian behaviour. With his hands and feet shackled he scavenged like a rabid dog barking outside the city walls, occasionally thrown scraps of food to perform tricks. Not for him the new attire and his own personal copy of the Protocol to be learned and chanted. He was banned from the hastily-built Studio, where the community now assembled each week to read and discuss the new philosophy. His was a figure of ridicule: testimony to the inevitable consequence of non-adherence to the Protocol and failure to embrace the spirit of the Prophet Giles. Not that the heretic cared. He wanted it all to end. He even asked to be euthanased, to register for an End of Life Pathway, but was refused. He spent his life at Ruth's grave, occasionally visiting his cottage for shelter and rest. Whisky helped to relieve the pain – a little – and Edward the converter, ensured there were ample supplies.

'There he is,' shouted the tour guide as he pointed to the hillside. 'Look – he's lying on the grave.' The group of fifteen or so pilgrims from the town and its environs peered towards where the heretic was asleep on a low mound of earth. There was no stone or plaque to mark the place where Ruth and her daughter were buried, because each time the heretic erected one it was quickly defaced and destroyed.

'Quick! Let's run,' shouted the guide as he urged his group up the hill. Once there he pointed at the bedraggled unshaven figure sprawled over the mound. 'There's the heretic, the man who was Chief. There he is. A so-called free-thinker, a man of loose morals. A man without the Protocol. There's the man who would have you think that *his* way was better than that of the Prophet.' The guide pointed once more at the heretic. '*That's* what happens to those that don't adhere: to those that won't comply.' He paused for a moment then addressed his group once more. 'Now, who won this week's prize. Who's first today?' he asked.

'*Me*! me!' replied a little girl jumping up and down. Her parents had dressed her in her best attire and bought her a traditional, child-sized Gilesian style hat for this special occasion.

'Okay then, go ahead.'

The girl who had won first prize in the *first throw* raffle then rather tentatively picked up a stone from the pile on a table in front of her and threw it as hard as she could in the direction of the heretic. It fell well short landing just a few feet in front of her but the throw was symbolic and there was loud applause and shouts of, 'Well done. Good shot.' The girl then stood back and rejoined her parents, flushed with her success.

The noise woke the heretic from his drunken slumber.

'Good morning, heretic,' said the tour guide, 'and how are you today?' The crowd chuckled. This guide was one of the best, combining traditional teaching with humour. 'Are you ready for your punishment?' The heretic briefly looked at the assembled crowd then simply rolled over and went back to sleep.

'Bless Giles,' said the guide, who then, as was laid down in the Protocol, threw the next stone. After a chorus of, 'Bless Giles,' from the rest of the group there followed a hail of missiles. Most were small, not large enough to kill but sharp enough to draw blood, while some were heavy enough to concuss.

'Take that, heretic!' said the little girl as she threw her second stone and when it glanced off his head there was a shout of, 'Good shot. Hooray. Bless Giles.'

Then one of the councillors stepped forward. 'Take this for leading us down the wrong path. The path of evil and destruction.' His rock stunned the heretic who shook his head and gazed unseeingly at the crowd which now surrounded him.

After five minutes the tour guide called a halt to proceedings.

'Right, ladies and gents, girls and boys. That's enough for today. We'll be back next week.' Then he led the group down the mountainside and back to the town.

The heretic, his near naked body now smeared with blood, his right eye swelling and half-closed, turned his face to the ground. He hoped that this time he would die, that he would not wake up. But it was not to be: he awoke an hour later, cold and shivering. Then, his shackles rattling, he walked down the well-trodden pathway to his cottage where he knew there would be whisky waiting.

* * *

'The donkey visited me again last night.'

'Lucky you,' said Lady Carter under her breath. She was on probation, allowed back into the Cabinet on the understanding that she would behave.

'Pardon?' said the P.M. looking at her.

'Nothing, P.M. Just a touch of wind, that's all.'

'Mmm. What did the donkey say *this* time, Lady Doreese?'

'Well, he said he thought I'd done rather well, actually.'

'Oh, good,' muttered the Minister who was on probation.

'I beg your pardon, Lady Carter.'

'Just the wind again I'm afraid, P.M.'

'You really should get something done about your wind, Lady Carter. It's most disconcerting. Have you tried carrots?'

'No, P.M.'

'Well I think you should. I used to have the most appalling indigestion, and they worked for me.'

'I will, P.M. I will, I promise.'

'Carry on, Lady Doreese.'

'Well, the donkey said that he had been on a pilgrimage to the place of his birth.'

'Oh, really, where was that?' asked the P.M., genuinely interested.

'Nowton, P.M. The donkey said it was disappointed. When he arrived there was no welcome. The place was drab, the architecture boring, there were no carrots, and there wasn't a single show on.'

'Did it get constipated again?'

'Nearly, but it managed to find some roughage in the form of sprouts.'

'Not good, I fear – the devil's vegetable.'

'Yes, indeed. He said they gave him colossal wind of the worst kind,' Lady Doreese wrinkled up her nose to illustrate her point.

'Yes. Not pleasant.'

'Well, if that's how the donkey feels then I suppose we'd better spruce the place up a bit. Can you do that for us?'

'A pleasure, P.M. In fact I've already started.'

'What have you got in mind.'

'Something tasteful, P.M. I think a kind of grotto, with donkey's favourite music, perhaps a show and, of course, a selection of vegetables.'

'Good, good.' The P.M. looked at his watch. Nearly drinks time he thought. 'Anything else to report.'

'Yes, I am pleased to that my last visit to Dalriada was a huge success and I can confirm that the Gilesian diaspora has spread far and wide across the whole of the known world. All pockets of resistance have been winkled out and destroyed… ' Her ladyship hesitated for the briefest of moments, '… rather – *converted*.'

'Excellent, excellent. And Protocol adherence?'

'One hundred percent, P.M.'

'Excellent, really first class. Well you've certainly done a good job. What about the Euthanasia Protocol?'

'Working perfectly. The average age of the population has fallen, USPELYs are well on target for the coming year, and we have reset the minimum age for euthanasia at sixty in order to grow the economy further. The extra work involved should ensure full employment and higher productivity for years to come.'

'What about the protected occupations such as our own?' asked the P.M.

'Well as Cabinet knows, those who run the system, like ourselves, have to be protected in order to ensure fair play and continuity. It would be ridiculous for *us* to be subject to the same age control Protocols as the rest of the population.'

'Quite, quite. Well that's all most satisfactory. To think all those years ago we used to worry about an ageing population and all that ridiculous nonsense about religion. All those unnecessary deaths caused by religious strife, culminating in the wars of theism. We have come a long way since those dark days, ladies and gentlemen.' The P.M. sat back in his chair, savouring the moment.

'Can you just remind us what happens to those who aren't converted or who don't wish to die at sixty?' asked the Minister for Babies.

'Careful, Lady Carter,' said the P.M.

'Just a thought, P.M.'

'Well,' said Lady Doreese, 'the Protocol deals with all that sort of day-to-day detail.'

'How?'

'Oh, I've absolutely no idea. It's all done automatically; no human is involved: that's the beauty of the system. The new chip has a life-completion programme, and a termination mechanism which can be reset remotely. An algorithm runs the age-control Protocol and automatically fires in to keep age at an optimal level.'

'I heard a rumour that a group of teenagers were killed... sorry, I mean Completed. Was that an error?'

'*An error*? Couldn't have been. The system is fail-safe.' Doreese thought for a moment. 'Come to think of it, I recall that in one of his visitations the donkey stated that some hooligans needed an accelerated pathway.'

'Oh, how very convenient.'

The P.M. looked at Lady Carter, not sure whether or not she had transgressed. Then, deciding in her favour, he turned to the Minister for Disasters, 'Now Gerry... ' he started but was immediately interrupted.

'Before you go any further, P.M. I can confirm that the weather is *shite*.'

# TEN

For three years the Enforcer watched Giles, the heretic, burn up inside with hatred and anger. The agony devoured Giles, every second of every minute of every day. Whisky barely dulled the pain, but allowed him to live in that half world: that crepuscular semi-existence that alcoholics inhabit. He came to anticipate the weekly visits: the tour guides with their pilgrims and even the stoning became a welcome distraction from the desolation that engulfed his soul. He started to join in, to play along: growling and grunting at the crowd on cue. He would run at them, shouting and waving his manacled arms till they drew back in alarm and then he would pretend to be cowed into submission by the rocks and insults. Soon people from far and wide travelled to the hillside to see the heretic and to hurl stones. The attraction grew so popular that the number of shows was increased to twice a week, and there were long queues.

Most evenings he returned to his cottage where there would be food. He neither knew nor cared where it had come from. Sometimes he ate; more often he did not. His hair and beard grew long, his skin became engrained with dirt while blankets covered his skinny, scarred body. He knew that he would die soon. No flesh could take such punishment for long; so he drank more and ate less: urging death on, faster and faster.

The heretic was sitting on the mound that was Ruth's last resting place, when he sensed, more than heard, someone approach. 'Giles. I've brought a visitor to see you,' said the Enforcer. Giles was staring along the length of the loch with his back to the speaker – a blanket over his shoulders and a bottle in his hand. He took a long swig and wiped his mouth with his forearm. 'It's not a stoning day, is it?'

'No. It's me, the Enforcer. You remember me: we sailed here together, had many adventures. You remember *me*,' the Enforcer entreated.

Still Giles stared. 'Are you a tour guide as well, now? Do you want me to growl, and spit, then squirm on the ground begging for forgiveness as you pelt stones at me? It's a good show.'

'*Turn around*, Giles,' ordered the Enforcer, becaming more assertive. 'I have someone who wants to see you.'

The heretic continued to stare at the rippling surface of the loch, the bouncing yellow and silver reflections that were his past. Then he heard another voice, one that was vaguely familiar.

'Turn around, Giles, I have come to see you.' The old lady's voice was weaker than he remembered but Giles instantly recognised its conviction and sincerity. 'The Enforcer has brought me to see you because he is worried about you.'

The boy slowly turned and there standing beside the Enforcer was the old woman from the hamlet at the head of the loch. 'Old lady, why have you come?' he said, and then, nodding towards a table a few yards away on which there lay a pile of rocks, added, 'the stones are over there.'

'How ungrateful, Giles,' said the Enforcer. 'The old lady has come to see you, to try to help you, and all you do is insult her. I have watched you wallow in self-pity and self-destruction for three years now. I have kept you alive with food and warmth. I clothe you with blankets when you are covered in snow, I carry you to the cottage when you are unable to walk; it is I who staunches the flow of blood and dresses your wounds and now I bring you a true friend. Don't insult her, Giles. It's time you came back to life, for you have grovelled in the gateway to death for long enough.'

Giles continued to stare at the grassy hummock in front of him.

'The Enforcer's right Giles,' said the old lady. 'You have a choice. You can continue in your present ways and soon achieve your wish of lying beneath the ground on which you now sit, or you may embrace a living future. Seek retribution for what happened to Ruth, Hope and Roger. My man is dead, but he trusted you. He had faith in you. He said that you were resourceful and resilient, that you could do something useful with your life: could change things for the better.'

The Enforcer looked Giles directly in the eye. 'Remember what the old man said. Be a sleeper, a mole, ready to emerge at the right time and restore sanity to an insane world.' The Enforcer paused, then added slowly, 'Giles, now *is* that time.' Giles said nothing but glowered at his visitors. 'There are two people in the world who care for you, Giles, two who continue to have faith, who do not see you as a fairground attraction. Those two people are standing in front of you at this moment.'

The old woman took a small step towards Giles who, like the wild animal he had become, began to retreat. 'You have degraded yourself, and by doing that you have shamed us all: Ruth, Hope, Roger, us, my dead husband and, of course, the old man who believed in you.'

The boy, who had called himself Giles, the Chief who had become a heretic, attempted to stand but stumbled and fell to his knees and broke down. It was then that his crushed and tormented soul finally and completely dissolved and despair wholly engulfed him. He shouted at the mound, '*Why did you leave me?*' and punched the hillside until his knuckles bled. The old lady knelt in front of him and, when he was exhausted by his passion, she embraced the heretic that was Giles. His filthy hair and blood-soaked blanket were enveloped by the love that issued from the woman. Then, from within the ashes of his crushed, tormented soul, phoenix-like, his desire was reborn and they wept together.

The Enforcer looked on, his face suffused with pleasure. 'Giles,' he said dispassionately, 'hold out your arms. It's time to cut those shackles that bind you to the past. It's time for us to leave this place.'

\* \* \*

When Mandy first heard of the events in the village at the foot of the loch she was furious that, yet again, the boy had survived. Edward was one of her finest missionaries and had converted scores of unbelievers, rooting out pockets of resistance and converting them, seemingly with ease. His view was that a dead Giles could become the focus for resistance as a martyr and that he was less of a threat alive: living as a heretic like a mad dog, the focus of scorn and ridicule, an example of what happened to nonbelievers. The only flaw in this otherwise excellent strategy was that Mandy had told Doreese, the GODOG, that he was dead and, if she ever found out the truth, Mandy would be finished.

Mandy considered having him assassinated but he was now so great a tourist attraction that the logistics of such an exercise were difficult. Even Doreese, on her last visit to Dalriada to celebrate the total integration of the two national Protocols, had asked to see him. 'Mandy,' she had said, 'I want to go and see the heretic – you know, the one people throw stones at. Everyone's talking about it in London and I want to see him for myself, perhaps even throw a stone or two. Is it true he grunts and growls like a real person?'

'I believe so, though that I haven't seen him myself. Up here it is deemed un-Gilesian for those like us – those in protected professions – to view the heretic. The show is more for the lower members of society – the unprotected, you know, children and those awaiting euthanasia, a kind of final pilgrimage – people like that.'

'Oh, that's a shame. But I do understand. Someone like me turning up might give the heretic some credibility, which would be undesirable.'

'Exactly, Lady Doreese.'

Thus, Mandy had avoided a meeting between Doreese and the heretic. But it had been a close call.

Doreese had then spent the rest of her time discussing the Nowton studio upgrade project, seeking details of the old man's appearance and behaviour from one of the few people who had actually met him. She then returned to London and Mandy concluded that by the time she next visited Dalriada the heretic, Giles, would probably be dead.

# ELEVEN

WELCOME TO NOWTON. BIRTHPLACE OF THE DONKEY. So read the sign on the platform, as Giles and the Enforcer alighted from the train.

'What's all that about?' asked Giles of his companion.

'The cult of the donkey seems to have originated from the Euthanasia Pathway that the old man requested, and has now been absorbed into popular Gilesian culture.'

'But it was a joke. The old man was being facetious.'

'*I* know that; and *you* know that, but it's extraordinary what some people will believe.'

'Do they believe that the donkey can talk?'

'Better than that, Giles. He is now the official mouthpiece of Giles the Prophet himself.'

'The old man would certainly have seen the irony in that,' observed Giles.

'The donkey has achieved almost mythical status by virtue of good marketing, helped of course by a vision or two from the Lady Doreese, may Giles bless her!'

'Ah! The parables of the donkey,' said the young Giles. 'Yes, very useful. Every time there's a problem, Doreese is conveniently visited by the donkey in a vision which then tells her that she's a good egg and really doing rather well.'

'Yes, it must be a great comfort to have a direct line to the one in charge, albeit through an ass.' And as he said this the Enforcer chuckled out loud.

The platform was busy, full of pilgrims visiting the Nowton shrine. Most were dressed in traditional fashion: an old overcoat – a red handkerchief displayed ostentatiously in the breast pocket – corduroy trousers and black leather shoes. The women wore hats, now often referred to as GODOGS. These were usually showy affairs, rather like large Yorkshire puddings with flora and fauna represented in their crevices.

The pair of them, Giles and the Enforcer, attracted some attention as they were both wearing blankets draped over their shoulders held at the waist by a belt, rather like a toga.

The two of them followed the crowd, which swelled until it filled the street as it reached the centre of town. As they neared the square where the Studio stood, they heard the first strains of Beethoven's ninth symphony, which grew louder as they approached.

'One of donkey's favourite pieces of music,' explained the Enforcer. Then – as they turned a corner and entered the square, the very same path that the boy had walked all those years ago, cold and hungry – they saw the Studio. No longer was it a small, humble, double-fronted building with a few adverts in its window. Surrounding buildings, including the little café he and the old man had frequented, had been demolished and it now stood alone, rising to three storeys and towering like an island in the centre of the square. Pilgrims paraded slowly around it in an anti-clockwise direction, awaiting their turn to enter. Every inch of the frontage was covered with flashing neon lights of varied colours and shapes. On the roof was displayed the outline of a donkey dancing to the music while munching on a carrot and smiling as it joined in with Schiller's *Ode to Joy*. Behind him was a massive hologram of the old man smiling benignly towards the crowds below.

'Mmm, nice,' said Giles.

'Tasteful,' replied the Enforcer.

'It's changed a bit since I was last here.'

Giles and the Enforcer queued with the rest of the pilgrims until eventually they reached the steps to the main entrance. Once inside, they pushed past those who were buying trinkets and memorabilia from market traders. On sale were all manner of souvenirs: framed pictures of the donkey and of the old man; key rings in the form of the Eiffel tower and a huge selection of carrots in all shapes and sizes, both real and plastic. CDs of the donkey's favourite music and shows were selling well, as were copies of the Protocol. These could be purchased separately, as CDs, or as part of an integrated package which included a cheap computer, some test questions and a picture of the donkey eating a carrot.

The noise of traders, pilgrims and music was deafening as Giles and the Enforcer pushed their way through the crowd to enter the relative quiet of the Protocol room. There, sitting row upon row, in front of computer screens, were dozens of pilgrims seeking answers to the questions they had brought along with them. Some had pages of questions, not just theirs but those of family and friends and they were madly scribbling down the responses of the Protocol to their queries. As soon as a computer station became vacant there would be a mad rush to claim it by those waiting.

'This is amazing,' said Giles the boy.

Quite something isn't it? Look! There's a fight breaking out over who reached that computer first. Let's move on.'

They passed through into another room where cakes were on sale, all accompanied by the mandatory vegetable to ensure bowel regularity. 'Remember the parable of the donkey,' they overheard one trader say when a small child requested a strawberry tart without its accompanying carrot.

Giles shook his head and gazed at the large screen on the wall. There, was an image of the old man. He was surprised by the resemblance. The picture was of a man: slightly younger, tidier and better looking than the old man had really been. There were fewer wrinkles in both clothes and flesh, but there was a definite similarity. Then the image changed and the events of the day were displayed. There were shows to be seen and a fast-track euthanasia programme for those from afar who had an elderly relative but no local access to a Studio. The rates were at a premium but the whole process could be completed in three hours, and there were over a thousand pathways on offer. Thirty clients could be processed at any one time and on a good day nearly a hundred pilgrims could complete their End of Life Pathway.

As well as all those facilities, the studio offered access to various other elements of the Protocol, including Protocol 24. On most days someone was twenty-foured and this spectacle always drew a large crowd.

'Well, Giles, what do you make of all this?' asked the Enforcer.

'I'm speechless. I just cannot believe how this has happened.'

The two of them then ascended a staircase, opened a door at the top, and found themselves on the roof. Giles advanced cautiously to the front of the building where there was a small parapet and looked down on the milling throng in the square below. The Enforcer stood a pace behind Giles and then, as the sun disappeared below the horizon and the evening grew darker, the pair of them were illuminated from behind by the immense neon image of the donkey imbuing them with a them a ghostly, portentous appearance. As they peered into the gloom below, some of the pilgrims saw them and began to point at the pair upon the roof. Giles took a step forward so that he was close to the edge of the parapet and slowly raised his arms. Gradually the hubbub from the crowd ceased and, when all was silent, Giles addressed the pilgrims.

'I knew Giles,' he said, just loud enough to be heard. There was a gasp of disbelief from those in the square below.

'I knew Giles,' he repeated. 'He saved my life when I was a boy.' The silence in the square was now complete.

'He didn't believe in the Protocols!'

On hearing this, there was a gasp and the crowd began to display its disapproval with hisses and shouts of, 'Shame!'

'He wanted the protocols destroyed! He said that he had created a monster that he could no longer control. What he wanted was that people should challenge the dogma, question the status quo – not simply adhere slavishly to some idiotic computer programme.'

This was too much for the pilgrims. Here was a strangely-dressed man who claimed to have known Giles personally, standing on the roof of the studio, the very home of Gilesianism, contradicting all that they had been taught: saying that their beliefs were not just flawed, but completely wrong. There was confusion in the square. Some shouted, 'This blasphemer should die.' Others chanted, 'Twenty four, twenty four, twenty four,' to the tune of colonel Bogey, while still others knelt, saying, 'He knew Giles: he must be enlightened.'

The heretic on the roof raised his voice and continued. 'Giles once said, "The protocol is an ass." ' But the younger Giles could no longer make himself heard above the noise emanating from the square below.

'Here, take this,' said the Enforcer, handing Giles the microphone used for the weekly addresses.

'*Yes.*' Giles, now audible, continued, 'I knew Giles as an old man. The donkey was a joke.'

Loud jeering now emanated from the crowd below.

'Yes! A *joke*. Something he made up to annoy the Euthanasia Practitioner in this very Studio. And then he died in a nearby hostel. *Of old age*. Believe me – I was there.'

Those in the square then held up their hands in salute, 'Bless Giles, bless Giles,' they chanted.

Giles the younger continued. 'The Protocol must be destroyed. The donkey is a figment of your imagination; the visions are an invention to protect the government. Go home and start to *think* again.'

There was a roar of disapproval and some of those in the square below began to hurl missiles at the two men on the roof.

'Just like old times,' said Giles as he turned towards the stairwell. 'Let's go and meet our fans.'

As Giles and the Enforcer entered the main lobby once more, the noise of shouting and trading gradually quietened. They were an impressive sight, dressed in their blankets, and their presence was unsettling.

Sensing that the moment was right, Giles began to speak once more. 'I came to this very studio with an old man called Giles. This is where he chose his pathway. He then chose to live, but was not allowed to. I am named after him.' Giles then rushed forward to where the traders had laid out their fares on display and set about pushing over the tables and stalls laden with their trinkets and mementoes. Pictures and toys tumbled to the floor accompanied by the crash of breaking glass and splintering furniture. Traders were astonished, uncertain whether to applaud or apprehend this iconoclast. One vendor, sensing the inevitable, grabbed a couple of expensive china donkeys then deliberately pushed over his own stall. In a final act of defiance, Giles lifted one of the fallen trestles and launched it towards a massive neon picture of the old man. After a few spectacular flashes and sparks all the illuminations were extinguished and even the donkey on the roof stopped dancing and fell quiet. There followed an eerie silence inside the studio, the only sound being that of Giles and the Enforcer crunching across a carpet of broken glass and debris as they walked slowly to the entrance of the studio where they stood on the topmost step.

'That,' said Giles the boy, '*That* is the way of Giles. *That* is what the old man would have done to this ridiculous place – *trashed it.*'

The pair of them then walked down the steps towards the crowd and as they approached, almost miraculously, the seemingly impenetrable wall of pilgrims opened to allow them to pass through.

After leaving the square they headed for a nearby hostel. 'Well, Mister Enforcer,' said Giles, 'overall, I think that went rather well.' And for the first time in years the Enforcer saw the old familiar cheeky grin creep across Giles' face.

* * *

News of these events quickly travelled far and wide. Mandy was horrified as her secret was out, while the head of D.I.E., the GODOG, was concerned about the civil unrest that followed. Most of those who had heard Giles' speech simply went home and naïvely sought advice from the Protocol: asking whether or not it should be believed. The Protocol replied, 'I am what I am, and must be obeyed.' Most were reassured but some began to question the *status quo*, the structure and the endless regulations; and met with like-minded people in secret and out of sight of a computer.

'Excellent news, Mandy, don't you think?'

Mandy's eyes widened. She had expected the GODOG to have her arrested immediately and Protocol 24 seemed the inevitable outcome. But here was Doreese sharing tea and cakes with her and expressing satisfaction at the events of the last few days.

'Not the riots, obviously,' Doreese continued. 'Those must be dealt with firmly. But the resurrection of the boy, after you had him Completed, can only be described as a miracle. It's a clear signal to me that Giles *was* the creator of the Protocols and that these truly have been sent to us from on high. It also means that the donkey is Giles' messenger and that my visions make *me* the chosen one.' The GODOG looked at Mandy with an expression of wonderment in her eyes. 'This is a sign. A sign that we must persevere in our mission. Don't you agree?'

Mandy couldn't believe her luck. Doreese had turned into a

believer, a true believer. She actually believed that the boy had been Completed and had come back to life. 'Absolutely. And a great relief to me, too,' said Mandy with feeling.

'Indeed so. Mandy. You must make contact with this new prophet and instate him as a Defender Of the Protocol.'

'But he's against the Protocols, GODOG.'

'Oh! Is he? Whatever. Instate him as a Defender of Giles then. Just get him onside, Mandy.'

'Certainly, GODOG.'

# TWELVE

Giles and his companion, the Enforcer, travelled the length and breadth of the land preaching the word of Giles. Not the philosophy of The Protocol, but the true words of the old man Giles. The words that Giles the younger knew: the concepts that he had debated with the man himself. He would quote from the letter written to him by old man and show his audience the signet ring that he had plucked from his dead hand. His aim was simple: to ridicule the Protocol and restore commonsense. As he travelled, his followers, originally numbering fifty or sixty, multiplied until hundreds regularly accompanied him wherever he went. After their conversion, Giles encouraged them to return to their towns and cities to preach the philosophy of reason and thoughtfulness. Those young disciples could be distinguished from traditional Gilesians by the toga-like blankets that they habitually wore and they began to speak of themselves as the Real Gilesians.

Neither Giles nor the Enforcer, however, was aware of the development of a sect which called itself the 'Brethren of the Donkey'. This group was appalled at what they saw to be outrageous attacks upon the Protocol, which they believed to be the embodiment of all that was true and must be adhered to, without thought or reason. They also believed in the parables of the Donkey and accepted them as incontrovertible fact. This essentially fundamental Protocolist group, developed a number of practices which set them apart. They dressed ever more starkly in traditional Gilesian fashion, refused cakes of all sorts, ate carrots at least three times each day and members of this sect became known to their detractors, as Asinines.

It was inevitable that friction would develop between these splinter groups and that trouble would ensue. The first that Giles, the Enforcer and their followers were aware of this, was when they heard that there had been a bombing. Unknown to Giles, a branch of Real Gilesians – his followers – had taken it upon themselves to plant a bomb in one of the main Protocol Studios in London. Many Protocolist lives were lost, computers destroyed and responsibility claimed. In retaliation, the Protocolists attacked an open meeting of Real Gilesians, indiscriminately shooting into the crowd, killing and maiming many. Not to be outdone, the Brethren of the Donkey joined the fray, indiscriminately attacking anyone who was not one of them.

Even though Giles preached restraint, the Real Gilesians then began publicly to destroy Protocol computers and to burn copies of the Protocol itself. One even killed a donkey. This inflamed the Brethren, who introduced a military wing to defend their faith, which the Real Gilesians soon matched with an army of their own, the RGA, and the conflict spiralled ever more violently towards chaos.

\* \* \*

As the chorus of, 'Bless the Protocol. May we serve it well,' died down, the P.M. looked across the table towards the head of D.I.E. 'Lady Doreese,' he said, 'I think you have some explaining to do, don't you?' The P.M.'s annoyance was exacerbated by a prolonged bout of dyspepsia. He knew that he needed yet another new stomach but was reluctant as it had only been two years since his last one. They don't seem to last as long as they used to, he thought to himself.

'Yes, P.M., it *has* been rather a difficult month.' Lady Doreese was wearing a rather subdued GODOG, with just a hint of barley and a small field mouse in its folds.

Lady Carter was similarly attired with a GODOG, but hers was, for once, slightly more extravagant. Hidden within its crevices was a small bird's nest full of fluffy chicks, while overhead, attached by a piece of bendy wire, was a starling which appeared to fly in circles whenever she moved her head. Lady Carter smelled blood. She began quietly. 'Lady Doreese, there is civil unrest; there are bombings and violence while one Gilesian sect fights another. Computers are being destroyed, Protocols are burned openly in the street and brother fights brother. To my mind, that's more than just a difficult month – it's a *disaster*. What on *earth* is going on?'

'Yes, what *is* going on,' echoed the P.M.

'Well luckily...' but Doreese was not allowed to finish her sentence.

'Oh, here we go,' said Lady Carter.

Doreese ignored the insinuation. 'As I was saying – luckily the donkey visited me again last night.'

'That *is* fortunate!'

'Yes, it *was* rather well timed.' Doreese looked in the direction of Lady Carter and forced a smile.

'What did he say this time? Eat more carrots?'

That's a point, the P.M. thought to himself, perhaps that's what I should do. Then he said out loud, his brow furrowed and his voice stern, 'Yes, what *did* he say?'

'Well, P.M. He said that this was all part of his grand plan, and that it would work out for the best in the end. He said that he himself once had to endure hard times to reach his sanctuary – and so must we. It is for the greater good, we must believe.'

'Well that's all *very* convenient isn't it?' Lady Carter was in no mood to pull her punches. 'What do we do in the meantime. Protocolists are fighting the so-called Real Gilesians, the Brethren of the Donkey are fighting the Realists and the Protocol fundamentalists seem to be fighting anyone they can find. *It's carnage out there.*'

'I'm not sure I want to live in a donkey sanctuary,' added the Minister for Disasters.

Doreese continued. 'P.M. if I may? I think the solution is to ask The Protocol.'

'Yes, absolutely. Of course that's what we should do.'

'Thank you, P.M. Anticipating your response and that of the Cabinet members I took the liberty of doing just that last night and I'm pleased to say that we have a solution.'

'Oh good. That's a relief. I was beginning to think we were in a spot of trouble there for a moment. Well done. What is the solution?'

'Well, The Protocol says that we should write another protocol to solve this problem.'

'That's not really a *solution,* is it?' said the P.M.

'A Protocol to end the Wars of the Protocols. *That's brilliant,* just brilliant! Why on earth didn't I think of that.' Lady Carter was at her most sarcastic. 'Tell you what, Lady Doreese, there's a donkey in the field behind my house, or maybe it's an ass. Either way I'll pop over this evening and ask its opinion. It'll give me better advice than we're getting from *you*, that's for sure!' The starling on her GODOG circled dangerously while one of the chicks looked in danger of fledging early.

'This new Protocol,' said Lady Doreese continuing undaunted, 'will be an anti-insurgent Protocol aimed at seeking out and destroying anyone who is not a Gilesian.'

'But *everyone's* a Gilesian – of one sort or another – that's the whole problem. They all believe in the same thing but still want to knock ten bells out of each other.' Doreese's tormentor then continued more calmly, 'Who do you want to destroy? The Gilesians, or the real Gilesians?'

'I don't know. Probably both. It's irrelevant: the computer can decide. Just as long as one of the protagonists is removed, all will be fine. You need two sides to have a fight you know,' she simpered.

'What about the Brethren of the Donkey?'

'Oh, the Asinines: what about them?'

'Well they need to be marginalised somehow. I understand that some of the worst atrocities have been perpetrated by them.'

Doreese paused, lost for words, so allowing Lady Carter to add, 'Lady Doreese, you really seem to be making up policy on the hoof.' Some around the table chuckled.

The P.M. had had enough. 'What are we going to do then? Here we are: the Cabinet, the people who rule the country, dithering when we are facing its most critical period for over a hundred years. In the face of this crisis all we can think of is, "We'll ask the Protocol," which then tells us to write *another* protocol!'

'Bless the Protocol,' said the Minister for Disasters.

'Bless Giles,' came the response.

'Bugger the Protocol. Bugger Giles. We have to make a *decision*!' The P.M. was growing excited and nearly thumped the table but thought better of it at the last moment. It was well past aperitif time, and he wasn't sure what was for supper.

'*Make a decision*, P.M.? Surely not!' said Lady Carter, 'We haven't done that in years.'

'What do you mean by, "make a decision?" ' asked Doreese.

'I mean – decide to do something, and then... ' the P.M. paused '... well – *do it.*'

'But that's what the Protocol does for us. *We* might get it wrong,' said Lady Doreese.

The starling bobbed and dipped ever more violently. 'You mean that we, we as individuals, should discuss how to solve a problem?'

'*Precisely*,' replied the P.M.

'Well, that's a new approach, I must say. I'm not sure how wise that would be, P.M. Remember there's an election next year.' One of the chicks fledged and landed on the table in front of Lady Carter.

'I want you all to give this a lot of thought. And come back with some solutions next week.'

'Next week, P.M.? *But that's only a week.*'

'Precisely.'

The following week they met again. The P.M.'s enthusiasm for radical change had waned considerably in the interim as his stomach had improved, so the Cabinet decided to do what the Cabinet usually did in moments of uncertainty – it asked the Protocol whether or not it should ask it what to do. The Protocol replied in the affirmative and then, when asked, advised that all those who did not support the Protocol should be deported. This policy was non-controversial as all groups concerned essentially believed in the Protocol, albeit in differing ways. The fundamentalist Asinises believed absolutely in the writings; the Gilesians also believed that The Protocol should be adhered to, but were sceptical about the donkey elements, while the Real Gilesians believed in the principle of written systems but felt that they needed to be interpreted. In other words everyone was correct. But sect fought sect and each splinter group sought to outdo the others with its cruelty and violence.

\* \* \*

'Mister Enforcer,' said Giles one day, 'I seem to have the inherited the King Midas effect. Except that everything I touch turns to blood.'

'It's not your fault, Giles. It's just the way of things. Everything goes round in circles. As sure as day follows night, peace follows war and with it, a belief that conflict will never occur again. But as the world turns people seek for a meaning: a goal, and that is created – whatever you want to call it – *something* is created. Once that happens there follows disagreement and disillusion. Then some believe in *the thing* more than others and become more fundamentalist, while non-believers become radical so that there is fragmentation and misinterpretation. This leads to inevitable conflict until darkness once again falls, the circle is complete and events start all over again.'

'Have we no control over this cycle of destruction?' asked Giles.

'I think not. There can be no doubt that religion is evil – but a necessary evil. Many have tried to control it and all have failed. Commonsense cannot prevail against faith.'

'Perhaps the Protocol *is* the right method of management then?'

'No, Giles, the Protocol has failed in exactly the same way as have all the religions which came before, and we are back where we started.'

'How *can* we restore commonsense?'

The Enforcer thought for a moment. 'The Protocol must be destroyed as it doesn't allow for any freedom of thought.'

'But it has kept the peace for nearly a hundred years.'

'Mmm, but, like all other beliefs, however well-intentioned, it is doomed to fail and is now causing more harm than good. It must be destroyed. It is the way of things, Giles. There can be no doubt that blood will continue to be shed as long as it exists. There is no point in blaming ourselves – blame The Protocol.'

The Protocol Wars continued and ravaged the world. Unimaginable cruelty was inflicted in the name of the Protocol. As well as the three main protagonists: the Protocolists, the Real Gilesians and the Brethren of the Donkey, numerous militant splinter groups formed, all with their own beliefs and codes, and all believing that theirs was the right path. Bombs were planted, innocent people maimed and killed, hostages were taken, tortured and killed. Brother fought brother, father killed son and country attacked country, all convinced beyond any shadow of a doubt that theirs was the true belief, that the obscenities they perpetrated were justified in the name of their cause.

Giles was inconsolable. He had hoped to bring thoughtfulness and consideration to society but instead there was conflict and violence. His own life and that of the Enforcer had been threatened on many occasions and try as he might, everything he said, all that he preached, just inflamed the violence and escalated the carnage.

'We must use the Protocol to stop this ridiculous sectarianism.'

Giles looked across the table to where the Enforcer was sitting, sipping a glass of wine. They were in his cottage by the loch and outside they could hear the sound of armed guards, smoking and chatting.

'No one will listen to us mere human beings any more, that's for sure.'

'It seems to me that we have a choice. We can either write a new Protocol, a Protocol to end all Protocols, above all others: the one *true* Protocol, urging peace and conciliation, or... '

The Enforcer interrupted, 'But surely that will result in yet another sect?'

Giles nodded his agreement, 'That's the risk.'

'Or?'

'Or somehow we shut down the Protocol altogether.'

The Enforcer thought for a moment. 'Even if you could do that it would lead to an intellectual and cultural vacuum. Our fellow human beings would have to find something else to believe in. Another prophet will come along and the whole sequence start over again.'

'As sure as the world rotates, the sun rises and falls and night follows day.'

'Does day follow night, or night follow day?' The Enforcer asked.

'It depends whether your glass is half empty or half full.' Giles laughed.

Some weeks later and without any warning, the computers started to shut down. One by one their screens became blank and the Protocol could no longer be accessed. To begin with the Practitioners and Monitors thought that this was merely a network malfunction but as more and more computers went down and the Protocol programmes became inaccessible the seriousness of the situation became apparent. Try as they might, the experts could not resurrect the Protocol, and when the last computer screen went blank, crowds with lighted candles gathered outside Studios across the land to hold vigils.

The Protocolists issued a communiqué accusing the Real Gilesians of this act of terrorism. The Brethren of the Donkey blamed the Protocolists who then claimed that this act of aggression was tantamount to a declaration of war, carefully not stating against whom. Each of the groups sought advice on how to act but without the

Protocol to pronounce, there was a stalemate: intellectual stagnation paralysed the world. Warring factions lost their sense of direction without which they no longer had a cause – righteous or otherwise – and they came together to share in their grief as they realised that their one common denominator – the Protocol – had made the ultimate sacrifice, it had died to save them.

'How did you do it?' asked the Enforcer.

'Simple in the end,' replied Giles. 'I just accessed the main Life Protocol, the decision-making section, and typed in, "There is no answer," and it asked, "Why not?" So I responded, "Because there is no question." ' Giles smiled at the memory. 'Then there was a great deal of whirring and all manner of symbols came up on the screen and the programme imploded and the screen went blank. Subsequently, every time anyone tries to access the Protocol the computer just shuts down.'

'What was the question you were seeking to answer?'

'What is the meaning of life?' Giles smiled once more.

'And the answer is?'

'There is no question.'

'And the Protocol couldn't cope with that concept?'

'No it was beyond its capability to grasp that there doesn't have to be a meaning to everything. Some things just *are*.'

'So is it dead?'

'Well, interestingly the final image was that of the old man waving goodbye. I think he's finally been laid to rest,' said Giles.

'Are you sure the Protocol's not just sleeping?'

'It looked moribund to me.'

# THIRTEEN

In the Cabinet room there was complete silence. All those present simply stared at the pile of books that had been the Protocol and the blank screen of the computer which had administered it. Some Ministers wore black armbands and every now and again there was the sound of sobbing.

'Well, what shall we do now?' the P.M. asked.

But no one could make a decision for the skill had been lost forever. They simply stared at the pile of books and the dark screen until the P.M. announced that it was suppertime.

And so the great Protocol dream collapsed and was washed away, like a flimsy bridge traversing a swollen stream. It disintegrated and was absorbed into the dust of the past, like so many good ideas and concepts before. Of course, society never quite recovered, just as it had never recovered from the Wars of Theism all those years before. Life could never again be the same. The populace no longer had direction, a goal, or a *raison d'être*. People gradually embraced the new order, a life without systems or algorithms, but for many years there was a vacuum, an absence of any sense of being, of anything to relate to. Initially the administration continued unchanged, but without the Protocol to guide them the Mandys, Doreeses and others like them were incapable of maintaining order in this new order-less world.

There were still some pockets of resistance, where communities clung on to the old world – living in the past – mainly in places like Norfolk and Dalriada. Small clandestine enclaves of Real Gilesians and even some fundamentalist Brethren of the Donkey met in secret: Protocolists without a Protocol.

The town at the foot of the loch, like most others, didn't suddenly change. The community still met in the Studio but instead of seeking the advice of the Protocol they would talk and discuss issues of the moment. Edward, the converter and his fellow missionaries had long since moved on to convert other towns and villages, so when Giles and the Enforcer returned there was no trace of them. Giles had wondered what he would do if they had been there: would he embrace them or kill them? He wasn't sure. Giles himself had changed irrevocably. Mentally and physically he was scarred. He had slaughtered the beast: fulfilled his brief – the mission passed on to him by the old man – but the price had been high. He had lost all that was precious to him. He was still a State orphan, a spectre, a sad ghost invisible to the authorities, but now he was no longer the innocent optimistic teenager who had been fed and clothed by the old man. He was now a disillusioned, middle-aged man. His hair was short and patched with grey and the scars of rocks and stones covered his face and body. He no longer felt confident that he knew the difference between right and wrong: no longer sure of his own destiny.

Giles and the Enforcer were sitting a few feet away from the little mound that was Ruth and Hope's grave. It was the tenth anniversary of the invasion of the village and of the terrible events that had followed. Below them the loch shimmered and shone in the evening sun while behind them the mountains rose imperiously towards the sky.

'Are there no good people left in this world?' asked Giles.

'Yes! Plenty. Bad people as well,' replied the Enforcer. 'It's just that it's very hard to know which is which. And of course you need the one to define the other.'

Giles was thoughtful. 'But there must be certain indisputable, characteristic features which define who is good and who is bad – what is right and what is wrong. For example, killing Ruth, Hope, Roger and the others was obviously a fundamental evil.'

'I agree, Giles, but it is also clear to me that the man who killed them thought he was doing the right thing. Does that make an evil act virtuous?'

'His moral compass had been exposed to a malevolent force,' said Giles.

'Again, I agree, but if he didn't know that, can you blame him for it?'

'Then surely it is for us to define what is right and wrong; for us to write it down to act as a template for peaceful co-existence.'

'The Enforcer smiled, 'Something like a Protocol you mean?'

Giles laughed, 'Yes that's it – let's write a Protocol.'

They were both silent for a while, comfortable in each other's company; and in the warmth of the summer's evening they talked about their lives and the Protocol. How it had been conceived in good faith but had grown into a monster, abused and misused until it became a tool of evil.

The first of the two shots shattered the back of Giles' head. His expression appeared to be one of surprise as he gently fell, face down on the hummock beneath which lay the remains of Ruth and Hope. As the Enforcer turned to look the second bullet hit him in the side of the head and he too fell, almost gracefully, on to the hillside. As the sound of the shots reverberated and echoed across the loch and around the mountains, a skinny figure with long lank hair and a bluish swelling over his left cheek emerged from below the tree line about a hundred yards away.

The man walked slowly towards the two corpses and when he had reached them he surveyed the lifeless forms lying on the ground in front of him. 'Consider yourselves converted,' he said quietly. Then, slowly he lifted his gaze from the bodies and looked out across the loch. Still holding his rifle in his right hand, Edward raised both his arms in a gesture of salute and shouted at the top of his voice, '*The infidel is dead. I have served you well. Long live the Protocol.*'